THE COINS OF JUDAS

Scott McBain is a pseudonym.
He lives in London and Panama.

THE
COINS OF JUDAS

Scott McBain

HarperCollins*Publishers*

This novel is entirely a work of fiction. The names, characters and incidents portrayed in it are the work of the author's imagination. Any resemblance to actual persons, living or dead, events or localities is entirely coincidental.

HarperCollins*Publishers*
77–85 Fulham Palace Road,
Hammersmith, London w6 8jb

www.**fire**and**water**.com

Published by HarperCollins*Publishers* 2002
1 3 5 7 9 8 6 4 2

A catalogue record for this book
is available from the British Library

isbn 0 00 651427 8

Set in New Baskerville by
Rowland Phototypesetting Limited,
Bury St Edmunds, Suffolk

Printed and bound in Great Britain by
Omnia Books Limited, Glasgow

*This book is dedicated to Di and Mike McDowell,
for all their friendship to the family down the long years.*

PROLOGUE

It is a most certain and most Catholic opinion that there are sorcerers and witches who, by the help of the devil, on account of a compact which they have entered into with him are able, since God allows this, to produce real and actual evils and harm, which does not render it unlikely that they can also bring about visionary and phantastical illusions by some extraordinary and peculiar means.

Malleus Maleficarum,
'Hammer of the Witches'

ST PETER'S IN ROME. SUNDAY AFTERNOON.

The heart of Christendom basked in the warmth of a bright August sun. Having lunched, with some olives and a little local wine, the tourists got off their air-conditioned coaches in the Via della Conciliazione and assembled in small groups for the afternoon's sight-seeing. The Germans patted their cameras, the Americans searched for the nearest gift shop, the British formed an orderly queue unasked and the French wondered why they were there.

Slowly, the tourists ascended the marble steps to reach St Peter's Square. As the press of humanity made its way forward, the coach operators waved red flags to direct them. Finally, they stood at the entrance to the Basilica, the elderly and the sclerotic on their zimmer frames having caught up.

The tour guides then took over. Expertly, they began their spiel. It continued uninterrupted across the flag-stones like the flow of a babbling brook, delivered in a multitude of languages. For Signora Rossi it was, perhaps, the two thousandth time she had said it, yet she delivered her monologue once more in a tone that sounded fresh, with all the gusto and hand movements that made an Italian an Italian:

'Behold St Peter's Basilica! The church in front of you, with its massive oval dome designed by Michelangelo, was consecrated in 1626. However, its history is much older. It is said to have been built over the original tomb of St Peter. You will recall from what I told you this morning [*they never did of course*] that much of Rome was destroyed by a great fire in AD 64 for which the Emperor Nero held the Christians responsible. As part of that persecution it is believed that St Peter was crucified, upside down, not far from this spot and that his burial place lies within the precincts of this basilica.'

Signora Rossi placed her ample hands on her ample hips and waited until the one or two interested people in her group digested this nugget of history. As usual, the rest fidgeted about, peered into their guidebooks, adjusted their bifocals and complained how sore their feet were. The pickpockets hovered around. Signora Rossi continued:

'The basilica contains eleven chapels and forty-five altars. It is 187 metres long and has more than 2.4 hectares of marble flooring. Among other things you will see Michelangelo's Pietà, the high altar at which only the Pope may say Mass and the throne of St Peter in Glory [*she paused to glare at a young couple locked in passionate embrace at the back of the crowd. They ignored her*]. Are there any questions before we go in?'

There was none. After a few exclamations of awe and amazement, the tourists made to enter. Of course, they mustn't stay too long. They had more visits that afternoon. It was an all-in-one-day tour, pre-paid. They still had to visit the tile shop, the Caffè Giolitti and the Trevi Fountain.

Meanwhile, Signora Rossi pursed her lips. The job was getting to her at last; she no longer enjoyed it. This was what Christianity had descended to. Sound-bite religion, day-tripper faith, young people hot with sexual desire even as they entered the heart of Christendom. What would their Saviour have made of it all? She dared not think.

Grinning, the pickpockets watched them shuffle in. Minus a watch. Signora Rossi's timekeeping would be out, again.

In another part of the Vatican, the pace was more sedate and the concern for religion more profound.

'Cardinal Benelli.'

The portly figure stood up from behind the ornate desk to greet his guest.

'Ah, Cardinal Hewson.' Benelli beamed at the American. He was as all Italians imagined good Americans to be: tall, broad-shouldered, with a large face and an enthusiastic smile. Also the grip of a baseball player, which made Benelli wince.

Hewson said in Italian, 'I'm sorry I'm late. I've just come from the church of Santa Maria Novella. It's the traffic.'

'Always the same in Rome!' Benelli chuckled and the

belly of the sixty-five-year-old mimicked his facial movement like a ripple across water. For the Cardinal was not one to forgo a good meal. He often joked in the company of laymen that, had he been invited to the Last Supper, he would have arrived early, though not for the best of reasons.

Food was one of the joys of Benelli's life and one of his small failings. For Benelli was a good cardinal, a fine administrator and bureaucrat, but no saint. As he confessed to God in his hours of personal introspection and prayer, so long as he got into heaven he was happy to stand at the back.

'The traffic's always dreadful,' he said, patting Hewson on the shoulder. 'It was like this when I came to the Vatican forty years ago. It will be the same when they carry me out.' He chuckled again, the chuckle seemingly open and carefree.

'Come.' Benelli took Hewson by the arm. He switched into English, although Hewson was fluent in Italian and many other languages; he was a very gifted man. 'There's no good reason to stay indoors on a wonderful day like this.'

The Head of the Inquisition or, to give him his modern title, the Head of the Holy Office, led the American Cardinal across his study and towards the large veranda windows. They stepped over the threshold.

'Let's try this way,' said Benelli, guiding his colleague.

The Vatican gardens were large and expansive. They were also beautifully maintained. Within the hub of a noisy city they comprised an oasis of calm and Benelli strolled there as often as he could, particularly in the cool of the evening.

'How was your flight?'

'No problem at all,' said Hewson, his Chicago accent

sounding harsh in the Italian environment. He looked at his companion, sizing him up. He'd not seen him for three years and they'd never been close.

Benelli was a good foot shorter than he, rotund, with an oval face on which a permanent smile seemed to be fixed. Although he appeared to be the epitome of joviality, Cardinal Hewson knew that this man of the cloth made tough decisions and was unafraid to speak his mind when occasion demanded.

Respected, feared, the keeper of the Faith, Benelli was the most influential figure in the Vatican after the Pope, since, as well as being Head of the Holy Office, he also held the post of Cardinal Secretary of State. Hewson wondered whether he'd be as powerful and successful when he took over these positions. He rather thought he would. Naturally, he'd make some changes. Stir things up a bit.

'Have they shown you everything?' asked Benelli. 'The Vatican's much larger than you think. You'll be confused for weeks.'

'I certainly will. I've been walking along endless corridors all morning. Surely there can't be any more to it?'

'Oh, the Vatican's full of surprises. It's a small city – more than fourteen hundred rooms – and it goes on and on. Not only the museums and the galleries, there're the living quarters for over a thousand people, including the Swiss Guards. Did they show you the libraries and the papal audience chambers?'

'Yes,' said Hewson.

'The Academy of Sciences and Radio Vatican?'

Hewson smiled. 'That too.'

'Good,' said Benelli. 'At least someone's following my instructions. What about the crypt under St Peter's Basilica?'

'Yes.'

'And the tombs of the popes?'

'Yes.'

Although he knew that the basilica was built over an old Roman graveyard, Hewson had never before entered the grotto located under the high altar of St Peter's. He and his guide had descended a number of levels, to beneath the foundations of the basilica itself. The grotto contained not only Christian, but also pagan tombs going back to the first century. For Hewson, it had been an awe-inspiring and deeply significant moment.

'Did you visit the tomb of St Peter?'

'No,' said Cardinal Hewson. He had his reasons.

'Oh?' Benelli glanced at him, puzzled.

'There was no time,' replied Hewson abruptly. 'In the past, when the Holy Father summoned me to the Vatican, I was only able to visit the papal apartments and the Sistine Chapel. So much is new.'

'It's the same for most people,' remarked Benelli with a sigh. 'This place is a great mystery. However, as my successor, you'll need to know the names of all the buildings and of everyone here. Not the simplest of tasks.'

'I wish I could decline the job.'

Benelli wagged his finger slightly as they crossed a lawn. 'Don't we all, but when the Pope orders, one must obey and, of course, there is a divine purpose to it. Anyway, there are *some* perks to the job. You have direct access to the Holy Father and you often fly around the world. It could be worse. Now, come and sit down.'

They sat on a bench in the garden with no one to disturb them. For a while neither said anything, being content to watch the flowers swaying in the breeze, the birds flitting from one tree to another and, towering above it all, the dome of the basilica. Then Benelli looked at Hewson. His gaze was shrewd and perceptive. Hewson realised that the last phase of his interview had been reached.

'Cardinal,' said Benelli, 'my job is a difficult one. One of the most difficult in the Church: the protection of the Faith. Although we've talked about this before, are there any final questions you'd like to ask me? Tomorrow, you'll be anointed as my successor and I'll depart to the monastery of San Lorenzo and into retirement, a simple priest again. However' – he leant closer – 'I wanted to talk with you, privately, even though you've read the briefing notes and chatted with my staff. Feel free to raise any matter you like.'

The tone was gentle and affectionate, like a true father to a son. Benelli knew that his position as Head of the Holy Office was not one any man would wish for, if he really understood what it entailed, and maybe Hewson was already experiencing the bouts of depression that had sometimes come upon him during his own tenure of that great office.

Hewson studied the older man in turn. How would he take his retirement after all his years of influence and power, with no bishops and priests to fawn on his every word? Poor Benelli, to be almost at the apex of it all then to be cast down again. Rather like the fall of Satan, Cardinal Hewson thought wryly. He said, 'Your job is a huge responsibility. To defend the Faith against false doctrine and those who seek to pervert the teachings of the Church for their own ends; to challenge the powers of evil – it is a superhuman task.'

'Especially so today.' Benelli began his sermon in earnest. 'Today, we live in a superficial and deceitful world. We've convinced ourselves that our existence is continually improving. However, never has there been so much poverty, so much abuse, so much starvation and despair. Never have people felt such loneliness and lack of fulfilment in their lives, both spiritual and personal. And never have there been so many false prophets and those who seek to destroy the Church.' He paused. 'We live in difficult times and we are, I believe, entering new and treacherous waters.'

Benelli sighed again (it was one of his habits) and gazed at the brilliant sheen of the flowers as they caught the sunlight. He continued.

'In previous eras, it was simpler. The paths of evil were very visible: the powers of sorcery, of witchcraft and of the devil. And so were those of the Church to combat them: the Inquisition, excommunication and the suppression of heretics. However, evil is a strange and infinitely subtle thing, Cardinal Hewson. For the very instruments the Church used in medieval times to oppose it, became twisted and perverted in their turn. The innocent were persecuted, the foolish and weak tortured or killed, and our Church was feared. The frightening image of those times lives on in the pages of history. Yet the essential task of the Faith – to fight the forces of darkness – remains. For the amount of evil in this world does not decrease and the contest is not a fair one.'

Hewson surreptitiously glanced at his watch. He hoped Benelli wouldn't go on too long.

'No?'

'No,' said Benelli firmly. 'The powers you have as Head of the Holy Office are limited while those of Satan are immeasurable and indeterminable. The Bible itself declares that the devil may appear in the guise of an Angel of Light and, indeed, he often does.'

'Surely you don't believe that?' People viewed Benelli as a practical man, a functionary, soon to be a celestial bureaucrat. Not an old-style conservative with hell and damnation high on the agenda.

'I *do* believe it.'

Benelli surveyed the statues of the saints on the colonnades of the Vatican and the dark shadows they cast. 'Even those the Church recognises as saints may have been the opposite in their time. The powers of darkness are powers of deception and betrayal, Cardinal Hewson, and I've no doubt some of those revered today as holy men and women were not actually so. While pretending to praise God they sought only their own self-advancement and glory. Evil snares human beings, even the most saintly, on their way to the Cross, and it does so when they least expect it.' He hesitated. 'But forgive me, I was digressing. What is your concern?'

'Er . . .' Hewson had lost the thread. 'My worry is that I may not be able to adequately shoulder this great office.' He watched as a young nun passed close to them. Her face was young and attractive in spite of her dress and cowl.

Benelli noted the grave aspect of his companion and felt pity for him. 'My son, do not be afraid. The Holy Father has chosen you for this task and I am sure that you will discharge it better than I. Prayer and a humble heart are the only things you require, though the latter has always eluded me, I fear. Have you any further questions?'

'Just one.' Hewson paused as if wondering whether to trouble him. 'It's rather odd. When I visited St Peter's this afternoon your assistant took me to the grotto. Nearby is a passageway not open to the public.'

'That's correct.'

'Your assistant unlocked the iron grate to this passageway and we went down a number of stairs, to a lower chamber.'

'Yes,' said Benelli. 'It contains the tombs of popes who lived in the first century. No one may visit it without the consent of the Holy Father.'

'I assume a person must be a priest to visit this place?'

'At the very least.'

'Ah,' said Cardinal Hewson and nodded sagely. 'That's what I imagined. Anyway, I saw a light at the end of the corridor and I couldn't help going towards it.'

He stopped and looked at Benelli, trying to divine his thoughts. But he wasn't able to.

'It was quite eerie. At the entrance to one of the tombs there was a light, or rather a number of candles. The tomb appeared to be relatively recent. Perhaps I was imagining things, but there was also a young girl there, praying.'

Benelli's face remained impassive, so Hewson continued, 'Your assistant motioned me to say nothing and to depart. When I asked him about this he told me I should speak to you or to the Pope. Who is the girl? Should she be there? She can't be a nun since she looks so young – only twelve or so.'

At first Cardinal Benelli was silent. He sighed more deeply than usual and Hewson was surprised to see tears welling up in his eyes. When he finally spoke his voice was hoarse and his tone one of the deepest sorrow. It was clear the earlier conversation had really been a prelude to this.

'The girl is allowed to visit the tomb at the express wish of the Pope. Only he can countermand the order. She should be left in peace.'

Benelli hesitated. Then he continued: 'Cardinal, all

institutions have secrets, the Vatican more so than others. Not only because of its very great age but because of its nature and the Faith it professes. For nearly two millennia our Church has held, and continues to hold, the secrets of the confessional: secrets of millions upon millions of human beings, saints and sinners, good and evil. These are human secrets. But our Church also possesses great spiritual secrets which go back into the mists of time.'

'There is something more?' Hewson asked when Benelli did not continue.

'Yes,' replied the Cardinal. 'I am afraid there is.' He lowered his voice. 'As my successor there are certain things you need to be told. Great secrets.' He paused again. 'Terrible secrets. None more so than the one I am about to disclose. Only three people alive know of it. The Holy Father, myself and one other.'

'The girl?' interjected Hewson.

Cardinal Benelli assented. 'It is a story of betrayal and it relates to Our Lord himself.'

Even in the warm garden Benelli felt a sudden chill come upon him.

Then he began: 'It concerns the Coins of Judas.'

THE FISH

CHAPTER ONE

> *They err who say that there is no such thing
> as witchcraft but that it is purely imaginary
> ... The devil has a thousand ways and
> means of inflicting injury and from the time
> of his first Fall has tried to destroy the unity
> of the Church and, in every time, to subvert
> the human race.*
>
> *Malleus Maleficarum,*
> 'Hammer of the Witches'

LIGHT.

It would be the first, and the last, thing that Paul would
remember after his illness started. He saw it flicker across
the ceiling through a gap in the curtain. Light. So in-
definably beautiful, so unconfined. He watched as the
beam penetrated the room, how it softened while it dis-
persed and, finally, its refraction into primary colours.
Where would humanity be if it didn't have light? A
people condemned to live in darkness. Light. As essential
as water yet, like water, so rarely appreciated.

Paul stretched out, careful not to disturb his wife.
There was silence in the house, and outside, in the exclusive San Francisco suburb, the faint hum of a car as it
passed along the private road. While he lay in bed that

3

Sunday morning, Paul perceived that he was the possessor of two wonderful things: light and peace. Together, they brought a deep sense of contentment. Paul considered this transitory state. It was a feeling relatively easily invoked yet, so often, it was thrust aside by the preoccupations of daily life. Besides, it was not something he was accustomed to. He was too driven for that.

Within a few seconds Paul's idyllic state dissolved and his consciousness slipped into first gear. Thoughts started to crowd in on him, displacing the wonderful sense he'd experienced of being outside himself, a free spirit unencumbered by human concerns.

Quickly, his mind summarised his agenda for the week. The Kramer trial, the article for *The Psychiatrist* magazine, those evaluations he and Ben had agreed to do at the San Francisco High Security Facility, the slot he was angling for on NBC news. Getting to the top of his profession, being the best criminal psychiatrist in the United States, this was the dynamo that drove Paul's ambition and he oiled its wheels liberally.

Paul focused on the sleeping figure beside him in bed, his train of thought switching to more personal concerns. He loved Marie. Well, that wasn't strictly true, he *had* loved her. When he'd married her, he had loved her. That was ten years ago when he had had a sudden urge to settle down and have kids, a thirties sort of thing that assailed men when they least expected it.

In Marie's case it had been different. She'd been a few years younger than him, straight out of university with an arts degree and looking for meaning, rather than money, in life. Of course, he'd swept her off her feet with his clever ways and his determination to win her even though her parents had opposed the match. Small-town, narrow-minded Catholics, they'd found him too ambitious and a man without belief.

Paul smiled faintly, recalling his former passion. Time, as always, altered the status quo. His love for Marie hadn't dissipated completely – but it had tarnished. He imagined it happened to every marriage these days, everything being so casual and fleeting. He still cared for Marie, of course, but the affairs he'd had over the past couple of years had altered his attitude. In some way he felt that he, and his body, belonged to others now, to a wider world, and not just to her. Not that he'd let on: she suspected nothing.

Also, perhaps he was wrong, but she seemed to have lost some of that self-confidence and resilience she once had. True, she was good at her job as a VP in the big charity for which she worked; she was no pushover – but with him, well, she looked at him at times in a slightly puzzled way as though they no longer quite connected, as if their worlds were drawing apart.

Besides, thought Paul, more bitter images rising from the depths of his soul, when their daughter Rachel was born, the fool who had masqueraded as a doctor had botched it. The compensation had bought them the house but now he had a loving, but less loved, wife. And one who was barren. That changed things a lot. For him and, he imagined, deep in her heart, for her as well.

'You awake?' There was a soft voice and a movement from under the sheets. Paul was silent, keen to go through his agenda for a while longer.

'Paul?'

Marie turned over in bed. A head of auburn hair nestled into his arm. He scrutinised her. It no longer was a beautiful face – not now, with the slight beginnings of lines and crow's feet – but it remained very attractive.

5

For a thirty-three-year-old woman her almost unmarked complexion, liquid brown eyes and high cheekbones set in an oval visage were something Paul could still be proud of when he introduced her to faculty members and others. Something else to boast about.

'Awake?'

'Um.'

'Remember,' she murmured sleepily without opening her eyes, 'we've the picnic with the Ingelmanns today. Florence invited us last week. We'll have to get up soon.'

'No. It's early. It's only seven.'

'Oh?' Silence, as Marie digested this welcome bit of information. Pity she hadn't asked before. Now she was too wide awake to get back to sleep. She tried to doze, but it was no good. She couldn't sleep any longer. She wondered what her husband was thinking. Probably about his work.

It had always been like that, even before marriage. A humble background had for him produced a thirst to succeed which seemed to be unstoppable. She understood his desire, but not its intensity, not now they had Rachel. However, Marie knew in her heart that he didn't forgive her inability to provide him with children. She'd failed him in some way and he couldn't accept failure in himself or in others: it was too intimately bound up with his ego.

Which was why Marie forgave him his casual affairs, though her knowledge of them drove a knife into her breast. Would he leave her? *When* would he leave her? Perhaps never. Oh God, that it might not be so, for she still loved him. Marie opened her eyes and looked at her husband. He smiled and her bitter thoughts temporarily departed. For better or for worse she loved him and she would keep to her wedding vows.

6

'She's asleep?'

'I'm sure.'

Marie sat up in bed and drew her silk slip over her head. Casting it onto the carpet she pulled the bed sheet over them so that they were hidden away in their own white cocoon. They started to make love. Her thoughts were concentrated on him, his on other women.

'Mummy?'

'Uh.' Marie exhaled slightly and groaned. It took a split second for her mind to return to the exterior world. Drawing back the sheet she looked across the room at the small and inquisitive child framed in the doorway, clutching her favourite doll.

'Rachel, honey, why don't you sleep some more?' Marie swept back her dishevelled hair as she moved across Paul's body to unlock herself from him.

'I can't sleep.'

Marie tried not to look too flustered. 'Well, that's OK, darling. Why don't you go downstairs? I'll be down in a minute.'

They lay in bed, every nerve straining to catch the sound of their seven-year-old daughter's tread on the stairs. After they heard the last footfalls, Marie turned back to Paul. They'd less than ten minutes before Rachel made a reappearance to complain she couldn't find her teddy bear. However, much could be achieved by then. Marie smiled at him. Paul raised his eyebrows.

'Women,' he muttered. Somehow, they could upstage men any day.

'Everyone ready? Ben's out in the car.'

Florence Ingelmann bawled out the words the moment she crossed the threshold of the front door. Immediately, she was surrounded by two attention seekers: one small girl and a dog. However, she took it all in her stride. She was used to the Stauffer household. With one sweep of her big fleshy arms she clasped Rachel to her and embedded the imprint of a massive pink lipstick kiss on her cheek. Then the family's golden Labrador was given a pat on his nose as he pawed frantically at her waist, keen to renew his acquaintance. The hazardous passage through the entrance hall completed, Florence swept on into the kitchen.

'Come on you two. Time to go.'

Before either Marie or Paul had got up from the breakfast table, Florence had enveloped them in her arms and squeezed them tightly. Once again, a sloppy kiss was attached to them, like the seal of approval slapped onto a supermarket item. That was the sort of woman Florence was. Larger than life, effervescent, unstoppable, and all packed within the confines of a five-foot-two-inch frame, topped with a mass of bleached blonde hair and a well-rounded physique that told all fitness trainers that they could look, despair, but not touch.

Eyeing the picnic basket, Florence seized it. She made for the entrance hall again, the gauntlet lying in wait for her, one member of which betrayed her presence by her giggles.

'Let's go, kids!' Florence yelled as she disappeared out of the front door.

Paul looked at his wife across the breakfast table, his buttered muffin still half in his mouth. He might be a professor of criminal psychiatry, a colleague of Florence's husband, Ben, and a well-known figure in his profession, but to Florence his thirty-nine years and several degrees counted for nothing. He and his wife were classified like their daughter and the dog, simply as kids. This had always irked him, since he had a well-developed sense of his own importance. Still, Ben was a supporter of his and he didn't have many.

Marie said gently, 'I think Florence wants us to go.'

Paul nodded. He could see everything was going to be premature today. And it was only eight-thirty on a Sunday morning.

The Ford sedan hurtled down the San Francisco highway with Ben at the wheel.

A lanky individual in his early fifties, with glasses and an absent-minded air, Ben was a professor of criminal psychiatry at the University of San Francisco and had been teaching courses there for many years longer than Paul. Despite this, and the fact that Ben was Head of Department and Paul's boss, the younger man always dominated things.

Why did he tolerate this state of affairs? Ben had asked himself this question many times, yet he knew the answer and he'd accepted it long ago. Because he was dealing with genius. He glanced across at Paul. His colleague was a handsome man, of medium height, with a full head of black hair and a visage a little too stark in its lines, almost ruthless, if seen in a strong light.

Self-opinionated, hugely ambitious, utterly exasperating at times: despite or possibly because of these character flaws, Paul had genius. A brilliant diagnostician who had a profound empathy with the criminally ill, Paul had the ability to express himself in academic articles and books with startling originality. He was not just impressive: in Ben's opinion, he would, in time, become as great a household name as Sigmund Freud or Carl Jung.

Other men would not have accepted this. Overcome by jealousy and a lack of self-worth, they would have sought to bring Paul down. It said much for Ben's humility that

9

he didn't. Instead, he did all he could to enable the younger man to excel at the university. Thanks to Ben they, and their wives, got on well. Good thing too, for Paul had no other professional colleagues who were friends. He was too brash for their taste.

Alongside their teaching commitments, Ben and Paul ran a private psychiatric clinic which catered for San Francisco's acting profession. They'd started it up only a year ago, yet it was already a lucrative business, given that most actors and actresses in the city were usually in, or out, of something – orifices, drugs, depression, jobs, stardom. And when they were, they invariably wanted to know – why me? At times Paul and Ben didn't know – but they could usually give a plausible enough explanation for money to be transferred from one pocket to another and everyone seemed to be the happier for it.

Ben appeared to like contrasts, for he was also the opposite in nature, and disposition, to his wife. While Florence was flamboyant and plump, the human equivalent of candy floss, he was tall and narrow; while she conversed like a twenty-four-hour speaking clock, he was silent unless forced to talk; while she was the life and soul of the party, he could turn a wedding into a funeral with his silence.

Yet this strange combination of opposites was their great strength and they were devoted to each other. Having no children of their own, Rachel Stauffer had become the object of their affection, a surrogate child that Florence endlessly cuddled and pressed to her ample bosom like a toy. Florence also adored Marie and Paul, though why those two had ever married was a complete mystery: their natures were so different.

Florence could see that for Marie, three essential components made up her existence: her husband, her child and her Catholic faith. Yet Paul shared only one of these. He loved Rachel deeply, but he had a withering contempt of religion and he needed no one to complement his being. He had a mind and personality as sharp as a razor that left others in no doubt of his self-sufficiency and his intellectual superiority. He would rise, or fall, like the morning star.

While Ben drove Florence gushed away to Marie and Rachel in the back, relaying the latest gossip from the gym, about which she had a comprehensive knowledge (of the exercise machines less so).

Unable to tolerate this verbal stream for long, Ben remarked, 'Don Eccles told me you've put in a request to do the Carl Jung lecture this year.'

'Yes,' said Paul.

'It would certainly be a coup if you get it.' Ben shifted in his seat. 'They've never invited someone so young before. They all tend to be in their sixties.'

'Exactly,' Paul retorted. 'The most prestigious lecture in psychiatry and they always give it to abject failures at the end of their careers who've only senility to look forward to.'

Ben grinned. Paul was right. However, that sort of truth only made enemies and Paul had a goodly number of those on the international selection committee. He wondered if he should tell him they'd already chosen Johann Hermanns from Basle. He decided not to. It would ruin their day out. Besides, there were other, more difficult issues to deal with. Did Paul know why Florence had fixed up the picnic?

'What topic would you speak on? Course, you could always turn it into an article if you're not chosen.'

Paul gazed at the contraflow as the cars hurtled by on the freeway. 'I thought something fairly controversial:

11

"Criminal Psychiatry and the Overthrow of Religion".'

'Wow! That would get them going. But remember most of the board of the university are religiously inclined. You don't want to damage your career prospects here.'

'So what?' said Paul. He could always get another job. He laughed, a relaxed laugh. Ben said nothing. They continued in silence.

'Turn left,' shouted Florence from the back, without missing a breath. 'Oh, and I was talking to Jenny Menteith yesterday at the Sorority League. Poor dear, her mother has been diagnosed with cancer.' Florence pressed a hand to her face in horror. 'Cancer of the throat, too. And such a beautiful voice.' She leant forward. 'Turn right, yes, right. We're almost there.'

Then she carried on with her soliloquy, inexhaustible. Rachel eyed her in fascination, amazed that a human being could talk so much without breathing. Florence must have specially fitted lungs. She'd ask her mother about it later.

Ben took the car down a small sandy track and they got out. The private beach lay before them, pristine white sand stretching down to the sea. With a shout Rachel ran ahead, the dog frisking about her legs. Anxiously, Florence hurried after her.

Marie caught sight of Ben's eyes. They sparkled with amusement as he watched his wife grasp Rachel's hand and lead her down to the water.

'Careful,' said Ben. 'She thinks the child's her own. She'll take her away from you one day.'

Marie smiled back. Florence had told her long ago that she was unable to bear children but, in her case, it was due to natural dysfunction, not the knife. It was this common link that had first drawn them together. Marie knew that Florence had accepted her burden, intellectually and philosophically, something Marie could not. Yet the motherhood instinct in Florence could never be fully suppressed and, as a result, she converted all the world into her own children.

Meanwhile, Paul made for the back of the vehicle. 'Let's get the picnic stuff out.' It was good of the President of the university to let them use his seaside retreat for the day. Of course, he'd want Paul to help him with something in return. 'By the way, Ben, have you read the latest article by Don Trautman, the "Psychiatric Evaluation of Female Prisoners Suffering from the Effects of Cocaine Addiction"?'

'Nope,' said Ben. 'Any good?' If Paul told him it was good, he'd read it. If not, forget it.

Gathering everything up, they strolled along the beach. It was going to be a perfect day. They could all feel it, apart from Ben. He dug his toes into the sand. He was thinking about the Kramer trial.

'My dear, you are *so* lucky.' It was late afternoon. However, Florence's voice had not gone out with the tide. It increased in volume, it diminished in volume, yet, like the current, it never quite abated. Marie wondered whether she also talked in her sleep. Poor Ben.

'I am,' she said.

'You have a beautiful daughter, a house that most people would kill for and a brilliant husband. God has blessed you.'

'He has,' replied Marie.

They sat watching Rachel playing in the surf. Paul and Ben had gone for a stroll. Florence paused. She cleared her throat cautiously. She'd approach the subject now.

Yet at the last moment, her nerve failed her. Although Marie was very confident and resilient with others, in

Florence's opinion, she'd developed a blind spot with respect to her husband. It hadn't always been like that. However, Florence knew nothing of Marie's anguish over her husband's infidelity nor of her determination to still keep the family together. So, of course, Marie must be worrying about the Kramer case. Florence would wait until her best friend raised her concerns of her own volition. So she remarked, 'Ben says Paul's latest book is doing very well. We both think that's wonderful.'

'Yes.' Marie said nothing more. There was a hush. Within a minute this had become so anathema to Florence that she burst out with: 'Marie, do you want to talk about Karl Kramer?'

Of course, she regretted it as soon as the words escaped from her mouth and she noticed her best friend's forehead crease with strain. Marie shook her head and turned away.

'I understand,' said Florence. Silly woman. She wished she hadn't spoken. Now she'd gone and spoilt things. In silence for once, they watched Rachel splashing in the sea with the dog.

'I don't want to discuss it.' Paul's voice was sharp and angry.

Ben stopped walking. He glanced back to where Florence and Marie were sitting in the far distance. He shrugged and then continued along the beach.

'Paul, I have to talk with you.'

'Not now.'

'Yes, Paul, *now*. The trial's tomorrow and if I can't raise the matter with you, who can? I'm your friend.' He paused. 'Is it true you're the only psychiatrist acting for the defence?'

'So what? Everyone has a right to representation.'

'Of course,' said Ben. 'I wasn't disputing that.' Paul began to walk away, but Ben caught up with him. 'All I'm trying to do is to give some good advice. This is a very high-profile case and the public are very passionate about it.'

'And?' Paul picked up some stones and hurled them into the sea. 'How many high-profile cases have you and I given professional opinions on? At least fifty over the last ten years. This is no different, I assure you.'

'But it *is* different. It's not just a question of serial killings. If this man gets off on the basis of your expert opinion and no one else is convicted you're finished. Do you understand that? The public and the profession will never forgive you. Is it true that Dr Lightman has withdrawn from the defence?'

'Yeah, and? He got cold feet at the last minute.' Paul looked at his companion almost scornfully. 'A little like you.'

Ben coloured. 'That's not true.' His voice had risen and he sought to calm it. No point in both of them getting angry. 'I pulled out after my own psychiatric evaluation. I came to the conclusion that Kramer did do it. I can't give evidence in favour of someone when, in my heart, I believe them to be guilty.'

'It's time to get back.'

Ben was losing. Still, he'd give it one more try. 'Let me put it this way. We both know that with certain types of criminal, there's a real danger that the psychiatrist empathises with them too much. You become drawn into their world and end up complying with them. Serial killers are a classic for that sort of thing. They are very manipulative.'

'Ah, so you think my professional judgement's been affected?' replied Paul coolly. 'That's the real issue, isn't it?' He stooped down to pick up some more pebbles.

'No, but what I am saying, Paul, is that Kramer is a strange and a dangerous man. I'm sure of it, both personally and professionally. You've visited him alone in prison so many times that you could be in danger of empathising with him. You need at least one other expert to support you, whatever the lawyers say. Don't go into this trial alone.'

'Or what?' Paul gave a big grin. 'It could be the death of me?' He went over and patted Ben on the back in a friendly way. It signalled that their conversation was at a close. Kramer wasn't able to fool Paul; he was quite sure. The real problem, if truth be told, was that Ben wasn't a very good psychiatrist. Also, he'd lost his nerve when the public began to bay for blood.

There was a shout behind them.

'Daddy, look what I've found!' Rachel ran along the beach towards them. She clutched something in her hands.

Paul drew her to him and inspected the shell intently. Ben was forgotten.

That night, while Marie was busy in the kitchen, Paul went into his study to start work on a lecture, the sound of Puccini's *Turandot* in the background. Gloria, the Filipina maid, came down the stairs.

'Rachel wants you to read a story to her before she goes to sleep.'

Marie nodded as she packed some cakes into a basket for a mothers' meeting the following day. She shouted through the door, 'Paul, can you read Rachel a bedtime story?'

Paul sighed and put down his pen. Then he went upstairs. His daughter lay in bed, pretending to be asleep.

Paul sat beside her and gazed at the simple beauty of her face, an angelic simplicity, the features perfectly formed. Within her small frame lay an innocence and unconditional love that no adult could hope to replicate. He'd do anything for her.

Paul waited. Within a few seconds Rachel opened one eye to check that he was still there. It was her undoing. Paul's fingers tickled her sides and she squealed and squirmed with pleasure. 'What story do you want, then?'

Rachel produced her favourite: *Little Red Riding Hood and the Big Bad Wolf*. Paul perched on her bed. Slowly, he read the tale. He was a dramatic reader and, at every twist and turn, his voice 'lived' the story, so that his daughter was soon hopelessly caught up. Paul glimpsed across at her. Her countenance registered that she was re-creating in her mind the fantasy he span, fear and uncertainty reflected in her mobile features while her moon-shaped eyes stared brightly into the half-darkness.

Paul paused as the wolf was about to meet its doom. 'It's time for some sleep. I'll read the rest tomorrow.'

'No, more.'

Paul leant forward to kiss her. 'Tomorrow.' He got up and made to turn out the bedside light, but she stopped him. 'Daddy!'

'Rachel, it's only a story. There are no big bad wolves. Besides, it's defeated by the little girl. Do you want me to look under the bed?'

She nodded and Paul did so. It had long fascinated him that children, especially the young, had the ability to comprehend a sense of evil without any explanation from their parents. He himself, from a very early age, had conjured up a world of ghosts and ghouls, monsters and witches, werewolves and demons, all 'lived out' and experienced in vivid nightmares. However, there was a perfectly logical explanation. Children extrapolated fairy stories in their imagination and then accorded a physical reality to them. Of course the image existed, but only in the child's fantasy. Image but no substance. All very logical. Thank God for psychiatry.

'See? Nothing there. Goodnight, sweetheart.'

Paul returned to work on his lecture notes. By the time he got to bed Marie was already asleep. He was glad. He'd had enough discussion about Kramer for the day. The matter was closed.

A few kilometres away in their more modest house, Florence and Ben sat side by side on the sofa and watched the evening news. As expected, it concentrated on the Kramer trial, which would start the following day.

The news commentator began his spiel. Was Kramer the serial killer who'd been stalking San Francisco for the past few months and had committed a series of murders that had appalled even a population hardened to violent crime? Or was he innocent – in which case a murderer was still on the loose? The public would soon find out.

Florence turned to her husband. 'Did you talk with Paul?'

'Not really.'

'What if Kramer's convicted?'

'*When* he's convicted Paul will lose his reputation.' Ben tossed aside his newspaper. 'It's as simple as that. Everyone thinks he's mad to put his status on the line but he's convinced the fellow's innocent.' He shrugged, pretending to be non-committal. 'Well, it's his decision in the end. Besides,' he concluded lamely, 'even murderers need good people to defend them.'

In Ben's opinion, Paul had been overconfident, too

quick to make a diagnosis. However, there was nothing he could do about it since it was his partner's call. No one had forced Paul to act as the expert witness for the defence and it was on his conscience that the outcome lay.

'I'm off to bed, hon.' Florence finished off her second slice of chocolate gateau and whipped cream.

'I'll be along in a minute.'

Ben turned off the TV. For a while he sat alone in the darkness, deep in thought. He was thinking about people. He'd always believed there was an extraordinary synchronicity between individuals and events. That is, during their life, people drew others to them – friends, workmates and even enemies – through their own unconscious desires and cravings. Subsequent events which happened to them then fulfilled, or destroyed, those desires and cravings. Why and how this occurred Ben didn't know and he thought it inexplicable to the human mind. It was like watching sheep being gathered together – but being unable to see either the shepherd or the dogs that assembled them.

So what had brought Kramer into their small world and lives? Was he just a much-maligned man or something more? Ben didn't know. But the truth was that he didn't like Kramer. He didn't like him at all.

And that worried him.

CHAPTER TWO

> *None of us stands outside humanity's black
> collective shadow. Whether the crime lies many
> generations back or happens today, it remains
> the symptom of a disposition that is always –
> and everywhere – present, and one would there-
> fore do well to possess some 'imagination in
> evil', for only the fool can permanently neglect
> the conditions of his own nature. In fact his
> negligence is the best means of making him
> an instrument of evil.*
>
> Carl Jung, *The Undiscovered Self*

THE KRAMER TRIAL. BIG NEWS IN SAN FRAN-
CISCO.

Five women had been gruesomely murdered in the
city over as many weeks; the manner of their deaths was
almost identical. A serial killer was on the loose, yet there
were no clues, despite a large police taskforce having
been assigned to the case.

Then Melanie Dukes was found floating face down in a
local canal one June morning, her body badly mutilated.
Ordinarily, her demise wouldn't have made the front
page, not on a Sunday. But this was different. Melanie
Dukes's death was the last straw for a population already

panicked by an increasing and seemingly unstoppable crime wave.

The people of San Francisco were outraged and it had immediate consequences. The politically adroit Mayor was forced to admit on TV that she was professionally embarrassed by the presence of the victims but no murderer, and she promised that 'everything' would be done. That left the Chief of Police contemplating alternative employment, so it was not long before he launched a huge manhunt. Yet more officers were drafted in to work on the case.

However, despite all the TV and newspaper publicity, extensive investigations and a high level of co-operation from the local public, no one was apprehended. A month passed without any new incident. It was clear that the murderer had gone to ground. But where? And why, after starting his frenetic killing spree, had the man suddenly stopped?

The public found this even more unnerving. They knew he would strike again, for the criminologists had assured them such behaviour was compulsive. The bars and discos of San Francisco became strangely silent. Fear dampened even the most active of spirits.

Then a name, almost fortuitously, cropped up. Suspicion began to focus on Karl Kramer, a trucker from Los Angeles. He was a violent man, a loner, someone whose very presence exuded a sense of unease. His current whereabouts also gave a possible explanation for the temporary let-up in the killings. One week after Melanie Dukes's murder, Kramer was arrested in the red-light district of San Francisco for stabbing a man to death in a bar-room brawl. Kramer alleged that he'd been acting in self-defence. However, he was found guilty of murder and sentenced to ten years, to be out in five with good behaviour.

Could it be that Kramer had got himself into jail to avoid detection for the serial killings? A possibility, albeit remote. If so, it was a high-risk strategy. Under California's 'special circumstances' rule, a person who'd already committed one murder faced the death penalty if found guilty of another.

There were other problems too. There was nothing in Kramer's background to suggest serial killing was his particular pleasure and the evidence against him was thin. No fingerprints, no DNA. In fact, no hard evidence, forensic or otherwise, apart from a single witness – the sister of the murdered girl. So, there it was: the fervent denial of Kramer that he had tortured and killed Melanie Dukes against the sworn evidence of the victim's relative, Laura Dukes, that she had seen him with her sister that fateful night.

A final factor weighed heavily in the scales of justice: the opinion of a criminal psychiatrist, a well-known professor at the University of San Francisco, Paul Stauffer. He'd become fascinated by the case and his opinion would be given on behalf of the defendant.

Kramer had one friend in the world after all.

Nine-thirty a.m. on a warm September day and the San Francisco court was packed with lawyers, journalists, spectators and ghouls.

Laura Dukes sat near the back in a seat reserved for the police. The court was a large, oak-panelled room with a high ceiling and a raised rostrum for the judge. There were padded seats for the jury and benches in tiers for the spectators. The scene reminded Laura of seats in a ringside. It was not that surprising. Criminal trials were not dissimilar from circuses. Only the mental agility of the performers distinguished them: though, sometimes, this was a close-run thing. Posturing, nit-picking, tricks and feints all in one show. Never was man's affinity to the ape more apparent. And someone was always for the high jump.

'Move along there.'

Laura's father had been dead two years and her mother was in an old people's home suffering from a degenerative mental illness. Laura had not told her mother about the murder: the poor woman could no longer recall her own surname. She'd suffered enough: only an unjust God could impose more. But God was like that, Laura thought bitterly, good at doling out the suffering. Enough to make humanity appreciate what he'd gone through.

That left Laura the sole person from the victim's family to attend the trial. She felt alone, afraid, and utterly depressed with life. She wanted it all to end.

'You OK?'

'Just about.' Laura glanced at the police officer. He was an African-American with grizzled hair and a kindly look. He touched her shoulder faintly by way of re-assurance and then went to help his colleagues to seat people.

Two rows in front of Laura Dukes a woman nudged her husband. 'Look, it's her.'

'Who?'

'At the back. Don't turn round too quickly. The sister of the girl who was murdered. Identical twins. Oh, isn't she pretty? Poor thing!'

The commentator's husband, a ponderous man with a large beer belly, swivelled round to look at Laura, who rapidly averted her eyes from his inquisitive gaze. He was a retired bookmaker who'd nothing else to do but to come to the courts with his wife on a regular basis and watch human misery as a spectator sport. He squinted at Laura, full of disrespectful curiosity.

Laura Dukes had been a twenty-three-year-old teller in a San Francisco bank, just as her sister had once been. Tall and attractive girls with blonde hair, slim figures and a passion for sports, she and her twin had been very popular at work, well known for their bubbly personalities. Their Friday and Saturday nights had invariably been spent in the bars and discos of San Francisco enjoying life to the full. Though not promiscuous, the twins had had a number of boyfriends and once, they'd even shared the same man. Laura had been the more outgoing; Melanie slightly more reserved. Two happy people with a passion for dancing, for men and for life. Then Melanie had been murdered.

'Silence in court.'

The fat husband turned back to his wife. The girl didn't look that unhappy. How callous could you get? He picked his nose.

'All rise for Judge Harrison.'

Laura watched as an elderly and stooping figure made to sit in his high judicial chair. She shook her head without thinking. How could this old man understand what it was like to lose a loved one to a maniac? What could he know of her personal tragedy and despair, locked away, as he obviously was, in his privileged lifestyle? Laura bit her lip; her mind was still racked with the guilt and the horror of what had happened. She closed her eyes to avoid the stares.

It had been a Saturday night. They'd gone to their favourite disco downtown – the Temptation of Eve – the one with the neon Eve encircled by a snake. It had been packed as usual, with people spilling out onto the sidewalk. It was Laura's and Melanie's sort of place: masses of young people out for a good time, eager to forget the tedium of everyday existence and oblivious to the dangers. However, the wolves were out there as well.

It was two in the morning. Laura had been ordering drinks at the long bar: she could recall it perfectly. Her sister, Melanie, had tapped her on the shoulder. Her features had been radiant, cheeks aglow from dancing, her voice slightly slurred from the alcohol. She'd giggled and whispered to Laura that she was going outside for a few minutes, their covert language for the beginning of something physical. Not full sex, but a grope was cool on the first night with a new guy.

Laura had nodded absent-mindedly while Melanie told her of her amorous plans. Her own thoughts were fully occupied with Danny, her boyfriend of five months, who was calling her for the next dance.

Melanie had pointed out her beau for the evening's fun. Laura had glimpsed the man as she balanced her drinks on a tray. He was standing well back from the bar, almost hidden in the gloom. *Almost* hidden, but Laura could still see him, as she did now in her mind's eye. Kramer had regarded her intently for a moment. Then he said, 'Hi,' in a soft tone. That was it, but enough for Laura to register the lilt of his voice, his large build, full lips and the ponytail.

True, she'd had a few drinks: a couple of vodkas and a Pearl Harbor tequila. Laura had admitted that in her statement to the police – but her visual recognition had still been there. She'd been tipsy but definitely not drunk. It had been Kramer who had gone with Melanie that night. She knew it. She would swear to it before the throne of God.

'All rise in court.'

Laura examined the jury as they filed in. Three

women, the rest men. She noted one man was in a smart suit. Perhaps he was a doctor or an accountant. The other jurors seemed rather like Laura – average sort of people with average sorts of lifestyles. What kind of justice would they dispense?

'The court is now in session.'

Laura's memory continued to flow as the jurors settled themselves down. That fatal night she'd watched Melanie leave the nightclub with Kramer, watched as he held open the door for her and watched as Melanie turned to give her sister a final wave.

It was strange but as Laura had stood there holding the tray of drinks, seeing them go into the darkness, she'd felt a deep sense of unease. More than that, in fact: a chill of fear, as though something, *someone*, had been trying to warn her. Of course, Laura had shrugged it off, as one did, and gone back to Danny. Would that she hadn't. It was the last time that Laura had seen her sister alive.

Two more hours had passed at the disco. Laura had wanted to go home, since her boyfriend was desperate for sex, but she couldn't find her twin. Not in the bar, not in the disco, not in the park outside the Temptation of Eve. That had baffled Laura, even in her drunken state. Mel wouldn't have left her. That was their agreement. Always stay at the disco, or go home together. Be safe.

So, Laura had rung Melanie on her mobile. Someone answered. It was a man's voice, Kramer's voice. Laura had asked to speak to her sister. He'd calmly replied, 'She's sleeping,' and then the mobile had clicked off. Laura had stood there in the disco car park, surprised by the briefness of the answer and its dispassionate, almost clinical, tone. However, Danny had been shouting at her to get into the car and in her befuddled state, she'd assumed her sister had taken her admirer back to their apartment for the night.

Yet, when they'd got there, there'd been no trace of Mel. Had she gone to the man's house? It was a possibility. Remote, but still a possibility.

Laura had slept badly that night. She'd had nightmares of being lost and utterly alone, of being separated from those she loved and unable to return home.

Early Sunday morning a passer-by had rung in to inform the police about a body he'd spied in the canal five kilometres from the disco. It was Mel, or rather what was left of her after the killer had slashed her to pieces. Once Laura had identified the body (they wouldn't let her see anything else but the face, the rest was too badly cut up) she'd started her descent into hell. Danny had left her within a few weeks, unable to cope with her tears, her rage and her burning sense of guilt.

Laura's prolonged sick leave from work had ended in her resignation and the medication she'd received from a succession of doctors had become a permanent crutch. Now, three months later, a shadow of her former self, she sat in a gloomy courtroom, waiting for justice. If only she had listened to her gut feeling, if only she'd stopped her sister from leaving the disco. It was her fault, really.

'Your Honour, I'm prosecuting counsel.'

Judge Harrison inclined his head and surveyed the rows of faces before him in the spectators' galleries. He knew what most of them had come for. Not just for justice, but to expend some of that terrible loathing they felt for Kramer – a man that the TV networks and the newspapers, with their over-hasty sense of justice, had already condemned as the murderer of Melanie Dukes and a serial killer.

The public wanted revenge – revenge on someone they couldn't comprehend but who caused them to experience evil thoughts in the depths of their souls; and they wanted the court to take that revenge for them. So be it. It would, but in accordance with the law. The man might be a murderer, convicted for killing a man in a bar-room brawl, but had he killed this woman?

'This court is now in session.' The gavel banged down.

CHAPTER THREE

There is an evil which I have seen under the
sun, and it lies heavy upon men.
Ecclesiastes 6:1

WHILE THE KRAMER TRIAL EXCITED the citizens of
the United States, at the Vatican events took a more
placid turn, as might be expected in an institution that,
to date, had spent two thousand years waiting for things
to come to fruition.

Cardinal Benelli was accustomed to spend the period
after dinner in his room in the Vatican, in prayer. If
truth be told, he sometimes fell asleep. He confessed
this, along with his other relatively minor sins (such as
a pleasure in good food), to Father Thomas, who was
also the confessor to the Pope. For like all human beings,
the Pope was not without sin and, since the earliest days
of the Church, he was subject to confession.

Invariably, the person chosen for the post of Father
Confessor was a simple monk or priest marked out by
his humility and sense of grace, for pontiffs were usually
all too aware that Christ's statement 'many that are first
shall be last; and the last shall be first', applied to them
as well. Human titles and dignities made no impression
on the divine.

There was a slight tap at the door and Benelli opened his eyes leisurely. It must be his assistant, reminding him that he had a meeting at nine.

'Come in.'

Benelli was startled to see that the person standing on the threshold was not his razor-thin secretary, who always approached him with a reverential air. Instead, his bleary eyes focused on a slight figure in his late sixties, with grey hair and a worn face.

'I'm sorry for disturbing you.'

'No, not at all,' said Benelli. He chuckled even though he was the faintest bit annoyed. He rarely saw the Father Confessor outside the confessional and to be caught in the midst of his sin was troubling. The simple monk in his brown habit and the Cardinal in his red robe looked at each other.

'How can I help you?' said Benelli, rising from his chair. An authoritative tone had crept into his voice, as if to remind the monk who was the more important of the two. Quite unintentional, of course.

'The Holy Father has invited both of us to visit the Vatican observatory this evening,' said the Father Confessor, his voice affectionate and untroubled by the put-down. 'There'll be an unusual conjunction of planets in the sky.'

'Oh?' exclaimed Benelli in surprise. He knew that the pontiff had taken a keen interest in the observatory since becoming Pope eight years ago. Why, Benelli was not quite sure. He rarely contemplated the sky; these days he had enough problems on earth.

Together, they went out into the night and waited for a car to take them to Castel Gandolfo, the Pope's summer residence, where the observatory was located. For August it was unseasonably cold and the stars were out in abundance. Benelli shivered.

He didn't know much about his companion. The Father Confessor had been the abbot of Cluny monastery in France. Then, about a year ago, the Pope had asked him to take up his new post. It was an unusual appointment since, ecclesiastically speaking, it was an inferior position to the one the monk held. However, he'd accepted it in the spirit of obedience. Benelli admired him in a slightly grudging way; he suspected he wouldn't have done the same.

'What will we see?'

'The Holy Father tells me there is a close alignment of Neptune, Mars and Uranus. It's quite rare.' The monk's gaze was steady.

'How interesting,' said the Cardinal, trying to sound enthusiastic. Not his cup of tea at all. They went inside.

The head of the Vatican observatory was a small man with a bald pate and beady eyes. With his clipboard, pens neatly arranged in his shirt pocket and bespectacled stare, he had all the indicia of a first-rate bore, which he proceeded to demonstrate.

'Your Eminence will,' he said, his weedy chest swelling up like a turkey-cock, 'of course, be aware that a conjunction is a close apparent approach between two celestial objects.' He swelled even more. 'And there is also a retrograde loop occurring – that is, in the case of Neptune and Uranus, the planets appear to move backwards, um, westwards, through the sky as they approach the opposite point from the sun. This takes some time. It will become even more apparent in a few weeks' time.'

The technician was delighted to display his knowledge to such an august personage. He glanced at the Father Confessor. Presumably the assistant; he didn't need to see it. Not important enough. The technician escorted the Cardinal to the telescope.

'You will notice . . .' He twittered on about various astronomical matters that passed, like the stars, over Benelli's balding head.

'I can't see a thing.'

'You need to focus it, like so.'

A sight appeared before Benelli's eyes. 'What is it?'

'A conjunction of three planets.'

Benelli still couldn't make anything out. Was there dust on the lens or was his eyesight dimming? He didn't like to ask. He stepped away, brushing his robe fondly. 'How often does this occur?'

'About once every two thousand years,' said the technician. 'The last conjunction was in AD 66. On the seventh of March to be precise. Of course, no one on earth would have seen it then.' He gave a braying laugh. 'Neptune and Uranus hadn't been discovered in those days. No telescopes, you see!'

'Of course,' said Benelli. He wasn't in the least interested in things cosmological: the administration of the Church had always occupied his attention. To change the subject Benelli tried to think of what had happened in AD 66. But he couldn't think of anything special. AD 67 was different: the presumed death of St Peter. In the event, it was rather a disappointing evening.

'Well, very interesting,' said Benelli, which he always did when lost for words. 'Very . . . interesting. And will the Holy Father be coming?'

'I don't think so.' The technician hopped about nervously. 'Only your names were given to us.'

'Wonderful.' If the pontiff wasn't coming, Benelli had to get back to his meeting. He parted from the Father Confessor at the door to the observatory. 'To the next conjunction!' The monk gave him a curious look.

Benelli gratefully returned to his well-appointed study

in the Vatican. He shivered as he took off his overcoat. How kind of the Pope to think of him. However, it had been an utter waste of time. He consulted his watch. He was due to see the Archbishop of Cologne at nine o'clock for a chat. Did they have any chocolate biscuits?

Benelli crossed over to the window and adjusted the top button of his cardinal's robe in a small mirror. Time to go. Then his eyes caught sight of a book on the table which had been given to him by the Father Confessor a few days ago, after his last confession. Benelli had had no time to read it.

He glanced at the title. *Abraham of Nathpar.* He groaned slightly. Oh dear, a mystic and an obscure one at that. Heavy going, no doubt. Better to leave it until the long vacation. Idly, the Cardinal flicked the tome open. Suddenly, his eyes fell on some words.

> *Be eager in prayer, and vigilant, without wearying; and remove from yourself drowsiness and sleep. You should be watchful both by night and by day.*

For some obscure reason the words unsettled Benelli. Especially the bit about the night.

CHAPTER FOUR

*He who justifies the wicked and he who
condemns the righteous are both alike an
abomination to the Lord.*

Proverbs 17:15

IT WAS THE SECOND DAY of the Kramer trial. Various
legal points had occupied the first. How boring.

In front of the court the TV networks from around
California had gathered, pantechnicons bursting with
equipment. Beside them were anchormen and -women,
primping and preening themselves with the self-
adoration of narcissists. Soon they would show off their
profound knowledge of the Kramer case to the viewers,
research undertaken by others and displayed on electronic signboards for them to read.

Inside the court, however, things were less dynamic and
breathy and the spectators were becoming restless. They
wanted action, otherwise, they might as well go home and
watch a crime series on the TV. Unexpectedly, they got it.

'Bring the prisoner in,' Judge Harrison ordered an
officer of the court.

There was silence. Then a sound of footsteps was
heard. The door opened and a number of the spectators
gasped involuntarily.

34

Karl Kramer walked into the room, his hands shackled in chains. He grinned at the assembly. A big man, with the build of a stevedore, his bulky frame and arms were engorged with muscles. His facial features were not unattractive either: a large visage with a well-shaped nose and dark eyes that were intense, almost female, in their composition and shape. His long, black hair was tied back in a knot. Not a male model, but he didn't look like a monster. More like the man on the local building site or a plumber.

However, the apparent normality of Kramer's appearance made him all the more frightening to the spectators. What could have gone on in that man's mind when he did what he did to that poor girl? How could anyone slice up another human being as he had, stabbing her more than forty times? Had this man no iota of remorse or guilt in him? And what did he do with the missing flesh? Eat it? The spectators shuddered at the thought and they passed judgement quickly. This monster was not part of the human race. He was quite different from them. They were sure of it. Let him die.

Kramer said nothing as he stepped into the dock. The silence continued.

Paul Stauffer and Ben Ingelmann were sitting in one of the witness rooms. It was a small room, shabby and painted a judicial grey. Just the thing to impress a potential witness and to remind him, or her, how bleak life could be.

Ben scratched his nose. He knew Paul was angry he'd come along, but Florence had begged him to. Besides, it was tragic to see that, after all Ben's hard work, his friend was about to throw away his career so lightly.

'Paul, are you sure about this?'

Paul looked up from some court papers on the table. He was beginning to get very irritated. He noticed that Ben's strands of wispy grey hair were thinning even more. Would he take early retirement? Perhaps that would be no bad thing. Paul could easily do his job and he'd make some changes to the clinic. Modernise it.

'What's the problem?'

'I'm still worried he could be faking.'

'Oh, for God's sake!' Paul raised his eyes towards the ceiling, exasperated. 'Listen, Ben, there's nothing in his behaviour or psychological assessments to indicate he's the serial killer. *Nothing.*'

Contemptuously, Paul tossed his assessment across the table. 'No previous convictions apart from the bar-room killing, no evidence he has abnormal traits, no indication that he hates women or that he has frequent attacks of homicidal fury. I accept he's a loner and, obviously, he's some violence in him but his psychological profile is negative for the type of behaviour you'd expect in this case. What do you want me to do? I can't decide he *might* have murdered Melanie Dukes on the basis of a suspicion or a hunch.'

'He's killed before.'

'Yeah, yeah,' said Paul in a caustic tone, 'another man in a bar-room brawl. So what? When drunk and under provocation. One stab to the heart and Kramer didn't deny it, though he claimed it was self-defence. No one exactly saw what happened, yet he was found guilty. Ben' – Paul's voice rose aggressively – 'it's a completely different crime from a person who seizes female victims, subjects them to prolonged torture and then, as his *pièce de résistance*, cuts them up with a knife.'

'I know, I know,' confessed his partner hastily. 'But I

don't think you should be so definitive in the witness box. There's a world of difference in saying, from a psychiatric perspective, that the man did *not* do it and saying that it is *unlikely* that he did it. It's just this case, this man, worries me.'

Paul glared at him. Ben turned away, embarrassed by his own behaviour. His colleague had a right to be resentful of Ben's poking his nose into his case. However, it had considerable ramifications for a city living under the menace of a serial killer, where there was a huge political, and public, impetus to solve the murders. On the other hand, even if he had interior doubts, Paul had agreed to act for the defence and to change his mind now would badly affect his reputation. That was the heart of the problem: either way he'd come in for intense criticism. Ben changed tack.

'What do you think happened?'

'He's telling the truth. He never met Melanie Dukes in his life.'

'And the evidence of her sister?'

Paul's hand cut through the air dismissively. 'What evidence? She *thinks* she saw Kramer and she heard his voice on two occasions. No other witnesses. The word of a girl who admits she'd drunk a lot that night against that of a convict. Not good enough to execute him.'

Ben drew in his breath. They'd reached the showdown. 'I just want to ask you one more thing. Personally speaking, not professionally. Do you have any doubts about this case?'

Paul focused on the questioning eyes. 'None whatsoever.' Then he looked away.

At that moment the phone rang. Paul took it. 'Kramer wants to speak to me. I'd better go.'

'Good luck,' Ben said. Nervously, he ran his hand

through his scanty hair as his erstwhile friend quit the room.

Karl Kramer blinked in the sunlight. He breathed in the purer air of the courtroom while his defence lawyer began his case. Four days of listening to the prosecution. Boring as hell. It was on the tip of Kramer's tongue to tell everyone just how pissed-off he was with the whole thing. But no, he must bide his time a while longer.

How could he divert himself? Karl perused the spectators in the courtroom. Finally, he located Laura Dukes right at the back. She knew he was looking at her. Lovely features. Just like her sister. Twenty-three years old, though she had the complexion of one much older. Probably the shock of her sister's death had aged her.

Surreptitiously, Karl winked at her. Laura Dukes hurriedly averted her eyes. Whore. Karl would remember that. If he ever got out he'd kill her as well. Of course, he'd take more time on this occasion. Her sister had died too quickly, he'd got carried away. But with Laura, ah, it would be different, he promised her.

While Kramer was thinking of more pleasurable things his attorney rattled on. Having opened his voice box, only death or a lack of cash could stop him.

'It is our case, members of the jury, that our client Karl Kramer never met Melanie Dukes, and that he certainly never killed her. He was elsewhere in the city, with a street prostitute, which he admits.' The lawyer coughed to get their attention. 'We also intend to call to give evidence Professor Paul Stauffer of the Department of Criminal Psychiatry at San Francisco University. He believes that our client's psychiatric profile does not reveal any indication that he would rape, or kill, women in the manner in which *poor* Melanie Dukes died.'

The lawyer paused after his emphasis on the word '*poor*'. Then he slipped in the poison pill. 'We may, per-haps, also note that Melanie was no sexual innocent and that, on her sister's own admittance, she'd had sexual relationships with a number of men. It was a considerable risk for her to take a lift in a stranger's car at that time of night.'

There was a sharp intake of breath from the spectators in the gallery as they expressed their disagreement and shock. So a twenty-three-year-old girl, by accepting a lift home, had provoked her murder? What did these lawyers and psychiatrists know about people or about life? Their faces registered their indignation; jaws clamped, eyes nar-rowed. They focused their venom on the defence lawyer. He continued:

'We do not deny, members of the jury, that Karl Kramer is not a very pleasant man, certainly not one you would like to meet in a bar after he's had a few drinks, but we assert that he is no serial killer.' The defence lawyer paused at this juncture. He gave just the right hint of a smile as if to say, I know he's bad. You know he's bad. But come on, he's not *that* bad.

Kramer inspected his lawyer and then his psychiatrist. Fucking idiots. Still, he didn't mind if clever people put up silly arguments. Why shouldn't they? They had to make money somehow. Who cared about the truth, anyway?

'And so . . . and so . . . and so . . .' the lawyer droned on.

Kramer leant over and whispered in an assistant's ear, 'I want to see the psychiatrist again this evening.'

Kramer observed Paul intently. The truth. Always diffi-cult, wasn't it?

Kramer had sat in his mother's bedroom watching her while she plied her trade as a prostitute in the slums of New York. Aged seven he had witnessed a dissatisfied client stab her to death with a sheath knife. By eighteen, Kramer himself had taken his first victim, a young girl whose disappearance was still not accounted for. But Karl made sure that no one ever knew of his past and he hid his seething hatred behind a mask of affable stupidity and heavy drinking.

At twenty-seven Kramer had moved to Los Angeles and had taken up work trucking goods from there to San Francisco. It was not a bad job and it had given him plenty of scope to practise his extracurricular activities. However, this past year, his assaults on women, and a few men, had taken a much more violent turn, as if something within him was propelling him further along the path of evil at greater speed.

Over the next few weeks the San Francisco police discovered five women's bodies, horribly mutilated, as Kramer had sought to find out what gave him most satisfaction, discarding the objects of his wrath with as much concern as a man might cast aside a cigarette butt into the gutter. It was only with Melanie Dukes that he had grown too bold. Normally, he would never go into the nightclubs or discos, preferring to waylay women late at night in quiet places as they came home from work or from bars. But in the case of Melanie Dukes he had gone inside and shown his face. He had made his first slip. That had got the police on his trail.

Yet it was Melanie Dukes who had given Kramer his greatest pleasure and his biggest thrill so far. The pleasure of asserting his power over another, the thrill of making the police look stupid into the bargain. It had been an irresistible temptation.

'What did you want to see me for?' asked Paul.

'How do you think the trial's going?'

'I don't know,' Paul replied patiently. His client wasn't very bright. 'We haven't heard all the evidence yet.'

Abruptly, Kramer chuckled. It was a full-throated chuckle, something Paul had never heard from him. 'I'm going to get off,' he said.

'You're sure?' Paul was taken aback. 'Why's that?'

'Because they're going to help me.'

'Who?'

'They are. And you,' said Kramer. He yawned and stared at the ceiling, bored with life.

'They? Who's they?' Paul was bewildered. 'I don't understand what you're saying.' This was unusual. Kramer was normally monosyllabic, just staring fixedly at him all the time. Conversation was beyond him. Very low IQ.

'Really,' said the killer as he manoeuvred gum from one side of his mouth to the other. He paused. 'Then you're gonna help me with my bar-room case.'

'Look, your lawyers haven't even put in an appeal on that one.'

'They will,' said Kramer in a nonchalant tone. 'And I'll get off that too.' Then he leant forward. 'You don't know what this is all about, do you?' He sniggered. 'It's about *you*, not me.'

'About me?' Paul looked at him in complete astonishment. What was happening? His client had suddenly found his voice and was talking in riddles.

'Uh, ha.' Kramer rose from his chair and beckoned to the guards as if they were servants. 'Day after tomorrow, I'll get off. Remember, they'll give you whatever you want. Oh,' he smirked, 'well done on getting the lecture.'

'What?' Paul stood up, even more confused.

Kramer walked clumsily towards the door in his shackles, his movements like a fettered animal. After he crossed the threshold he looked back over his shoulder and gave a big wink. 'Tell Laura Dukes I'll be seeing her.'

That night Paul sat alone in his study for a long time. What was happening? Until that very last conversation with Kramer he'd been so sure he was innocent. Yet that final remark, when Kramer had said it, Paul had been startled. Was he subtly telling him he'd killed the girl? Or was it just a throw-away comment, since Kramer had obviously seen the murdered girl's sister in court and would see her again the following day?

'Goodnight, Daddy.' Rachel climbed up on his lap and pressed her face to his. She could see that he was preoccupied. 'Will you read me a story?'

'Not tonight,' he replied. Paul watched her walk through the door up the stairs.

Kramer had also said, 'You don't know what this is all about, do you? It's about *you*, not me.' What did he mean by that? Did Kramer realise that this case would make, or break, Paul's reputation? That Paul had a vested interest in it and he couldn't back out now? And what was the point he'd made about the lecture? Did he mean the Carl Jung one which that supercilious bastard Johann Hermanns had got?

Marie came in. 'You all right?'

Paul nodded.

She hesitated. 'Paul, can I talk to you?'

Her face was drawn. Probably some of the people at work, those self-righteous charity bigots, had got at her again for his representing Kramer. But he didn't want to know. They'd argued about it before. There was nothing further to be said on the matter. Full stop.

'I have some things to do. Let's talk later.'

Marie could see he wasn't in a co-operative mood. Perhaps later, in bed, they could discuss it.

'I'll read Rachel her story.'

Marie departed from the room. Suddenly, Paul realised he wasn't so sure about Kramer any more. Perhaps he was the serial killer after all. Things might be so very different from what he'd thought. Or was he just over-reacting?

Anyway, what was he going to do about it?

CHAPTER FIVE

The earth is given into the hand of the wicked;
[God] covers the faces of its judges – if it is
not he, who then is it?

Job 9:24

THE PROSECUTING LAWYER JABBED HIS finger at
the prisoner and began his summing up.

'We contend that this man – take a good look at him,
members of the jury – this monster, murdered a young
woman in the most horrific fashion. Having kidnapped
her he killed her. Then he mutilated her body, gouging
her eyes out. Finally, he tossed her corpse into a canal.'

Kramer frowned. They never got it right. He'd taken
Melanie's eyes out *before* he killed her. Attention to detail,
huh, and this man was meant to be a lawyer. He hoped
the suit would go further into the killing bit, he liked to
rehear the gory details.

The spectators ogled him, their faces pinched white
with morbid shock at the callousness of the crime. They
hated him, they wished him dead, but so what? Who were
these nonentities anyway? Just nobodies, living humdrum
nobody lives. Trash. Kramer gave the judge a sympathetic
smile. Boring job, he imagined. They must pay him well
to listen to all this rubbish.

'You have heard the oral and written evidence of Professor Paul Stauffer for the defence, who is very strong in his opinion that Mr Kramer doesn't have a psychological profile to suggest he could have killed Melanie Dukes. However, you have also heard our expert . . .'

Blah, blah, blah. Kramer looked again at Laura Dukes in the back row. He wondered whether her naked body would be as good to hold as her sister's had been. He bet it would.

Two days later the jury gave their verdict. It was a stunner.

NOT GUILTY.

The court erupted into mayhem. Karl Kramer stood up when they announced it. He didn't smile. He'd been thinking of other things. Of the people he'd tortured since his youth. Still, he was pleased with the verdict. They weren't going to execute him after all. Good decision. He didn't particularly want to die yet. There were a lot more things he wanted to do. Like get acquainted with Laura Dukes.

Kramer stared across at her. She was crying and the rest of the crowd looked stunned. Still, the jury weren't to blame, he thought. Donkeys led by fools. They'd just got it wrong. Shame about that. Never mind, they couldn't win against him and his kind. Kramer turned round in the box to go back to the cells.

'Is there anything you'd like to say, sir?' a pressman called out to his departing figure.

'Er, yeah.' He pulled the chewing gum from his mouth and tried to look serious. 'I'd just like to thank my team. In particular, Prof Stauffer.' He winked at Paul, who was putting notes into his attaché case. 'He always knew that I was innocent. He was sure of it.'

Kramer sniggered. The psychiatrist seemed uncomfortable for once. But Kramer didn't mind endorsing the

Prof. Stauffer would soon have the criminal underworld queueing up for his expertise. And much, much more, if what his mistress told him was right. Praised be evil. In thy name.

They led him down to the cells.

As the murderer got off, the victim's sister started her sentence.

Laura Dukes leant over the basin in the courthouse restroom and was violently sick. Women entered and left but no one sought to help her. They didn't know what to say or to do. Eventually she bathed her face in cold water and studied herself in the mirror. Not the prettiest of sights, but it didn't matter. Nothing really mattered for a long time. She gritted her teeth and went out into the corridor. She thought of her sister.

'Laura.' The prosecuting counsel came up and took her arm. He led her to a bench. 'You OK?'

'He got off.'

The attorney was a well-dressed man in his late fifties. However, with a flaking skin he looked much older. He said, 'Laura, I'm sorry, we just didn't have the evidence.'

'But what about *my* evidence? I saw Kramer. I heard him. I identified him in a line-up. What more did they want?'

The lawyer shook his head. 'It just wasn't enough, Laura. I'm sorry. The jury must have concluded that it was a case of mistaken identity by you.' He patted her hand. 'What can I say? You know, and I know, that he's as guilty as hell. Yet, the psychiatric evidence in his favour was very strong. They had one of the top people from the University of San Francisco, Paul Stauffer. He was firm in his opinion.'

They observed Paul, who'd exited the courtroom and was waving goodbye to the defence lawyer. Outside, the massed ranks of the media were waiting for him.

Laura's eyes narrowed in fury. 'Kramer's guilty. You can *see* that. It's so obvious from his behaviour. He's done this before. I know it. He's the serial killer.'

'Laura, please calm down,' said the prosecuting counsel in a hushed voice. He didn't want the cameras taking pictures of her in this state; they'd crucify her. 'We had no evidence, that's the problem. And the courts need evidence to go on, not just your opinion.'

But Laura Dukes would have none of it. Beside herself, she got up and ran after Paul. She caught up with him at the end of the corridor. They were alone.

'How much did they pay you?' Laura's face was tense and drawn with loathing.

Paul didn't intend to say anything. However, on an impulse, he felt angry with her, imposing on him like this. It spoilt his satisfaction at having won. He replied curtly, 'What I normally charge. Thirty thousand dollars.'

'To lie.'

'I didn't lie.'

Incensed, Laura's voice rose in pitch. 'You lied. You know in your heart that the monster tortured and murdered my sister. He's evil.' She pointed her finger at Paul accusingly. 'You know. Yet you hide it behind all your jargon and your fancy language. That's what they pay you for. You liar.'

Paul said calmly, 'I spoke what I thought was the truth.'

'I don't believe you.'

Paul shrugged. He started to walk away towards the TV cameras, towards his destiny. Meanwhile, the prosecuting attorney rushed up. He caught Laura Dukes by the arm. 'You shouldn't be discussing the case with him. Leave him. It will only make it worse.'

'Do you know how I feel?' she screamed down the corridor. 'Do you know?'

Paul didn't turn round. Surreptitiously, he adjusted his tie.

Her lawyer grabbed her. 'Laura, please. We'll take you home.'

Violently she turned on him. 'So, what do you want me to do? How do I face this?' she shouted. 'That was my sister who was ripped to pieces – not just a piece of flesh. Is that justice?'

Her counsel gaped, for once at a loss for words. Then his professional persona asserted itself again. 'Laura, I know a good psychiatrist. You need help to cope with this.'

'Huh, a psychiatrist for me too?' She thrust him aside.

Late that night, Laura Dukes sat in the front row of pews in a church not far from the spot where her sister's body had been recovered from the canal. The lights twinkled at the altar. The place was silent.

However, in her mind a tempest raged. She cursed God. Why had he made her? And why had he made her sister – to die in such a horrible fashion? Why? Revulsion and hostility boiled and surged through her.

Why do the evil always get away with it in this world? Why are they – the killers, the child molesters, the maniacs – why are they always protected while the good suffer? Why? *All I want to know is why.* She gazed at the altar as she questioned the Almighty. Surely, supreme and divine being, you can tell me? It's a simple enough question. It can't be that difficult to answer.

However, the candles burning at the altar gave her no response. Nor did the man on the cross. There never was an answer. That was the whole, bloody stupidity of it all, thought Laura. The God that never answered. Damn him.

Laura Dukes knelt down. And she prayed – her final prayer. 'God, if you really loved me, if you really ever cared for me or my sister, then I pray for this one thing. That you will take revenge on Karl Kramer. That you will make him suffer. And that you will make that lying psychiatrist who helped him suffer. But you won't do that, will you? You won't make them suffer.'

Laura Dukes glared at the crucifix in righteous anger. She knew the real reason why her God wouldn't answer. Because he had chickened out on life at thirty-three. No starvation for you, no rape, no torture, a family around you when you died and lots of hangers-on. A quick death – a few hours on a cross. But for me? How can you repay me for a future life of suffering? To lose my sister in this way? Knowing that, when Kramer gets out in a few years' time, he'll probably come after me as well, and I'll be the next victim? What will you do about it, man on the cross? *What can you do, O Christ?*

Ten minutes later Laura got up. As she gave up her seat, so she gave up her faith. For she knew the truth now in her heart. There was no loving God in this world after all. He was just another trick, another figment of the imagination, in a world of con tricks. There was only evil, pure and boundless. Laura walked down the steps of the building. Then she went to the hospital to say goodbye to her mother. The old woman bade farewell in an affectionate way, having no idea who her daughter was. Even in that, the Almighty had failed them, again.

That night Laura Dukes committed suicide. She

drowned her sorrows and herself, in the same canal in which her sister had died.

Paul put down the phone. Quietly, he entered the living room. It was approaching midnight. Marie was reading a magazine, her feet curled up on the sofa. She noticed his expression and then exclaimed in alarm, 'What is it? What's wrong?'

'Laura Dukes killed herself. An hour ago.'

'Oh my God.' Marie's hands rose to her face in horror.

Paul said in a neutral tone, 'I think we'd better go to bed.' There was nothing more to do.

'Paul, it wasn't your fault. You had to give the evidence as you saw it.'

That night, as Paul lay in bed, he heard the soft sound of Marie praying and he knew whom she was praying for. He closed his eyes. In life there were winners and there were losers. Kramer won, Laura Dukes lost. He'd been found not guilty by the jury and she couldn't accept it. So what was Paul supposed to do?

He turned over in bed. Of course, the case had been difficult. Even he had begun to doubt Kramer at times – particularly after that last strange meeting he'd had with him before the verdict. But by then it had been too late, hadn't it? Anyway, Paul wouldn't be providing assistance to him on the bar-room killing. He was sure Kramer had been properly found guilty of that one.

Tomorrow, the TV networks would be out with a vengeance. Paul would face accusations that he'd caused Laura Dukes's suicide in some way. However, he could defend himself. The girl had obviously become mentally unhinged by the trauma of her sister's death, that was all. His mind idled onto other matters. He wondered

50

whether he should put on the new suit he'd bought a couple of days ago. With the yellow tie? Or the red one he'd sported on the first day of the trial? Did TV viewers notice that type of thing?

Paul slept soundly. Marie continued to pray long into the night.

'Get in.'

Kramer grinned and threw himself down on the bed. Behind him the steel door closed. He walked about his cell in the San Francisco High Security Facility. It was good to be back home for a while. In a couple of months, when the political furore over the trial had calmed down a bit and they thought he wouldn't be attacked by other prisoners, they'd move him to a less harsh environment. Little did they know that Kramer could easily look after himself. He always had, thank you very much.

The warder peered at him through a grate. 'Your psychiatrist will visit you in a few days.'

'Oh yeah?' Kramer didn't care if he came or not. Paul had done his job.

Kramer stretched out on his metal bed. It had been a good day. Avoiding the death penalty, that was something to celebrate. Now he only had his sentence for the bar-room murder to complete. What was five years in prison for killing a drunk? Karl would find plenty of things to occupy himself with. He'd write to that pretty sister of hers, pretend to be all contrite, of course. And when he got out, well now, Karl would carry on as always. He couldn't do otherwise, his mistress wouldn't let him. In the meantime, there were plenty of inmates to victimise, plenty of young prey. A veritable feast. He was glad he'd come to earth.

Karl Kramer closed his eyes. He thought of Laura

Dukes. Mentally he undressed her, savouring his cruelty
as he tore her to pieces. Soon, he slept.

By his side stood an Angel of Darkness.

CHAPTER SIX

Because sentence against an evil deed is not
executed speedily, the heart of the sons of men
is fully set to do evil.

Ecclesiastes 8:11

CARDINAL BENELLI CONSULTED HIS WATCH. It was
time to sleep. He read the last few words:

But when I looked for good, evil came; and when I waited
for light, darkness came.

He put down the Bible on the chair beside his bed. He'd
finish the chapter from the Book of Job tomorrow night.
It always made depressing reading. Poor Job. That the
innocent should suffer was one thing, but that God
should allow suffering to be deliberately inflicted on
them was particularly terrible.

Benelli turned out the light. In fact, it had been a
long and depressing day. In the morning he'd met a
delegation of priests from Burkina Faso who'd brought
with them details of the massacre of Christians there. It
was horrifying to contemplate the depths of evil to which
humanity could sink. But what could Benelli do besides

make pious statements and pray? It seemed so ineffectual in the light of their agonies.

Then, in the afternoon, he'd chaired a committee meeting on the financial state of Rome's churches. The coffers were bare once again. In the case of the Vatican, in particular, they'd inherited a treasure house, the maintenance costs of which soared every year. Then there was the recent expulsion of priests from China ... but he didn't want to go on.

Benelli said his prayers, which took some time. At the end he added a few requests for himself. Nothing too selfish, of course. Just the fervent hope that the meeting of the Ecumenical Commission, which he had to chair on Thursday, would go well. Those evangelicals were so troubling.

He settled back to sleep. However, tonight, he was unable to do so. The same had happened the last few nights. What *was* the matter? It couldn't be the usual worries of work. Perhaps he was just getting old. Should he take a sleeping pill? No. He closed his eyes.

Slowly, he lapsed into a dream. Or was it a vision?

Benelli found himself gazing up at the stars; where he was on earth he had no idea. He became transfixed by the immensity of the cosmic picture unfolding before him. Stellar formation after stellar formation, endlessly unravelling like a great, unfathomable mystery. As they did so he began to comprehend a little of the awesome passage of time. Not just a few years. Hundreds of thousands of years. Millions upon millions of years. The absolute insignificance of man in all this became firmly impressed on his mind.

Captivated by these images, in his trance, Benelli experienced a profound spiritual awakening. He felt as if he had been thrown into a warm pool of water hidden away in a mystical world that no one could find. The exhilaration was utterly transcendent.

For an instant Benelli perceived with absolute certainty that mankind, the most insignificant spiritual form in the cosmos, was, in some extraordinary way, the most significant. That God had planted within humanity the key to it all. The key to the Creator himself, to eternal life. It was overwhelming. All would be revealed. Benelli's whole being rose up to marvel at the majesty of it. Then he discerned something else. It was both terrible and tragic in its purport.

Suddenly, the Cardinal awoke. He sat up, fearful and disoriented. In the distance he could hear a dog barking. His mind was still half filled with his revelation. Why had the Pope told him to visit the observatory? He got up. What was that? He stopped. Words came flooding into his consciousness. Words that the first occupant of the papal throne, St Peter, had declared:

> *There is one thing, my friends, that you must never forget: that with the Lord, 'a day' can mean a thousand years, and a thousand years is like a day. The Lord is not being slow to carry out his promises, as anybody else might be called slow; but he is being patient with you all . . .*

Benelli stumbled out of bed. He went down on his knees, truly frightened. It was as though a messenger was seeking to tell him something. But he could not, did not, want to accept it. With all the strength of his will he tried to reject it, a reluctant prophet. He begged, 'May it not be so. Not now. Not while I live.'

Slowly, the vision faded from his mind. Benelli remained on his knees.

CHAPTER SEVEN

Unclean spirits . . . are the enemies of the human race, rational in mind, but reasoning without words, subtle in wickedness, eager to do hurt, ever fertile in fresh deceptions, they change the perceptions and befoul the emotions of men, they confound the watchful, and in dreams disturb the sleeping.

Malleus Maleficarum,
'Hammer of the Witches'

A MONTH HAD PASSED SINCE the end of the Kramer trial and the suicide of Laura Dukes.

For Paul, it had been an extremely busy period. He was the man of the moment. There were endless TV interviews, a couple of chat shows, demands for books from publishers. He was also heavily involved in advising the San Francisco police on tracking down the serial killer now that Kramer had been found not guilty.

The public, and most of his fellow psychiatrists, accepted that Paul had been right. Pointedly, Ben had said nothing. Paul realised it was sour grapes, but at Marie's insistence he didn't press the matter. Kramer was obviously not the serial killer, and he'd been a model prisoner since the trial. He'd told the national press that he was trying to find God and he'd joined a basket-weaving class in prison. In fact, Paul had agreed to give evidence for him in his appeal against the bar-room killing, so he might be out in a few months, if successful.

It had also come to light that Laura Dukes had had a minor breakdown after a bust-up with a boyfriend when she was sixteen. She had been a more disturbed young woman than they'd thought. Pity the welfare people hadn't discovered this before. The strain of a trial seven years later must have been the final straw. Still, Paul reflected, that was just the way life turned out. If people wanted to kill themselves, it was difficult to stop them.

One other good thing happened to Paul . . .

The university hall began to fill up. It held over a thousand people and the seats for the lecture that night were on an invitation-only basis. The guests came from around the globe. Ben watched as many famous names from the world of psychiatry and criminal psychiatry entered the auditorium, the men in tuxedos, the women in glistening evening wear, all gathered for a major social event. To host the Carl Jung lecture was a triumph for the University of San Francisco and, since the location of the event depended on the identity of the keynote speaker, it was also a testimony to the ability, and growing renown, of Professor Paul Stauffer that he'd been chosen.

After the tragic death of Johann Hermanns in a plane crash in Munich, the international committee had decided to break with precedent and choose Paul Stauffer, aged only thirty-nine, to give the principal address. This was an astonishing move – revolutionary even. Brilliant, iconoclastic, not one to tolerate fools, he was a dark horse. But the committee had actually done something right for once and, as Ben and others at the university recognised, it was unlikely the committee would have cause to regret their choice. Paul was guaranteed to provide a *tour de force*.

'Ben!'

'Hi, Marie. Where's that misplaced husband of yours?'

'Oh, don't worry,' laughed Marie as she adjusted the strap on her pale blue evening dress, 'I made sure he got here.' She pointed to her spouse, submerged among the mêlée. 'And there's your wife.'

Ben nodded glumly. Florence had cornered Sir Harold Pickerton, the greatest criminal psychiatrist of his age. Marie could see that she was in full verbal spate and the poor man was pinned to the wall. He was assenting furiously while Florence held forth on the joys of their holiday to the battlefields of Scotland the previous year, wholly unaware that Sir Harold's English ancestors had almost been wiped out to a man by the Scots at Bannockburn when they'd inadvertently fled in the wrong direction.

A bell rang. Everyone went to take their seats.

'Such an interesting individual. So knowledgeable,' trilled Florence to Marie as they sat down. 'Of course, I told him that your husband was a genius, my dear.'

Sir Harold, somewhat recovered from his conversation and reliving the trauma of an ancestral massacre, mounted the podium. He asked for a minute's silence in memory of Johann Hermanns. Then he introduced their speaker for the evening. Marie sat transfixed as Paul stepped forward to the lectern. Composed, he set down his papers and began in a confident and friendly voice:

'Ladies and gentlemen, I am a professor of criminal psychiatry here at the University of San Francisco. I'm also senior consultant to the San Francisco High Security Facility, which houses some of the most dangerous and violent people in this country. As a result, my area of expertise for many years has been the study of those whom the general public often characterise as monsters, whose crimes fill the front pages of the newspapers and for whom our citizens demand the death penalty. Serial killers, child rapists, cannibals, torturers, mass murderers: these are my patients – though I'm more cautious about calling them my friends.'

There was a mild ripple of laughter in the room. What was friendship anyway? Psychiatrically speaking, of course.

Paul continued, 'In my lecture today I want to analyse the role religion has played in distinguishing good from evil acts and how this has affected our approach towards regulating criminal behaviour.'

He leant forward, his voice assured and inviting. The audience were hooked.

'The basic tenet of my lecture is that the religious concepts of good and evil, which have played a pivotal role in Western society to date in regulating human behaviour and punishing criminal conduct, have *no* role in modern psychiatry. Today, with modern drugs and therapies, we should evaluate criminal behaviour using medical, as opposed to moral, terms. This will enable us to salvage even those criminals currently regarded as morally defective by society and fit for nothing but death.'

'So far, so good,' said Florence in a loud stage whisper.

Paul then considered in detail the place of religion in society from the point of view of regulating human conduct. For centuries the Church had sought to monitor and control the most basic aspects of people's daily lives – for example, in relation to marriage, to divorce, homosexuality, adultery, the age of consent, legitimacy, etc.

'Indeed, in medieval times,' said Paul, 'the Church even prescribed the basic sexual position people must adopt, the missionary position being deemed the only one appropriate.' Paul smirked. 'Presumably Eve experienced this after the Garden of Eden.'

The audience laughed loudly – a sophisticated and mocking laughter. It was going to be a witty speech. How droll. No place for religion in modern secular society, banished by science. Marie blushed. Paul could never resist getting a dig in at the Church.

When the laughter had died down, Paul pursued his theme of religious dominance down the centuries. How the Church ensured that conduct it did not approve of was either punished by law or was made subject to moral censure such as excommunication. How the Church had used instruments of torture and burning at the stake on those whom it deemed guilty of challenging its right to dictate the moral order – whether they were heretics, dissenters, witches or sorcerers.

'None of this repression worked. None of it was necessary. In the name of God, the worst injustices were perpetrated. However, today at long last, we have come to realise that tolerance and understanding, not persecution, is what is needed. We are progressively emancipating ourselves from the mumbo jumbo of dogma. We realise that it is not for religion or the Church – and that means *any* church – to regulate many aspects of private and consensual human conduct. Nor to damn people if they do not conform. Medicine, together with the advance of science, has played a huge part in this emancipation. For example, by telling people afflicted with leprosy or schizophrenia that theirs is a medical condition – not a punishment from God.'

Paul paused to let his words sink in. He continued,

'Today, in our country and in many others, we no longer fill our mental asylums with young unmarried mothers, we no longer ostracise homosexuals, we no longer punish adulterers. Why? Because we recognise that their activities do not, in fact, threaten the foundations of society and that simply to categorise such people as evil or depraved misses the point. *People have a right to be different – even radically different – providing they do not cause harm to others in their actions.*'

There was faint applause. The audience liked what they heard. True, the thesis was not original, so far. However, it was clear, succinct and thought-provoking.

'So, today,' continued Paul, 'our prisons and mental asylums now hold a more restricted category of patient: the truly sick and not those whose moral, sexual or religious beliefs differ from those of the majority. I contend that this category can be further reduced through drugs and counselling. In the case of serious crimes in particular we must determine the illness that drives them to it – for it is an illness, a lack of mental balance.'

Again, there was slight applause. Paul realised he was now approaching more contentious ground. In modern society people could accept that religion should not be allowed to punish private consensual behaviour. But to assert that people who committed horrific crimes were not evil, were not morally depraved as such but merely sick, was a more debatable issue.

'This then is where we approach the great taboo: murder. However, even among murderers there are categories which must be distinguished.'

Paul detailed his experience in working with people who'd committed murder in a family context or under the influence of drugs, and how their personalities and mindsets were quite different from professional killers or psychopaths. Religious beliefs often reinforced the rejection of these criminals – further alienating those who most needed help.

'I welcome the fact that the public is slowly beginning to accept that those who murder in certain situations have a right to be rehabilitated into society after a period of time. For example, women who kill their partners after years of physical and emotional abuse, children who kill other children without really knowing the true consequences of their acts, mercy killings and others. This is a great advance and one that has only occurred over the last twenty years. And, despite many churches continuing to damn these people, we in the profession have sought to help them and will continue to do so.'

Twenty minutes had passed. Paul knew that the audience was with him. Now for the thin ice – the area where there was no firm consensus among psychiatrists and where the public had a very different perception.

'We are left with the hard cases: paedophiles who kill children as part of their quest for sexual gratification; people who massacre their school- or workmates; torturers who eat the flesh of their victims; serial killers who murder by numbers; professional assassins. What do we do with these people? Destroy them in revenge? Throw away the prison key?'

'Yes,' said a female voice distinctly. It came from the centre of the audience. There were a couple of other murmurs in support.

There was stunned silence, then Paul regained control. He continued in a faintly sarcastic tone.

'My answer is "no". Once we have put aside our religious moralising and personal revulsion over these acts, with medical treatment and counselling even those categorised as irredeemable by society can be rehabilitated. *The people who commit these shocking crimes are, in my experience, not evil.* This term has no medical significance. They are individuals invariably affected with mental illness, with psychiatric disturbances, with social and societal deprivation and they react accordingly. It is this we must emphasise and appreciate, since to act otherwise is to damn with no prospect of redemption.

'So, in conclusion, I look forward to the day when religious terms like good and evil are no longer used when judging very serious crimes. Instead, the terminology of medicine, treatment and training should be used. Many, if not all, of the "monsters" of today can be reformed citizens of tomorrow, if we stop demonising them and try to help. Our insight is all.'

When Paul had finished, he received a standing ovation. For the first time in many years the profession had heard a good speech which was clear, eloquently put and not just self-adulatory. At the end of the conference, he was surrounded by admirers.

'My dear,' Florence turned to Marie, 'I must hurry to congratulate him. But who was that dreadful woman who shouted out "yes"?'

The keynote speech over, the guests retired to the bar for the night. Paul's face was soon flushed with alcohol and the praise of well-wishers. Marie managed to kiss him before he was dragged off for an earnest discussion with a Romanian psychiatrist who believed that eating turnips was the answer to the psychotic condition. Indeed, he had tried it on himself and he now felt fine.

Towards midnight, the crowd at the bar thinned. Ben and his wife approached Paul through the throng. Marie followed.

'We're just off home,' said Ben. 'Congratulations again.'

Florence bestowed a kiss on Paul with the force of a liposuction machine. 'Magnificent!' she exclaimed. 'You really are coming up in the world. Very grand.'

'Thanks,' said Paul. He smirked. 'That's enough praise for one night or else my head will get too big. Let's go. Oh, I need to pick up some things from my office. Back in a minute.'

Marie watched him depart. For some reason she felt uneasy. With all his fame now, where would that leave her?

Paul walked across the university compound into a brick and glass tower block. There was a loud buzz as he opened the main door with a pass key. The corridor lights went on and he climbed three flights of stairs, all dimly lit.

He felt contented. His lecture had been a success. He was truly on his way to the big time. The Kramer case had started it all. He strolled past the rooms of his colleagues, their names etched in black paint on the glass-panelled doors. Hah, he'd do much better than they.

And Marie? It was time to re-evaluate their relationship. He was sorry, of course, but he'd didn't think she'd be able to cope with his success. What he needed now was a younger and more ambitious woman. Naturally, he'd seek custody of Rachel; she'd get a better start in life with him. She required his drive and self-confidence, key components in getting to the top. That's the way the world was, wasn't it? Survival of the fittest and all that? Paul had no complaint.

Finally, Paul halted outside his office. He fumbled in his pocket. He felt drowsy from the alcohol and the aftermath of the adrenaline flow. His mind was still on his speech as he bent down to the keyhole.

'Excuse me.'

The voice was so close that Paul dropped the key in shock. It took a split second for his mind to adjust. He discerned the person beside him in the twilight. She was slim and blonde, but not young – at least not that young. It was difficult to gauge her age. Not a student, but not yet in her thirties. Slightly flustered, Paul stooped to pick up the key from the floor.

'I'm sorry. I didn't hear you. Can I help?'

'I listened to your speech.'

'I hope you enjoyed it,' Paul said.

'It was great. You were much better than Johann Hermanns would have been. We were rooting for you.'

'Rooting for me?'

'To get the lecture.' She smiled and drew a hand through her hair. 'We knew you would. Just knew.'

Paul glanced at her again, puzzled. He tried to open the door. For some reason the key didn't fit. 'Oh, many thanks.'

'Course, I didn't agree with all that you said about good and evil in an absolute sense,' continued the woman, her voice soft and low.

'Yes, well, er . . . ?'

'Helen.'

'Helen.' The key fitted. 'Look, won't you come in?' said Paul. 'Or, perhaps we could meet tomorrow. I'm not at my best for philosophical arguments at the moment; my head's rather befuddled with the drink.' He laughed. Helen laughed along with him. It was a companionable laugh, easygoing.

'I just wanted to congratulate you on your speech, that's all,' she said. She made no effort to enter his room.

'And to disagree with me.'

'Perhaps,' she said. 'Anyway, Kramer was right.'

'Right?'

'About you giving the speech.' Then she continued: 'I have to leave. Night then.'

Paul was bewildered. There was something that intrigued him about her, even in his befuddled state. Her poise and the knowing look. Not sexually knowing, just knowing. How did she know what Kramer had said about the lecture? Or had Paul misunderstood?

'Sure you won't come in?'

'No, I must go.' She started down the corridor. Then she turned. He couldn't make out her face in the twilight. 'See you at the dinner,' she called out breezily.

'The dinner . . . ?'

But she'd gone.

Paul closed the door to his room behind him. He shrugged. Strange woman. He'd hardly understood a word she'd said. Yet, in some way, he hoped he'd see her again. She might be interesting. He switched on his desk lamp and began to search for a file. Then, on a sudden whim, he crossed the room. He'd invite her to visit him tomorrow. Paul opened the door and went down the corridor to the top of the stairs. He leant over the balustrade. 'Helen?'

Silence. Paul listened for the click of her heels. Nothing. He frowned. She couldn't have departed so quickly: it was only a few seconds since he'd bidden her goodnight. He went down the stairs, cursing under his breath, since, for some reason, the corridor lights had gone out. Groping his way towards the main door, he tried it. It was locked. Naturally. She wouldn't have a pass key and, even if she had, he'd heard no buzzer.

How had she gone? She must have used one of the emergency exits on the other landings. Paul ascended the steps again and checked the doors on the first and second landings. They were locked and bolted. That left the third landing. He approached the heavy steel door and thrust down the handle. It was also locked.

A whiplash of fear ran through him.

It took a few seconds for Paul to override this primeval human sensation. He walked back to his room, consciously ignoring the fact that there was no other way out. By the light of the desk lamp he gathered up the papers he needed. He must go. Marie would be waiting for him.

Besides, he wanted to be out of the building.

CHAPTER EIGHT

*What is even worse, our lack of insight
deprives us of the capacity to deal with evil.*
Carl Jung, *The Undiscovered Self*

'HAVE YOU ANYTHING ELSE TO CONFESS?'

Although it was an essential part of the rite, Cardinal
Benelli sat in the prayer box and meditated on the words.
He had confessed his usual sins. A tendency towards
pride, not unexpected, perhaps, in the second most
senior person in the Vatican. A tendency to criticise other
priests at times when he should have had more charity.
A tendency to eat too much. Involuntarily, he caught
sight of his paunch.

'No, Father,' he said.

The Father Confessor started on the penance and then
gave absolution. Cardinal Benelli always tried to listen
carefully to him and to take his words to heart. However,
this time, he was not listening. He was preoccupied.

He still had a confession to make.

But this was a different confession. Different from
earthly sins, and very much more complex. It related to
the dream he had had a month ago. About the stars.
Well, it was a dream only, wasn't it? Yet it still troubled
him. When he'd knelt to pray that night he had been

quite sure there was something more: a spiritual message directed to him in particular. However, by the next morning, his feeling of certainty had gone. He doubted it and, little by little, the clarity of his vision had diminished.

There was a slight noise as the door to the confessional was opened. Cardinal Benelli got up as well. He stepped outside and into the private chapel of the Pope. It was a small but beautifully decorated room, hidden away within the confines of the papal apartments. Before their gaze was a large cross carrying the tortured body of the Saviour. Natural light flowed through stained-glass windows set into the ceiling. They depicted the Ascension in vivid colours. The ambience was wonderful, one of deep spiritual peace and unfathomable mystery.

'I beg your pardon for any sins I may have committed against you.'

Benelli nodded. The Father Confessor always said this after his confession and it was quite touching. The Cardinal looked back at the pale blue eyes of the monk while they focused upon him. Benelli was sure this man had committed very few sins in his life. Why was it some people seemed to be so much more spiritually advanced than he? Was it the penalty of his secretly enjoying high ecclesiastical office? The sin of pride, the greatest sin of all?

They started to walk out of the chapel. The Father Confessor noticed that the visage of the Cardinal had become more drawn and tense these last few weeks, as though he were carrying a heavy burden. He halted.

'Is there anything else you would like to tell me?' he said quietly.

Benelli hesitated. A great desire came over him to seek the Father Confessor's advice. But he musn't. Certain things could be discussed only with the Pope. No one else. No other human being. That was the oath he'd given when he became Head of the Holy Office. It couldn't be broken.

'I'm fine.' He gave a false smile.

The Father Confessor opened the door and Benelli began to pass through. Of course, he wouldn't tell the Pope either. The Holy Father was too busy to be troubled with Benelli's petty worries. He had hundreds of other problems to deal with – the administration of a Church of more than one and a half billion people – not the uncertainties of one old man.

Benelli stood in the doorway of the chapel and glanced back. Did he have a confession to make? Had he neglected to convey a spiritual message? To speak of an extraordinary legend hidden in the mists of time?

The chapel door closed. Benelli had no confession.

CHAPTER NINE

Now let us examine how the devil can,
through local motion, excite the fancy and
inner sensory perceptions of a man by appari-
tions and impulsive actions . . . Although the
devil cannot directly operate upon the under-
standing and will of man, yet . . . he can act
upon the body, or upon the fancies belonging
to or allied to the body, whether they be the
inner or outer perceptions.

> Malleus Maleficarum,
> 'Hammer of the Witches'

IT WAS FALL. New arrivals at San Francisco University, another year.

'He did say nine-thirty?'

'Yeah, relax.'

The group of first-year students milled outside Paul's room chatting in a desultory fashion. Some sat on the floor while others leant against the brightly painted wall, their books and satchels beside them. They were mostly between eighteen and twenty although there was one older man, distinguished by a fleck of grey in his hair.

The majority of students had jeans and tee shirts on,

although a couple of the girls were in frocks. They were very self-conscious, anxious to make a good initial impression, just as most students started out. However, these neophytes of psychiatry would soon develop a more judgemental approach towards themselves when they realised that their patients could see though their mild affectations and foibles with razor-like clarity and exploit them ruthlessly to their advantage.

'I hear he's great to work with.'

'Really laid back.'

'Hot property after the Kramer case. How he got him off was amazing.'

Dave Rattinger, from Colorado, a soccer player with light blond hair and a winning personality, approached one of the prettier girls. He wanted to make a hit with her, but reckoned it would take time. She was shy. He could tell by the way she held the textbook defensively against her breasts, obscuring them from sight. Still, she looked good enough for him. Worth a try. He'd left his former girlfriend back home. He began the conversation.

'Are we off to the Facility today?'

'No one's told me.'

Dave persisted. 'A friend of mine says he does that to all the students on their first day. Takes them to the Facility to give them a fright.'

'Oh,' said the girl, pulling on a cigarette as she leant against the wall. She paused. 'My name's Suzanne Delaney.'

'Dave Rattinger. From Denver.'

'Cigarette?'

'Thanks.'

'Here he comes.'

Paul strolled along the corridor. He was dressed in jeans and an open-neck shirt, carelessly academic in appearance. He gave a mock look of astonishment at the small audience before him. Then he grinned. 'You must be keen. I didn't expect anyone so early.'

He unlocked the door and beckoned them in. 'Sit yourselves down. Anywhere you can find space.'

It was a large room with a desk in one corner, free-standing bookshelves, a sofa and some chairs in the centre. The side tables had papers piled up on them and the walls were hung with a number of artefacts that Paul had accumulated in his twelve years of teaching and practice. A machete given to him by one murderer, now cured (at least in his own estimation). A Noh mask from a Japanese professor of psychiatry who had visited Paul on an academic exchange programme. Prints of Bedlam, the English lunatic asylum, by the eighteenth-century artist Hogarth. Many other small *objets d'art* – from African totems to framed newspaper extracts recording particularly horrific crimes on which Paul had given psychiatric advice. Nothing on Kramer though. It was a case Paul preferred to forget. He had his reasons.

The students went over to the artefacts and began to discuss them. Paul didn't call the class to order. The pieces were a good introduction to the subject and always provoked interest and inquiry.

Suzanne sat down on the sofa and lowered her own books from her breast area to her lap. Dave Rattinger promptly sat down beside her. She groaned inwardly. Why were the creeps always attracted to her? Because she had an innocent-looking face that exuded the vulnerability of a teenage girl? Or because she had a stunning bosom which she showed off to good effect when she wanted to?

Suzanne smiled at Dave, a sweet but dismissive smile. One that said, 'Stick to self-abuse.' Dave smiled back

73

hopefully, quite oblivious to her subliminal message. As a psychiatrist he'd have to do much better in reading human nature.

Meanwhile, Paul rummaged among the papers on his desk. 'Right, we should have twelve people. Can we have a quick name call, please?'

'Bob Treital, Donna Jackson, Art Jacovits, José Ramirez, Dee McKenna, Dave Rattinger, Suzanne Delaney, Brad Hanson, Laura Kuo, Sally Akers, Greg Parsons and Emil Buzek.' Everyone introduced themselves self-consciously, trying to sound cool.

Paul grasped a wooden chair. He came and sat to one side of the circle.

'Well, at least we start out with a full complement. Welcome to General Criminal Psychiatry, Part One. I'm teaching this course though, for a couple of lessons, my colleague Prof Ben Ingelmann will fill in.'

He contemplated the dough from which he had to make leaven bread.

'You'll find *my* course is rather different from others on the campus. In criminal psychiatry I want to give you as much practical experience as I can, as well as get you through the theoretical claptrap. Have you got hold of the texts I recommended for your preliminary reading – Carlton and Brown and my own work on criminal psychiatry?'

Various tomes emerged from bags.

'Good.' Paul waited until all was quiet. 'OK, I intend to start the course off with a flavour of what it will be like at the end of it, when you graduate, *if* you graduate, in four years' time. Then you can get a feel early on whether this is really the subject for you. So, today, we're going to visit San Francisco High Security Facility, the top high-security prison in the country.'

There was a deep intake of breath. So it *was* true what the older students had told them. They were going to the bad house, the really bad house. Even in the most cynical of the students hearts quickened.

The Facility. Would they see Paul Horrath, the mild-mannered Arkansas man who'd dispatched ten people in the woods over a decade by means of ritual slaughter, cutting out their tongues? Or the rat girl, Jennie J. Lee, who poisoned her relatives with thallium? Or Vincente Buzzolini, the Sicilian mafia's top enforcer in the States? Or Tommy Earle, the ex-butcher who had an appetite for young children? A mixture of ghoulish thoughts and a palpable sense of fear flowed through them.

'Before we depart, please listen carefully,' said Paul. 'We are going to one of the special areas. There you'll meet a number of people who have committed very serious crimes. The first big surprise you'll get is that the inmates in the Facility will seem, and usually are for most of the time, very normal indeed – just like you and me. They don't have crosses on their foreheads marked "Danger" or staring eyes that bulge out at you, which is the general public perception of dangerous criminals.

'The second big surprise you'll get is that the prisoners have seen many groups of eager students just like you – so don't expect them to behave like guinea pigs or to be remotely impressed.

'The third thing is that we're going to attend an art exhibition they're putting on. The purpose of this exhibition is not that you get into earnest discussions with them about their crimes – which is usually the last thing they want to chat about. OK, is that understood, everyone? Now, it's important that you know something about the individuals you'll be encountering.'

Paul went to his desk and picked up various red

folders. 'Here are background notes on the inmates you'll be meeting today. Read them on the bus and give them back to me before we enter the Facility. We'll start off at ten-thirty outside this building. I suggest girls wear jeans.'

'Why?' said Sally Akers, a stir of feminism arising.

'Because they will touch you up if you wear a skirt,' replied Paul succinctly. 'Now, any questions?'

'Are they all men?'

'No. Men and women, with a ratio of about two to one. As you may know, women, statistically, are much less likely to commit violent crimes.'

'Will there be murderers there?'

'Sure. Please read your folders. A couple of murderers . . . er, one in for infanticide, an arsonist, the rest for rape and other serious offences against the person. Next.'

'Will it be safe?'

'Perfectly safe,' said Paul. 'We've never had problems in the five years we've taken students there. Although all these people have been violent, they are not regarded as such at present. In a number of cases they are also under medication. However, don't walk about unaccompanied. And keep in sight of the staff, who will be in the blue uniforms.'

'Is it their artwork?' someone said above the noise that had broken out.

'Yes,' replied Paul. 'A few of them are quite gifted. The exhibition's in D Block of the prison.' Paul raised his voice. 'You can leave the art room and wander around the ground floor of the block. But don't go any further.' He knew, for the first ten minutes, they'd be so attached to his coat tails he'd feel like a mother duck. Then their visceral fear of the unknown would begin to abate.

'But I don't see any famous names,' Bob Treital said,

his tone despondent as he flicked through the thin red folder.

'Famous names?'

'Yep,' said Bob, switching gum to one side of his mouth. 'The really evil ones. Like Gary Snyder, the cannibal man of Texas.' He grinned.

Paul gave scornful smile. 'I'd prefer it if you don't use the word "evil". It's a moral rather than a psychiatric term. The people we are dealing with are ill or disturbed in some way. And Mr Snyder is not currently categorised as a violent patient. The very opposite. The only people you'll be seeing today are those who have been categorised as non-violent. Dangerous or violent prisoners will be locked up in their cells.' He assumed a serious face. 'Of course, Bob, if you would like to meet Mr Snyder alone, it can be arranged.'

Bob Treital gulped. His self-assured grin abated. Perhaps alone would not be the best idea. Not at the moment. 'Er, no. Just asking.'

'Fine,' said Paul. He continued: 'We'll spend a couple of hours at the Facility and then come back by bus. Don't take anything apart from what you're wearing and these folders. You'll be searched at the main entrance and as we go into D Block. OK, that's it, people. See you outside at ten-thirty.'

Somewhat nervous now, the students gathered up their things and went downstairs. A couple of the girls departed to get changed. Half an hour later the bus started off while the students avidly read the contents of their folders. There were intakes of breath and gasps as they sought to relate the placid faces in the photographs with the appalling nature of their crimes.

'How could he do that?'

'Poor women.'

'Animal.'

'Shoot the bastard.'

Paul had heard it all before. It was a perfectly normal reaction. Fear distorted one's perception and judgement. Quite understandable.

'Do you ever become afraid?'

Paul turned round in his seat. He looked at the pretty girl with a freckled face and large dark brown eyes.

'Suzanne?'

'Yes. Suzanne Delaney. Don't you ever become afraid in your work?'

'No, not really,' said Paul. 'The majority of the people I deal with may be inherently violent, but they're usually predictable in how they react. We use drugs to alleviate most of their symptoms. I haven't been attacked yet, if that's what you're asking.'

Suzanne touched him lightly with her hand. 'I'll stick close to you,' she said.

Paul laughed. She'd be fun to have in the class, he suspected. Nice figure.

The San Francisco High Security Facility was located outside the city in the desert. It had a wide area of land around it without any population. Not that people would want to live near it anyway: the notoriety of the prisoners held within its confines was sufficient to conjure up fear and alarm in the stoutest of hearts.

That said, the large and aggressive Warden of the prison, Hanlon Dawes, maintained that the Facility (or the Zoo, as he privately called it) had never had an escapee – or at least one that had got out alive. Hanlon Dawes used it as his standard gag when he sought re-election before the State Prison Committee at its triennial review, and it always went down well.

What Dawes didn't tell them was that there was an unwritten rule in the prison that any prisoner who tried to escape would be shot dead. The prisoners didn't officially know this but, as in all prisons, the rumour filtered among the inmates and they got the point, whatever their IQ. So few attempted to leave unasked. That left many of them with the option of a life behind bars or, for those who were unlucky in the lottery of the judicial system, execution. In California, where consumer choice was important, the condemned person could either choose a lethal injection or gas to be finished off with – the latter to cater for those who were squeamish with needles. The coffin and the final mug of coffee were thrown in free.

'There it is.'

Dave Rattinger whistled slightly as the outline of the Facility loomed over the desert horizon. There was only one dusty road that led towards it. The absence of any other buildings or forms of life gave the stark impression that the road itself was a journey of no return. To a living hell.

'Everyone,' said Paul. 'Please have your identification ready and leave your folders on board.' He got out of his seat and went to stand by the driver at the front. The bus pulled up before massive steel gates. From inside a bunker two heavily armed guards stepped out.

'Everyone off.'

The occupants got out and the bus drew back twenty metres. A guard told Paul and the students to pass through a small side entrance. Bob Treital observed the faces of the warders as he did so. They were thickset, impassive, hard. All humanity had gone from them. His cockiness was diminishing by the minute.

The students walked through a narrow wire passageway

and into a small hut. A man greeted Paul. 'Morning, Prof. New fodder for us?'

'Just visiting,' Paul quipped back.

They passed through a large scanner machine similar to those found at airports. The warders made them place on plastic trays any keys, pens, coins, rings and hair clips they had on them. Soon the students felt stripped of their individuality. Only their clothes remained. It was an unsettling feeling.

'Go through to Sector Two.'

Another wire enclosure, another inspection. This time male and female guards searched them with small hand-held scanners. All the while a guard stood behind a screen, a gun cradled in his arms.

'What's this?'

Donna Jackson went crimson at the sound of a bleep. 'It's a nipple ring,' she stammered.

'Do you have any other metal on, or in, your body?'

'Yes.'

'Where? Your private parts?'

'Yes.' Her voice went dry at the intimacy of the question.

'What is it?'

'A stud – er, two.'

The female guard barked, 'Go next door. You'll have to take them out.'

Meekly, Donna stepped aside, mortified with embarrassment. Paul noted this with interest. Now she would begin to feel how the prisoners felt. Privacy was a forgotten word in this establishment. There were many other words that were also left outside the prison gate: kindness, hope, love, freedom, identity.

'Proceed to Sector Three.'

Paul and his group passed the final entrance gate and

then down a long corridor. From there they stepped through the threshold of a heavy steel door. The sight before them was impressive. Up to now, it had been outbuildings with endless coils of wire around them and, further out, a wide-open space with watchtowers and electrified fencing which surrounded the perimeter of the Facility. Now they were within the prison proper. They stood in a massive courtyard, enclosed by twenty-five-metre walls with sheer sides that were impossible for any person to scale. There were four blocks in the courtyard, marked A to D in large black letters on the side of each building.

Although the students didn't know it, there was one more block. Underneath where they stood was a chamber, E Block, to house the most dangerous prisoners of all. For these lost souls, the light of day was never seen – only filtered light. Paul had been to E Block many times. However, only he and Ben Ingelmann had passes, and there was absolutely no chance that a student, or any other person not personally vouched for by the Warden, could visit those cells. Truly, those who had committed terrible crimes did pay a price for their sins. Entombment alive.

'D Block. Follow me,' a guard said to them, bawling from force of habit.

In single file they passed down a long corridor, one guard at the front and one at the back. More gates, more electronic doors, more guards. Surely, no one could escape from here, thought the students. In truth only one had. He'd managed to get to the outer gate by taking a prison visitor hostage. Then, on the instructions of the Warden, he'd been shot dead. The hostage had also died, but that was a price the prison authorities regarded as acceptable and the precise circumstances of the unlucky victim's death were glossed over by the bureaucracy. Nothing to write home about, unless you were the hostage's widow, in which case you'd already received the news – a sympathetic call from the State Governor.

'Hello, Professor.' A breezy woman in a white coat came up to Paul and shook his hand. Thin and wiry, with a worn face and grey hair tied back in a bun with an elastic band, Emma Breck was the Senior Psychiatrist at the Facility. Fifty years old, unmarried, tough and resilient, she had been working in the institution for more than a decade. 'They've just started the exhibition. You're among our first guests.'

She viewed the gaggle of students with a pleased eye. It was nice to see fresh faces and eager voices again in this, the home of the zombies. She directed them into D Block, a rectangular building with only one corridor leading into it so that it could be closed off in case of emergency. The students stood on the ground floor and looked up.

It was a depressing sight. There were two more floors above them, with heavy prison doors bolted into the walls on each landing. Wire netting stretched from the banisters, to prevent inmates casting themselves over the sides as they came out of their cells. Suicide was frowned on by the authorities here, unless it was assisted. Then they felt in charge.

'The art exhibition's in here. Yes, just to the right.'

The ground floor of D Block had no cells but was given over to communal rooms as well as to a guard post. Dr Breck led them in. After the trauma of passing through so many gates and the process of gradual dehumanisation, it was a relief for the students to see some vestiges of normality again. Indeed, apart from the bars over the windows, the art room was almost indistinguishable from the school classrooms they had been studying in not so long ago. Paintings lined the walls and in one corner there was a stand of plastic cups of orange juice and a tray of biscuits. Then, of course, there were the inmates themselves, some behind easels, others conversing with a handful of visitors who comprised, in the main, doctors and psychiatrists from out-of-state universities and foundations.

The normality of the situation hit the students, just as Paul had predicted. No monsters here. A few men and women dressed in blue jeans and shirts talking quietly or dabbing at pictures. An air of calm reserve, like a small-town convention for middle-aged voters, with only the glad-handing mayor being absent.

The artwork reinforced this impression. No crude scenes of violence. Instead, self-portraits, boats bobbing on the sea, baskets of flowers, plenty of swirling colour. For the patients were painting what was outside of them, not the unacceptable horror within. In their paintings, they endlessly re-created the world in an idealised image: tranquil, calm, ordered.

As the students watched the prisoners their fear began to dissipate. They realised they'd been crowding around Paul as if for protection. Self-consciously they began to separate and move towards the pictures and the artists. It was all right. These people were part of the human race after all. Different, but still part of it. Recognisable, at least outwardly.

'Do you paint much?'

'No, not really. I've just started. I'm not very good.'

The woman smiled at Dave Rattinger. He smiled back. She started to explain why she liked bright colours and scenes of waves crashing against the seashore. Dave nodded. She was older than her photo, about forty-five, motherly. A child killer. She'd stabbed a neighbour's child to death and sat by it as it died. Then she'd gone upstairs to do the same to the young boy's sister. She'd done it because she was tired of hearing their noise through the walls. And now she was discussing the early work of Vincent Van Gogh with Dave and wondering why he had liked such strong shades of green.

'Can I get you some orange juice?'

Donna Jackson turned to the enquiring young man with a slight stammer. He was twenty-three, a couple of years older than she was. Handsome with babyish features.

He stared intently at her – first at her face, then at the V of her groin. Strangely, Donna didn't feel embarrassed. Rather, she felt pity. He wouldn't have had a woman since he came here and he'd never have one for the rest of his days. If life had been different, they might perhaps have gone out together. Who knew? He was handsome enough.

'Thank you.' She watched him go to the table and get some juice. Then he came back to her. Nervously, his eyes looked at her face and then back to her sexual parts. He'd been imprisoned for a series of horrific rapes where the victims had been strangled. Yet to Donna he appeared so innocent in the light of day: there wasn't an inkling of the violence and cruelty behind his placid mask of studied normality. What had driven him to it? What was he really thinking about while he was talking to her?

An hour later the room was alive with conversation and laughter. The natural sense of fun in the students and the desperate desire of the inmates to have normal human company again was like a tremendous force of pent-up energy that was released. The students' fear disappeared as understanding formed. So far so good.

'Paul, I want you to come and see someone,' said Emma Breck. 'They brought him in yesterday. Psychopath, eighteen years old. Killed his family with a knife and a baseball bat. I'd be grateful for your opinion on his recent evaluation.'

'Sure.' They left the art room and ascended the metal stairs. On the third landing, Breck led Paul into a side room. A teenager was there, in leg irons and handcuffs. Paul and Emma sat down and Paul began to talk to him.

As time passed, down below, the students had fully recovered their self-confidence and their boisterousness. They had forgotten where they were. A few tried their hand at painting.

'Would you like to look around?'

Suzanne Delaney contemplated the thin girl with a worn face and vacant eyes beside her. Mary Driver. They were nearly the same age. She'd been involved in a number of gangland killings in which she'd lured men to their deaths at the hands of her demented boyfriend, now also dead. The red file Paul had given them indicated that she had a low IQ and was easily manipulated. She was also a good artist, as the drawings of desert scenes attested.

'I'd like that.'

They went out of the art room into the corridor. Mary showed her the other rooms on the ground floor: a well-stocked library and a games room.

'These are for the men. In our block, C Block, we have the same.'

They talked easily and Mary was forthcoming about her daily life, though life was scarcely a description of an existence in which she was often locked up alone for twenty hours a day six days a week.

'Does anyone visit you?'

'Neah.'

They started up the stairs to the first landing. All was calm. From the art room below the sound of laughter drifted up.

'Where are the other inmates?'

'In their cells.'

'It's so quiet.'

'They are told to be silent when visitors come.'

'Oh,' said Suzanne. They walked past the heavy steel doors of the prison cells, their blank faces disclosing nothing of the occupants behind. Mary was asking Suzanne about her shade of lipstick. She seemed such a pathetic creature. Almost incapable of having committed a crime.

'How do you survive here?' said Suzanne.

'I do favours.'

'What sort of favours?' asked Suzanne, curious.

'Just favours.' Mary paused and then said darkly, 'Everyone does favours to survive.'

They carried on walking and discussing makeup, the thing that Mary missed most about being inside. Her sentence was for life. After a few years she wouldn't worry about appearances any more. No point in keeping up a pretence.

'This is Sean Patrick's cell,' Mary said conversationally as they passed it. Suzanne started. The name of the mass murderer brought her back to her senses.

'I must return.'

'In a minute,' said Mary. 'And this is where Jerome Stinson, the axe-killer, is.'

Suddenly, Suzanne felt a sinking feeling. An inner voice, very clear and strong, was telling her to go back to the art room now. Something terrible was about to happen. She turned, but not quickly enough. Mary Driver blocked her path. Savagely, she pushed Suzanne against a cell door. To her horror, it started to open.

'And this is Karl Kramer's cell. The serial killer.'

'No!'

With that her guide thrust her inside. Everyone had to do favours to survive, and this was hers. Mary Driver ran back down the corridor, screeching with manic delight.

As Suzanne picked herself up from the cell floor, a man got up from his bed. With utter horror Suzanne recognised the face, but by then Kramer had embraced her in his arms.

A piercing shriek reverberated throughout the prison block. It had the timbre to it of a wild animal caught in a trap. Pure fear. Paul shot up from the table at which he sat. *'Oh, my God.'*

The next few minutes were a bewildering intermingling of events, most of it dictated by panic. The massive steel door half-way down the passageway to D Block slammed shut, activated by an electronic signal from a guard. As a result, no one could get in, or out of, the block. They were trapped.

Two warders rushed into the art room. Frantically, they separated the students and guests from the inmates. The former they locked in the art room, the latter they pushed out into the corridor. At the same time steel grilles on each of the stairways slid across to seal off each landing of D Block.

By this time Paul had reached the first floor where Suzanne was. As he raced along it, he could see the faces of his students peering up at him from the ground floor, their expressions full of alarm and fear. Paul was closely followed by a warder. But they were too late. At the far end of the corridor stood Kramer. He had a makeshift wire noose around Suzanne's throat.

'Well hello again, Professor,' he beamed. 'I've just met one of your students.'

Since his acquittal for the Melanie Dukes murder, Kramer had been back in the Facility, serving his sentence for the bar-room killing. They were due to move him to another prison soon. However, Karl was not a happy man. The suicide of Laura Dukes had affected him deeply. She'd escaped him and that annoyed him very much since he'd been carefully arranging the details of their future relationship when he got out of prison.

For Laura it was a good thing that she died when she did, for the torture and death that Kramer was planning for her was beyond all human conception. For Kramer, though, it was bitterness and gall. Now that he'd been acquitted of her sister's murder, he was able to drop the pretence he'd been maintaining for the last few months and the dark side of his nature rose to the fore.

A couple of weeks had been enough for him to impose his will on the other inmates, since they knew better than any judge or clever psychologist what sort of man the real Karl Kramer was. They could feel it emanate from him and, in some cases, they knew the symptoms from personal experience.

Kramer had decided that, since he was in prison for a while, he might as well enjoy himself. And it was nice to meet his old psychiatric evaluator, Paul, who had helped get him off. He bet that Paul was regretting it now, or that he soon would. Still, that was tough. Kramer never remembered help from others and never returned it – that wasn't his style.

'Stay where you are,' Paul told the prison guard. Slowly, he walked forward. The sight was chilling. Kramer held Suzanne tightly in front of his own body, his back against a blank wall. About her neck was a thin sliver of wire which he'd tightened so that her jaw was pushed upwards and to the right. Like a chicken about to have its throat cut.

Kramer peered out from behind his victim's head, his eyes gleaming with menace and suppressed excitement. He let Paul and the warder get within three metres. Then he said in a calm voice, 'That's close enough.' He tightened the wire noose.

There was total silence in the prison. In their cells the prisoners could detect something violent was about to happen. They could sense fear and terror pervade the air and they exulted in it. It brought back to them memories of times past. They waited expectantly.

'Karl?' Paul scrutinised the killer. It must be obvious to him there was no possibility of escape. So what was he doing? Probably he wanted to play with the girl, but how far would he go?

In his guts, Paul began to acknowledge he'd made a bad mistake about this man. Ben was right. He had been deceived by him after all; it was quite incredible how clever Kramer had been. No hint of this for months, yet now Paul could feel the violence steaming from him like heat.

Paul needed time to coax Kramer into giving up his victim, but even as he watched, he knew the Warden would be authorising a marksman to come to D Block and kill Kramer if necessary. And if a hostage was in the way . . . well, so be it. Prisoners needed to be taught hard lessons.

'OK, Karl. I think that's enough,' Paul commenced

in a mild tone. 'This is one of my students. Her name is Suzanne. She's very scared. Please let her go now.' He couldn't see Suzanne's eyes since her face was to one side, but he could imagine her terror.

'Yes, she is afraid,' said Kramer quietly. 'Very afraid. I can feel that.' He pressed his stubbly face against hers and gave her a slow, wet kiss. 'It turns me on.'

'What are you going to do?'

'Who knows?' said Kramer as he leered at them. With his spare hand he unclipped Suzanne's bra. Then with a brutal movement he tore her blouse from her back. He was enjoying himself, and he had not enjoyed himself for quite some time.

Suzanne stood close against his body, half naked, her torso free and exposed. Kramer looked at the onlookers with scornful amusement. He knew what Paul and the guard were thinking. Despite their fear and concern, the men were staring at the victim's breasts and in their minds, just like his, were erotic thoughts. Kramer knew it; he sensed it. He wanted them to feel what he was feeling – the violence, the cruelty. His pleasure, her pain.

From the cells came a fell chorus, the cries shrill and harsh, almost wolf-like in their tone. The inmates could not see or hear what was happening, but they could feel it vibrantly, as if they had tapped into a line of atavistic and irrational savagery that subconsciously flowed between them. They cried for sheer joy as they told Kramer what he should do to his unknown victim.

The students in that same building heard their cries and they shivered. Within seconds the veneer of civilisation had been torn aside and underneath was exposed the dark side of mankind: the cruel, the irrational, the immoral animal instinct of their ancestors, alien and terrifying, but an instinct that, deep within the innermost recesses of their psyche, all the people in that building, inmates and visitors, knew in some way and, to some extent, shared. A few felt the palpable presence of evil, strong and powerful. But not Paul because, of course, he rejected such things.

'Please let her go now.'

In the distance, there was the sound of a steel door opening. A prison marksman was on his way. Paul knew it. So did Kramer. He crowed triumphantly. It was then Paul was sure he was going to kill Suzanne.

'Well,' said Kramer, sticking his tongue out at the awestruck people in front of him. 'So nice of you to come, Professor, to look at the exhibits. But it's always more fun to look at the exhibits together, isn't it? Then we both know just how we feel.'

His hand slowly released itself from Suzanne's breast and then began to paw at her body. The bystanders stared at her frail torso in the arms of this monster. They were both repulsed yet attracted by the contorted human exhibit. It was like a painting by the English artist, Bacon, the subjects trapped within their own cruelty and submission.

Footsteps sounded on the stairs. Kramer giggled, his teeth glinting in the harsh neon light. With his spare hand he now loosened the button of Suzanne's jeans and pulled them down so that they almost straddled her knees. Kramer knew what they were thinking, his audience before him. Their horror was real, yet voyeuristic, their pity for the girl now mixed with an aroused pleasure. They could begin to understand his own thought process.

Paul heard a slight click. Behind him, from the corner of his eye, he saw the guard raise a rifle. He would go for a head shot.

However, the murderer understood exactly what was intended and he kept his head very close to the girl's. If the guard fired now, he might easily kill them both. So the guard wouldn't shoot. Kramer knew that. Too scared. First time. Kramer continued to lick away at Suzanne's neck, like a wolf caressing its prey before he ate it. The bulge in his trousers pressed hard against her back. His spare hand moved from behind her as he unzipped himself. Public rape – now that was something he hadn't tried yet.

The marksman clicked off the safety catch. There was a sound of footsteps on the metal staircase. Another guard had arrived with an order from the Warden to fire.

The outcome was not what Paul had expected. He swivelled round, to beg the prison marksman not to shoot. As he did so, his heart lurched. For behind the heavily padded figure was someone else – the very last person Paul expected to see.

She stood there, directing her gaze at Kramer. Then she switched it to Paul. It was the mysterious woman he'd met in the corridor that night after his lecture. What was her name? Helen. Paul was astounded. She had on the white overalls of a physician. She must be a psychiatrist working in the prison. How come he'd never met her before?

Swiftly, Helen turned her eyes back to Kramer. Paul's gaze also swivelled back to the serial killer, all this having taken place in the space of a millisecond.

A most extraordinary thing began to happen.

The self-satisfied expression on the face of Kramer changed. He started to sweat, his features contorting – at first in puzzlement, then in fear. The visage of the murderer finally became rigid as if fixed on a point beyond human vision.

Little by little, Kramer's free hand, which had been about to part Suzanne's legs from the back, moved across his crotch and to his side. It was clawed, the muscles standing out rigid from the flesh, as if it was being compelled, inch by inch, to concede its desired position by a tremendous force. Kramer's other hand, which held the noose, also began to relax, the fist prising open. It was a remarkable spectacle and Paul looked on, flabbergasted, without the slightest clue as to why this was happening.

With the noose slackened, Suzanne was able to see ahead and her frightened gaze alighted on those watching. Her terror marginally abating, she became conscious of her nakedness and tried to cover herself with her hands.

Paul watched while the killer unwillingly released his grip on his victim. The face of the murderer was screwed up in agony, the eyes bloodshot, as if invisible barbs were being pushed deep into the sockets. It came to Paul what was occurring. Kramer must be suffering a massive catatonic reaction to drugs.

As soon as the noose fell away, two warders rushed forward. Thrusting Suzanne to one side, they hurled themselves at Kramer and wrestled him to the floor. His resistance was gone. Suzanne bent down to draw her jeans back over her nudity and then burst into tears. Emma Breck, who'd arrived on the scene, ran to comfort her.

Paul stood, lost. What he'd just witnessed seemed unreal. As if he'd been watching a film in slow motion. Yet, what had happened was real enough. It was still before him – the mêlée, Kramer's suddenly frenzied struggles as they dug a needle into his arm to sedate him, Suzanne's pitiful weeping. It had happened. It was real. It was this world.

Paul turned round to ask Helen what she made of Kramer's reactions.

She was not there.

CHAPTER TEN

The demons ensnare us by means of creatures formed not by themselves, but by God, and with various delights consonant with their own versatility . . .

The demons seek to ensure that they will be so enticed by men; and they do this by first misleading human beings by their subtle cleverness, either by breathing a secret poison into their hearts, or even by appearing to them in the deceptive guise of friends, making a few of them disciples of their own, and teachers of very many others.

St Augustine, *The City of God*

THE BUS RETURNED TO THE university campus. Paul's students were subdued. Although they knew something had occurred to Suzanne, they'd seen nothing of her humiliation by Kramer. Paul had asked the prison authorities to drive her back on her own so he could talk with her privately before she faced the onslaught of their questions.

When the bus stopped, he turned to face his students, interested to find out what effect the disturbance had had on them. If they wanted to be criminal psychiatrists they'd have to get accustomed to the unexpected and to the violent.

'I'm sorry about what took place this morning,' Paul told them. 'It was a more realistic introduction to the world of criminal psychiatry than I'd anticipated. I look forward to meeting you again next Wednesday. Unless, that is, you've decided to switch to the classics or history of art.'

There was a ripple of laughter. Having recovered from the shock, they were all experiencing the elation of having been in, but having escaped from, a traumatic situation. Riding high on an adrenaline surge.

'Really really wild,' said José Ramirez as he got out of the bus. 'I'll be back for more, man.' Better than marijuana any day.

The students departed, chattering away excitedly. Paul sat on a bench to gather his thoughts. It was a beautiful afternoon and the university campus lay spread out before him in all its greenery. Behind was the building where he worked and, in front of it, a great expanse of grass where students lolled about as they gossiped and took in the sun. It was all so tranquil, civilised and predictable. A different world to that from which they had just come, the land of the caged and the damned. It had been an interesting day.

What an appalling error in not locking Kramer's door. How could it possibly have happened? And how had Kramer got hold of wire to make a noose? If he knew the Warden, Hanlon Dawes, someone would suffer for it. And who was this mysterious woman, Helen?

More worrying, Paul had seen Kramer as he really was. Perhaps Paul shouldn't have given such a positive assessment of him at his trial. Diagnosis was such a tricky subject. That said, it was the jury who decided on the verdict, not him. He refused to feel personally responsible for this man's acquittal. They got it wrong, not him.

Besides, Paul couldn't allow any doubts. It could get out to the press and TV networks and his celebrity status would be jeopardised – a hell of a mess. So it was important not to jump to any conclusions too hastily. Kramer wasn't a threat to the public at present, being in prison. Paul would keep him under observation. He quickly steered his mind off the uncomfortable subject.

'Professor!'

Wearing borrowed clothes, Suzanne got out of an unmarked prison car and came across the grass towards him.

'Suzanne. What can I say? Do sit down.' Paul eyed her carefully. What would happen if she thought the university was to blame? There would be a scandal and Suzanne could recover damages against them. A fear of lawyers, and litigation, came upon Paul. Murderers were one thing, lawyers another. Only one was capable of redemption in his eyes.

'Suzanne, nothing like this has ever happened before. There will be the fullest investigation, the Deputy Warden has assured me. I'm very sorry.'

Though her face was still deadly pale she gave a bleak smile. 'It's OK, Professor. I'll come to your next lesson.'

Paul breathed a sigh of relief. She had guts. 'Call me Paul.' He put his hand on hers; it was soft but still icy with fear. 'Would you like some tranquillisers? I can get you some.'

'No. I told the prison people I just wanted to go home.'

'Of course,' said Paul as he got up from the bench. 'I'll drive. You're not in a fit state to drive yourself.'

In the Mercedes he said to her, 'You were very brave. You kept calm, the first rule of a criminal psychiatrist.'

'I didn't feel it. It all happened so quickly.' Suzanne swallowed hard. 'Would he have killed me?'

Paul hesitated for a fraction of a second. Sometimes, lying was acceptable. 'No,' he said, 'I don't think so. If he'd intended to, he'd have done that earlier on. I'm sure Kramer was playing with you to mock the prison authorities. He made no attempt to leave the prison or to negotiate. He just wanted to demonstrate his power to the warders and the other inmates. You see, he's trying to assert his status in the prison. It's an important function, like an animal marking its territory.'

'Why?'

'To survive,' said Paul, getting into professorial mode. 'Prisons are dangerous places, even for killers. There's always someone else who wants to prove they're king of the jungle. That's what the public forgets. These people do suffer. Whatever crimes they've committed come back to haunt them in some way or another. They live in fear not only of themselves but of others.'

'But he could have killed me.' Then, more softly, 'He's killed many other people.'

'You don't know that. He killed a man in the bar. He was acquitted of the Melanie Dukes murder.'

She hesitated. 'You don't think he's the serial killer?'

'Of course not, there's no evidence of it,' Paul said sharply. 'I don't think he'd have seriously hurt you. Anyway, he let you go.'

'But why me?'

'You just happened to fall into his clutches.'

Suzanne nodded. She said, 'Terrible how bad luck strikes, isn't it?' She stared out of the window at the passing traffic, the lanes full on a normal San Francisco weekday. 'Everything's fine and then disaster strikes. That's what scares me so about life. It happens so rapidly. You can be fine one minute and your world's turned upside down the next. Like God's playing with you.'

Paul swerved slightly to avoid another car. 'Did Kramer say anything to you?'

'No.'

'It's the violence he is . . . er, he *may* be hooked on, the sense of being in control. It's like a drug. Such people have to dominate others. Their way of getting high.'

There was silence. Emma Breck had found Suzanne a new top and sweater. Her face was particularly lovely in its paleness. Haunting. He thought of her naked body and his emotions as he'd gazed at her, imprisoned in Kramer's arms. He was only human, after all. Paul frowned. He was becoming as bad as his patients. Too much empathy there.

'We should talk about this further. At the moment you're experiencing delayed shock, so you'll feel very calm, even elated. The fear and depression will hit you later on. Why don't you come and stay with my wife and me for a day or so?'

'No, really, I'm fine . . . Paul.' She gave him an open and affectionate regard. She had beautiful hazel eyes and an unmarked face with no lines or crow's feet. The face of a twenty-two-year-old, bursting with health and vigour.

'Or perhaps you could stay with a boyfriend?' Why was he so inquisitive?

'I don't have one.'

He said nothing more. The Mercedes swung into the student residential area. Suzanne pointed out her block and Paul pulled up outside. Just before she got out, he said, 'Come and see me tomorrow. Promise. I'm worried about you.'

Her eyes focused on his. He could see a hint of amusement in them. 'Perhaps,' Suzanne said. She got out and glanced back through the window. 'It's not your fault.' Then in a soft voice, 'Paul, don't worry. I'm not going to sue anybody.'

'You read my mind!' he said.

'Yes.' They both laughed.

Simultaneously, their eyes locked on each other's, registering forbidden subliminal desires. They were quickly suppressed.

Paul watched her cross the grass and disappear inside the student block. She had courage, that girl. He liked that. He drove away, reluctant to acknowledge his feelings.

He liked Suzanne. A lot.

'I know, I know,' said Ben when Paul entered their psychiatric clinic. He stood by a filing cabinet in the reception area, his elbow leaning on it. 'I know what happened.'

Paul followed Ben into his room and his colleague flopped into a leather armchair behind his desk. He had an air of studied calm, although he was very worried. He scratched his nose.

'Are we going to get sued?'

'Hey, relax.' Paul went through the story.

Ben shrugged. 'Well, at least it gives the students experience of what working in top-security prisons is like. And the girl?'

'Badly shaken, but not stirred. It's OK, I'll see her tomorrow and go through it with her.' Paul exuded confidence.

'Good idea,' replied his partner, more cautiously. 'Anyway, I don't think Kramer will be a problem for a while. The Warden's ordered him to E Block. He doesn't like people messing about in his prison.'

Paul shrugged. He'd no doubt that a considerable amount of brutality went on at the Facility. However, it was always impossible to prove. Accidents occurred with regularity to those prisoners who became too difficult to handle and the suicide rate at the prison was high. Paul suspected that the guards were happy to help the inmates resolve their personal problems.

Ben contemplated Paul. He should raise the subject of Kramer with him now; it must be dealt with. He was certain now Paul had misdiagnosed him and Kramer was the serial killer. However, he wasn't over-keen to discuss the subject today. Feelings could get high and it would hit Paul's ego badly as well as have some nasty repercussions for the university and their clinic. Their reputation would be savaged by the press.

'To more important things,' said Ben. 'Apart from handling all your fan mail after your celebrated speech,' he made a slightly comic face, 'next week, Florence and I are going to Aspen for ten days before my classes start. We're going on Monday. Don't say you've forgotten?'

''Course not,' Paul replied, though he had.

'It'll be great,' Ben went on, full of enthusiasm. 'I could do with a rest and I've no doubt you'll be able to man the fort in my absence.' Both of them knew that. No concerns there.

'Sure. We'll take a holiday later.' Paul made towards the door. 'There's a new psychiatrist on D Block. A woman. Did you know?'

'No one told me. What's she like?'

'I only caught a glimpse of her today. I'll make some inquiries.'

'Good idea. And don't forget you and Marie are coming to our dinner party tomorrow tonight.'

'I haven't forgotten. I've some calls to make.'

Paul exited Ben's room rapidly. He didn't want to talk about Kramer either. As soon as he reached his office the phone rang. It was the Deputy Warden of the Facility. He sounded nervous, which meant Hanlon Dawes was on the warpath.

'Inquiry's underway. Starts Wednesday. We've suspended three officers and moved Kramer.'

'How is he?'

'Less cocky than he was. Seems to have hurt himself quite badly when we moved him from his cell. Is your student all right?'

'She'll be fine. How did it happen? The prison door, I mean.'

'We're still not sure. As you know, each cell door is electronically controlled. The guard swears he never pushed the button to open Kramer's cell and the computer printout registers nothing. It seems the door, quite literally, opened by itself. That's impossible, so we've suspended the guard and asked the boffins to investigate. They'll get to the bottom of it. Thanks for remaining so calm.'

'No worries,' said Paul. Then he enquired casually, 'Who was the woman psychiatrist?'

'Who?'

'The woman just behind me when Kramer let go of the girl. I wondered when she started working on D Block.'

'I don't know,' said the Deputy Warden. 'We've taken on no extra people. I'll make some inquiries.'

'Thanks. I'll like to chat with her.'

Paul put down the phone. He stared out of the window

up at the sky. Large storm clouds were gathering. Nothing unusual in that. Yet, they were gathering in a way he couldn't possibly conceive.

They were gathering around him.

THE EVIL NET

CHAPTER ELEVEN

*There are three kinds of folk whom God will
permit to be tempted and troubled by the devil
. . . the wicked for their horrible sins, to punish them in the like measure; the godly that
are sleeping in any great sins or infirmities
or weaknesses of faith . . . and even some of
the best, that their patience may be tried before
the world.*

James VI of Scotland, *Daemonologie*

THE CONVENT OF SANTA CRISTINA lay outside the
town of Benedetto in northern Italy. Located on a moun-
tainside, it opened out onto some olive groves that overlooked the sea. The convent had always been a small
community, the home of an order of nuns that had been
established by St Cristina in the fourteenth century with
a vow of silence. The buildings were of local stone with
a simple coat of whitewash and they blended in with the
strong, clear light of the landscape.

Clambering up a rough-hewn path a visitor would cross
a vegetable garden and then through an arched gate
whose oak door was much bleached by the sun. Inside
was an inner courtyard, in the centre of which was located
a well. Vines grew up the surrounding walls. Besides a

dormitory and a refectory there were no other major buildings save for the chapel around which the life of the small community had revolved for centuries.

In the convent all was plain and unadorned, and was silent apart from half an hour during the day when conversation was permitted. However, strange to relate, even when talk was allowed, the nuns rarely conversed for they had little to say and their facial expressions and slight movements of the hand were usually quite sufficient. Their lives were full of serenity and in that they found a profound happiness.

This nunnery had no claim to fame. It was never visited by the public and only once a year did its superior, the village priest, attend to hear the singing of prayers by the nuns in memory of their founder. In truth, the place was forgotten – by the local people, by the bishops, by the great cardinals in Rome. And yet, in the humblest of places on earth lay hidden the most extraordinary things and people. Of some of these mysteries only the Holy Father knew.

It was early in the morning. Outside, it was pitch-black. Within the chapel, there was only the flicker of light from two candles on the altar. All was silent. Yet the watches were being kept throughout the hours of darkness, as they had been since the foundation of the Faith.

The nun at prayer, Catherine of Benedetto, was a plain woman in her late fifties. She had been at the convent for all but the first eighteen years of her life. A life spent in contemplation. A wasted life, the scoffers and the worldly-wise would say. But for Catherine it was not so. She had been blessed beyond ordinary human beings, blessed with great visions and with great faith. And for Catherine this was a gift beyond all price, beyond all human cravings and possessions. It was a gift from an ever-loving God.

Although Catherine told no one in her small community of her revelations, save for the mother superior, the other nuns knew of her sanctity: it was so strong that its presence was felt by those around her. Her gift was also their secret blessing and they thanked God for it.

It was the third hour of the morning. Catherine of Benedetto lay stretched out before the altar, her physical form without movement and, it seemed, without life. Her spirit was elsewhere, lost in cosmic mysteries far beyond human consciousness.

It was then that a frightening vision came to her, so devastating in its purport that she cried out in agony. She struggled with the foe to divine its true meaning. Long and savage was the battle and many times she thought that the enemy would sever her from the world for ever. When she came to herself again, she woke the mother superior and divulged what she had seen.

Three days later a man appeared at the door of the refectory. In silence he listened to Catherine. Then he started back down the rough-hewn path. Near the foot of the mountain he stopped in an olive grove. There, he wept bitterly.

'What have I done? What have I done?' Cardinal Benelli cried to himself and to the sky. 'I have failed. I have ignored a message given to me and this humble servant of God has shown my weakness and my failing. Forgive, oh forgive me.'

The distraught man continued down his rocky path. There was not a moment to lose. For Cardinal Benelli, the Head of the Holy Office, had not the slightest doubt that the woman who'd stood before him was a living saint and that what she had said was beyond all spiritual questioning. She'd also told him the thing he most feared.

'A Coin of Judas has come into the world.'

CHAPTER TWELVE

For man does not know his time. Like fish
which are taken in an evil net and, like birds
which are caught in a snare, so the sons of
men are snared at an evil time, when it sud-
denly falls upon them.

Ecclesiastes 9:12

MARIE LED RACHEL INTO THE LOUNGE. The dinner
with Ben and Florence was at eight; she had plenty of
time. Paul would meet her there.

'Do you want to see your programme?' Rachel nodded.
Marie switched on the television set. 'OK, darling. I'm
just going to get dressed.'

As she climbed the stairs Marie hummed to herself.
She was looking forward to the meal. They hardly went
out now, what with the increase in Paul's workload and
the clinic being so successful. As a result of the Kramer
trial he'd become a household name. She wished he'd
spend more time with her and Rachel but at least he
seemed fulfilled in himself. Perhaps they would stay
together after all.

In the kitchen there was a rattle of pots and pans.
Gloria, the Filipina maid, was preparing supper. In the
lounge, Rachel watched television and played with her

toys. Her cat was sprawled out on a rug before the hearth. Everything was the epitome of normality in a happy household.

A few minutes later Rachel glanced up from dressing her favourite doll. A frown crossed her face, since something curious was happening. Both the picture on the TV and the volume began to fade, very slowly. Rachel watched it, fascinated, until the comic strip was replaced by a blank screen supported only by the faint hiss of background static. Then there was a click as the electricity supply to the television cut out.

Rachel considered this. Then she went back to what she was doing, unworried. The television was an adult toy; her mother or Gloria would know how to resuscitate it. However, this curious event was soon followed by another.

The young cat, who had been dozing on the rug, sat up abruptly. It rose to its feet, its ears straining forward, its eyes gleaming as they focused on an object approaching Rachel.

'Ginger,' said the child fondly, 'come here.'

But the cat wouldn't; it continued to focus on a presence behind Rachel. A moment later, its back arched and the hackles rose along the full ridge of its spine. The animal now stood rooted to the spot, its lips drawn back in a hideous gesture of defiance while it hissed and clawed violently in the air at an imaginary foe. Disconcerted, Rachel turned to look behind her, but there was nothing.

'Ginger, what's the matter? Come here,' she said in an uncertain tone.

However, her pet was fully occupied and, unknown to Rachel, fighting a losing battle to defend its young mistress. It now went into a frenzy, spitting viciously and backing away. Then it bolted out of the room with a yelp.

Rachel looked round the room, very frightened. She didn't feel well. She thought about getting up, but her sense of unease abated and she began to pick up her toys again. She didn't glance behind her this time. Had she done so she would have perceived the image of a woman.

Upstairs, Marie undressed. She entered the bathroom annexed to the master bedroom to take a shower. Her mind was occupied with things she had to do at work the next day.

Suddenly, she cried out in shock.

At the end of the bathroom, by the window, stood a woman. She was blonde and willowy in appearance, of an indeterminate age. Her gaze was fixed on Marie's face; the look was impassive without a flicker of emotion.

'Who are you? What are you doing here?' Marie stared back at the intruder, dumbfounded. She grabbed a robe to cover her nakedness.

The woman didn't reply. Her eyes remained implacable. Marie backed away. In a choked voice she said, 'Get out of my house, now.'

Turning, she ran across the bedroom to the landing outside.

'Gloria!' she shouted, the panic plainly detectable in her voice. 'Can you come here?'

Within a few seconds the maid appeared at the bottom of the stairs, clutching a mixing bowl. 'What's up, Mrs Stauffer?'

'There's someone in my bedroom.'

'In your bedroom?' The maid hurriedly ascended to the first floor. They went into the bedroom, then the bathroom and finally the other rooms. Both of them felt frightened, as most women were in San Francisco at that time – Karl Kramer being found innocent of the murder of Melanie Dukes meant that a serial killer was still lurking about, and they could be the next victims. Yet, there was nothing.

'She was there. I saw someone. I'm sure.'

'Who?'

'A woman,' said Marie, gulping a breath of air. 'In a red evening dress. By the window. She was staring at me.'

The maid's visage reflected her puzzlement. It didn't sound like a serial killer or even a burglar. They returned to the bathroom and surveyed it. The double-glazed window was shut tight.

'Let's search the house.'

Hastily, Marie put on her clothes and, together, they went through the house. Downstairs, Rachel had not moved from her former position. However, her posture was involuntary since her whole body was now rigid with fear as she clung to her doll. Gloria glanced into the living room but failed to notice the child's condition.

'It was nothing,' said Marie with a nervous smile after they'd searched everywhere to no avail. 'I must have just imagined it. How utterly amazing. Sorry to have alarmed you, Gloria.'

The maid, a young woman fiercely devoted to Marie and her daughter, remarked, 'Not to worry, Mrs Stauffer.'

'I've been feeling ill all day,' said Marie. 'It was just a trick of the light. There's no other explanation, is there?'

Marie went back up the stairs. An hour before she had to set out for Florence's dinner party. She turned on the shower and returned to her bedroom to undress. An instant later she fled back to the bathroom.

She vomited violently.

*　　*　　*

'You're early for once! Incredible!'

Ben led him into the house. There was a loud buzz of conversation and they headed towards it. Florence emerged from the kitchen. She kissed Paul heartily.

'Hello, my love. So nice to see you. Now, please phone Marie. She won't be coming, she's not feeling well. Nothing bad – just a small stomach upset.'

'Oh,' replied Paul and frowned.

He rang the house and Gloria answered. Marie was sick and had a mild temperature; she'd gone to bed. Did he want to talk with her? No? The maid would phone him if Marie awoke. Paul returned to the kitchen and Florence thrust a glass of wine into his hand. 'Poor thing. Come and meet everyone.'

They passed into the large living room. Paul was introduced to the other guests: the local doctor and his wife; a couple from the university who taught English; Florence's nephew and his new girlfriend; the director of a very modern art gallery in town and his male partner. And finally an old friend of Ben's who was a civil engineer. The wine was in full flow and everyone was boisterously talking politics and the latest scandal involving a Republican senator.

'Of course, it would have to be bondage,' said the art gallery director blithely. 'That's politicians for you. They always say they're tied up with someone.'

'Food's ready,' commanded Florence. They paraded into the candle-lit dining room. The doorbell rang.

'Ah,' exclaimed Ben, 'our final guest. I'll get it.'

Paul found his allotted seat by the doctor's wife and began a polite conversation. As he did so an individual came into the room. Florence emerged from the kitchen and did the honours for the rest of the guests.

'Professor Helen Jones, another psychiatrist, I'm

afraid. The chair opposite Paul, my dear. Ben, more wine.'

Paul looked at Helen out of the corner of his eye as she greeted the other guests and sat down. 'Hi,' she said with a friendly smile. Caught up in conversation with the doctor's wife, Paul was able only to mouth back a silent 'Hi' across the table to her. So, Helen *was* a psychiatrist after all; the mystery was solved. How come she'd disappeared from the prison so quickly? He was looking forward to talking to her about Kramer.

The evening went swimmingly, as did all Florence's parties. Mountains of food, the constant refilling of wine-glasses and an amusing spectrum of opinions and guests combined to ensure that the laughter was full and prolonged. The art gallery director stole the show with his outrageous descriptions of the private lives of his clientele, so-called 'post-reductionist artists', and the lengths to which they would go to secure an exhibition.

'My dear, he not only seduced the gallery owner's wife and daughter but went to bed with the owner as well. It's true, it's absolutely true, I swear,' the director shrieked. 'All for the sake of art!' The foie gras trembled on his fork.

Soon, conversation was in full spate. Paul barely managed to get a word in with Helen, who'd been commandeered by the doctor on one side and Florence's nephew on the other. She looked very fetching in a low-cut red dress with a black silk scarf about her neck. He couldn't help glancing at her from time to time.

Ben tapped his wineglass. 'Everyone, I'd just like to propose a small toast to my esteemed colleague for the excellence of the Carl Jung lecture he's just given at the university.'

They congratulated Paul.

Ben continued: 'And now we will all have to bow and scrape to him. Having demolished the concept of religion in psychiatry, we must pay homage to the new god who has arisen and who knows all the secrets of the criminal mind. To Paul.'

Good-humouredly, the others toasted his good health. 'Tell us more,' they said, and so Ben briefly described the content of the lecture.

'You say religion and superstition have had their day? That science has the answers and not the priests?' asked the doctor.

'In a nutshell,' replied Paul. 'Naturally, I was dealing with the field of criminal psychiatry but, for me, it applies as a general proposition.'

'God doesn't exist, then?' inquired Helen as Florence topped up their wineglasses for the seventh time.

'Nope,' said Paul, digging into his dessert. 'There's a rational explanation for everything in the universe, for every illness, every event, every thought.' He put down his spoon. 'Even for the formation of the universe itself. It's one of the great truths we're learning in modern society.'

'I see,' said Helen, sounding unconvinced. 'And, if you don't believe in God, then you don't believe in the devil.'

'Right again,' Paul replied. 'You see, these concepts have simply been used by the Church for centuries to manipulate people and to keep them subservient. A useful exercise in mind control to get the masses to do what you want, by telling them what's good for them and what's bad. But the reality is that there's no God and there's no evil power.'

'Oh, I know some *wicked* people,' said the art gallery

director with a salacious chuckle. 'Don't tell *me* about evil, darling.' Everyone laughed.

Paul took a gulp of red wine and continued. 'What we need to do is to discard this junk and re-look at society in a scientific way. Whether killers should be executed, whether abortion or mercy killing should be crimes, whether things like blasphemy should continue to be a legal offence. All these issues need to be analysed from a scientific basis, without all the mumbo jumbo and religious argument that usually accompanies them.'

'Mumbo jumbo?' queried the doctor.

'Absolutely,' said Paul, getting into his stride. 'Funny, isn't it, that the Church —'

'So, when we've swept moral dogmas out of the house,' interrupted Helen, 'what have we left?'

'A happier society,' said Paul. He tucked into some more apple pie and went on. 'Look at the past. The Church told people to burn witches, that women were subordinate to men and that other religions should be persecuted.' He ticked off more infractions on his fingers. 'It told people not to eat meat or have sex on a Friday and not to work on a Sunday. It told people that unmarried women should be treated as outcasts, that suicides should be buried in unconsecrated ground, and that the Pope was infallible. Also, that mad people were possessed and that the sun went round the earth. All great stuff.

'But what did it achieve in helping society? True, it built great palaces for cardinals and bishops to live in, with everyone else working their backs off to keep them in the luxury they were accustomed to. But all it did, ultimately, was make for a divided society.'

He paused, his hands held out as if he were lecturing to his psychiatry class once more. 'You see, to *rule* over people, you have to persuade one section of society that they are different, that they are the elect and that they will receive certain benefits or punishments if they do, or don't do, as you say. You then pit them against another section of society and, of course, you set yourself up as the judge. It's easy to bring about, as you can see so clearly in all these fad religions of today. Of course, it's all a lie and a cheat.'

'So there are no eternal truths?' said the art gallery director with a little moue. 'My dear, what a disappointment.'

'Course not,' replied Paul. '"Eternal truths", in fact, only have a limited shelf life. Don't you think that our forefathers genuinely believed that human sacrifice was necessary to get good crops, just as we no longer do so? Don't you think that some religions genuinely believe that having more than one wife is OK, just as other religions believe that it's not?

'It is all relative. What we're convinced of in one century we reject with equal fervour and conviction in another. It's a merry-go-round that simply leads to confusion and bloodshed. We need a better basis to determine whether the principles of religious belief have any foundation. Otherwise, it's baloney, with each sect claiming that they alone "know" the truth and that everyone else is wrong. Religion is the same as art – it's a work of genius or it's a con trick. It depends on whether you're selling the picture or painting it.'

They clapped.

'Well, you *are* a modern man,' said Helen mockingly. 'You have all the answers. I wish I did. But suppose that science itself is relative and depends on a perception of the world which is a subjective one. I mean, suppose our understanding of our own existence is just a vision invented by our brain. A brain that can provide any number of images, each as real as the other, if properly tuned.'

'Balls,' said Paul dismissively. His voice was getting louder. 'Though it's an argument sometimes made. Scientific truth remains so throughout all ages. The earth goes around the sun and always has done. It's just that people in earlier periods of civilisation didn't have the final facts before them. Once all the facts are assembled you achieve certainty. Newton did far more than Christ in establishing the reality of our world.'

'But he believed in Christ,' protested the doctor quietly.

Helen shrugged, happy to drop the conversation. However, the well-lubricated guests wanted to hear more of Paul defending his viewpoint. They urged her on. Helen examined him with a coy smile.

'Since you're happy to dismiss the existence of God and the devil I imagine you also don't believe in the soul, or life after death. No world but this one.'

'You've guessed it,' said Paul. 'The rest is comforting nonsense to help us get through our existence. People talk of God but they've never seen him. And he doesn't seem to be much help when he's really needed. Try having a philosophical discussion with a man about the love of God when he's in an aircraft about to crash, or entering a gas chamber. I think you'll find his approval ratings of his creator aren't very high at that moment. And try telling a multiple murderer that God is looking after both him and his victim.'

'All talk, though,' replied Helen. 'Brave words, but I've always found people are anxious to deny these things until it comes to the hard point.'

'What do you mean?' said Paul, surprised.

'Well, suppose there were some eternal truths after all,' said Helen teasingly. 'What would you give to learn them? Ten years of your life? Your life? What would you give to prove the point?'

'Oh, a bet, *wicked*,' said the art gallery director, slipping his hand onto his boyfriend's knee.

The guests looked at Paul expectantly. 'Hang on,' continued Paul, the drink affecting the fluency of his argument, 'you should be the one persuading me to take part. I've put forward my argument, that's proof enough. You've got to reveal yours. What will you give me to play the student?' He clasped his hands in mock supplication. 'You see, I'm meant to be the teacher.'

Underneath the table Helen's leg brushed against his. Paul was not sufficiently sober to know whether it was accidental or intentional. He didn't really care. Everyone laughed with him, caught up in the childish game of pushing the matter to its logical conclusion.

'Let's see,' she said, her voice becoming mock serious. 'How can I tempt you?' Helen pondered. 'Let's just say a kiss and some silver.'

'Clever,' said Florence's nephew. He hoped the meal would end soon, he felt desperately randy. He regarded his female companion. They'd met only a couple of days before on a blind date. Would she, wouldn't she? Odds on she would tonight, with her cheeks as flushed as that. He poured her more wine. 'Clever, a good biblical allusion there. The kiss by which Judas betrayed Christ and the silver by which he was sold.'

'Kiss, kiss, kiss!' The art gallery director was in his element, his face a great red blur. 'Give her a kiss. Get the first part over with, for *God's* sake!'

Helen got up and went round the table to Paul. Florence had gone out to get some more food and Ben more wine. The conversation had taken a blasphemous turn which neither of them was happy about. However, they didn't want to offend their guests, so they remained in the kitchen.

Paul felt supremely at ease and amused to be in such good company. When Helen approached him he realised she wasn't joking; she really would kiss him. She reached out and took his arm to draw him to her.

As she did so, something within the very core of Paul's being warned him to be careful. It was an unconscious reflex, a sort of inner feeling of disquiet, as though the joke had gone on long enough. 'Stop now,' the inner voice said. Yet Paul couldn't resist completing the party game. He genuinely believed in what he was saying. And it was only a game, after all. No harm could possibly come from it.

'It's a good job my wife's not here,' he said while Helen's lips moved towards his.

'Don't worry,' replied Helen blithely, 'at the heart of every relationship is betrayal. I know.'

Marie awoke. The house was in darkness; it was the early hours of the morning. She'd slept badly, an intermittent and disturbed sleep, and she felt hot and feverish. Stretching out her hand in bed she discovered Paul wasn't there. He must still be at the dinner party. No matter, she hoped he was enjoying himself.

She gave a slight sigh as she remembered something. Incredibly, she'd forgotten to say her rosary. Drilled into saying it as a child, it was as much a part of her as any other reflex. Strange how she'd forgotten it. She felt too lethargic to switch the light on. Tomorrow. She'd say it tomorrow. Surely God wouldn't miss one day. It didn't really matter. The sky wouldn't fall in.

Marie tried to go back to sleep. Then, with a groan, she flicked the light on. Bleary-eyed, she fumbled about for her rosary, its small white pearls and silver cross. It was her mother's; she'd given it to her daughter the day she'd died.

She sat up and cried out in horror.

The rosary lay on the bedside table, the white pearls discolouring even as they smouldered.

When Paul kissed Helen he felt the warmth of her tongue as she slipped it deep inside his mouth. It was sensual and overpowering; it touched his own tongue, entwining with it. He smelt the subtle perfume of her body scent. Everything around him was forgotten. He wanted to be with her, with Helen. He didn't hear the mock cheer of the dinner guests, nor the entrance of Ben back into the dining room, his friend wryly shaking his head. He knew nothing of their thoughts. His senses carried him away.

A vision came to him. He was standing on a cliff of unimaginable height. A powerful wind was blowing in his face. Paul felt supremely in command of himself, unaffected and unaffectable by any living thing. Like some Apollo, his body lithe and naked. Slowly, he cast himself off the precipice in a spectacular dive. Imperishable, he fell. About him there was darkness and stillness, eternal in its depth. Then his trance broke.

Helen stepped back. 'One kiss is enough.' She returned to her side of the table.

'But,' cried one of the guests, 'where's the silver?'

Florence's nephew grasped a silver-plated candlestick. 'What about this?' However, no one laughed. They looked at Helen somewhat aggrieved, as if she'd spoilt the fun. 'I don't think I have any,' she said.

'Oh, shame,' cried the gallery director, fishing in his capacious pockets. 'Luvvies, I must have something here.'

From a purse on her lap Helen extracted a small vanity case and drew an object from it. They watched as Helen flicked the coin across the table to Paul. It gleamed brightly in the candlelight. Paul caught it.

Instantaneously, the candles went out. They were left in semi-darkness. They gasped. The perfect high drama to end the evening.

Child's play.

'Wonderful party, as usual.' The doctor and his wife wended their inebriated way down the garden path towards a waiting taxi.

'Really enjoyed it.' Florence's nephew kissed Florence on the cheek and hastily got into his car. His girlfriend slipped in the other side. She hoped they'd stop at the nearest hotel. She wanted sex, and now. It was as if she were being consumed by a fire of lust. Why, she didn't know or care. They roared off down the drive.

The other guests also departed from the house, the art gallery director collapsing into an inconvenient rose bush. He managed to resurrect himself with help. Paul was saying goodnight to Ben when he realised Helen wasn't there. He could see her strolling down the drive. He grasped Ben's hand.

'Wonderful food.'

'Sorry Marie wasn't able to come.' Ben paused. It was as good a time as any to raise the subject of Kramer, since his colleague was clearly in a genial mood.

'Helen, wait!' Paul quickly turned. 'Thank Florence for me.' With that he rushed off.

Ben watched him go, annoyed with himself for having

let the opportunity slip. He went back into his house and closed the door. The party had got too boisterous for his taste. And for some reason he didn't feel well. Perhaps it was too much wine?

Soon, Paul caught up with Helen. He was slightly out of breath. 'I've hardly had a chance to chat with you all evening, and there's a lot I want to discuss.'

'Oh?'

'Can we meet up soon?'

'You want to see me?' she said. Her eyes gave away nothing. They were cold.

'Of course,' continued Paul impatiently. 'I also need to talk to you about Kramer for the inquiry. I imagine you'll be there. What medication was he on?'

'He wasn't on any.'

She started to walk away and Paul followed her. The cold air and the alcohol made him feel light-headed.

'Can I get you a taxi? No one walks in San Francisco at this time of night.'

'Why not?' remarked Helen quizzically. 'There aren't any serial killers about that I know of.' Then: 'Your wife's waiting for you. *Poor* thing.'

The remark was soft but incisive, the stress on the word '*poor*' uncannily like the voice of the defence lawyer in the Kramer trial. It sobered Paul up and he stopped in his tracks.

'I have to go now.' Her expression softened. 'Of course we'll meet again. I've bought your apprenticeship, haven't I?'

Paul grinned. He liked her sense of humour, a woman who was used to getting her way. He searched in his trousers.

'I've lost your coin.'

'Impossible.' Helen stepped up to him. She kissed him

farewell. It was a kiss both sensuous and tender, but different from the previous one. A kiss of betrayal.

Between a servant and a master.

CHAPTER THIRTEEN

*But the power of the devil is stronger than
any human power. There is no power on earth
which can be compared to him who was
created so that he feared none.*

Malleus Maleficarum,
'Hammer of the Witches'

ST PETER'S BASILICA, eleven o'clock at night. Tourists, pilgrims and staff had long since departed. All was quiet. A monk stood by the side entrance with a key. He watched as Cardinal Benelli approached from out of the gloom. Unlocking the door, he let the Cardinal in.

As he did so, Benelli asked: 'Have Cardinals Graziani and Vysinsky arrived?'

The monk nodded.

'And the Father Confessor?'

'No.'

Benelli stepped inside and the door closed behind him. Within St Peter's Basilica there was profound quiet and a deep velvety darkness, save for the candles flickering at the high altar in the far distance.

The Cardinal sat down in a pew at the back of the church for a moment to collect his thoughts. He felt anguished. What would he say to these people? How could he adequately explain? It was so difficult, for what he knew, and what he was now responsible for, was of extraordinary significance.

Benelli wished he had been spared this particular cross. He felt so unworthy, incapable of dealing with this matter of the most profound spiritual importance. Contrary to popular belief, those who were appointed cardinals were rarely of a saintly disposition, and Benelli recognised this in himself. For saints were little concerned with the outward trappings of the Church, or with the wear and tear of administrative duties. They had no interest in clerical ranks and titles that others so earnestly sought.

Instead, cardinals tended to be solid men – good, worthy administrators – but not those with the deepest insight into the workings of the spirit. So why had the Pope chosen him for this task? Surely, he should have asked someone like Catherine of Benedetto; she would know of the powers of light and darkness and of how the Coins of Judas could be opposed. But not him.

Benelli sighed in anxiety. Then he got up. It was time. As he walked down the long aisle of St Peter's Basilica, he reflected on the past and on this, the final resting place of the Apostle on whom Christ had laid the greatest burden of the Faith, the simple and impetuous fisherman of whom the Saviour himself had declared:

Thou art Peter, and upon this rock I will build my church; and the gates of hell shall not prevail against it.

It was St Peter alone who could deal with the Coins of Judas and all the evil they embraced. Would that he were here in this time of peril.

As he walked down the aisle Benelli looked about him.

This building – the massive edifice crowned by that immense hemispherical dome – was one of the most famous in the world. However, although architecturally imposing, even more so was its strange and mysterious history, which was scarcely known to people in the world outside.

This huge structure, solid and massy as it was, was of relatively recent construction for, in 1506, the warrior Pope, Julius II, had commanded the greatest commission of his age: the tearing down of the old St Peter's and its replacement by a magnificent new building. The pontiff had spared neither genius nor expense to ensure that his instructions were fulfilled. He ordered one of the greatest architects of the time, Bramante, to prepare designs for the cathedral, and the poor man was driven on by a Vicar of Christ unsatisfied with anything less than artistic perfection.

On Bramante's death, the pontiff commanded Raphael to be the architect and, when he died, Giocondo and Sangallo helped complete the great work, each time more modifications and adaptations being made. Finally, one of the greatest figures of the Renaissance, Michelangelo, then seventy-one years old, was appointed to design the famous dome.

The new basilica took 120 years to complete. When it was finished it was one of the glories of the Faith. In fact, it was so impressive that, over time, people tended to forget this mighty church had replaced an earlier one – one that Julius II had ordered to be torn down because it had become structurally unsound. This was the older St Peter's Basilica, begun by the Roman Emperor Constantine around AD 320. He, in turn, had built his church over a Roman graveyard where St Peter, it was said, was buried after his crucifixion in about AD 67, the precise date of the Apostle's death being unknown.

There had been a huge outcry among the Roman people in 1506 when Pope Julius had ordered the old basilica to be torn down. However, Julius triumphed and the building was demolished, for his spiritual mandate could be questioned by none; the pontiff was answerable only to God. That said, there was one small matter, almost forgotten in the annals of history, that even the Pope himself did not have the temerity to change. A historian of the time, Egidio de Viterbo, recorded it thus:

> *Pope Julius built this absolutely splendid church which may be considered the equal, not of the lesser stars, but of the sun itself. He placed it, he said, over the very tomb of St Peter, the Apostle who described the glory of God. Bramante, the principal architect of the period employed by Julius . . . tried to persuade him to move the Apostle's tomb to a more convenient part of the church but Julius told him he could not and said repeatedly that the shrines must remain where they were, and forbade him to move what should not be moved.*

The architect was never told why the tomb of St Peter should not be moved. He concluded that the Pope must have his reasons and he wasn't anxious to challenge God's anointed representative on earth. Even if he had questioned the pontiff on this matter he would have received no reply since Julius kept this secret to himself – a secret that had been passed down from one pope to his successor since the foundation of the Church.

It related to the Coins of Judas.

Benelli approached the high altar. He genuflected and started down the stairway to the confession, the name for the crypt under the altar. From there he would step down, via a secret passageway, into the grotto and to the tomb of St Peter.

As Benelli did so, he walked back in history, like a simple pilgrim, to the very beginnings of it all. For below the present high altar of St Peter's, consecrated by Clement VIII in 1594, lay other, older, altars, now hidden. The altar of Callistus II inaugurated in 1124 and, beneath it, the altar of Gregory the Great inaugurated in AD 594.

This was only the start of the antiquities of Christianity. Below that altar lay the monument erected to St Peter by Constantine after his battle at the Milvian Bridge outside Rome in AD 312, when he fought against the Emperor Maxentius to determine who would rule the Roman world.

In the afternoon of that fateful day of 28 October, the outcome of which would have such a profound effect on the development of the Christian religion, Constantine saw in the afternoon sky a shining cross more brilliant than the sun with the words 'By this sign you shall conquer.' Ordering his troops to place the sign of the cross on their shields and banners, Constantine won a mighty victory. As a result, when he became Emperor he proclaimed Christianity to be the state religion of the Roman Empire.

However, in AD 320, when Constantine wanted to construct the first basilica of St Peter's to recognise his new religion in Rome, he was faced with an acute problem. The place where he was determined to site it was an old Roman graveyard on the side of the Vatican hill and it was a criminal offence under Roman law to violate graves. So Constantine had all the tombs in the graveyard carefully filled in with compacted soil and rubble to create a level base, while preserving the tombs themselves within the earth. On top of this he built the first St Peter's.

But why? Why the effort to move more than one million cubic feet of earth when this undisputed ruler of the civilised world could simply have had the law changed and the pagan graveyard razed to the ground in order to build this, his own monument to the greater glory of God?

There was a reason. A profoundly spiritual one. In that dusty graveyard on the outskirts of Rome lay the tomb of a man. A man who, by any reckoning in any period of human history other than the Christian era, would have been regarded as a person of no consequence in the annals of the mighty and the powerful.

A poor fisherman. An old Jew.

St Peter.

Over the centuries it became lost in legend as to whether the tomb of the Apostle actually existed under the basilica dedicated to his name, and pope after pope adamantly refused permission to excavate below the high altar to determine the truth of the matter.

Sixteen hundred years passed. Then, in 1939, alterations were made to the burial crypt under the high altar to accommodate the body of Pope Pius XI, who had recently died. Digging by workmen unearthed the pavement of Constantine's basilica and, beneath it, a layer of graves and sarcophagi that had been sunk below the floor of the old church.

Would they be allowed to dig further? Only one man had the power to permit this. Miraculously, after the ecclesiastical prohibition of so many popes, the new pontiff, Pius XII, ordered a search to be made for the tomb of St Peter. In 1940 they rediscovered the Roman graveyard and its tombs – untouched for almost two millennia.

It was these tombs that Cardinal Benelli made for, located under the very foundations of St Peter's. He came at night so that no one would see him. Silently, the Cardinal passed along the ancient street excavated more than nine metres below the high altar of the basilica, past the graves of the pagan dead with their richly painted frescos and stunning mosaics. As he did so Benelli recalled the earliest records about the first Apostle and the manner of his death, for they contained a key to the mystery of the coins.

After the resurrection of Christ, it was St Peter who led the Church and became its first Pope. He was an emotional and headstrong man, but one saturated with the love of God. So great was his spiritual power that the sick were laid on the ground before him in the hope that his shadow might fall on them as he passed, and so cure them.

During his ministry St Peter travelled widely, though the precise details of his movements were uncertain. In AD 43 he was arrested by Herod Agrippa I, yet he escaped from prison by miraculous means. Later, he presided over a Church Council in Jerusalem and he may have become the first Bishop of Antioch. Finally, in AD 64, a great fire swept through Rome and destroyed much of the city. The Christians were blamed for this by the mad Nero, anxious to find a scapegoat for an act probably committed by himself.

St Peter was forewarned of the search for him and he could have fled Rome and escaped his gruesome fate of crucifixion. But he did not. He went to his death with others in the Circus of Nero for the amusement of the mob, choosing to be crucified upside down in deference to his creator.

The night of his crucifixion, his body was taken down from the cross by his disciples and covertly taken away. This was a dangerous task since Nero had instigated draconian measures to destroy the Christians and their new religion. Because of this, the burial of the Apostle was hasty and in a place unlikely to attract inquisitive eyes: a trench in a Roman graveyard. Only those who had been close to St Peter knew of the whereabouts of his tomb and they marked it with secret signs.

When the Roman oppression against the Christian Church had lessened slightly, in AD 160, Pope Anicetus, the tenth in papal succession, raised a shrine over the grave in which St Peter had been buried. This comprised a small chapel and it was built into a red-brick Roman wall that had been erected over the trench some time after St Peter had been laid in it. Pilgrims continued to mark the burial spot with signs and prayers.

As the centuries passed, the first altars of the Catholic Church were erected above the tomb of St Peter, including the altar in the old Basilica of St Peter. Finally, when Pope Julius II commanded the new basilica to be built he ensured the new high altar was placed directly above the grave of St Peter, *even though the latter, as a result, would be hidden more than thirty feet below ground.* Why?

As Pope, Julius knew a mighty secret. The grave of that great Apostle contained not only the bones of one whom Jesus loved. It contained a vast spiritual power that only St Peter, the one whom Christ had foretold the very gates of hell could not prevail against, could defeat.

Within the grave, and in the arms of the Apostle as they buried him, his followers had placed a chalice filled with holy water. In that vessel lay many pieces of silver.

Coins by which the Light of the World had been betrayed.

*   *   *

Cardinal Benelli continued to walk down the Roman passageway. Finally, he stood by a simple red wall. Beside it were Cardinals Graziani and Vysinsky. They looked tired. They were elderly men and, as usual, they would rise for Mass at five the next morning. Yet sleep was out of the question, for the Holy Father needed to be advised on a matter of supreme importance.

They waited for one more person. Benelli watched as the Father Confessor proceeded down the underground road towards them. He'd been rather aggrieved when the Pope had indicated the monk should attend their meeting since his ecclesiastical rank was less elevated than their own. However, the Holy Father's word was law and it could not be gainsaid.

The four men gathered. Before them, beneath the red-brick wall, lay the tomb of St Peter. They had come here at the request of the Pope so that they might discuss the spiritual crisis they were faced with. Although even the Vatican was not safe from the great powers of evil, those unseen spirits who watched over the world and trafficked in its misery, within its confines there were, perhaps, one or two places that even an Angel of Darkness would not dare to penetrate.

Benelli looked at his colleagues. Three simple men, not saints, not Angels. How powerless they were. A profound grief came over him. After bowing his head in prayer, he began.

'Beloved friends, we have a problem that the Church has not had to face for a thousand years.' He paused.

'*A Coin of Judas.*'

CHAPTER FOURTEEN

*This then is our proposition: devils by their
art do bring about evil effects through witchcraft, yet it is true that without the assistance
of some agent they cannot make any form,
either substantial or accidental, and we do
not maintain that they can inflict damage
without the assistance of some agent, but with
such agent diseases, and any other human
passions or ailments, can be brought about,
and these are real and true.*

Malleus Maleficarum,
'Hammer of the Witches'

MARIE SAT AT THE BREAKFAST TABLE, her food
uneaten. She felt nervous and unsettled as she waited
for Paul to come downstairs.

Outside, Rachel was playing with the dog. Marie didn't
know how to broach the subject with her husband. He'd
be very dismissive of anything supernatural. That was
the way he was. He'd laugh at her. Also, the more she
thought about it, the more she realised it had to have
been her imagination. Or, rather, a nightmare. There
was no other explanation, was there?

Yet, despite its absurdity, an inner voice told Marie

that she had seen a woman in the bathroom. Then there was her rosary. She had seen it discoloured. However, when she awoke this morning, she couldn't find it. She sighed. Was it a portent of future things? Marie cast her eyes over the front page of the news. They were still searching for the serial killer. She thrust the newspaper away from her.

'Hi, darling.'

She turned as Paul hurried into the kitchen. There was a sound of noisy barking outside. He glanced at her and gave his usual grin. Marie felt relieved. Everything was back to normal.

'I have to dash,' he said, straightening his tie. 'I'm already late.'

'Do you want any breakfast?'

'No.' He rummaged through his attaché case. 'Damn, you haven't seen my evaluation of Julian Brennan?'

'Who?'

'You know, the son of Toni Brennan, the film star? Er, he was in *Powers of the Flesh* and something else.' Paul closed his case. 'I must have left the thing at the university. I'll be late for my lecture.'

Paul left the kitchen and Marie followed him into the hall. 'How was the dinner last night?'

'Great. Feeling better?' He looked at her inquiringly, but she could see he was distracted. There was a harassed expression on his face. He opened the front door.

'Paul?' Unease threaded through her voice.

He turned. 'Um?'

'You haven't seen my rosary, have you?'

'Your what?'

'My rosary.'

'No,' he said, completely bemused. 'Of course not, I never touch it. Look, darling, I have to go.'

'OK.' She kissed him. 'See you later.'

Marie watched him drive off. She stepped back into the house, feeling happy. Everything was back to normal; she'd imagined everything after all. She went upstairs. Quickly, she changed into a suitably impressive business suit, since she had a board meeting at work. Then she returned to the kitchen and tapped on the window.

'Rachel, time for school.'

A minute later, her daughter appeared. 'The dog won't come in.'

'Leave him then.' Outside, the Labrador was barking furiously. Marie left a note for the maid to feed him when she arrived in the afternoon.

'Got your gym kit?'

'Yes, Mummy.' Rachel skipped to the car and Marie opened the passenger door. She strapped her daughter in and walked round to the driving seat.

'My running shoes?' said Rachel, searching in her satchel.

Marie muttered under her breath. 'I'll be back in a minute.' She made towards the house.

When Marie opened the front door she felt a draught of very cold air. She stopped, curious as to where it could have come from. The house was also silent, profoundly so. She couldn't even hear the grandfather clock that ticked away noisily in the living room. However, Marie's consciousness didn't reflect on these matters; she was too preoccupied with getting to work.

Closing the door, she crossed the hallway and ascended the stairs. A sense of disquiet grew in her mind. It rapidly evolved into a distinctly unpleasant feeling that someone was watching her. Marie reached the landing and made for her daughter's bedroom. As she did so, she began to experience a sharp burning sensation in the pit of her stomach that made her double up in pain. She gripped onto the banister. 'What is the matter with me?' she thought.

It was then she heard a noise. It was a soft crump, like the tread of a man; it came from their bedroom. Marie stood rooted to the spot with fear.

Someone else was in the house.

Slowly, Marie made towards their bedroom. She went in. The room seemed to be as normal. However, an object was lying on the carpet. A coin. Curious, she moved towards it.

At that instant she felt as if someone had dealt her a savage blow to the back of her head. Marie collapsed onto the floor, gasping for air. In rapid succession, her sight blurred and went; then she could no longer feel, smell, or hear. The parameters that defined her human existence began to shut down. Images flickered into her mind. One was of Kramer, another of a woman pinioned in his arms. There were more, but not of Marie's world. Finally, a dark curtain descended. She saw and perceived nothing. 'I am dying,' she told herself. Then, 'I am in Hell.'

It was some minutes before she came to. She felt punch-drunk and groggy as if her brain had sustained a shocking blow. Gradually, her consciousness reasserted itself and her senses started to return to normal. She peered round the bedroom. It didn't seem like her room, her world, at all. It resembled something so distant, so false. A stage set.

'Mummy?' Rachel's anxious cry from the car penetrated the bedroom window.

'I'm coming.'

Her body aching, her spirit drained of strength, Marie staggered downstairs, her mind still in turmoil. What was happening to her? And why? At the front door she started back. Silently, tears began to stream down her cheeks. Inside the house by the front door lay the cat, Ginger. It was dead, her rosary savagely twisted round its neck. A thought flitted into Marie's mind and then vanished.

Someone, *something*, had moved into her house.

Paul sat in the conference room of his clinic. He felt uneasy.

This was one meeting he wasn't looking forward to – with Toni Brennan, film star, Hollywood cult figure, man of the moment – and total prick. Paul surveyed the two unappetising specimens of humanity lounging in the plush office chairs in front of him. Two fiends: one, little more than a walking drug ingestor, the other, his reptilian manager.

Paul could also see there was going to be lots of drama and histrionics today – and all he wanted was some peace and quiet on a Thursday morning. Why had Marie looked so unhappy when he'd left her? Was she still unwell?

The histrionics began early.

'Do you *know* what time it is? Why are you twenty minutes late? That's not what I'm fucking paying you for.' The balding actor started up from his chair and banged his hand on the table violently. 'What I *am* paying you for is to get my fucking kid off!'

'Toni . . .' His manager grabbed the actor's arm. 'I'm sorry,' he said to Paul. 'Toni, Toni, come and sit down.' He gave a leery grin. 'My client's very overworked, Professor Stauffer. A new film, you know. Huge amount of creative talent needed. Lots of brilliance. Toni's the new De Niro. He can get a little overwrought at times.'

The manager licked his lips. He was a cadaverous man, used to skimming money off people whom others wouldn't touch. His client's behaviour was nothing new to him. With a drug addiction as serious as Toni Brennan's the actor would either be out of a job or dead within a year. But that was the future. At present Toni was the darling of Hollywood and there were rich pickings to be made before the body finally rotted.

Paul regarded his client, all colour unco-ordinated, earrings and heroin-narrow eyes. Dressed like a twenty-year-old but going on forty. Not a man to worry about retirement – a word too long to spell.

Paul raised his eyes slightly. 'Mr Brennan?'

'Er, Toni, yeah it's Toni.' The actor tried to switch back to Mr Nice Guy again.

Paul watched the actor's fingers as they trembled lighting a cigarette. Then he opened his report. 'Well, Toni,' he said quietly, 'your son, Julian, has problems. He's exhibiting all the classic signs of serious maladjustment: arson at school, wrecking cars and,' Paul paused, 'taking drugs.'

'That's nothing to do with me.' Toni flounced into his chair. '*I'm* not the problem. It's his fucking mother.'

Paul pursed his lips. Not the problem, he thought, but the cause. Who'd want a father like that?

'And,' snarled Toni, 'it wasn't my son who burnt down the school. You've spoken to him, he's not capable of that. Look,' the tone became whining, 'I need a psychiatric report that says my boy's OK. That's all I want. Do you understand?' The tone became belligerent again. 'That's what I'm fucking paying you five hundred bucks an hour for. I'm not the one who needs treatment.'

Paul assumed a grim aspect. It was a waste of time discussing things with Toni at the moment. He'd wait until the heroin he assumed the actor had taken a few minutes before began to wear off.

'I'll talk to your son again,' he said.

Paul walked out of the conference room and into another. Toni's wayward offspring sat with his feet on a table, reading a pornographic magazine. He was dressed in white jeans on which he'd scrawled obscenities with a red marker pen. What creativity! Self-mutilation would come next. Following in the erratic footsteps of good old Dad. Julian was fourteen years old, small for his age, with a face older and more aggressive than his years. He gazed up at Paul idly. 'What did my dad say?' He blew a balloon of bubble gum.

'He wanted me to talk with you.'

Julian sniggered and turned back to his magazine. 'Fuck that. I told you, didn't I? I didn't burn down the school.' The voice was sullen and bitter.

Paul sat down. 'I think we should discuss your father.'

'No way.'

'Why not?'

'None of your business, is it?' Julian had no desire to approach the heart of the problem.

Paul stared across the room. This was not a difficult case. It was obvious what the problem was: an addict for a father who threw money at him one day and then ranted and raved at him the next. A mother who'd left years ago to be replaced by a bevy of teenage girlfriends whom the boy couldn't have any affection for. This child was a human disaster who doubtless lived in a vast, tastelessly decorated Hollywood-style mansion. Lonely, bitter and frightened. Good for a film script; pity it was a human being's life as well. But then, were some human lives worth saving?

'So you don't want to talk to me?'

'No.'

'Fine.'

Julian turned back to his magazine, surprised at having scored such an easy victory. Paul returned to the conference room.

'Well,' commented Toni Brennan, 'he's normal, isn't he? And if he's not normal, then *I'm* not fucking normal.'

The mortuary eyes of the manager and the narrow, slit eyes of his client contemplated Paul. They defied him to contradict them.

Paul was about to tell the father where to go. He couldn't help them and he didn't want to. However rich this film star was, however famous, however much talked about, there were some sleaze bags for whom no amount of money was worth the effort. Of course, Ben would be more sympathetic. But Paul's view had just hardened. Definitively. He opened his mouth to speak.

At that moment he had a vision. Or was it an hallucination?

Paul saw the man before him as he really was. Not the human being, the two-bit suddenly successful actor Toni, who couldn't cope with himself. Rather the emotions and feelings that flowed out of his scrawny human frame. It was like opening a Pandora's box of the senses. Paul could feel waves of melancholy, rancour and despair emanate from the actor. They flowed across the table towards him like music, or waves tumbling on the seashore. Paul received them not in his head, not as an intellectual impression, for he couldn't see or hear anything. Instead, they were vibrations that magically entered his own being.

He sat there, overwhelmed by this wholly unexpected and unique experience. He was absorbing, like notes from a piano, a chord of fear, another of jealousy, another of rage. They issued from Toni Brennan and they converged to convey an overall sense of malice. It was fascinating: a Bach fugue, but of the inner being.

Paul's consciousness abruptly clicked back into play. He must be on a drug trip. Had they put something in his coffee? He wouldn't put it past them.

'Well, are you going to write the report?' Toni leant forward, his tone urgent.

Scarcely a second had gone by. Paul observed the manager and then the actor. Had they seen anything? Felt anything? No, their expressions were still the same. Nothing had changed. Paul must have been in a reverie. Yet, even as he spoke, he could still feel the vibrations. He tried to define them further. It was as though he were standing in a deep river pool feeling the water swirl about him. A strange feeling, but not disconcerting. A new sense. More than that – this wasn't coming from Paul's thought process, from his consciousness. It was coming from *elsewhere within him.*

'I haven't decided yet.'

'What do you mean, haven't decided?'

'I want to see your son again next week,' said Paul crisply. 'Then I'll give you my decision.'

'Now look, you.' Toni jumped up, highly agitated. 'I'm not being pissed around so you can screw more money out of me. I need the report for his court appearance this week.'

'Mr Brennan, the purpose of these visits is not to screw money out of you. It is to help your son.'

'Well, then, *he* can come back next week.' Toni threw up his hands theatrically. 'I'm busy.'

'I want both of you to come back.' Paul continued to focus on the actor. The emanations from him had changed again. Anger had been replaced by fear. It had a different tonal quality – shriller, more intermittent. Paul could feel its resonance. The father was scared about him discovering something. But what?

With a mutinous glance the film star got up. He wanted to tell the psychiatrist to go hang himself, but they needed him to get Julian off the arson charge and Stauffer was the best since the Kramer case. An arrogant bastard, but the best. Also, Toni needed another fix. He had to get out of here.

'We'll be back, don't worry,' said the manager. He smiled his oily smile. Good, more fees, he thought. He charged by the hour.

The son appeared at the door of the conference room. 'See you next week,' snarled the father to his shrink.

Paul watched the deeply unpleasant trio walk down the corridor. He could still feel impressions flowing from the actor. However, this time he could also feel them emanating from the son as well, strong and powerful. Waves of very deep animosity; and they were directed towards the father. At that instant, a terrible thought came to Paul. It was so shocking he tried to dismiss it from his mind as quickly as possible. However, it remained there, like a certainty. He knew what would happen to Toni Brennan. The son would kill the father. Soon.

But what the hell was happening to him?

'Mrs . . . ?'

'Stauffer. Marie Stauffer.'

The patrolman sucked in his breath. He was a fat man, badly dressed and badly shaven. He didn't care how he looked or what people thought. He didn't like his job either but it paid well, since he was a crooked policeman.

'Where did you see the cat?'

'There.' Marie pointed to the carpet in the hall. 'The cat was there.'

'Yeah,' said the patrolman. He picked his teeth with the tip of his finger. Stupid woman. Still, she was pretty. About thirty, he reckoned, with dark hair, a svelte figure and a generous mouth. The patrolman studied her lecherously. Her husband was a lucky man, assuming she had one.

Most of the women in this area were divorced or separated. Middle-aged women with a big house, one or two kids and a husband who'd run off with the secretary. So what did they do? Sat in the kitchen, dreaming of better days and waiting for the monthly alimony cheque. With time and an unused body on their hands. He often tried to proposition them. He'd been disciplined about it a number of times, but he didn't care. If they only knew what he got up to anyway. Well, what every human being got up to in this world really – lying, cheating, stealing, betraying. That's why they were here.

'Uh, huh.' He clicked his jaw. 'You found the dead cat inside the front door, you took your daughter to school and returned. But the cat was gone. So you called us.'

'Yes,' said Marie patiently. She didn't like the look of him, but he was a police officer.

'And no one else has the key to your house?' He blew his nose on a dirty handkerchief.

'No. Apart from my husband and the maid, and they haven't been in.'

'I'll look around.'

'Please do,' said Marie.

The patrolman inspected the rooms at a leisurely pace. He was certain what her problem was. Fear. These last few weeks he'd been called out on numerous occasions by women. They knew there was still a serial killer loose, so they got wound up. He couldn't blame them. If he had a chance, he'd carry a machine gun around with him in this city.

'Well,' he said curtly. 'It's obvious your husband or maid discovered the cat was dead and moved it.'

'No,' said Marie firmly. She could see he didn't believe her, and she daren't tell him about the rosary or the fact that she also couldn't find the dog. 'Officer, I've phoned the maid; she knows nothing about it. And my husband is never at home during the day. I saw the cat. It was dead. When I returned from the school its body wasn't there any longer. Someone must have entered the house – twice – to put the cat there and then to remove it.'

The patrolman sneered. 'Talked with your husband, uh? Called in a neighbour? Taken a photo or something? Look, who'd break in to your house just to steal a dead cat? I know there're sick people in this city,' he ran his tongue over his chapped lips, 'but most stick to burglary. Uh, let's just check upstairs and see if anything's been disturbed. You go first.'

The patrolman watched as Marie ascended the stairs, his eyes fixed on her posterior, his thoughts elsewhere. Abruptly, he blinked. He thought he saw someone on the landing above them. He blinked again, but there was nothing. Must be a trick of the light. He started to climb.

'Attack her.' The command was incisive; it whispered directly into his ear.

'What?' said the patrolman, out loud. Shocked, he turned round to see who'd spoken and then back again. 'Did you say something?'

Marie turned at the top of the landing, startled. 'No.'

The patrolman blanched. He'd distinctly heard a

woman's voice, but he couldn't have. As he reached the top of the stairs the instruction came again, but this time *inside* his mind. 'Attack her,' it whispered, repeating the words softly and insistently. The patrolman had heard this inner voice before, usually when he stole things or bore false witness in court. However, this one was very loud and commanding. It mimicked his own.

Together, they entered the master bedroom. The patrolman pretended to look around yet his eyes kept returning to Marie as she stood by the bed. Marie glanced back at him. She wrapped her arms about her body. Why was he looking so strangely at her? She felt vulnerable and frightened.

'There's no one here,' said the patrolman out loud. He moved towards her. In his thoughts, the temptation had become more subtle. It was obvious this woman wanted him, wasn't it? He could feel it, see it in her eyes. She wanted sex. Besides, who'd know if he touched her?

Marie backed away. However, the patrolman, in the grip of forces he knew nothing of, started to raise his hand, to seize hold of her. You'll get away with it, the inner voice told him with glee. No witnesses. I promise.

Simultaneously, the phone at the bedside rang. It shattered the spell. Marie fled to it and picked up the receiver, her hands trembling. 'Gloria!' She burst into tears. 'I've been trying to contact you. Come over immediately.' She looked up, her face white. 'There's no need to stay. Please leave now.'

The patrolman glared at her as he recovered from his daze. Had she read his thoughts? Impossible. Still, the call had spoilt his evil desires.

'Er, all right. Call if you need me.' He grinned feebly. Descending the stairs he walked to his car and got in.

He reversed down the driveway. As he did so he squinted into his side mirror. Standing in the middle of the road was a large man with a knot in his hair. He seemed familiar, well-known. The patrolman blinked. When he looked again, the figure had gone.

Upstairs, Marie started to cry uncontrollably. She knew something was happening, yet she couldn't properly comprehend it. Not surprising, since it transcended rational thought.

The devils were moving in.

Hanlon Dawes got up. The distinguishing features of the Warden of the High Security Facility were the build of a marine and the character of a bully.

'Hi, Paul.' The greeting was brusque as always; Hanlon hated administration as much as he hated prisoners. 'You know these people. Emma Breck, Senior Psychiatrist, Darrel Bartlett, my assistant, Pat Harbison, Head of D Block and . . . Jeff Eichenberger, Security Systems, who work the computers in the prison.' The tone was withering. 'Sit yourself down.' The Warden pointed to a seat behind the Formica-topped table. 'By the way, your student's recovered, hasn't she? No problems?' He eyeballed Paul.

'Er, she's fine,' replied Paul. He cursed himself for having forgotten to visit Suzanne for two days now. He lied. 'It gave her a bit of a shock, but she's better now.'

'As *I* anticipated,' said the Warden. 'Well,' he said to the hapless attendees, 'what the *hell* went wrong?'

Pat Harbison commenced nervously: 'Sir, all the cell doors are electronically controlled. They can only be opened by a guard inserting a password and pressing a key.'

'I know that,' replied the Warden. 'I'm not an idiot. Get on with it.'

Harbison went white. 'The warder on duty, Schramp, is sure he didn't push any key to open Karl Kramer's cell. And the computer people tell me that there's no record of his having done so.'

The Warden shifted his glare to the computer systems operator. He liked nerds even less than the prisoners or administration. The list of things Hanlon Dawes didn't like was as long as his arm. 'Well?'

'It's true, sir,' said Eichenberger in a strangulated voice. He plucked at his glasses. 'No instruction was given to open Kramer's cell door. We're still not sure what happened.'

'Not sure?' Hanlon Dawes exploded. 'Kramer gets out and nearly rapes a woman visitor and you're not sure? We could be facing a massive lawsuit and you're not sure?' His face and neck suffused with blood. 'Schramp's fired. And you,' the Warden directed his wrath at Eichenberger, 'you'd better check your computers because if this happens again you're out of here as well.'

The Warden continued savagely: 'I want a statement on what happened from each of you on my desk by ten a.m. tomorrow. Without fail.' He got up. 'Paul, I'll talk with you.'

They stepped outside into the corridor. Dawes checked to see no one was there. Then he brought his face close to the psychiatrist's. 'That guy Kramer, he's the serial killer,' he said in a low voice, tapping Paul on the chest with his finger. 'You screwed up.'

'What do you mean?' replied Paul arrogantly. This man was just a prison officer. What did he know of complex psychiatric matters?

Hanlon Dawes gripped Paul's arm tightly and led him down the corridor. 'Because I've spent thirty years working with scum,' he said. 'And I'll tell you something. The other prisoners are frightened to death of him and that's saying something in this zoo. The way he attacked your student was no isolated incident. Our nasty little friend knew exactly what he was doing.'

'I don't think so.' Paul didn't like being told off by his intellectual inferiors.

'Now listen, mister.' Hanlon Dawes threatened him with a finger. 'You may be a hot-shot psychiatrist, but you'd better get your act together. You find out how we can get this animal Kramer back into court or else you're out of here as well. No more visits. Remember, a girl committed suicide because of your smart-arsed opinion and' – he paused to accentuate his parting words – 'I've got an election coming up.'

Hanlon Dawes stomped off. Paul watched him go. That was his relationship with the top man gone; five years of visits blown away.

Yet, within half an hour, Paul himself was to experience the same exasperation and ill temper.

'Pat,' he exclaimed angrily, 'I'm the psychiatrist, remember, I'm not crazy. I *saw* a woman. She was behind me. She was staring at Kramer, for God's sake. I met her last night. Her name's Helen.'

'There was no one, Paul,' stammered the Head of D Block. 'Look, there's a way to prove it. Let's go through the security camera tapes.'

They painstakingly reviewed them all. No woman there; Paul had to admit it. Besides Suzanne Delaney and Emma Breck, there'd been no other woman on the landing when Kramer had held Suzanne hostage. Just Paul and the two guards. Pat shrugged wearily.

'Forget it. It was an understandable mistake, what with all the drama and everything.'

'I want to talk to Kramer.'

'Now isn't a good time.'

'I want to talk with him.' Paul's voice became ugly. 'If not, I'll go to the Warden straight away.'

'Are you threatening me?' said Harbison, shocked. He'd never seen the psychiatrist behave like this.

'Yes.'

A dreadful place of filtered light and white walls, E Block was located beneath the main prison courtyard. Here they put those who had committed crimes almost beyond imagination. It presently housed some of California's most notorious killers.

They included Chris Cooper, who'd tortured people in bizarre satanic rites that involved drinking their blood; Dave Urch, a psychopathic killer of more than twenty young children; Jerzy Palubicki, a nurse who had injected patients with a range of poisons; Hank Jacobsen, who shot dead fifteen people in his workplace because someone got his monthly pay cheque wrong; Abdul Kali, who blew up an aircraft of holidaymakers to draw attention to a political group he was a member of. A roll call of the damned.

Paul had visited these inmates and tried a variety of psychiatric treatments on them. Yet their minds remained disassociated from the reality in which they lived, imprisoned in an inner world that was both destructive and impossible to penetrate. People without a shred of compassion, mercy or remorse. E Block was where Hanlon Dawes had ordered Kramer to be put in solitary for three months, a padded cell to himself, seeing no one for twenty-four hours a day, seven days a week.

The guards led Kramer in chains into an empty room where they handcuffed him to a wall. Paul came in and sat down.

'Oh, surprise, surprise,' crowed the murderer sarcastically. 'It's my psychiatrist come to ask about my health.'

Paul said nothing. He waited for the warders to go, keeping well back from the chained figure on the wall. Then he shut his eyes. As he did so, he experienced a massive jolt, like an electrical surge, radiating through his being.

What Paul had felt that morning with Toni Brennan and his son he now felt with Kramer. But these sensations were different, far more dramatic. If the vibrations from the actor and his child were similar to those experienced by a person adrift in turbulent waters, with Kramer, he was caught up in a hurricane. Paul could feel cruelty and malevolence streaming out of him. Deep and profound, these feelings were directed at Paul, trying to penetrate his being as if he were a small boat on the sea that Kramer was seeking to hole and destroy. It was a frightening experience, pitiless and unrelenting. Paul immediately opened his eyes.

'So you feel it, too,' said Kramer. He licked his lips.

'What is it?' Paul asked.

'Who knows?' The tone was contemptuous. He knew, but he wouldn't tell.

Paul shut his eyes again, experiencing the turbulence, trying to fathom some meaning from it.

'Who was the woman?'

'What woman?'

'The woman who stood behind me when you attacked the student,' said Paul. 'Helen. You saw her. I know you did. Who is she?'

Silence. Paul could feel a change in the impressions emanating from the killer.

'You're frightened of her, aren't you Karl? She made you release the girl. But how can she possibly do that?'

Although Kramer said nothing, the vibrations were more eloquent than any words. Within the arching waves of cruelty there were profound troughs of fear. Kramer was afraid. A serial killer who instilled the most hideous terror in others was himself afraid. But of what? What on earth could cause him such fear?

'Guards!' Kramer bawled out. 'Take me back to my cell.'

The warders returned and began to unchain him from the wall. Kramer stared fixedly at Paul. As he shuffled past him, he bent down to whisper some parting words. 'Look for the mark, sucker.'

Paul drove home from the Facility. It took him a long time since he got caught up in the rush hour; yet it gave him time to think. Something was wrong with him. Well, not wrong; that in itself was inaccurate. He was experiencing a strange hypersensitivity. But why? It couldn't be the result of external stimuli; he'd taken no drugs, no drink and wasn't on any medication. Brain malfunction, then? No. His sight was fine, no headaches, no blackouts, no memory loss. Depression? The opposite. His mind felt sharp and clear. Extraordinarily so, in fact.

However, there *was* a problem. The woman Helen, that was the problem. Both Paul and Kramer had seen her the day Suzanne was attacked. Yet no one else had. More oddly, Kramer was scared of her. It made absolutely no sense. Nor did Kramer's parting comment. What mark? What did it mean?

Soon, Paul pulled into the driveway of his house. It

was a beautiful sunlit evening, just before twilight. A memory to treasure. Then Marie was running down the drive, tears streaming down her face. She grasped at the windshield.

'It's Rachel.'

CHAPTER FIFTEEN

The evil that comes to light in man and that
undoubtedly dwells within him is of gigantic
proportions, so that for the Church to talk of
original sin and to trace it back to Adam's
relatively innocent slip-up with Eve is almost
a euphemism. The case is far graver and is
grossly underestimated.

Carl Jung, *The Undiscovered Self*

CARDINAL BENELLI STOOD WITH THE two cardinals
and the Father Confessor beside the tomb of St Peter
and told them the story of the coins.

The Gospel writer, St Matthew, recorded how Christ
was betrayed. The chief priests and the elders of the
people gathered in the palace of the high priest, Caiaphas.
They took counsel together to arrest Jesus by stealth and
to kill him. The opportunity soon came. One of Christ's
twelve disciples was Judas Iscariot, a common thief. Before
Judas took bread at the Last Supper, Satan entered him.
Then, he went to the chief priests and asked them: '*What
will you give me if I deliver him to you?*'

They gave him thirty pieces of silver. That night Judas
went to the Garden of Gethsemane with a mob and there,
by means of a kiss, he betrayed the Light of the World.

Jesus was taken by the chief priests and elders of the people and delivered to Pilate, the Roman governor, for crucifixion. St Matthew also recorded that, when Judas saw what he had done:

> . . . he repented and brought back the thirty pieces of silver to the chief priests and the elders saying, I have sinned in betraying innocent blood. They said, What is that to us? See to it yourself. And throwing down the pieces of silver in the temple, he departed; and he went and hanged himself.
>
> But the chief priests, taking the pieces of silver, said, It is not lawful to put them into the treasury, since they are blood money. So they took counsel, and bought with them the potter's field, to bury strangers in. Therefore, that field has been called the Field of Blood to this day.

Cardinal Graziani looked at Benelli sharply. 'Are you saying these coins of Judas still exist?'

'Yes, and they have immense power. What I am about to tell you is known only to two people: the Pope and the Head of the Holy Office. It has been handed down from the beginning of the papacy to all those who have occupied the chair of St Peter. It is, perhaps, the most intimate secret of the Church.'

The expressions of the cardinals registered the deepest alarm. No one in that small audience wanted to hear any more. It was a secret too ghastly in its ramifications to contemplate. However, Benelli had no option. He was commanded to divulge it. Contemplating the plain red wall in front of them he began:

'In this world there are many things which bear witness to the truth of the Gospels – tangible evidence of divine events. The bones of a saint, the bloodied garment of a martyr, the writings of a father of the Church. These objects comprise the human manifestation of a divine truth and each is imbued with a tremendous power of good. But of the other side, of the powers of evil and the means by which they might be invoked, the Church has been silent throughout the centuries. Intentionally so, to prevent the misguided and the foolish from doing great harm to themselves. Most of all, the Church has been silent about the Coins of Judas.'

Benelli sighed. Even as they stood by the tomb of St Peter in this, the innermost sanctuary of the Church, he felt anxious, as if other, unseen, presences were there, listening to his words.

He continued: 'Our Lord was sold for thirty pieces of silver, each imbued with the greatest of evil. After his resurrection, St Peter led the Church. He alone knew of the destructive nature of these coins and one of his responsibilities was to gather them in. Against him, and him alone, they had no force, for Our Lord himself had said: "Thou art Peter and upon this rock I will build my church, and the *gates of hell shall not prevail against it.*"

'What happened to these coins? The Bible tells us they were used to buy a field, called the Field of Blood, outside Jerusalem, to use as a graveyard to bury foreigners in. The name of the man who sold this land to the chief priests is unknown and the coins he received in payment were soon scattered throughout the Roman Empire.

'It was an enormous task to recover them. Yet the first Apostle did not falter in his duty. In the course of his travels he was led by a series of revelations to where they were. Some surfaced in Antioch, some in Rome, some in Corinth. Always they were found in the possession of the rich and powerful, the cruel and the dictatorial. Throughout the remaining years of his life St Peter searched for them and, as each came into his hands, it was drained of its evil power. Yet, even as he tracked them down, the Angels of Darkness did all that they could to thwart his designs. They did so through the Roman Emperor, Nero, one of the most benighted men who ever lived.

'As you know,' said Benelli, and his hand stretched out across the tombs of the pagan dead behind them, 'it was Nero who blamed the Christians for the great fire in Rome and who tried to wipe out the early Church.' Benelli recalled the words of the Roman writer Tacitus on the fate of those souls:

> *Their death was turned into a diversion. They were clothed in the dress of wild beasts, and torn to pieces by wild dogs; they were fastened to crosses, or set up to be burned, so as to serve as lamps when daylight failed. Nero gave up his own gardens for the spectacle in which he dressed up as a charioteer.*

'One of those fastened to a cross was St Peter. He was crucified by Nero before he had recovered all the coins.'

'How many were recovered?' asked Cardinal Vysinsky.

'All but eight,' answered Benelli. 'When St Peter died he was buried here' – he indicated the tomb before them – 'and in his arms were placed those twenty-two coins. They are contained in holy water, in a sealed chalice, to be undisturbed for the remainder of time. They no longer have any force. For the Scriptures told the truth: not even Satan's power could prevail against the Father of the Church.'

'And the other eight?' Cardinal Graziani asked. His face was gaunt with shock at what he was hearing; his aged hands trembled.

'Five more are accounted for. However . . .'

A bell tolled in the basilica above them, for it was the twelfth hour. The air became very cold. Benelli looked at the Father Confessor. Who knew what dark messengers had gathered around them? He hesitated.

'Go on,' said the monk quietly.

'The history of the coins I can only divulge to you in the presence of the Holy Father,' said Benelli, 'but I'm commanded to tell you something of their nature. The Coins of Judas look like simple Roman coins, a silver denarius bearing the face of Tiberius Caesar, but they can only be wielded by a human who is ensnared by evil. Otherwise, they have no effect.'

'Ensnared by evil? In what way?' said Cardinal Vysinsky.

'One who has sold his soul to the devil.'

The two cardinals looked at him aghast. They crossed themselves.

'Throughout the centuries,' continued Benelli grimly, 'despite the wickedness of men, there are relatively few prepared to sell their souls to evil when it comes to it, and to do so willingly. Even the dictators, the torturers, the murderers, the assassins, the blasphemers of this world are cautious over such things. Within the putrefaction of their own minds something still warns them: "Take care, go no further, for you will damn yourself for eternity." Yet there are a few who have crossed into the Abyss even while on this earth, as the coins have proved.'

'How can this be?' asked Graziani.

Benelli felt exhausted. A tiredness was overcoming him that sapped him to the marrow.

'It is the free choice of man. Any part of God's creation can reject him. But by denying him they ultimately deny themselves. In so doing, all that they are and all that they love – for love cannot belong to evil – is extinguished as though it had never been. Both their body and soul will become as nothing, for, in the end, they are no longer themselves. They are wholly possessed and they become part of the powers of darkness. They work for a different master.'

Cardinal Vysinsky croaked, 'But why would any man wish to sell his soul for such a coin?'

'For control over mankind, and for knowledge. For a period of time a Coin of Judas will give its wielder the vision of an Angel – until they are wholly taken over and their being destroyed. The more powerful the coin, the faster this occurs. With these last coins the period of enlightenment, and the eclipse of the soul, will be brief.'

'What do you mean the more powerful the coin?' asked Cardinal Graziani. 'Do these coins have different degrees of power?'

Benelli nodded. 'Originally, all had the same amount of power but, as each is destroyed, its influence flows into the remainder. The evil becomes ever more concentrated as the coins revert to their source. To the one who rules the Field of Blood.'

There was silence.

'Who can resist them?' breathed Cardinal Graziani finally. His aged face was wreathed in sadness. Truly, this night had been the longest and most painful of his life.

'I do not know,' said Benelli, his voice leaden with sorrow. 'However, the Holy Father now seeks our advice on this matter.' He hesitated, unwilling even to declare it.

'*One of the last Coins of Judas has come into the world.*'

CHAPTER SIXTEEN

So also the intellect can be darkened by a bad angel in the knowledge of what appears to be true . . . therefore, when devils enter the body, they enter the powers belonging to the bodily organs, and can so create impressions on those powers.

> *Malleus Maleficarum,*
> 'Hammer of the Witches'

IN THE HOSPITAL PAUL AND Marie hurried along a bright green corridor. There was a swirl of activity about them. A drug trolley collided with a bed being wheeled in for emergency surgery. A clutch of nurses rushed by, about to start their evening shift. A young man, with a head bandage and a hangover, sat disconsolately on a wooden bench, unaware his girlfriend had just died on the operating table and that his driving days would be over for a long time. Paul gritted his teeth. He abhorred hospitals. He hated death.

They arrived at the children's ward. Before they went in, Paul turned to Marie. They'd scarcely spoken during their journey to the hospital. She was very pale.

'They say Rachel fell off a swing? Is that all? No other details?' he said testily.

'That's what they told me at the school,' Marie replied.

'Why wasn't someone watching her?'

'They saw a woman walking past her when it happened, but she didn't stop. She wasn't a teacher.'

'Typical. No one helps anyone else in this city.' Paul was feeling uncharacteristically angry. Normally, he would be quite calm, but not today. It was a bad day.

Marie hardly noticed. She'd been trying to make sense of the events of the last twelve hours but she couldn't, since they led her to an unpalatable conclusion. She also felt unwell, her body heavy and lethargic, her mind unable to concentrate, as if drained of energy. What was happening? Could she be having a mental breakdown? But it was so unexpected, as if a black cloud had suddenly descended on her.

They entered the accident department. A doctor came forward and shook hands with them.

'We're going to keep your daughter in for observation tonight. She's had a nasty blow to her head.'

He was a young, ginger-haired man who looked as if he was fresh out of medical school. Not someone to inspire a great deal of confidence.

'Of course, you'll do a brain scan?'

'Er, yes,' the medic replied with a slight smile, uncertain as to whether Paul was also one of his profession. He had that look about him. 'You can never be too sure.' They entered a room. 'Here she is. We've sedated her, since she was in pain. She's been asleep for the last half-hour.'

Rachel's head was swathed in a bandage. She looked so peaceful.

'Mrs Stauffer? Can I have a word with you concerning Rachel's details?'

Marie got up and went outside with the doctor. Meanwhile, Paul focused his complete attention on his daughter. He cared for her more than anyone else in the world.

Paul closed his eyes. Within a few seconds he felt sensations emanating from her body, but these were quite different from those he'd experienced with Kramer or the film star. The vibrations that flowed from Rachel were soft and undulating, like the gentle swell of a vast ocean. They were Rachel's innermost expressions of love – the love she bore for her father and for others.

Paul was profoundly moved by them and tears welled up in his eyes. How could this possibly be? How could he experience the existence of his child in this way – her inner presence and emotions? He looked away. He didn't want to believe it; it was impossible. Even as Paul experienced these waves they began to change. They became turbulent, presaging the arrival of a mighty storm. Rachel moved restlessly in the hospital bed, her spirit troubled.

'You all right?'

Paul shuddered at the sound of his wife's voice. 'Yes,' he said curtly. He got up. 'I'm going to talk with the doctor.'

But he lied. Going outside into the corridor, Paul hurried past the surgery and made towards one of the wards. As he did so, the power of the Coin of Judas acquired a greater hold over him. Surreptitiously, its spiritual energy filtered into his being, dampening his senses to make them less capable of resistance. Like a great snake, an angelic force emerged from its cosmic prison, stealthy and invisible.

Walking through the wards Paul didn't feel his normal self. He experienced a lightness, a fragility in the world around him, as if it didn't really exist. Once, in a medical experiment, he'd taken the drug mescalin. Within a short while he'd experienced a strange and wonderful distortion of reality. Green carpets became super-green, flowers acquired an iridescence of colour, artwork became a molten mass that seemed to lurch out of the picture towards him. However, what Paul was experiencing now was quite different: a true vision. The carpets, the walls, all inanimate objects remained the same to his sight: the drab remained drab, the bright remained bright.

But in the case of human beings, what a transformation! In the children's ward he could perceive their auras. Like magic they appeared before his eyes, emanating from the children, towards and through him. Vibrations no longer, but light of an overwhelming intensity. Brilliant diamonds that refracted into their constituent colours: the lightest sky-blue; the purest blood-red, the most sunlit yellow; the deepest sea-green.

He sat on the bed of a young girl. Although in a coma, a brilliant light, warm and comforting, streamed from her, its intensity almost blinding. Dying to one world, her being was effortlessly augmented in another.

In an old people's ward the colours were less pure and intense. Here, sadness, anger and other human emotional disturbances seemed to weaken the force and diminish it. Still, the aura remained.

Finally, Paul made his way to the bowels of the building. He passed through a door marked 'Morgue'. Inside, he opened a freezer. Without unzipping the body bags of the corpses he stood beside them. There was nothing. No vibrations, no colours. The human husks produced nothing. So whatever it was, Paul reasoned, died with the body. He must be seeing their life force.

Just then an attendant wheeled in a corpse. Paul gasped, for an aura still emanated from it. Very weak, but still there.

'When did he die?'

The man flicked a ticket attached to the toe of the deceased. 'Two days ago. Suicide with a razor.'

'Can you see anything?'

'See?' replied the attendant, bemused. 'Did you say, "see"?'

'Oh, nothing.'

Paul started to open the fridges and check the dates of death. What did it mean? When people died the aura didn't leave them for three days, yet it became progressively weaker. Within three days, it had gone or at least Paul could no longer perceive it. So, whatever he was looking at was not a life force as such, but it was a force, and one that remained for a time after death. What was it? And *why* could only he see it?

Paul turned to close the door to a freezer. Then it happened.

Without warning, his body crumpled under him and he collapsed onto the floor. He experienced an agonising pain around his heart and his senses started to flicker, then fade away. An instant later, his frame started to convulse frenetically. It was terrifying; he no longer felt in command of his own being; it was as though huge forces of energy had been unleashed within him and were fighting for control: armies on a battlefield. I'm going to die, he thought. This is what death is like – eternal darkness and fear. Then he felt no more.

'Wake up.'

Gradually, his sight returned to him. He focused once again.

'Helen?'

She knelt beside him. He felt desperately ill. 'Have I had a heart attack?'

'Course not.' The tone was flippant. 'You just felt faint.'

'No, it was more than that,' he gasped. 'What are you doing here?'

'I want to ask you the same question.'

'It's too difficult to explain.'

'Really?' Helen helped him get up. 'You'll soon feel better.'

And Paul did. It was extraordinary, but once he sat in a chair with her comforting hand on his shoulder, his nausea and dizziness abated. He felt a warm and sustaining glow. Outside, twilight became night.

'I have to go now.' Helen looked at him closely, her eyes locking on to his, to take away his memory of her. Suddenly, she said, 'Your wife's coming.'

Paul bent down to pick up his wallet, which had fallen from his top pocket. When he looked up again, Helen was gone. The morgue doors opened and Marie ran through them followed by a nurse.

'Where have you been? We've been looking for you everywhere.'

Late that night, Marie sat in the living room of her house. It had been an extraordinary day and she felt overwhelmed. They'd helped Paul upstairs to the emergency department and the doctors had run some tests on his heart. But they were negative and he'd kept insisting he'd only felt faint. Paul had given no explanation as to why he'd been wandering about the hospital, nor why he'd entered the morgue. On returning home he'd gone straight to bed, so she'd had no chance to tell him of the other strange events.

She gazed across the room. The woman in the red dress, her rosary, the cat, the threatening patrolman, Rachel in hospital and now Paul ill. What did it all mean? Also, there'd been a garbled message on the phone from Gloria, their maid. She'd gone to visit a friend – Helen someone – and wouldn't be back for a few days. It was not like her to go off without notice, and her voice had been very curt. Another strange event. Perhaps she should wake Paul now and discuss these matters with him.

Just then the phone rang. Marie jumped and picked it up.

'Sorry to ring you at home, Paul,' the voice was soft, almost caressing, 'but I couldn't get hold of you today.'

'Who's speaking?'

'Oh.' There was a puzzled pause. 'I want to speak to Professor Stauffer. It's Suzanne.'

'Suzanne who?'

'One of his students. He was going to come and see me today. At my apartment.' The tone remained intimate, as if speaking about a very close friend. 'Tell Paul to come tomorrow.'

'Look, I'm afraid he's been ill, and I don't know anything about . . .'

'Tell him to come.' There was a click as the receiver was put down.

Marie pondered the strange call for a few moments. Then she went upstairs. She felt nauseated and utterly exhausted. It would be OK when she had Rachel back with her. She passed her daughter's empty bedroom, then the spare room where Paul had insisted on sleeping that night. As she did so, she remembered something else she'd forgotten to ask her husband about. The coin she'd seen on the bedroom floor that morning. Marie had searched for it, but it had gone.

Slowly, Marie undressed, her mind a whirl. And the phone call? Was Paul about to start another affair? She couldn't face any more. She loved him, but this time, she'd leave him and she'd take Rachel with her, come what may.

Marie turned out the light. She lay in the darkness. As she did so, her deepest anxiety surfaced into her mind, like the drip of a secret poison. It was quite irrational, quite inexplicable, and there was no reason to fear it at present. But there it was, lurking like an evil spirit in the depths of her troubled heart.

She was afraid she might die. Soon.

CHAPTER SEVENTEEN

God will judge the righteous and the wicked,
for he has appointed a time for every matter
and for every work.

Ecclesiastes 3:17

IT WAS AN EXTRAORDINARY MEETING, even for an
institution that was two thousand years old. Cardinal
Benelli looked about him. They were in the private
chapel of the Pope located in the heart of the Vatican.
The doors had been closed and Swiss Guards posted
outside. They sat in the centre of the chapel underneath
the stained-glass window depicting the Ascension. Four
people. The pontiff in white, two cardinals in red and
the Father Confessor in his simple brown cassock.

'Cardinal Graziani is unable to attend,' said the Father
Confessor. 'He is very sick.'

'I know,' said the Pope gently. 'We will continue alone.'

Benelli looked across at Pope John XXV. Of medium
height, slim, with a deeply lined face and a wonderful
smile, he was much loved. A man of peace, a mystic, he
was now in his late seventies. Although Benelli saw him
almost every day, he still had the feeling of being in the
presence of a very special human being, a link between
the physical and spiritual worlds.

The Pope closed his eyes in prayer. Then he gazed towards the altar.

'We should begin,' he said.

With nervous hands, Benelli picked up the ancient document he'd taken from the papal safe only a short time before. It had been written in Latin nearly one thousand years ago and its vellum pages were very frail.

Benelli began his summary. 'The history of these coins is a terrible one. They have only one purpose. Just as they were used to betray Christ, so their true purpose is to betray, and to destroy, the Church which he founded. Each coin, wielded in the hands of one who has sold his soul to the devil, will seek to destroy the papacy itself.'

There was a profound quiet.

Benelli continued, 'It is not known why St Peter was unable to find the remaining eight coins during his life. However, down the ages, these coins have resurfaced, one by one. When they do, they attach to a human being. Soon, that person is wholly possessed by an evil spirit, to his eternal destruction. *When* these coins resurface and *why* they attach to particular individuals, we don't know. The history simply declares this to be a cosmic mystery. It says, however, that the entry of these coins into the world is always presaged by major natural phenomena such as volcanic eruptions, famine, plague.'

Benelli started on the history of the coins. It went back almost to the beginnings of Christianity.

'The first of the eight remaining Coins of Judas not destroyed by St Peter came into the hands of the Roman Emperor Diocletian. Under its pernicious influence he initiated a persecution of the Church in AD 303. It was the most systematic attempt to wipe out Christianity the Roman state ever undertook. Proclaiming himself the son of a god, Diocletian ordered the clergy to be seized.

Many of those arrested were torn to pieces in the Colosseum. Others were horribly tortured and sent to work in the mines. Worse, the Emperor forced even the pontiff himself, Pope Marcellinus, an old and sick man, to offer incense to the gods.'

At this Benelli halted, his voice hoarse with emotion. When he was sufficiently recovered he continued.

'Poor Marcellinus. He failed the Faith of which he was the foremost living representative. It nearly destroyed the Church. Later, he repented and he was beheaded in AD 304 at the command of the Emperor. The following year, Diocletian issued an edict to suppress Christianity. It became a licence for wholesale slaughter.

'Yet,' Benelli continued, 'prematurely aged and forced into retirement, Diocletian died in AD 316 before the coin could complete its work. The Coin of Judas was recovered from his corpse and secretly placed in St Peter's tomb, together with the twenty-two already there.'

Cardinal Vysinsky shook his head with pain. He could hardly bear to hear more. Since he had first heard of these coins he had been living a nightmare.

'The second coin came into the hands of the Roman Emperor Julian, commonly called the Apostate, a man much influenced by dreams throughout his life. Julian had a bitter contempt of Christianity. He called it the trickery of the Galileans and the resurrection "a monstrous tale". Once he became Roman Emperor in AD 361, he publicly converted to paganism. He disenfranchised the Christians, had their churches burnt and persecuted them relentlessly. More importantly, he desecrated the remains of the saints. In particular, he searched everywhere for the tomb of St Peter, to destroy it. Soon he emulated Diocletian in his ferocity . . .'

'Why was he not able to destroy Christianity?' asked the Father Confessor.

Benelli shrugged. 'We think he trusted in the power of the Coin of Judas too soon. Also, given its nature, it betrays even those who wield it. Just as Christianity was about to face its greatest peril, Julian received a mortal wound from a spear when he and his troops fought the Persians in AD 363 outside the walls of Ctesiphon, below modern-day Baghdad. Who cast the spear was never known. However, it was called "the lance of justice" by some, and Julian's final words to his greatest enemy as he lay dying at the age of thirty-two were, "*Thou hast conquered, O Galilean.*"

'Once again, that particular Coin of Judas was recovered and placed in the tomb of St Peter which was, by now, hidden deep below the high altar of the first basilica. As for the Emperor Julian, within a few years of his death, it became a common rumour throughout Rome that he'd agreed to serve the devil in return for becoming Emperor. St Jerome called him the betrayer of his own soul.

'It was some centuries before the next coin surfaced, for the power of evil is patient beyond all reckoning. The third coin was held by a general in the Saracen army. In AD 846 he, and ten thousand other Saracens, landed in Italy. Meeting almost no opposition, they entered Rome and expended their hatred of Christianity to the full. They stormed old St Peter's and destroyed everything they could, even stripping the high altar. In particular, they searched for the Apostle's tomb. Yet, the history records that it escaped them, for they could not discover exactly where it lay hidden.

'The fourth coin – and remember each is more powerful than the previous one – came into the hands of one who used it to take over the papacy itself. As you well know' – Benelli looked searchingly at his small audience – 'Pope John XII was a scandal to the Church both in his public and his private life. Using the coin, he became Pope in AD 955 at the age of eighteen. That "dissolute boy", as writers of the time described him, dedicated himself wholly to debauchery, and the Lateran Palace where he lived was openly described as a brothel "which the devil attended, welcomed with toasts".

'The battle against him was fought both on the earthly and on the spiritual plane. Eight years after becoming pontiff he was deposed by a revolt in Rome and Leo VIII consecrated in his place. But the power of the coin was not to be thwarted and John returned to the Vatican. Excommunicating Leo he savagely revenged himself on those who had opposed him.'

'Yet he was struck down,' said the Father Confessor.

'Yes,' said Benelli, 'felled by a stroke in the act of adultery in the papal apartments. He died at the age of twenty-seven. The history records it was openly declared at the time that he was a servant of the devil.'

'And what of the fifth coin? Was that in more recent times?' asked Cardinal Vysinsky.

Benelli nodded. 'This coin is the most puzzling of all. There is a mystery to it and the history itself tells us little. The man who held the fifth coin was Sylvester II, who was pontiff from AD 999 to 1003. Of him there are many legends, all very disturbing. In his youth he studied among the Saracens in Spain and was well known for his investigations into astrology, mathematics and magic.

'The history declares that Sylvester was said to have entered into a pact with the devil: his soul for the papacy. In quick succession he became Archbishop of Rheims, Archbishop of Ravenna and then Pope. Once he became head of the Church his name became notorious as a black magician and it was only after enormous effort that he was driven from Rome and the papal throne in AD 1003. He returned but died shortly thereafter.

'This is the tale of the five coins,' said Benelli. 'Three more remain.'

Quietly, Benelli folded the ancient parchment and placed it on a side table. Both the Pope and the Father Confessor had closed their eyes. In meditation or despair?

Cardinal Vysinsky coughed. 'Where are these five additional coins that were recovered after the death of the Apostle?'

'Four of them lie in, or above, the tomb of St Peter beside us,' replied Benelli, 'and they no longer have any power or effect.'

'And the fifth?'

'In the tomb of Pope Sylvester II, as he commanded on his deathbed.'

'Why was that?' queried Vysinsky. 'Why was this fifth coin not also buried next to St Peter?'

'We don't know,' replied Benelli. 'But we are trying to find out. However, it is difficult. These events happened one thousand years ago.'

'That means there are still three other Coins of Judas remaining in the world besides that of Sylvester II,' continued Cardinal Vysinsky, 'and if what is said of them is true, they must be very powerful indeed.'

'Yes.' John XXV opened his eyes. 'And the situation is worse than I feared. The history records that, on his deathbed, Pope Sylvester II made a very disturbing prophecy. He said each of the last three Coins of Judas had a truly awesome force.'

'How so?' asked the Father Confessor.

Benelli was silent.

'How so?' The question was repeated.

The Pope himself supplied the answer. He said softly: *'They can summon Angels of Darkness into the world. Against whom no human power can stand.'*

CHAPTER EIGHTEEN ·

*The devil has power over all those who follow
their lusts.*

Malleus Maleficarum,
'Hammer of the Witches'

PAUL ENTERED HIS CLINIC IN downtown San Francisco. Ben accosted him at the door to his office.

'Bit late isn't it? We had a meeting at ten to evaluate a patient. Did you forget or something?'

'I had to go to the hospital early this morning. It was Rachel.'

'What's up?' asked Ben anxiously. 'Is she ill?' If anything happened to Paul's daughter he'd never hear the end of it from his wife.

'She's fine. She banged her head when she fell off a swing at school yesterday. They took her in for observation overnight.'

Paul stared at his colleague. He could perceive light emanating from him as clearly as he could the sunlight coming through the window.

'Ben, I've been seeing things,' he said abruptly.

'Seeing? Did you say *seeing* things?'

'Yes, seeing things.'

His partner looked at him as if he'd gone mad. 'Seeing what? Whatever do you mean?'

Paul explained about his ability to discern light emanating from people, like some form of aura or astral force. His colleague cut him off in mid-flow. Paul was teasing him as usual.

'What nonsense! You're the last person to believe in that. Sounds like the effect of medication or hallucinations brought on by stress. Not stressed, are you?'

'Must be the sleeping tablets I'm taking,' Paul lied. 'I'll check with my doctor.'

'You were beginning to get me worried. I need you to cover for me when we go on holiday. I don't want to postpone it. Oh, I have a message for you. That woman Helen phoned. You know, the one at the party. She said, "Congratulations on getting what you want." '

'What does that mean?'

'Er,' said Ben, 'I never asked. I thought you'd know. Probably the Carl Jung lecture.'

'Probably. By the way, how did Helen get to your dinner party?'

'She phoned me just after Marie said she couldn't come. Said she'd met you on the Kramer case and she wanted to discuss something with you. On the spur of the moment I decided to invite her to the dinner. That was all right, wasn't it?'

'Sure.'

Paul watched Ben depart and then entered his own office. He stared out of the window for a few minutes, pondering the ambiguous message Helen had left. Impulsively, he picked up the phone and dialled a number.

'Hello,' a husky voice answered.

'Suzanne, it's Paul Stauffer. My wife left a message

saying you'd phoned last night. Sorry about not coming to see you before, but things have been very hectic. I thought I'd visit you this afternoon. Providing you're awake, that is. What time do students get up these days?'

'I'm busy studying in bed, Professor.' She laughed merrily. 'I'd love to see you. That would be great. I thought you might call.'

'Say four o'clock?'

'Oh, I'll be ready by then.'

Suzanne put down the phone. Her bedroom was in darkness, the curtains firmly drawn. She turned to her bed companion. All that could be seen in the gloom was the upper part of a torso. Suzanne stroked the exposed flesh. The figure stirred.

'He's coming over.'

Her partner sat up. Then she gave her a kiss.

'I know.' Helen smiled. 'Congratulations.'

'Come on in.'

Paul stood in the doorway of the student apartment. Suzanne stepped lightly to one side so that he brushed past her to enter the room. She was wearing a simple red dress which showed off her lithe figure to its best effect. In the background, soft music emanated from a CD player.

'Hi.'

'Hi. I'm sorry I'm late. I got held up, as usual.'

The furniture in the room was trendy and inexpensive. A sofa and a couple of armchairs. A coffee table. Books in no particular order lying in a bookcase, a silk jacket draped over the back of a chair. In one corner stood a wine rack, a few bottles of wine lodged in it. The place was untidy and homely, as well as being youthful.

'A drink?'

'Beer, if you have any.'

'Course.' Suzanne went into the tiny kitchen adjoining her room. She came back with some cans and handed him one. She nestled down in the armchair opposite him. They drank.

'I'm fine now. I've got over the shock.' Suzanne's eyes were moist with excitement and the memory of it. 'I was *so* frightened when the cell door opened and Kramer came towards me. I thought I was going to die. I was paralysed and he took over.'

'I did tell you not to wander about,' said Paul.

'I know,' said Suzanne. 'I just got carried away.'

'Now you realise how careful you have to be when dealing with the criminally ill. Always expect the unexpected.'

As he spoke, without thinking, Paul dug his hand into his pocket and his fingers touched a coin. From its rough sides and embossed head he was sure it was the coin Helen had given him. But how had it possibly got there? He hadn't seen it since the party and he thought he'd lost it. For some curious reason, Paul didn't draw it from his pocket; he didn't feel inclined to mention it to anyone.

'Has the prison found out what happened?' Suzanne offered him some ginger biscuits from a tin, munching one herself.

'Not yet,' said Paul. 'They think it was one of the warders who opened Kramer's door by mistake, but I'm more worried about you.'

'Honest, I'm fine,' replied Suzanne breezily. 'It would take much more to finish me off, believe me.'

The music stopped and Suzanne knelt down by the side of Paul's chair where the CD player was located. As she put a new disc into the machine she looked up at him. Her expression was open, unashamed and seductive. Paul glanced at her and then away. However, his eyes were dragged, almost unwillingly, back to her face. They looked at each other a second time. The look was of mutual desire. Paul got up from his chair.

'I'd better be going.'

Suzanne also stood up. He watched her long, slim legs straighten as she raised herself from a crouching position.

'Must you?' she said. The music began again, slow and dreamy. Its sensuousness beguiled him. Paul closed his eyes. When he opened them again he saw light emanating from Suzanne – a deep bright red. It flowed towards and through him, netting him with its sexual desire.

'Don't go.' Her hand rose to caress his face.

'I'm married,' he said. 'With a child.'

'I know.' She kissed him lightly on the lips. 'Stay with me.'

'What about your boyfriend?'

She gave a mischievous smile. 'None. I told you. I don't have one.'

Paul sighed as he gazed on his temptation. As the music rose in volume, Suzanne silently undid the tie of her dress. The gossamer sheath slipped to the floor. She had the barest underwear on. Placing her arms round his neck she began to kiss him, her tongue gently prising open his mouth. Then she stood back. Casually, she undid her bra. He'd seen her breasts before.

'I'm all yours,' she whispered with a cynical laugh.

In the small bedroom, Suzanne loosened the thong about her thighs and it fell to the carpet. Paul could see the reflection of her firm buttocks in the mirror behind her. He quickly drew her onto the bed, oblivious to all else but an intense craving to satisfy his loins. Soon, a soft growl radiated from Suzanne's throat, like the purr of a wolf. They were alone, his adultery secret from the world and his wife.

Almost.

In the middle of his sexual exertions, had Paul looked with the eye of the spirit, he would have noticed a figure standing in the corner of the bedroom. Helen contemplated the couple, an expression of triumph on her face. Suzanne turned her head towards her mistress and grinned.

Then she concentrated on her victim once more.

'I bet you're hungry!' Marie lifted Rachel into the car. 'Does your head still hurt?'

'A bit,' replied Rachel.

Marie pulled out of the hospital grounds. Paul had left home early that morning, so she'd hadn't had a chance to talk with him about the matters dominating her mind. However, she'd discuss everything with him that evening, come what may. Meanwhile, Rachel's own face was a pattern of childish indecision as she debated whether to confess her secret. Finally, she said, 'I saw someone last night.'

'Oh, yes?' said Marie in a bright tone. 'Saw someone? In the hospital?'

'A woman woke me in the night. She told me I must come with her. I was frightened.'

'Darling, it was a nurse. One of the people in green uniforms. Did she give you any medicine?'

'No, it wasn't a nurse.' The seven-year-old shook her head adamantly. 'She had a red dress on, and blonde hair. It was the same woman who pushed me off the swing.'

'Pushed you off the swing? But you told me you fell.'

'She made me fall,' cried Rachel emphatically. 'She stopped the swing in mid-air.'

'Honey, that's not possible. You're making things up again. What did she look like?'

Involuntarily, Marie slowed down the car, her anxiety increasing as her daughter, in a matter-of-fact voice, described the same woman Marie had seen in the bathroom on the evening of the dinner party.

'What did you do when this woman told you to go with her?' Marie's throat was dry.

'I said I was waiting for my mummy.'

'What did she say then?'

Rachel looked straight ahead. 'She said my mummy would die soon.'

With a stifled cry, Marie pulled the car over to the side of the road. 'Stop it,' she shouted at her. 'Stop it, Rachel. No one woke you, no one said those horrible things.' She leant against the wheel of the car, pleading. 'It was only your imagination. Nothing is going to happen to your mother, I promise.'

Rachel scrutinised her face, unconvinced.

Marie drove fast back to the house, her hands gripping the wheel in shock. Her thoughts were frantic and uncontrolled. This woman had something to do with Karl Kramer or the serial killer. She meant to do them harm. Or was this Paul's new girlfriend? Was she stalking them, and did Paul know? What was happening? She was going mad.

Marie entered their house. She pushed Rachel in front of her. 'Darling, go and play with your toys in the living room.'

Hurriedly, she went into the kitchen and dissolved into tears. Her hands jerked convulsively as she tried to sit down at the table.

'Mummy!' There was a scream. She ran.

Rachel was standing in the middle of the living room. Before her, near the wall, was a woman: the same one Marie had seen upstairs in the bathroom. She was dressed in a simple robe and she beckoned to the child. Although the shape and form of the woman was human, Marie's senses told her something was dreadfully wrong. She was looking at *something*, not *someone*. At an image slightly hazy in the dim light, without shadow. A phantom, a spirit.

'Darling!' Marie muffled a scream. 'Come to me.'

But her words were unheeded. Rachel started to walk towards the figure. Then in a horrific movement her feet levitated straight off the ground. She began to walk in the air as Helen beckoned.

Marie screamed. As she did so, the phantom vanished and Rachel fell to the ground. Marie ran to her sobbing child.

Marie was utterly incapable of words. She had seen the impossible. Yet her senses told her it had happened. It was real. Things began to fit into place. Clutching her child, Marie reached for the phone, but Rachel put a restraining hand on her mother's even as she pressed the keys. 'Mummy, don't do that.'

'Why not? I'm contacting your father.'

The child spoke the truth. 'Because he's causing it.'

CHAPTER NINETEEN

The act of riding abroad may be merely illusory, since the devil has extraordinary power over the minds of those who have given themselves up to him, so that what they do in pure imagination, they believe they have actually and really done in the body.

Malleus Maleficarum,
'Hammer of the Witches'

AFTER MAKING LOVE TO SUZANNE, Paul fell asleep, exhausted by his sin.

Yet this sleep was quite distinct from any other he'd experienced before in his life. It was a wakeful sleep and an extraordinary one at that. While he slept Paul felt his body move. Not his physical body – it continued to lie in bed, inert and dead to the world. This body was different. It was his spirit form – one he never believed existed.

Paul contemplated the scene as if he was standing in a corner of a room, a spectator to the events that unfolded. Slowly, an apparition materialised from his body. It was a greyish substance and it drifted upwards like a plume of smoke exiting from the top of his head. It shimmered slightly in the darkness. This 'presence', for there was no other way adequately to describe it, coalesced into a shape. Though its appearance had a similar outline to that Paul possessed on earth it was quite different from the hard, solid flesh from which it had arisen. It was more fluid, a sheath of light.

Before his spirit form assumed its final shape, Paul was no longer a silent bystander. He felt himself inside the manifestation, which enfolded him like a cloak, a means of transport to enable him to journey on astral planes just as his physical body enabled him to live within the confines of the world.

Another change occurred. Paul still thought. However, this process was now effortless. His mind, or rather the spirit formerly imprisoned within his human frame, was no longer fettered by the agonisingly slow movements of a foot moving, a hand lifting or a heart beating. There was no sense of energy being used, of tiredness or of weight. For his spirit did not hunger or thirst, did not grow old, did not remember or forget. It simply was. Despite this, a human being on earth called Paul still existed. He knew this because he 'saw' his physical body recumbent on the bed – an empty bottle from which the genie had escaped.

He began his strange odyssey into the spirit world.

Paul ascended onto the first astral plane. The change was no different from sloughing off an old coat, yet this was a human coat. He felt no fear or concern, for the power of the Coin of Judas had, unbeknown to him, already overwhelmed these human warning devices. During his ascent the vast store of mental energy formerly directed towards preserving his human form began to turn in on itself, to discover a secret world *within*.

Suddenly, Paul was in his office in the university. It swirled before him. Had he consciously thought of it he would have realised it was night. Yet night and day no longer had any significance to him; he saw the darkened room with the same clarity as though it were bathed in bright sunlight. In fact, with greater clarity, for the objects before his gaze – the furnishings, the books, the desk – had an added lustre and sheen. His everyday sight had been superseded by a heightened perception. A super sense.

Paul began to 'walk' about his office, though there was no physical movement as such. Instead, everything appeared within his purview as if he were in the centre of a circle and it revolved around him. His feeling of excitement was compounded by a sense of wisdom flowing into his being. A dusty mansion in his mind had magically been reopened to enable him to alight on unimaginable treasures within. Freedom indeed.

Where next? His mother's house. Instantly, Paul was there, downstairs, in the homely old kitchen. Cups and dishes set out on the sink, a worn tea towel that had fallen from its peg, breakfast laid out for the morning. And on the dresser, a box of chocolates for a neighbour's birthday. Yet Paul knew he could not possibly be in his mother's house, at least not physically, since 'home' was four thousand kilometres away, in Connecticut. But in spite of that, he was there.

Paul saw the reclining figure of his elderly mother in the bedroom upstairs, her eighty-year-old body lying in a foetal position, sleeping quietly. Paul could see that the energy which sustained her existence on earth was weakening. His mother would die very soon. Comprehending this did not shock him. There was a certainty to it which caused no pain. Her arrival on earth and her departure were ordained since the beginning of time. Paul did not question this, as he would once have done. It was inevitable.

The prison next. The High Security Facility came into view as though he were proceeding down the dusty road towards it. He passed within, the walls no longer impeding him. Like water in an ocean, he travelled with the flow, without restraint. Paul studied the warders: as they chatted in their communal canteen, as they stared at the monitors of the Facility's elaborate security system, as they ate, slept and defecated. He was a silent witness to the acts of man.

He had become a watcher.

D Block was bleak and still, the only movement being the security cameras noiselessly rotating on their axes. It was here Paul 'saw' three warders removing an inmate from a cell. He was a well-built fellow, his arms and body heavily tattooed. Despite being handcuffed, and having his mouth taped, he was struggling violently in the hands of his captors, who were pushing him along the landing. Paul recognised the guards; one nursed a black eye.

The struggle increased. A warder lashed out at the legs of the victim with a baton and he collapsed to the floor. Blows then rained down on his unconscious body. Finally, they dragged him into the lavatories to continue their punishment beating. Paul 'saw' them on their sinful journey. Yet he felt nothing – no outrage or revenge. He was just a spiritual witness, without human passions.

Paul passed down to E Block, hidden in the bowels of the earth. Nothing could hinder him.

In a corner of his cell, Karl Kramer slept. He twitched continually, perhaps caught up in a nightmare in which he, for once, was a victim. Then the movements ceased and the monster awoke. Rapidly, Kramer turned over in bed and peered about him. In the subterranean darkness, Kramer could not physically see any human being. However, having descended far along the paths of evil, he could detect the power given off by a spirit form and he knew something was there. The killer got up quickly, and Paul could see alarm spread across his face. Kramer must be afraid of him.

But Paul was wrong.

There was someone else Kramer was afraid of.

Paul also began to experience fear. It was a different fear to that on earth – more acute, more profound. A terror that pervaded the very essence of his being. Had an intruder stepped into his home at night Paul would have been alarmed, but this was different, a thousand times worse. This feeling was as if someone were trying to step *into* his own being, into his spirit. And it wasn't Kramer. From behind the killer in his cramped cell, on another astral plane, a path opened up. Something was progressing along it, coming towards Paul. A shadow, pitiless and without mercy. Drawn by the coin.

'Be careful.'

The voice was so close that it was beside him. Immediately, the image of the prison and Kramer vanished, to be replaced by another: that of Helen.

Helen's spirit body was not like Paul's, which, to him, seemed to be a greyish monochrome. But hers – oh, what richness, what texture! Her image was that of a young woman in her late teens with long, flowing blonde hair. A Greek maiden, like those portrayed on ancient vases. Ageless and timeless.

'It's a vision,' Helen told him, but no words as such came from her lips.

'What?'

'The spirit form you see me in. It's your perception of me. Like your own.'

'Mine?'

'Yes. You can change the appearance of your spirit

body. It will change anyway the further you go out on the astrals.'

'How did you get here?'

She laughed heartily; or rather, Paul felt her laughter. 'The same way as you, stupid. I left my human body.'

'So where am I?'

'You are out of your body, in spirit. On the first astral plane.'

'How many astral planes are there?'

'Nine.'

'And after that?'

'Hungry for knowledge as usual. I chose well. I'll tell you later, but we must go now.'

'Why? How do you know all this? Why have you brought me here?' A hundred and one questions ran through Paul's mind, but no answer came.

Unexpectedly, the backdrop changed, and he was in Kramer's prison cell once more. The menacing presence behind Kramer was very close to him, as if it could reach out and touch him, possess him – body and soul. Yet Paul didn't know that the spirit who controlled Kramer was one and the same as the beautiful woman who'd just materialised before him. A moment later they were no longer in the prison cell. Instead, they were in a bedroom.

'Who did that?'

'I did,' said Helen.

'You changed the vision?'

'It was time to go.'

'Why?'

Helen ignored his question. 'Look where you are now. Then we must continue. You have a lot to learn.'

'Learn?'

'You have a task to perform.' Helen smiled indulgently.

'Let's start with someone you know in the world – to help you perceive the changing nature of reality.'

They were in the bedroom. Paul viewed the sleeping figure. It was Suzanne. Her face was turned towards him, calm and peaceful in her sleep. Paul contemplated the youthfulness and innocence of her features. A man was lying beside her. He recognised himself.

'Don't approach your own physical body. It can have harmful consequences.'

'Can I touch her?'

'Try.'

Paul touched Suzanne but she did not move. Helen laughed. Her thought had a mocking and amused resonance to it. 'You have to go higher up the astral planes before you can influence her physical body,' she said. Helen kissed her secret lover on the cheek and Suzanne stirred slightly. 'See, you need greater power. With that you attain ever-increasing states of reality. Let's go.'

'Where?' Paul didn't like her effortless sense of superiority; that was his vice on earth.

The scenery changed. Now they were standing at the top of a mighty waterfall. The water fell in great torrents into a pool below. In the distance two mountains loomed up into a sky that was crystal-blue in colour. The slopes of the mountains were covered with trees, though Paul didn't recognise them as being the same as any he'd seen on earth. The colours in this scenic view were far more enhanced than those on earth. Paul could detect no animals or signs of human presence.

Helen instructed him. 'Each ascent to a higher astral plane is preceded by a vision. Without it you can't progress any further, since you don't have the wisdom or the power.'

'Are the revelations the same for everyone?'

'No,' said Helen. 'As with all things in the spirit world, the greater the insight you have, the more the picture develops and unfolds. The reality does not change, the perception of it does.'

'Do you see the same as I do?'

Helen ignored him. Her perception of hell was not to be divulged. If he truly saw what she did, he would die immediately. 'Jump.'

'Jump?' Paul looked down from the top of the waterfall. Foaming waters thrashed below him.

Helen said, 'It's only a vision. You'll pass onto the second astral plane.'

Paul paused. 'I can't.'

'You can,' said Helen impatiently. 'Nothing can hurt you. You are simply passing into another reality, like the one we've just left.'

Paul felt uncertain.

'What do you see below you?'

Paul directed his thoughts. Hundreds of metres below, there lay a pool of water. Its centre was turbulent but at its edges all was quiet. He described what he saw.

Helen nodded. 'Focus on the centre of the pool.'

Staring into the water, Paul saw a bright light that diminished into the depths, like a tunnel. 'If I jump, will I die? Physically die?'

'No,' replied Helen. 'The coin will protect you.'

'The coin?'

'The coin I gave you. It has immense power over the astrals. We must go on. Stop being a coward or I'll leave you here.'

Paul jumped.

When he hit the pool, his location changed. Once again he was in Suzanne's bedroom. Yet this time, there was a difference – an enormous qualitative difference.

His human faculties and emotions had returned to him, but in the interim, they had heightened hugely, both in substance and intensity. Like an industrial power plant, long disused, these cerebral pistons cranked into action at a frenetic pace, ever faster, ever more potent.

Paul cried out in his amazement and surprise. He could hear, and feel, Helen's soft laughter resonating through him.

'Your perception will continue to heighten if you obey me. It gets much better – much, much, better,' she said. 'Go on, kiss her.'

This time, Paul lay down beside Suzanne. It seemed he had a physical body once more – one that could experience pleasurable sensations but, itself, was without pain or stress. He could hear Suzanne's soft breathing, feel the smooth touch of her red lips, caress her body, nuzzle her breasts, all the time without Suzanne feeling it – though, to him, the sensations were as real as if he had been making love to her then and there.

At Helen's command the vision changed as she used the coin to raise him up the astral planes. They were now in a grove. The trees, their foliage thick and dense, allowed only fleeting glimmers of light to penetrate to the earthen floor. It was carpeted with pine needles, from which arose a heady scent. The trees looked ancient, their bark covered with moss and creepers. In the distance Paul could hear the soft trill of birdsong and, about him, there was the gentlest of breezes. So this is the Greek Elysium, he thought. He could remain here for ever.

Paul turned to Helen and his breath, had he breath, would have ceased. For before him was Helen of Troy, or rather all that he could imagine of her. A finely chiselled beauty as perfect as a statue, the lightest blue eyes, fair blonde hair and so slender. Further, this beauty was unmarred by any earthly imperfection wrought by old age, by suffering, human sickness or death. Instead, it was a spiritual essence, and her being radiated a delight and joy to his perception that no aesthete or philosopher could ever hope adequately to describe.

Helen smiled at him and her eyes danced with pleasure. Things were going well.

'Your sight is getting better,' she commented. 'And you're looking better, thank God. Not so sickly.'

Paul examined himself. He was so very different from on earth. His limbs were golden, bronzed by an unknown sun, slightly taller, his chest more broad. But it was his eyes, or rather the vision that came from them, that had achieved the greatest change. Looking out from the wood, Paul effortlessly stared across a vast sea. An island lay on the remote horizon, its sandy foreshore and woods untended by human hand. Paul had a desperate longing to visit it.

'Helen, let's stop a while. Is this all real?'

'Of course. It's *a* reality. The universe has much more than human reality. It has millions of them. How boring it would be if the earth was all that there was.'

'But I mean that island and where we are standing now. Is it real?'

'Yes, stupid. It existed in human time, long ago. But this is nothing. I want to show you things that have only ever existed on the spiritual plane. Look out of the grove in this direction' – she pointed with her hand – 'what do you see?'

'I see a path. It winds away into the hills. Where does it lead?'

'To the third astral. Start walking.'

Helen began to move towards the path. However, Paul

hesitated. So Helen went ahead and stood beyond the grove of trees, in the dazzling sunlight. She undid her tunic, offering her body to him, beckoning enticingly. With a shout of joy, Paul hurled himself out of the grove and into the unknown light.

They were back in Suzanne's small room, watching the sleeping figure. Helen said, 'She's all yours.' Then she disappeared from his sight. At least, Paul thought so, though in fact she never left the coin, whether in the human or spiritual world. She was its guardian. She held it for her master.

Paul kissed and embraced Suzanne. To her, it was a dream, a figment of her imagination, but for him, on the astral planes, the sensation of each kiss and each caress he received from her was a thousand times greater than on earth. Stunningly beautiful, warm and sensual, Suzanne's being effortlessly melted into his, his spirit experiencing a pleasure and stimulation which could never be replicated in this world. It was bliss and he longed for it to continue for ever. A perfect dream with the immediacy of reality.

But it was not to be so. All too soon Helen's spirit reappeared.

'We must leave.' With that, Paul's rapture started to blister and corrode. He experienced a sense of being flung down a black tunnel. Fleeting images of a grove and a waterfall loomed up before him. Then he was back, truly back, in Suzanne's bedroom once more.

He awoke feeling violently sick with a terrible noise resonating in his ears. Helen stood beside him.

'What are you doing here? Where's Suzanne?'

'She went out and left you sleeping. It's very late at night. You must go back to your wife. She's been waiting for you.'

'But am I dreaming or awake?' Frantically, Paul clasped his own flesh. 'I am alive or dead?' He panicked. In what world was he? What was happening? How had Helen got into Suzanne's bedroom?

'You are awake. In your world. But you must stop your wife from leaving your house, Paul. Go home now.'

Marie stood on the landing, a suitcase packed. It was two in the morning and Paul still hadn't returned. He was with another woman; it was obvious. Rachel and she would go and stay with Florence for the night. And then? Marie was too weary to think. However, she needed to consult a divorce lawyer.

There was something more.

The appearance of the spirit and Rachel's levitation had convinced Marie something very strange indeed was happening. Her rosary, the animals, the behaviour of the patrolman, the manifestation she and Rachel had witnessed; to her these constituted clear evidence of the presence of evil, and against their power Marie realised she had no adequate means of defending herself.

Also, she knew they were connected in some way with Paul, but she couldn't divine how. She still loved her husband despite his many faults. However, she also loved her daughter and she had a duty to protect her. So she must choose.

'Rachel?'

Her offspring was awake and sitting on her bed.

'It's time to go,' said Marie, falsely trying to inject a note of play into her voice. 'Florence will be so happy to see us, won't she?'

The child nodded. Unlike her mother, and with the non-rational perceptiveness of a child, Rachel could feel the actual presence of evil and its initial manifestations –

the baleful images, the tormented cries, the overwhelming fear of death. They had already penetrated her unconscious mind and they terrified her. Indeed, it was time to go.

Together, they went downstairs, about to begin their journey into exile. Then, on impulse, Marie went into the living room. Extracting a Bible from a bookcase, she opened it at random.

'Why? Why?' she whispered.

She started to weep as she read the text from the Book of Job. So it had to do with Kramer after all.

'*Vengeance is mine; I will repay, saith the Lord.*'

CHAPTER TWENTY

First that devils are spirits . . . and that the
devil, whether he be many or one is . . . a crea-
ture made by God, and that for vengeance.

Reginald Scot,
The Discoverie of Witchcraft

'CARDINAL BENELLI!'

It was late evening and Benelli was attending a
gathering of German priests on a private visit to the
Vatican. They encircled him in one of the audience
rooms, full of respect, catching his every word. Benelli
rather enjoyed these occasions. Not that he was taken in
by this false adoration . . . or was he?

'Cardinal!'

Reluctantly, he caught sight of the slim figure who
stood near the wall, overshadowed by the medieval
tapestry.

'I have to go.'

Passing self-consciously through the crowd, Benelli
approached the Father Confessor with a distinct sense
of annoyance. Really, he had important things to do,
could not the monk approach him at a better time?

'I must speak with you alone.'

Benelli studied his face. It bore not only a look of

suffering but one of great concern. A sense of foreboding came over him. The Father Confessor quickly drew him into a sideroom and they stood in semi-darkness. Statues and works of art provided a gloomy backdrop.

'Cardinal Graziani is dead.'

'Dead!'

Benelli was aghast. He knew Graziani had been ill and that he'd been unable to attend their meeting when the history of the coins had been recounted, but dead, no! An impression of the kindly old man flickered before his eyes.

'How? When?'

The Father Confessor's voice was subdued. 'He died just twenty minutes ago.' He paused. 'In agony. They'll announce it as a stroke. He was delirious at the end. Only the Pope and the papal physician attended.'

Benelli's grand demeanour of a few minutes before was replaced by consternation. Had Graziani been experiencing the same nightmares as Benelli had? The same inability to sleep? The same internal voices, as the evil spirits sought to enter his consciousness? One look at the Father Confessor's face and he was sure. They were under siege. It had begun.

'Did he mention the coin?'

'Yes.'

'What did he say?'

The Father Confessor's eyes never left the Cardinal's face. 'He said it will come to Rome but not at all in the way we think. It will come secretly and in disguise.'

'But what does that mean?' said Benelli helplessly. 'Did he say nothing more?' Why was the monk staring at him so?

'No.'

'But . . . but what do you think he was trying to say?'

The Father Confessor was silent for a moment. 'I don't know. In the past these coins were held by powerful men, the last two by pontiffs. This time it may be different. We must go now. The Holy Father wants to see you as soon as possible.'

Benelli walked beside the monk. He was shell-shocked. Somehow, he had not believed that these awful things would happen.

'And Cardinal Vysinsky?'

'He is ill,' replied the Father Confessor. The tone was grim.

Together they ascended the stairs and hurried through a number of the Vatican apartments to reach the private study of the Pope. Benelli's thoughts were confused and troubled. As Head of the Holy Office he knew of evil spirits and how they acted. Contrary to popular belief, they rarely appeared. Instead, they sought to molest and trouble the human mind, and they did so with an astonishing subtlety, one that invariably outwitted their victims.

Mimicking the internal voice of human beings they always led their victims astray, playing with a non-human virtuosity on human cravings and hubris. 'Did that man not insult you?' they would whisper; 'Take revenge', or 'Be rich, be powerful; you're much better than they are', or 'Seize what you can in this world. Lying, cheating, stealing, betraying, it's all part of the natural order, my friend, so you just go ahead.' Their threats, their suggestions, their appeals to evil were relentless and without count, so much so that human beings soon thought this was just a part of their normal thought process. But the end purpose was always the same. To falsify, to distort, to sow enmity between humans. To turn the soul from God.

As their forces built up in the human psyche, so did the intensity of their persuasion. Hating, killing, despising – these were their trademarks, and Benelli knew them well. But what startled him now was the extraordinary way in which they could paralyse and harm even the most virtuous. If Graziani had fallen, would he not be the next victim of these armies of the night?

'Perhaps I should speak with the Pope alone,' he said to the Father Confessor.

They were about to enter the inner sanctum.

'I wouldn't recommend it,' replied the monk, for once contradicting his more august colleague. 'If we are divided we fall.'

Benelli was about to reply, but it was too late. They entered the papal chamber and John XXV rose from his chair. His face was drawn and his words brief. 'The situation is very serious. Cardinal Benelli, I order you to visit the Tower of the Winds.'

It was raining heavily and, in the darkness, as Benelli moved across the piazza, his umbrella and red robes were tugged by a November gale. He glanced at St Peter's Basilica to his left and carried on. He was proceeding to an almost forgotten part of the Vatican to which no person could have access without the express consent of the Pope.

Truly, the Vatican was a strange and a mysterious place, he reflected, not only in its physical layout but in the secrets it contained. It could justifiably be regarded as a house of many mysteries. Having crossed the piazza, Benelli passed through the Leonine walls, the final defence against the Saracen invaders in AD 846 as they searched for the tomb of St Peter; then through the Gate of Anne and into the heart of the administrative sector of the Vatican. A few priests encountered him *en route* and they inclined their heads respectfully.

Soon, Cardinal Benelli reached the courtyard known as the Court of the Belvedere. He turned to his right and climbed some stone steps. He breathed heavily as he did so; he was feeling his age. At the top he pushed open a large wooden door and crossed the threshold into a library.

The Vatican Library, the library of the popes, comprised a massive collection of more than forty kilometres of records in a multitude of languages, some of which went back to the very foundations of the Church and many of which had never been read by modern scholars. Benelli progressed down the length of a large room. It was full of book stacks, its ceilings brightly adorned with scenes by sixteenth-century artists. Within the book stacks lay serried ranks of ancient tomes bound in parchment, the bindings inscribed in small, handwritten Greek and Latin letters.

Who knew what treasures lay here, still to be unearthed by modern man? Ancient maps disclosing the location of long-forgotten churches as well as pagan temples and palaces. Secret reports compiled by ecclesiastics down the ages, reporting on the political events of their time, containing a judicious mixture of gossip, devotion and personal prejudice. Mysterious parchments recording secret journeys made by learned monks in the dark ages on behalf of the Vatican to the great Chinese and Mogul empires in the East, as the Church sought to determine whether the Apostles, and Our Lord himself, ever journeyed there. Finally, records of the challenges to the Faith. Of heresies and sects, of witchcraft and demonology, of the paths that linked the human and the divine worlds. But it was not these tomes Benelli sought.

At the end of the chamber, the Cardinal opened another door and went down a narrow and dimly lit corridor. What was not generally open to the public and what was much more difficult to inspect were the Vatican's Secret Archives. They comprised another thirteen kilometres of documents concerning the governance of the Church, and this library, founded in 1612 as an institution in its own right, was quite separate from the Vatican Library itself. The Secret Archives could be visited only with the approval of the Prefect, as the Head Librarian of the Vatican Library was called. This privilege was given (and rarely at that) only to theological scholars for the purpose of specific research. No general browsing was permitted.

At the end of the corridor, Benelli arrived at an office where a solitary light burned. The Prefect stood up when the Cardinal entered. His room was small and cramped, a mahogany panelled study lined with books. A large picture of the Virgin Mary gazed down serenely from behind a desk. The Prefect was a thin and desiccated individual. With age, his face had become as lined as a used parchment, the perfect foil to the rather portly Cardinal.

It was eleven o'clock at night and the library had long been closed. However, the Prefect had been told to expect the visit of the Head of the Inquisition, the older title by which he preferred to think of Benelli.

'Cardinal.' The librarian inclined his head slightly in obeisance. From under his robe, Benelli extracted a letter.

'Here is the papal order.'

The Prefect looked at the signature and the seal of the present pontiff. Then he read the letter written in Latin. There was no doubt as to its authenticity and its intent. The Prefect pursed his lips. He folded the missive and handed it back to Benelli.

Normally, the Tower of the Winds, the inner sanctum of the Secret Archives, was his domain. Only the Head Librarian could enter it – and solely for the purpose of ensuring that the books within were adequately protected against fire and water. He had no authority to read any of the works contained in the Tower and, unlike his medieval predecessors, this Prefect had never sought to do so, obedient as he always was to the commands of his sovereign lord, the Pope.

'I'll escort you to the bottom of the stairs,' said the Prefect. 'We'll need a torch.' He opened a drawer in his desk and took one out. Quitting his office, the pair departed along the corridor; no word was exchanged between them; each was engrossed in his own thoughts. Soon, the light emanating from the Prefect's sanctum was lost. They walked in darkness, with nothing more than a pencil beam of light to shepherd them.

Unlocking a door, they entered the main part of the Secret Archives. Essentially, this comprised two long corridors without windows, each filled with bookcase after bookcase of bound documents, rising from floor to ceiling. One of these corridors led to the base of the Tower of the Winds.

The Prefect's and the Cardinal's footsteps echoed on the silent stone. While they walked, they passed miles of records stretching back into the mists of antiquity. Records of the Senate of Cardinals who had advised the Pope since the sixteenth century. Records of the Sacred Rota, one of the ecclesiastical courts. The Registers of Petitions, seven thousand volumes of requests to the Pope from supplicants from all over medieval Europe.

Finally, the Prefect and the Cardinal came to a halt.

Two doors faced them. Behind one lay a huge safe containing some of the most important documents of the Vatican, dealing with political and religious events in centuries past, when the temporal power of the Church was so much greater than today. The Prefect stopped before the other door. It was of oak, worn and of great age. 'I'll wait here, Cardinal Benelli. The Tower of the Winds is before you.'

The Prefect unlocked the door with an old key and passed the torch to Benelli. He glanced at the anxious face of the Cardinal in the light of the beam. He was puzzled why such an eminent person would want to visit so late at night. This place in particular – one so strange that the Prefect himself never dared enter it save in daylight. But who was a simple librarian to question the orders of the pontiff? May God's will be done!

Benelli took the torch and began to ascend the winding staircase, his shoes scratching slightly on the stone. The Prefect watched him depart, the light fading into a Stygian gloom. The Cardinal stumbled a number of times as he ascended. He was now in the oldest section of the Archives and the least visited. Here the most ancient and most problematic of Church documents were kept, many in code, for the eyes of the Pope or his specially appointed representative alone. They included no fewer than five thousand Papal Registers, containing handwritten copies of the official letters of the popes as well as intimate details on the lives of the pontiffs, recorded by specially approved papal historians.

The stairway was steep and narrow, for the Tower had no lift. It also had no lights, a protection against fire and thieves. As a result, it was never visited in the dark. Never? Well, only when the circumstances were wholly exceptional.

Finally, Cardinal Benelli reached the top of the stairs. He was twenty metres above ground. He paused to catch his breath. The air had a musty and dank smell about it. It was also pitch-black. Benelli crossed the threshold and entered the Room of the Meridian.

This room had been so named since it was built as an astronomical observatory – though not for Galileo, whose signed confession that the earth did not move around the sun was located in another part of the Vatican Library. Benelli lowered his torch. Cut into the floor was a zodiacal design oriented to display the rays of the sun as they entered through a slit in the wall. It was here that the calculations for the Gregorian calendar had been made in 1580.

In the centre of the Room of the Meridian was a small table. Benelli put down his flashlight and looked round. Chained to the walls were a number of iron storage chests fashioned in the fourteenth century. Each had a massive and unsightly lock. Within them were located some of the most tantalising documents in the history of the Church, blandly described in the Secret Archives of the library as 'Miscellanea'. Chests full of political and religious intrigue, of trials for sorcery and black magic, of scandals touching the private lives of the popes. Secrets. Dark secrets.

Benelli sighed. From his pocket, he extracted a silver crucifix which the Pope had given him that evening. It glinted in the torchlight. He felt comforted and he said a brief prayer. Then he went to the chests. The Pope had told him in which to look and had supplied him with a key. Benelli knelt down beside one of them. As he did so, he felt the hackles rise on the back of his neck. He was not alone. It was no human presence but a cosmic one.

A watcher had arrived.

Opening the lid of the chest, Benelli peered within. There were many folios, one on top of the other, spotted with age. On their white vellum bindings were stamped titles in Greek with various cyphers and dates marked beneath. These were deliberately enigmatic so that even the librarians would not know what the folios contained.

After a short search Benelli selected the volume he was looking for. It was almost two feet in width, like a great register. Benelli took it to the table and sat down. No one had read this tome for more than five hundred years. This was attested to by the large seal Pope Sixtus IV had affixed to it in 1476, which seal the present Pope had ordered to be broken. Benelli put his hand on the volume. Then he closed his eyes and said to himself the opening lines of a prayer of exorcism: 'Remember not, Lord, our offences, nor the offences of our forefathers, neither take thou vengeance on our sins.'

About him the room grew colder. Benelli could feel the presence of evil spirits in the room now, but he could not see them. They would disclose themselves to him if they wished. Benelli leant forward to kiss the cross. Finally, he opened the book. It was a report on witchcraft. Yet it was one that was quite different from any other in the Church's history. For it was a report on witchcraft committed by a very powerful man indeed. The Vicar of Christ himself.

Pope Sylvester II.

Gerbert of Aurillac was born in AD 940 and educated at the Benedictine monastery of Aurillac in France, then in Spain. He was marked out from youth by his great talent for scholarship and learning. He became Bishop of Reims in AD 991 and then Archbishop of Ravenna.

Finally, in the inauspicious year of AD 999, he was conse-crated Pope, taking the title Pope Sylvester II.

Pope Sylvester II was a strange man by all accounts. An expert in logic and mathematics, he was also deeply versed in the wisdom and magic of the East, which he'd learnt when he'd studied in Moorish Spain.

Sylvester was credited with introducing Arabic numerals into Europe and the invention of the pendulum clock. However, from the very beginning of his papacy, he also acquired a terrible reputation for sorcery. His notoriety was such that rumours spread throughout Europe, to be recorded by Church historians and gossipers long after his death.

It was no less than Bartholomew Platina, the famous librarian to the Vatican who, in his work the *Lives of the Popes*, published in 1479, solemnly affirmed:

> *Sylvester the Second ... the devil helping him with an extraordinary assistance, got the papacy on this condition, that thereafter he should be wholly the devil's, by whose assistance he had arrived at so great a dignity.*

Platina had acquired this information by secretly looking in the very book Cardinal Benelli was about to read. For his disclosure of such secrets he was punished and the Pope of the time, Sixtus IV, ordered the closure of this part of the Secret Archives even to its librarians. On the book itself the Pope placed his seal, declaring the punishment of death to anyone who sought to open it other than by the express permission of a pontiff. Why so draconian a measure? The folio contained not only a description of the life of Pope Sylvester II, but also his last confession.

It was a central tenet of the Church that a confession

by a person on their deathbed was one made in the presence of God and it must never be disclosed to another human being. In the case of Sylvester II, however, the Church had been forced to make a very rare exception, for two reasons.

The first was that it was not known whether the final confession of Pope Sylvester II was made in the presence of God or of the devil.

The second was that Sylvester II had wielded the last Coin of Judas to have come into the world.

Benelli broke open the seals to the book and began to read the tiny letters of the priestly chronicler.

It was a frightening tale. Of the accusations against Pope Sylvester and his trafficking in black magic. Of the extraordinary powers he was said to possess and his ability to outwit, and destroy, his enemies. Of the spirits he was able to command and a large black dog that always followed him. Of his end and his burial outside the Lateran Church in Rome rather than the Basilica of St Peter.

One writer summarised the legend thus.

[Sylvester II] *signed his soul away to Satan, and was rewarded by becoming Pope. Raised to power and shockingly abusing it, Sylvester II was naturally anxious to know how long he would live to enjoy the sweets of office. The answer was on the face of it reassuring in the extreme. As long as he abstained from celebrating high mass in Jerusalem, he had nothing to fear.*

Forewarned was forearmed. Sylvester II had little difficulty in passing a self-denying ordinance on the subject of visiting the Holy Land, and giving himself up wholeheartedly to a wicked and luxurious life. But he who

*would sup with the devil needs a long spoon. Dispensing
the sacrament in an unfamiliar church in Rome, the
wicked Pope felt his strength rapidly ebbing and also
realised that he was surrounded by demons on all sides.
On hearing that the name of the church was the Holy
Cross of Jerusalem, he knew that he had been tricked and
that his hour was at hand.*

*The shock broke him. There and then he made an open
confession of his guilt, and uttered the most solemn and
touching warnings against commerce with evil spirits. He
then commanded that . . . after his death his body should
be placed upon a bier of green wood drawn by two virgin
horses, one white and the other black . . .*

*Great was the sensation when this strange funeral pro-
cession drew up at the Lateran Church; greater still the
terror when loud cries and groans were heard proceeding
from the coffin. Then a deathly silence fell and Sylvester
II was laid to rest.*

Benelli read on, anxious to see whether this Pope, in his
lifetime, had in any way sought to refute these venomous
accusations against him. While he did so the Cardinal
felt a movement of air in the room. It came up the stairway like a northerly wind and it started to ruffle the pages
of the book. He reached out and held up the silver cross.
The breeze died down. Then a flicker of light appeared
in the stairwell. Benelli knew he mustn't stay long. Soon,
other powers, mightier than the watchers, would come.
He started reading the confession.

*I, Simon of Lyon, a monk of the Order of St Benedict, make
this statement in the year of Our Lord One Thousand and
Three. On the 12th day of May I was ordered to attend
the Holy Father, Sylvester II, who lay dying in the Vatican*

apartments. I did so and I now repeat the nature of the last confession given by that poor man.

While he read, Benelli became anguished to the depths of his soul. For the last confession of the Pope was an appalling one – a confession the like of which the Church itself must not have heard since Judas threw the thirty pieces of silver back onto the steps of the temple.

Pope Sylvester confessed that he had acquired, from a mysterious beggar, a coin which he soon discovered, by virtue of its immense cosmic power, was one of the thirty pieces of silver that Judas Iscariot had received as blood money for the betrayal of his Saviour. The Pope also recounted that there remained three more Coins of Judas in existence in this world – each of which would be more awesome than the last.

The monk to whom Sylvester's confession was made recounted that, in his very last moments on earth and exercising his full authority as Pope, the dying Sylvester commanded that the Coin of Judas he possessed should be buried with him and that on no account was it to be placed in the tomb of St Peter. But why? There was no explanation.

The official record of the final words of Pope Sylvester II was set out in the *Lives of the Popes* compiled by the librarian Bartholomew Platina. Sylvester commanded his corpse to be cut into pieces, saying:

> *Let him have the services of my limbs, who before sought their homage; for my mind never consented to that oath, nay, that abomination.*

However, Benelli could see now that these were not his final words. The dying man had said something more, never revealed to the world, but only to his confessor. Benelli read these final words. Then he sat back in shock. When Pope Sylvester II had uttered them, had he been moved by the spirit of God or by the wiles of the devil? Were his final words a trick or the absolute truth?

Suddenly, Benelli started up. On the threshold of the Room of the Meridian, a monstrous hound materialised. It approached slowly, its jaws yawning open in a feral snarl. Benelli raised the silver crucifix above his head and cried out in a loud voice, '*Exorciso te immunde spiritus.*'

Nothing happened. Then the beast vanished. Hurriedly, Benelli locked the book back in the chest and quit the room. As he started back down the stairs the torch went out.

'Cardinal, are you all right?' the Prefect called up anxiously from the base of the Tower.

There was no answer, for Benelli was fully occupied. As he was descending the stairs he saw the shadow as it began to form only a few steps behind him. It had the physique of a man, but the visage of a demon, and it was bathed in a yellow, spectral light. On its brow it bore its mark of satanic power. Terrified, the Cardinal held up the crucifix and shouted out: 'I command thee, evil spirit —'

In that instant, a murderous force hurled Benelli off his feet and down the stone steps. He cried out as he fell. Finally, he lay at the base of the Tower, his ankle twisted under him, his head badly gashed.

'Cardinal!' The Prefect searched for the torch. It emitted a feeble light. He looked, panic-stricken, at the drawn face of his companion, blood seeping from a head wound. The frightened Prefect stooped over his body. 'I will get help.'

'No,' croaked Benelli aloud. To himself he whispered,

'Do not go, it will kill me.' Then, 'We must leave here. There's no time to lose. Get me up.'

Hurriedly, the Prefect locked the door to the Tower. Before he did so Benelli attached his silver crucifix to the inside. Together, they passed back through the Secret Archives and then into the Vatican Library proper. The Prefect continually expressed his worries about Benelli's ankle but the Cardinal's mind was on other things.

Still in shock, Benelli recalled the final words he'd read in the confession of Sylvester II. For that Pope had murmured some more words to his confessor as he lay on his deathbed after the administration of extreme unction. His final words on earth. A terrible prophecy:

No living being can withstand the last three coins. If one is held by the person closest to the Pope the Church itself will fall.

Cardinal Benelli began to weep. There was only one person in the Vatican who could be said to be closest to the Pope.

Himself.

CHAPTER TWENTY-ONE

*All theologians speak of . . . evil spirits who
appear in the shape of a man, a woman or
some animal. This is either a real or actual
presence, or the effect of imagination.*

Bouvier, Bishop of Le Mains,
Dissertatio in Sextum Decalogi Praeceptum

PAUL AWOKE IN HIS OWN HOUSE. He stretched out
in bed and realised that his wife wasn't there. There was
nothing to worry about. She'd gone with Rachel to stay
at Florence's for the night and had left a note; it had
happened before.

He reflected with pleasure on his sexual activities with
Suzanne the previous evening. He'd got back late and it
had been a stroke of luck that Marie hadn't been there
– even though Helen had told him to keep her in the
house. Paul's mind turned to more uncomfortable matters. What should he do about Marie? Divorce was on
the cards. And Rachel?

'Hi!'

His train of thought shattered, Paul gazed towards the
bathroom door. She stood in the morning light, attired
in the same tunic he'd seen when they'd visited the grove
on the third astral plane, though her features didn't

mimic the perfection of his dreams. Was he awake or still dreaming?

'You don't remember?' Helen turned and disappeared. He blinked his eyes.

'Paul.' Helen had reappeared in the bedroom.

'How come you can do that? Why can't I?'

'Because,' said Helen, 'you have to go much higher up on the astral planes before your physical and spirit bodies can appear in different places at the same time. Bilocation takes some practice, as the saints have found out. Want to learn?'

Helen looked at him inquiringly. If only he understood the true nature of the coin. But they mustn't arouse his suspicions before they gained a greater hold over him. The forces of the master of the Field of Blood were pouring into his soul.

'What body of yours am I seeing?'

'My spirit body, of course,' said Helen smugly. 'My physical body's tucked up in bed. It can't go through walls.'

'Your physical body?'

'Let's just say it's one I've borrowed for a while.'

Paul stared at her. He wasn't just talking to a figment of his imagination. He pondered, trying to keep calm.

'Paul, it's real,' said Helen impatiently. 'This is not a dream, or just your imagination. You are awake and it is *real*. You are seeing my spirit body, just as you did when Kramer attacked the girl. It's a different reality to one you've experienced before – but it's still a reality.'

'But why can't others see what I can?'

'Because the coin gives you the power. Otherwise, it would be impossible for you since you need to have a deep faith in spiritual matters.'

'How do you know all this? Who are you?'

'Later, later,' Helen said petulantly. 'You can see me. So can your wife and child since I've deliberately chosen to reveal myself to them. I don't think much of Marie, by the way – you need a woman with less religion and more guts.' She blew him a light-hearted kiss. 'I've got just the person in mind for you.'

Paul continued to goggle at her, still not wholly convinced. Helen groaned. Show a human being a miracle and the first thing they did was question it. Didn't they realise they were the most stupid of God's creations? 'OK, if you still want proof, smart arse, why don't you contact your mother? Did you visit her house last night or not?'

With that, she vanished. Paul reached for the phone.

It took just ten minutes for his understanding of reality to change dramatically. Ten minutes and his mechanistic view of the universe, all human theorems and rules and measurements, collapsed about his ears, like the tinkling of broken glass.

Paul talked to his old mum. Four thousand kilometres away, in a perplexed voice, she confirmed all he'd witnessed the previous night. The bottle of pills by the bed, the washing-up towel that had slipped to the floor, the small box of chocolates she'd so carefully wrapped to give as a present to the next-door neighbour – details it was quite impossible for him to have previously known, or seen, by any human reckoning.

Paul put down the phone and went into the bathroom. As he buried his head under the shower, he considered what might be happening to him. A thought came into his mind. He remembered a book he'd read on mysticism many years ago when a student.

Among other things its author had noted that mystical experiences, being paranormal, could never be adequately described to a third party: they had to be personally experienced. Also, they provided a startling insight into the deeper nature of the cosmos – a realisation that the human intellect was not even scratching on the surface of things. Finally, the writer had noted that these experiences were invariably passive in nature – they contained the sensation of being taken over by a higher power.

'Damn.' Paul had dropped the soap. He bent down and picked it up. It was curious too that most mystics, Christian and otherwise, were adamant that their experiences of heaven and of hell lay *within* the human psyche and *not* outside it. Sometimes their trance states were also accompanied by supernatural visitations or prophecies.

Paul reached for a towel and stepped out of the shower. He'd always believed that people who spoke of these things were, quite simply, deluded. However, even when he'd read that book Paul had been conscious the mystics and saints were very consistent in their delusions, which was unusual. But what else had he witnessed last night that could prove the existence of the spirit world?

Paul skipped breakfast. Revving up the car, he hurtled down the drive. At the end of it, he flicked on the indicator to turn right, to the university, since he had a lecture on Freudian analysis to deliver at nine o'clock and he was already late. Then, on impulse, he thrust the wheel violently to the left. He'd another appointment; he'd just decided.

'Prisoner in D Block, cell number twenty-five.'

The guard at the High Security Facility checked his identity card and ticked a rota list.

'Sure thing, Professor.'

Paul sat down in one of the prison waiting rooms.

The guard returned a few minutes later, accompanied by Emma Breck. He gave a watery smile. 'I'm afraid it won't be possible today. The inmate's been taken ill.'

'I want to see him.'

The guard glanced at Breck then at Paul. 'Sorry. Like I said, he's ill – he's in the infirmary.'

'Get me Pat Harbison.'

The guard shrugged and left the room. Emma Breck remarked quietly, 'Paul, we've been friends for many years. I suggest you leave this particular prisoner for a few days. Is there anyone else you'd like to see?'

He scrutinised her expression. 'You know what happened, don't you?' At that moment Harbison came in.

'You wanted to see me?' The tone was affable and unconcerned.

'Yes,' said Paul, making the tone of his voice equally good-natured. 'I want to chat with you about the condition of the prisoner in cell number twenty-five. Last night, you and two of the guards, Williams and Barlansky, took him from his cell, bound and gagged. Half-way along the corridor, Williams smashed him in the back of the legs with a baton, and when he was unconscious on the ground, you all laid into him. I just wanted to ask – did you enjoy it?'

Harbison gaped inanely, overcome with shock. Finally, he closed his mouth and his countenance betrayed his fury. That bastard Williams must have blabbed. 'This is none of your fucking business,' he snarled. Throwing back his chair, he marched out of the room.

'Paul, I don't think you should have said that,' said Emma Breck, terminating the ensuing silence. 'You're losing favour here with people at the top. There's a lot that goes on in this place which should remain undisclosed. Be careful.'

'But it's true?'

She gave a hasty nod. 'They said the prisoner attacked them when they took him out of his cell. It was a lie. He'd have been so doped by the sedatives I gave him that afternoon he couldn't have lifted a finger.'

'So why?'

'He'd assaulted a prison guard earlier in the day – it was their way of teaching him a lesson.' Emma Breck put her hand on Paul's. 'Take my advice. Leave now. Let things cool down for a while, OK?'

Paul left. At the gates, the Deputy Warden met him. He had a brief message from Hanlon Dawes. 'The Warden orders you to take three months' leave of absence from visiting the Facility. I'm sorry.' He liked the psychiatrist.

'I see.' Paul got into his car without saying a word. He started back down the single road. He must talk to Kramer again, since he was the only other person who could see Helen *and* who obviously knew something about her and her powers. Paul would return, whatever the prison authorities said.

But he'd come back in the way they least expected.

Florence Ingelmann contemplated Marie. She was very worried. Something was wrong with her closest friend. However, Marie had refused to tell her what it was, despite Florence's persistent yet kind questioning. The furrowed brow betrayed Marie's deep sadness and angst. She always chatted to Florence about everything. Why not now? It must be something to do with Paul or Rachel, surely?

'Would you prefer it if we don't go on our ski holiday? We could postpone it for a day or two,' said Florence, 'or even cancel it.' She poured another cup of coffee. If truth be told, she was a bit nervous about skiing.

'No, you go.' Marie hesitated. 'But if I phone you, would you return?'

'Certainly. We'll always help you both, you know that.'

Marie nodded. 'Thank you,' she said, almost in a whisper.

They both looked towards the little girl standing in the doorway, with her slight figure and long blonde hair. Could they have witnessed the scene now as Paul did, they would have seen waves of bright light flowing between the mother and the daughter, reflecting their unconditional love and affection. They would also have seen the love that Florence had for them both. As long as Florence was there, she'd defend them to the death.

'We must go,' said Marie.

'I understand,' said Florence. Rachel would be late for school. Together, the small group went towards the front door and walked to the car. Florence kissed Rachel once more, fervently clasping her to her capacious bosom. 'See you soon, my darling,' she said. Then moved by an unconscious prompting (and her complete inability to be kept in suspense about anything) she exclaimed: 'It's about Paul, isn't it?'

Tears formed in Marie's eyes.

'He's ill? Very ill?'

Marie nodded. 'But you must say nothing to anyone.'

Florence watched the car depart from sight. She was overcome with melancholy. Perhaps he had cancer. Perhaps he was dying. Reluctantly, she started to pack for their holiday. One thought rattled about in her emotional mind.

Should she tell Ben about Paul's illness? Could she ever keep a secret?

*   *   *

The object of Florence's worrying returned from the High Security Facility to the clinic. Ben approached him as soon as he came through the doors. His face was flushed and angry, a most unusual occurrence.

'Paul, what *is* going on? Did you forget you had an appointment with that Hollywood actor and his son? They've been here for over an hour and are furious. They're threatening lawsuits and everything. The university also phoned to find out where you were for your morning lectures. What's happening? And I'm meant to be going on holiday this afternoon.'

Paul ignored him. He went straight into the conference room. Toni Brennan was there, together with his son and the manager. On the arrival of an audience, the actor began his finest thespian performance. He'd spent the last hour polishing it up.

'Where the fuck have you been, eh? What the *fuck* do you think I'm paying you for? Who the *fuck* do you think you are?' He was in full spate, ire and viciousness ejaculating from him in great streams. If only he could have acted like that on screen, he would have gained an Oscar for his accurate portrayal of a drug-addicted actor collapsing in on himself.

'Shut up,' said Paul.

Then a truly strange thing happened. Toni Brennan shut up. Even his son and his lawyer looked at Paul in complete astonishment. They were witnessing some sort of miracle.

'I'll speak with your son.'

'Fuck me,' said Julian as they walked into a separate conference room. 'How did you do that? I can't get him to shut up. You must have shot him in the arse.'

'Sort of,' said Paul. He also didn't know how he'd managed to make the actor silent, but he knew that whatever power he had within him was growing and he liked it. 'I've only one question for you. Did you burn down your school?'

'Course not.'

'I see.' Paul could discern the sensations coming from him and could interpret them easily now. He knew the boy was lying.

'That's all I have to say,' continued Julian.

'I'll be back in a minute,' said Paul, unconcerned. He went to his office and closed the door. He needed to find out what the real problem was with this wretched specimen of a teenager.

Helen had told Paul that the coin she'd given him had immense power. He extracted it from his pocket. It looked like an old Roman coin. It was strange that he was able to locate it only at certain times. At others it was as if he'd forgotten its very existence. He closed his eyes.

Slowly, a vision came to him. Although Paul didn't know it, Helen was beside him as this was happening, since it was her influence, not his, which was operating the coin.

As Paul's spirit form swiftly left his body, his inner sight clarified. He was inside a house. Toni Brennan's house. It was a huge and sprawling mansion, garishly decorated with pink carpets on the floor and puce wallpaper. Not unexpected. Toni Brennan's taste was as overblown as his talent.

Paul ascended the stairs. Or, rather, the stairs appeared before his eyes as if he was standing in a circle while things came into view. Now, he was on the landing. He could see the master bedroom in which the actor was accustomed to sleep with one of his many girlfriends. The boy's sleeping quarters were down the corridor.

Julian's bedroom was large and rectangular in shape. It overlooked a spacious lawn. The blinds were down and the sun filtered through the vents, catching a haze of dust in its beam. In the centre of the room was a double bed with a duvet crumpled up in a corner. The place hadn't been tidied in weeks and, on the floor, lay a mountain of shoes, comics and clothing. The walls were plastered with posters of naked women. Julian was going to be just like his father: a rebellious young teenager who'd soon develop into a self-destructive young man.

'You need to go back.'

Paul turned. Helen stood in the doorway of the bedroom, with a short Grecian tunic, her long blonde hair and an achingly beautiful face glistening with a cosmic light.

'You need to go back,' she said though no words as such came from her mouth. 'I know what you're looking for, but you need to go back.'

'Go back?'

'Yes, back in time. What you're looking for happened in the past. On the sixth astral you can go back in time.'

'Where am I?'

'On the third astral plane,' she remarked condescendingly, as if speaking to a stupid child. 'You need to go further out on the astrals.'

'How do I do that?'

'Open your hand.' Paul did so and the coin lay in his palm.

'Normally, a human being can ascend to the sixth astral only after great trial and effort.'

'Trial and effort?'

'Yes,' said Helen. 'Through magic or as a result of profound spiritual wisdom. But in your case, Paul, it's different. With the coin you can easily go there.'

'Why's that?'

'I'll tell you later. Just concentrate. The coin will do the rest. You see, it exists now both on the physical and spirit planes. It is beginning to take effect in this world.'

Paul stared down at the coin. Gradually, an image materialised before him. He was standing in a walled garden, though the wall wasn't of brick. Rather, it resembled bronze and it exuded a dazzling yellow light. All around there was a profusion of trees and flowers that Paul had never seen on earth. Their brilliance and luminosity was so intense it hurt him to contemplate them.

As Paul's insight widened he discerned that each flower, each tree, was unique in its every facet; and its size altered depending on the depth of introspection with which he considered it. Each contained a world within itself. Worlds within worlds.

In front of Paul a doorway appeared, as if set into the garden wall. He walked towards it and stood on the threshold. If he stepped through would he ever be able to enter the world of men again?

'Resist.'

The instruction flashed into his mind. The order was not his; it had come from elsewhere. He hesitated on the threshold. 'Resist. Turn back,' a voice continued. 'They are deceiving you.' The voice was that of a woman, quiet but insistent. He saw the image of a nun standing by the door.

'Ignore it,' screamed Helen. He could hear her strident and disparaging tone overriding that of the other. 'Go on. You must go ahead, Paul, otherwise you will die. Trust me.'

After a further moment of hesitation, Paul made a conscious choice and stepped across the portal. With that, the impression of the garden evaporated and another came to him. It was like a film rewinding but without all the jerks and whirr of an actual film. No sense of time passing, or of going back in time. Just actuality.

It was night, in the human calculation of things, a month before Paul had ascended to the sixth astral. Paul was now in Toni Brennan's house, upstairs on the landing. Toni's son, Julian, was lying on his bed, smoking a cigarette in the darkness. Paul could see him as clearly as if he were standing in the room and it was daylight. He watched, bewitched, like a moviegoer watching a picture. However, this was no picture. It was what had once happened on earth.

Down the corridor from Julian's room, the door to the master bedroom was half open. His father was lying on the huge, black-satin-covered bed with a teenage actress. They were both naked and had just made love. The young girl lay on her back staring listlessly up at the ceiling while Toni injected himself with a shot of heroin, a rubber band clamped tightly about his arm. After a few moments of drowsiness, he slumped backwards into a drug-induced sleep.

Lucy, the young actress, pushed the flabby and inert body away from her. Paul could read her thoughts. She was bored. Heroin wasn't her scene. Besides, she was finished with Toni. The bastard still hadn't given her the film part she wanted despite frequently giving her another part she didn't. She lay on her stomach and closed her eyes. She wished life would get better, but it never seemed to. That was the problem. If something could get screwed up, it did.

Hearing a slight noise, she turned towards the doorway: The boy, Julian, stood there, in boxer shorts, his hair tousled. With curiosity and desire he eyed her naked body. Disdainfully, Lucy turned away from his devouring gaze, drawing a bed sheet over her slim form. What to do?

For a while she studied the recumbent torso of the father, the over-white flesh, his mouth open and snoring. Half-way to a corpse and not much further to go. Out of the corner of her eye, Lucy glimpsed the boy. Their ages were close, perhaps three or four years apart. The son was a younger, fitter, more attractive incarnation of his father. Quite cute really.

Lying back on the pillows, Lucy gave in to her temptation. With a half-smile of revenge, she got up from the bed, pulling a satin sheet in front of her. Hearing her footfalls Julian drew back into the darkened corridor. However, Lucy pushed open the bedroom door wider and approached him, her complexion still flushed from her recent bout of lovemaking. She stood close to the boy and let the sheet gently slide to the carpet, to reveal her nudity.

'Are you influencing them?' Paul asked.

Helen shook her head. 'No. It's their own free will. Watch.'

Julian ogled his temptress, stunned and abashed as his fantasy was fulfilled. Then he seized her, his lust unstoppable. They made the brief journey to Julian's bedroom. On the bed Lucy let him do as he wished, giggling at his impatience. She was happy to be with someone her own age at last whose tastes were normal. She wanted satisfaction tonight and she'd get it.

The illicit lovers thought they were alone. Yet, there were unseen spectators to this display of unrestrained human passion. Paul and Helen beheld every aspect as if they had stood beside the creatures that fateful night. Silent and terrible spirits, they discerned not only the physical act but also the invisible energy spurting from them as their mental desires coupled as surely as their bodies.

'Not bad,' said Helen in a mock stage whisper to Paul, 'for the first time. But it gets better.'

As the lovemaking came to its climax, the actor arose from his bed in the master bedroom, unsteady but conscious. The cuckold was appearing on the scene. Shame about the timing, but Helen had helped with that one.

Toni shuffled down the corridor, unnoticed by anyone save the watchers. The rest was a real-life drama in which the actor revealed his thespian talents. Hamlet's ghost made his belated entrance. A click of the light switch, the lovers startled like frightened deer, their disengagement from coitus, unrestrained cries of wrath.

'Now you know what happened, are you going to tell Julian what you've seen? About his big secret?' Helen sniggered at her fellow bystander. 'Bet you'll be a coward.' Then she was gone.

Suddenly, Paul was back in his office again, sitting in his chair. He noticed the clock on his desk. Not a second appeared to have passed. So travel on the astral planes was outside the context of time. But did the vision lie? Was this the true explanation for the rift between the father and son?

Paul stepped back into the conference room. Julian didn't bother to look up from his comic strip. Paul knew he must be careful about broaching the subject matter, given its heady amalgam of passion, guilt and shame. So what should he say? A battle seethed inside his being, between his old persona and the new one – between the Cain and the Abel hidden deep within him. Contradictory thoughts fought for supremacy. Yet the contest was an uneven one. By now the coin had penetrated deeply into the marrow of Paul's spiritual being, warping his critical faculties. Absorbing its odium, he sowed in his soul what he must inevitably reap.

'Well, Julian, I think I know what your problem is,' he said dispassionately as he sat down.

'Yeah?'

'I think you screwed your father's teenage girlfriend and he caught you at it.'

Julian looked up, abashed.

'Yes,' continued Paul, 'a young blonde girl with pert breasts and a small tattoo of a bird on her inner thigh. She started it, didn't she, tempting you as she did? She was the one to blame. But then it was your turn, wasn't it? Shame on you,' he mocked savagely. 'Shame on little Lucy.'

The boy stared at him. An instant later, his complexion altered from astonishment to blind hate. His father, or the girlfriend, must have spoken to the psychiatrist. They'd betrayed him.

Paul adjusted his tie as the boy fled from the room. He felt no pity or mercy, for the coin did not contain these things. So Helen did not lie. Interesting.

Outside, all hell broke loose as the manager tried to separate the father from the son, the latter screaming maniacally. At last, when Julian had been dragged from the clinic, kicking and screaming, Paul stepped out into the corridor and approached his client. Poor Toni. The drug-eaten actor who had turned the amazing gift of life into a disaster movie for himself and others. He was silent now – a feeble spectator to the havoc unleashed before him.

'I'm afraid I can't treat your beloved son, Mr Brennan,' Paul said with heavy irony. 'I don't know what's wrong with him. But I'd be careful if I were you.'

'Why?' queried the actor.

'Because he will kill you,' said Paul, his voice icy with certainty. 'Now, have a nice day.'

CHAPTER TWENTY-TWO

*There exist unclean and wandering spirits,
whose heavenly vigour has been overlaid by
earthly soils and lusts. These spirits, burdened
and steeped in vices, have lost the simplicity
of their original substance; as some consolation for their own calamity, these lost spirits
cease not to conspire for others' loss, to deprave
them with their own depravity.*

Tertullian, *De Anima*

SISTER MARTHA, THE MOTHER SUPERIOR of a convent on the north side of San Francisco, looked out of
her study window. Rachel was walking in the garden
below, her hand clasped in that of a nun.

The elderly woman turned back from the scene to
converse with her unanticipated guest. She quickly sized
up Marie, as she did everyone she met. Early thirties,
educated, softly-spoken. From her demeanour she probably had a kindly, but determined nature and was very
protective of her child. Why on earth would a woman
like this come to their convent to recount a story of
demonic possession? She didn't fit the character type.

During the course of a long religious life, Sister Martha
had experienced people who'd come to her with such

problems. In the case of the vast majority it was clear what their illness was from the outset – and it certainly wasn't possession by evil spirits. Mental illness, the effects of drug trips, deep depression, brain damage, evangelical hysteria – these were all easily detectable. So, too, when possession was invented to escape from some gruesome crime or event that an individual was unable to cope with – murder, incest, family torture or betrayal. These dark secrets eventually came out and, in most cases, they could be resolved or, at least, some form of relief given.

However, demonic possession was a matter much more sinister and frightening. It touched at the very roots of human existence in this world and at the cosmic forces of good and evil. Sister Martha had no doubt Satan existed; no one within the Church did. Yet even to reflect too much on this was, itself, a dangerous thing. For the powers of evil were not constrained by the human mind, and could easily overwhelm it – affecting even those who foolishly thought they could dabble in the occult with impunity. They were wrong: the devils entered silently into their hearts and often waited a long time to wreak their destruction.

Sister Martha turned her attention from such a murky topic. She was sure that the person before her was neither the subject, nor the object, of possession. However, she had to convince the poor woman of this. She could see it would take more than words, since this particular soul was adamant.

'Marie,' she said quietly, 'I've asked Father David to talk with you. He's a priest with experience of these things. Are you really sure you want this, though?'

'I'm sure.'

'Quite sure?'

'Yes.'

So Sister Martha called to one of her nuns and asked her to invite Father David in. They could hear Rachel's childish laughter drift up from the garden below.

The man who came in the room a few minutes later was not what one might expect an exorcist to be. No muscular Christian, no brawny figure who would wrestle with the powers of darkness and hurl them down. Instead, Marie saw before her a stocky figure in his early fifties dressed in a brown cassock of the Dominican order, a rope cord about his waist. A film producer would have been disappointed in him. No cinematic presence here, not even a handsome face; it looked like a gnarled potato, saved only by a warm smile and eyes that wavered from hers.

Father David shook Marie's hand and they talked for some minutes. He rose from his chair.

'You're mistaken, Marie. It's true that there is a spirit world as well as a human one and that evil spirits can sometimes manifest themselves. However, the phantom of a woman you've described doesn't sound like one. Also, I suspect that your husband is as bewildered as you are about all this, *if* it did happen.' He emphasised the last words slowly and carefully.

'But my child saw it as well as I.'

'I know,' continued the monk smoothly. 'And I accept that poltergeists are possible. These are spirits that can be activated by a young child. They move things, they dislodge things but they don't mean any harm. They are spirits that are lost, they are neither in this world nor in the next. Why they're trapped we don't know, nor why they come or go. Rarely are they harmful and they often delight in being near children.'

'Why Rachel?' Marie asked.

'Oh, it won't have anything to do with Rachel personally,' said Father David in a breezy tone. 'I believe it's because she's a child; that's the reason. Children give off a wonderful feeling of love, much more than adults. That's what attracts these spirits, like moths to light.'

'But my husband – it has something to do with him, I'm sure. And the Kramer case.'

The monk had heard of the case. He'd also heard of Paul Stauffer and he was certainly not going to take on a famous psychiatrist; it could do untold damage. Yet he could see this woman was very determined. Doubtless, she loved her husband very much.

'Marie.' He raised his hands as if to pacify her. 'From all you've told me, I think you do have a problem.' He paused. 'You're very worried about losing your husband to another. That is producing your trauma. You need to talk to him about this.'

Marie shook her head. 'Yes, but this has nothing to do with the events I've described. I saw the woman. She means to harm us.'

The priest ignored her and his tone became dismissive. 'Please reflect on what I've said. Now, would you like me to talk to Rachel and set her mind at rest as well?'

When Rachel entered the room the priest took her hand. 'I want you to tell me what you saw, little one.'

So Rachel gave him a description of the mysterious lady and her long flowing blonde hair. The priest looked at her and his eyes twinkled with affection and amusement. 'And she doesn't remind you of any of your teachers at school?'

Rachel shook her head decidedly. 'Oh no, she was much more beautiful.'

'But she frightened you?'

'Yes,' said Rachel, 'because she wanted to take me away.'

'I see,' said the priest. 'Well, I don't think you'll come across her again.' He stood up; the matter was at an end. Case closed.

'She had a coin,' Rachel added.

'You didn't tell me,' said Marie, looking at her daughter quizzically. 'What kind of coin?'

Father David frowned – the child was becoming very imaginative. He had to go soon. There was a dying patient to attend to.

'Shall I draw it?'

'Yes, that's a good idea. Now, I really must depart,' he said. He patted Rachel on the head and shook hands with Marie. 'I will be back in a minute when I've collected my things.'

He left the room to gather up some books. On the way back he stopped outside the door. Perhaps it was best to leave them to it? On impulse, Father David poked his head round the door for the last time.

'Bye, then.'

He smiled at Sister Martha, Marie and the child seated around a table. Then he spotted the drawing. Slowly, Rachel turned towards him, her face radiant in a trance-like state.

'Oh, my God.' He blanched. The child was trying to tell him something and him alone.

Hurriedly, Father David beckoned the nun and Marie outside. 'Perhaps Rachel should stay in the convent for another day or so. It would be good for her. In fact, I insist.' His voice became authoritative. 'Marie, I'll visit your house after all. Just to put your mind at rest. Stay here, I will be back soon.'

'Thank you, Father.' She clasped his hand.

Father David hurried down the stairs, already late for the dying man. But that was not on his mind. He was alarmed. The face of the child had been illuminated by a light not of this world. And, of course, it was possible for a child in a trance to draw a perfect replica of a silver denarius of the time of Christ. But would the child really have written, as if stamped deeply into the coin, the letters 'SMRM – *Salva me, Redemptor Mundi*'?

The last words the traitor Judas Iscariot said before he hanged himself from that tree.

Save me, O Redeemer of the World.

CHAPTER TWENTY-THREE

*For we are not contending against flesh and
blood, but against the principalities, against
the powers, against the world rulers of this
present darkness, against the spiritual hosts
of wickedness in the heavenly places.*

Ephesians 6:12

THE MORNING AFTER HIS VISIT to the Tower of the
Winds, Cardinal Benelli struggled to sit up in bed. He
wasn't well. It wasn't just the fall down the stairs of
the Tower that had knocked the stuffing out of him. The
real reason was fear.

There was a tap on the door and his private secretary
came in. He gave some papers to the Cardinal to sign.
Official business must go on. Benelli took them, but
didn't read them. His mind was on more important
things.

'Your Eminence.' The secretary coughed. 'Cardinal
Vysinsky is still unwell. The Holy Father asked me to
inform you.'

Benelli waited until the secretary had gone. Then his
face became dejected. With the death of Graziani and
Vysinsky ill, their numbers were depleting. Already it was
destroying them and they didn't even know where it was

or who wielded it. That was frightening enough, but what he'd learnt last night in the Tower of the Winds was even more disturbing.

Betrayal. That was at the heart of these coins. Judas had betrayed his Saviour and one of them would betray the Pope, if the last words of Pope Sylvester II on his deathbed were true. But would it be Benelli? Please, God, no. The Cardinal was agonised. How good a Christian was he, after all? Not that good, he knew. And he'd failed to pass on the initial message about the coins. He was the weakest link. He must tell the others of this, admit the truth.

He closed his eyes with weariness. Although the coin had yet to surface, already Benelli felt its presence. He'd been unable to sleep last night, as he had the past few days. When he did, the whisperings had started. The blasphemies, the temptations, the infernal laughter – he heard them close to his ear. At present the voices were external, as if invisible messengers had been sent to attack and wear him down. What happened when they came from within, *inside* him?

'Cardinal?'

The Father Confessor stood by his bed.

'I'm so sorry,' said Benelli. 'I must have dozed off.'

'It's all right,' said the monk. He sat down on a chair. 'I've brought you the Sacraments.'

After he had administered them Benelli started to feel stronger in himself. 'Is it happening to you?' he blurted out. He was loath to admit his weakness before a man who, try as Benelli might to emulate him, would always be better than the Cardinal in so many ways.

'Yes.'

'But I mean the dreams, the whisperings, the temptations?'

The monk nodded. 'But you should close your mind to them. Let them pass by. Do not fight them.'

'Can you see them?'

'Some of them.'

Benelli shuddered. Apart from the spirit in the Tower he had not seen them yet. What would happen when he did? These spirits were far more powerful than any he'd experienced in his life before. If they could attack him even when he opposed them with a crucifix blessed by the Pope, what could they not do? He hesitated. Then he told the truth.

'I am very afraid.' He looked into the calm blue eyes of the monk. They reflected compassion.

'So am I,' replied the Father Confessor simply.

'What will happen?'

'The power of the coin is growing very fast,' said the Father Confessor. 'We need to destroy it before it is too late, but we still don't know its location. We've seen the human being to whom it's attached itself, though.'

'You have?' Benelli was surprised. 'Where?'

'Not I. Catherine of Benedetto has seen the man, but she doesn't know where he lives. She has tried to tell him to resist it. However, it seems he cannot.'

'Why?'

'It is very powerful indeed. Besides, this man craves it.'

'Does he understand its true nature?'

'No,' said the Father Confessor in a downcast voice. 'But he soon will.'

'But we must do something,' said Benelli. 'We can't just wait. Surely we can find it? There must be some clue to where this man is on this earth.'

'Do you not know it yourself?'

'I?' said Benelli. He sat up in bed in alarm. 'How

should I know it?' His voice quickened and he began to perspire. 'You, the Holy Father, the nun – you know of these spiritual things. I am not a mystic, just a cardinal.'

'But you had a vision.'

'That's true,' said Benelli in anguish. 'I saw the stars, I saw the presence of a coin, I felt great evil. And I failed to tell the Holy Father because I did not believe that the legend of the coins was true. But,' he continued helplessly, 'I saw nothing else.'

'I understand. It's just that these revelations often contain much more than one thinks. The history says that the appearance of these coins will be evidenced by natural phenomena. I thought you may have recalled something.'

'No, no,' insisted Benelli. 'And the nun, Catherine, has she seen anything?'

'I'm afraid not.' The Father Confessor rose from Benelli's bedside. 'I will come and see you tomorrow.'

'Don't worry, I'll be up by then.'

'Then I'll leave you with the newspaper.'

Benelli glanced at the folded newspaper. It was *The New York Times*. He never read it; he preferred Italian newspapers. The once self-assured Cardinal watched the Father Confessor depart. Now he was even more anxious. Did the monk and the Pope think that he was hiding something? Were they testing him? How terrible. Oh, if only all this would go away, if only . . .

That afternoon the doctor revisited his patient. He gave Benelli some tranquillisers and insisted he sleep for a while. They drew the curtains in his small bedroom and left him alone. But Benelli did not want to be alone, and he could not sleep. His dreams had become nightmares. This time he was in the Tower of the Winds, he was falling down the stairs, he was looking up at the stars, he . . .

Suddenly, Benelli awoke. Grasping for the light switch, he turned on the lamp. He *had* seen something in his trance after all. Now he remembered. Something frightful, something that might foretell the location of the coin.

Hastily, he got out of bed to tell the Father Confessor. As he did so, the newspaper slipped to the floor. Benelli groaned when he caught sight of a headline on the front page. The monk had already guessed.

'Heavy tremors in the San Francisco area. Earthquake warnings.'

CHAPTER TWENTY-FOUR

*The devil leaveth other marks upon their body
. . . and these, the devil's marks, be insensible,
and being pricked will not bleed, and can
often be in the secretest parts, and therefore
require diligent and careful search.*

Reverend Richard Bernard,
Guide to Grand Jurymen

'I THOUGHT YOU WERE NEVER COMING. What kept
you?' Suzanne kissed Paul lingeringly as he entered her
apartment.

'I was held up,' replied Paul with a grimace. 'By a
second-rate actor with a troublesome son. I won't be
seeing them again, though.'

Suzanne was wearing a short red skirt and a Lycra
blouse that combined to show her legs and cleavage to
best effect. After their initial embrace, she drew the top
up over her body. Paul glimpsed the outline of her neck,
her dark hair cascading back over it. She turned to him
so that he could touch her heavy, tawny breasts before
she pressed them against his body.

'Where were you this morning?' She drew him into
the bedroom. 'You had us for a psychiatry lecture. Everyone was waiting for you.'

'I went to visit the prison,' replied Paul as he undressed. 'What happened to my lecture?'

'Well, we stayed around in your room for a short while. Then that other professor, Ben Ingelmann, phoned. He told us to go home. He apologised and said he couldn't teach us himself since he was just going off on holiday. We all thought it was very funny.' She paused. 'Have you told your wife about us?'

'Er, not yet.'

Suzanne gave him a knowing smile. 'I understand.'

Paul pushed her down onto the bed, stripping off her short skirt. They made love many times. Each time she clung to him and demanded more, as insatiable as a succubus. Afterwards, they lay back on the bed.

'Why don't you sleep? I'll wake you up before it gets too late.'

'I have to go home,' replied Paul reluctantly. 'I've hardly seen Marie all day. She went to stay with friends.'

'But you're not worried about your wife, are you?'

'No,' Paul replied after a pause. It was strange, but he wasn't worried about her. She'd sort of slipped into the back of his mind, become more remote.

'Please stay a little longer. Please.' Suzanne grasped onto him, kissing him fervently. Then she turned over in bed and lay on her front. Outside, twilight became night, though neither of them noticed.

Idly, Paul's hand stroked the mounds of her buttocks, which were firm with no cellulite. Then he spotted an imperfection on her body. It was a mark like an ancient glyph, burnt into the flesh on her right buttock. It glimmered slightly in the dim light given off from the bedside lamp.

'What's that?'

'What?' Suzanne turned her head slightly.

'The mark.' Paul ran his finger over it. It was like a cattle brand.

'What mark?' Suzanne placed her hand on her right buttock. 'There's no mark.'

'Suzanne, there's a mark there. I can see it.'

She looked at him, baffled, her fingers touching the very spot. Then she giggled. 'You're teasing me, there's no mark.'

A strange and unpleasant feeling came over Paul. He could see that she was telling the truth. Yet there *was* a mark, a brand on his lover's body, and she didn't know it. Suzanne turned over quickly. Paul now admired the youthful smoothness of her belly. She began to stroke him, a finger caressing the side of his face. Paul watched her expression.

'Suzanne,' Paul said quietly. 'When you were attacked by Kramer in the prison, there was a woman in the corridor. She was standing behind me.'

'Woman, what woman?'

Trying not to lose patience, he continued, 'Don't play games. There was a woman behind me. She signalled Kramer to let you go. He didn't do it of his own free will. She had blonde hair.' Suzanne's gaze was growing increasingly bewildered. 'Her name is Helen.' Paul continued, 'She wore a white coat. Oh, come on, Suzanne, you *must* have seen her.'

'Paul, I didn't see any woman. I don't know why Kramer let me go. I'm just happy he did. Let's make love, just once more.'

'But there was a woman, and you have a mark.'

'Oh, yeah?' Her tongue slowly moved down the length of his body, kissing his belly button. 'Really? Let's try something else.'

After more amorous activity, Paul fell into a deep

sleep. In his dream, Helen was standing before him.

'Where am I?'

'Look.'

They were standing on the edge of a great cliff. The hallucination was similar to the one Paul had experienced when Helen had kissed him at the dinner party. On that occasion, however, Paul had discerned only the cliff on which he stood. Now, on the other side, across a vast expanse of space, he could make out the outline of another cliff rearing up, equal in height to the one on which he stood.

Paul directed his sight down the side of the cliff facing him. It took an age, since the precipice was so immense. Finally, a ravine at the bottom became visible. The moment it did so, Paul stood directly beside it. By comprehending it, he was already there. No descent was needed.

'The reality is appearing before you,' said Helen. 'The coin is producing it.'

The image of the coin appeared in the palm of Paul's hand, though he'd no idea how it had got there. He surveyed the unfolding scene. At the bottom of the ravine, where he and Helen now stood, there flowed a mighty river, its waters wending their way into the far distance. This river had no rocks and no foam. Instead, bounded only by the sides of the cliffs, it flowed its way from an unknown source to an unknown destination. Helen and Paul stood on a tiny ledge of rock just above it.

Judging by the standards of Paul's world this was no river, it was as vast as an ocean. However, as Paul's spiritual powers augmented, so did his perception of the cosmic scale of things. Now he could apprehend the river's immense size as well as its being bounded by cliffs on both sides.

'Where are we?'

'On the seventh astral,' said Helen. 'Very few humans can reach here. Only sorcerers and mystics. This is your world and your time. Look into the river.'

Paul looked into the profundity of the deep blue waters flowing past him. After a while, he began to divine an outline of the world on the riverbed. Yet this map was like no other, for it altered even as he looked at it, the tiny grains of sand which seemed to comprise it shifting but a fraction, the slightest of slight movements. It was his world, held within the callipers of time. Paul understood that this vision alone could appear to his eyes in a myriad ways and still not repeat itself. Also, that to every human and spiritual being, this sight would appear different. Ever changing, ever fluid: the flux of human destiny.

Paul revelled in this knowledge, even as it swelled within him, driven by the incalculable power of the coin. Why this was happening he did not know. Helen did.

The thirty Coins of Judas contained the deepest wisdom. A wisdom that went back into the eternal darkness – before man existed, before the Field of Blood, before the orders of Angels were conceived – when Satan, in the celestial form of Lucifer, the morning star, walked in the presence of God.

To Paul's improving sight, the semblance of Helen also transmogrified once more. Her spirit body became brighter, the hair no longer blonde but a shimmering silvery colour. And the face too, beautiful, beyond any human description of beauty. For it was ethereal, a face without blemish, a face that even Helen of Troy would have envied. A timeless face, incapable of mark or wear. Almost angelic. Almost.

'This river,' said Helen, 'is what the Greeks called the

River Lethe, the river of forgetfulness. Human souls swim through it into your world below. As they descend, they pass through time. Where we stand, vast ages can be seen. However, once the soul enters the water, time speeds up until your world is reached. While this occurs, these souls forget the past. Their eternal memory fades.'

'Is it their choice to enter the world?'

'Yes,' said Helen, 'just as it was mine and yours. Everything is choice.'

'And if I descend will I forget the past?'

'No. You have the ability to return to the world without being overcome by forgetfulness. The coin alone gives you this power.' Helen continued, 'You see, it contains a wisdom that existed before the formation of the river itself. An imperishable wisdom that came from the divine.'

'The divine? Who? What?' Paul begged her to tell him more, but she wouldn't. 'Not now. Fix your attention on the sight before you. Here you can behold the history of the race of man.'

'All of it?'

'Yes, all of it, apart from the minds of those on earth who possessed a greater spiritual power than you have now.'

'What is beyond this?'

'There are more revelations,' said Helen. 'I can take you to the ninth astral. No being can go any further while still in human form. After that the orders of Angels begin.'

'Can you go there?'

'No,' she said, 'for I still inhabit a human body, just as I've done for the last two thousand years. I still exist on earth, though not always in the same body.'

Paul scanned her visage closely. 'Can I go beyond the ninth astral?'

'Yes. Only you. That is, if you so choose.'

'Why?'

'Because,' said Helen in a beguiling tone, 'of the power of one who loves you. It is his power that is contained within the coin. Now let us descend. Enter any period of the past that you wish.'

'And the future?'

'The future, no. The future is not known even by the Archangels.'

'They exist?'

Helen smiled. 'Did not scripture tell you?'

Paul contemplated the river. It was so calm and placid. He longed to throw himself into its inviting waters, to feel its awesome force. To sink into an ocean that could not drown him but which would bear him as he willed. He turned back to Helen.

'The girl, Suzanne?'

'Well?'

'She has a mark on her.' Paul almost felt himself hesitate, though there was no hesitation as such since their communication was not via any human thought or word. 'She is your possession?'

'Yes,' said Helen, 'she belongs to me.'

'You can make her act according to your will?'

'Yes. On earth people can possess things. Here, people can possess souls. Would you like her?' said Helen. 'I know that you enjoy her. She can be yours. My gift to you.'

'And Kramer?'

'He belongs to me as well,' said Helen.

'So Suzanne and Kramer were used to bring me here?'

'Yes, they were part of my design.' Helen had no desire

to tell him that her own power over human beings was limited to those who toiled in the Field of Blood, the children of darkness. Nor that she was only the guardian of this Coin of Judas, not its master. She'd tell him later. All in good time, in human time.

'Why?'

'To save you,' said Helen. 'But you can see these things for yourself. It is your choice. Nothing is forbidden to you. Nothing in the whole universe.'

'By who?'

'By the one who loves you.'

Paul turned away. Somehow, he knew that Helen was lying, that she was hiding something from him. Yet a desire for things hidden to man infiltrated him, filling up his spirit. In doing so, it increasingly displaced Paul's love for Marie and his daughter. He was acquiring a thirst: an insatiable thirst for cosmic wisdom. A thirst which could not be quenched by all the knowledge in the world.

Paul dived into the river.

Floating. The most wonderful sense of floating on calm and untroubled waters. Without fear, without sense of time, without obligation, without responsibility. Floating. Then, after so long, so eternally long, to feel a subtle change. To be like a leaf drifting in a still pond, an almost imperceptible sense of movement. Aeons passed.

Then, again, a change. To be like the branch of a tree gently swaying in the wind. Aeons passed. More movement, like the soft falling of snow from the sky. Then faster. Like the rain beating down, like the flick of the tail of a trout, the running of a rabbit, the racing of a dog, the crawl of a child, the cry of a human being, a glint of sunlight.

To be conscious of time hurtling by. To be back in the world. To feel the gunning of the temporal engine like a mighty train speeding along the tracks. Back into human reality.

'Where are we?'

'I don't know,' said Helen. 'It was your choice, not mine.'

Paul was in the garret of a small castle overlooking a lake. Outside, the water lapped up against its sturdy foundations and the banks on the far side of the lake were covered with linden trees. It was summer. Within the garret itself, books lined the walls. There was also a solid mahogany desk, stained-glass windows, some pipes on a stand. Paul noted the titles of the books: psychiatry, philosophy, astrology, religion. Where in the world was he?

Paul's spirit passed through the walls of the castle and into an enclosed courtyard. An old man was sitting in a wicker chair, his feet perched on a footstool. Paul stared at him. He still couldn't fathom out where he was, so he re-entered the study and inspected a calendar pinned to the wall. It said 15 May, 1958, the letters in French. And? Paul noted a letterhead on the desk. Understanding came to him. He was in the residence of Carl Jung in Böllingen, Switzerland.

'Trust you to pick a psychiatrist,' said Helen.

Paul was mesmerised. He was in the home of a man about whom he had read so much, who had been his guru when he studied for his degree in psychiatry. Now he saw the rather rotund and elderly figure sitting in the sunlight without the slightest perception that he was being watched, puffing away contentedly on his pipe.

'Typical,' observed Helen. 'He's reading one of his own works.' She glanced up at one of the overhanging trees. Paul watched as a leaf dropped onto the book. The great man grunted and brushed it aside with his hand. He was reading *The Undiscovered Self*. He seemed to be enjoying it.

Helen shook her head. 'Personally, I preferred Freud. He had better ideas on sex. Worrying about his archetypes, though. We're not as bad as all that.'

Another leaf fell. Jung closed the book and slowly got up from his chair to prepare some lunch.

'Can you change things in the past?' Paul asked.

'Sometimes,' said Helen. 'But not all things. And not on this astral plane. You need to go much further out. Now, you've had your boring selection. Time for something more lively. My turn. Let's get back to the good old days.'

They were in a different time and place. Paul was standing in a stadium. It was like that for modern-day dog races, an elliptical circuit with a seating capacity for more than a hundred thousand people. However, in this case, the stadium was being used for chariot racing and it was the last race of the morning. The chariots hurled down the track, the horses' eyes bulging as they were ferociously whipped on. At one end of the arena was an obelisk, about which the chariots tore. As they did so, the audience sprang up and down in their seats, cheering on their favourite team, the blues or the greens.

It was a warm July day just before lunch and the Circus of Nero was almost packed to capacity, yet people still pushed through the entrances, clutching their tickets, eager for the afternoon's entertainment. Paul didn't recognise the stadium – not surprisingly, since, within thirty years of this spectacle, it no longer existed. But, by noting the dress of the people, the marble columns bearing the insignia of legions, and the size of the arena, over a hundred and sixty metres in length, Paul guessed that he was in one of the circuses of Imperial Rome.

'I was here,' said Helen, conversationally. 'I had a wonderful time that afternoon, the weather was just perfect.' She sighed. 'Much better than in your period of history. People really enjoyed themselves. They made the best out of life and got on with it.'

Paul stared down into the arena from a balcony. The next feature was about to start. The crowd was restless and expectant. Mothers petted their babies and put them to the breast; their husbands gossiped about the latest news from the provinces and smacked their children for throwing half-eaten melon slices on the poorer section of the crowd.

All Rome was there: the Emperor, senators, centurions, businessmen sucking up to clients, lovers, thieves, hustlers and soothsayers. Beneath the lowest arcade of the circus vendors sold cheap wine and fruit from their stalls. Everywhere there were prostitutes, male and female, adult and child, of every colour and disposition, from all over the Empire, offering their fleshly wares.

The management prepared for the next spectacle amid the noise and hubbub. It was a feature everyone enjoyed. Plenty of action. Great for the kids to watch.

The victims led by the soldiers across the yellow sand into the centre of the ring were mostly young. They were almost naked; their bodies glistened in the sunlight from the oil that had been put on them. As they entered the arena the older youths tried to form an outer circle around the women and children. One old man was carried out on a wooden pallet and then roused with a few kicks, to prepare for death in an entertaining fashion.

A blast of trumpets rang out and there was a hush among the fidgeting crowd. Everyone, audience and victims, looked towards the huge metal gates located at the north and south sides of the circus. They began to rise slowly, the rope winding around creaking wooden barrels. Finally, the audience drew in their breath with a murmur of excitement as the lions shot out. As usual, there was a tense moment as the animals accustomed themselves to the open space and to the vast, expectant crowd. The participants sized each other up.

Then the sport began.

The crowd heard a piercing scream, and a blonde-haired child of not more than six or seven broke from the human pack that remained huddled in the centre of the arena. She started to run towards the walls, vainly seeking sanctuary. This distance seemed short to Paul, as he stood, in his vision, with Helen on the steps of the Circus of Nero, but for the child it was immeasurable.

The crowd gazed down at the running figure while they sipped their wine. The girl's movements were swift, her naked body crouching low. Her heels dug into the sand, still blotched a blood-red from where they'd dragged dying horses away. The human's running skills were wonderful to behold, supremely natural and animal-like, a small creature fleeing in utter terror of its life.

Meanwhile, a starving lioness let out of a pit by the northern gateway crouched down. Then it started to pursue her. The audience watched, spellbound, as the animal raced across the arena – muscles rippling on its great flanks, limbs superbly co-ordinated to give it maximum velocity, muzzle thrust forward and low. As it prepared to kill its jaws opened. The child did not see this. She did not turn round as she fled.

The lioness approached its prey in a great arc, its speed rapidly increasing as it carefully judged when the two would meet. Suddenly, the little girl looked back at her killer. Then she raised her head upwards to the sky, screaming out in despair. The walls of the circus would never be reached – not in this world.

The victim swerved in a last desperate attempt to save herself. However, the lioness had already projected this jink into its trajectory and there was a massive jolt as two hundred and forty kilos of flesh thundered into the victim at forty kilometres an hour. She would have been tossed up into the air had the lioness not already secured a firm grip on her right shoulder with its jaws.

They tumbled into the dust. Like lightning, the lioness loosened its initial bite. Expertly it turned the body underneath its own, its paws raking deep into the flesh. Within a second the jaws clenched around the neck and throat of the girl. Then the back teeth bit in, at three tonnes per square inch, severing at one swoop the cervical bones and wrenching the head from the torso. There was a looping gush of blood and the frenetic convulsions of the corpse. Starving, the lioness sat down and began to devour its prey. A delighted roar went up from the spectators.

'Habet!' 'It's got her!' 'How quick!'

The others in the ring watched the slaughter of one of their number in silent horror. Then their unearthly screaming began as they fled to their deaths, the remainder of the lion pack closing in. The final cries were drowned out by the roars of the crowd, hoarse with excitement and blood lust.

'Iugula!' 'Kill!' 'Verbera!' 'Strike! You missed that one!'

'I was sitting over there,' said Helen idly. She pointed out the spot. It was very near to the Imperial box. Close to it were two seats whose occupants Paul was unable to see, as if they were hidden in a heat haze. He assumed one of the occupants must have been Helen.

'Who were you with and why can't I see them?'

Helen hesitated only fractionally. 'Oh, I can't remember. Anyway, as I told you, you can't see those further out on the astrals than you are at present. But that's Emperor Nero, of course.' She pointed to an empty seat in the imperial box. Then to another. 'And that's where his mother, Agrippina, used to sit. Oh!' she squealed, 'and there's Claudia, the bitch.' She pointed to a woman silently watching the carnage.

'Who?'

'His latest conquest.' Helen shook her head. 'I never liked her. He got rid of her as well; she'd no sense of humour. So where do you want to go now? Or would you like to see the rest of it? The best is yet to come. The crucifixions will be tonight. Nero always likes to give the crowd a good finish. There might be someone you know in history there. An old fisherman.'

Paul surveyed the spectacle, drinking in the scene.

Suddenly, Helen gasped and her face twisted in pain. The illusion about them began to dissolve rapidly. 'My power!' she screamed, 'My power!'

Simultaneously, Paul descended into the throes of agony. It was as if his human body, wherever it was, was being forcibly dragged from one point in time to another, across a vast distance. The past dissolved in a blur; the present did not yet exist. There was darkness and confusion, an inability to perceive anything. He was caught up in a swirl of waters, lost in a whirlpool. He had no sense of being.

Finally, he awoke.

He was back in Suzanne's bedroom. She lay beside him, sleeping peacefully. Helen was nowhere to be seen.

Although Paul didn't know it, she'd gone to challenge Father David and Marie, who'd just reached Paul's house.

Paul blinked. It had been just a dream, hadn't it? Of course it had. He leant over the recumbent figure of Suzanne and drew back the sheet. On her right buttock he found the mark of servitude again. But this mark was different. It had *changed*.

He lay back in bed and experienced a frisson of the purest delight. It must be his mark. Deep within his being he realised that the revelations he'd been experiencing were as true as reality. And this woman, Suzanne, had become his slave. He was her master, body and spirit.

Paul kissed her. A kiss of possession. A kiss of Judas.

CHAPTER TWENTY-FIVE

[Freud] confessed to me that it was necessary to make a dogma of his sexual theory because this was the sole bulwark of reason against a possible 'outburst of black occultism'. In these words Freud was expressing his conviction that the unconscious harboured many things that might lend themselves to 'occult' interpretations, as is in fact the case. These 'archaic vestiges' or archetypal forms grounded on the instincts and giving expression to them, have a numinous quality that sometimes arouses fear. They are ineradicable for they represent the ultimate foundations of the psyche itself.

Carl Jung, *The Undiscovered Self*

FATHER DAVID AND MARIE GOT into his elderly car. He'd decided to say nothing to her of his concerns. It would cause her great anguish and it might be precipitate.

He'd tried to contact Cardinal Benelli, his ultimate superior, since he and other experts in exorcism had been ordered by the Vatican only two days before to inform them of any cases of possession in which a coin was referred to. However, the sharp-tongued official to whom Father David had spoken had said that Benelli was ill and couldn't speak to anyone. So Father David had left a message.

He somehow doubted the Cardinal would contact him. After all, why should he? Father David had always served in minor clerical posts and, in his thirty-five years as a monk, he'd never visited Rome once. He was an insignificant person in the great scheme of ecclesiastical things, at the bottom of the clerical ladder. There it was.

'I'm sorry about the condition of the car,' he said. 'It was a gift from a parishioner and I'm very grateful for it.'

'Please, you don't have to apologise.'

'You have a lovely daughter.'

'Yes, I adore her.'

'And your husband, he's fond of children?'

'Oh, yes,' Marie replied. 'He loves her more than all the world. Have you met my husband?'

'No,' continued Father David. 'Though I've read one or two of his books. I don't think he's a great fan of religion.'

Marie hesitated. 'Let's say that he doesn't believe in it. He thinks it's all nonsense.' She looked somewhat embarrassed. 'I'm sorry.'

'Please don't apologise. He's perfectly entitled to his opinion. And you?'

'Oh, I believe,' she said.

'Why?'

'Why?' They were speeding down the highway. 'Because I know that God exists,' Marie said. 'I just know inside me, that's all. And when I look at the stars or at Rachel, I am sure of it. I don't read any religious books, though; I just say my rosary every night. And you?'

The priest laughed. It was a robust laugh. He was a practical man and had little time for theory either. 'I'm the same, though I have one or two books to read as well. All part of the job.'

'What is this coin my daughter and I saw?'

Father David's face became serious. 'I don't think we should talk about these things now.'

They continued down the road in which the Stauffers lived, and into the driveway. Marie's home loomed up in front of them. 'Very impressive,' said the priest quietly.

It was a large house of two storeys, set in its own grounds in an exclusive part of the city. The style was modern and functional, all glass and wood. It had been designed by one of California's best-known architects.

'Yes,' said Marie. 'We've lived in it for four years. I love it here.' Then, wistfully, 'I used to love it here.'

'And you soon will again,' said Father David in a confident tone. He stepped out of the car. He was ready for the task in hand.

The Church accepted the reality of evil spirits and their ability to possess man and beast. The Bible frequently recorded the casting out of demons from those who were possessed and most people knew of the famous incident in the Gospel of Matthew where devils were commanded by Christ to leave a possessed man and to enter a herd of swine, which then ran over a cliff. However, the modern Church was also very cautious about these matters – since the vast majority of alleged demonic possessions were falsehoods or trickery.

Yet since very early times, there had been exorcists – that is, trained priests, appointed to exorcise evil spirits. These men were carefully selected by the Church, individuals methodical and highly circumspect in their approach. They reported to a cardinal in Rome – a man whose nature was sufficiently discerning to sift the false from the true, like chaff from grain. Cardinal Benelli.

'Will your husband be in?' They strolled towards the front door. Outside, it was twilight.

'No,' said Marie. 'He usually gets back from the university much later. He always has a lot to do.'

'I can imagine.'

They crossed the threshold and stood in the hallway. All was calm.

The demonic possession of human beings was relatively simple to detect. Generally, evil spirits would react to the touch of the cross or other divine objects, as if seared by fire or scalded by hot water. This had nothing to do with the object itself, but with the presence contained within. Devils felt the spirit of holiness with which it had been imbued. However, these relatively simple indicia of evil were not foolproof, for the gradations of evil spirits were many and those deeply immersed in evil could remain unaffected.

Manifestations were often a more reliable guide than the touch of a cross. For the natural world was subject to laws that did not bind the spiritual and Father David himself had witnessed things that defied explanation: children who spoke in tongues of ages past, the inexplicable levitation of objects of great weight, mysterious writings on walls and floors, the physical presence of forms that were part of the cosmos but not of this world.

Father David had only to close his eyes and he could often see these spirits as he carried out his exorcisms. Sometimes they were pitiful creatures, cowering with the baleful eyes of beasts. At other times the manifestation comprised the actual figure or face of a dead or a living person – like a mask – but often horribly distorted by fear or hate.

Then there were the powerful forces of evil, those that had descended far into the depths of malice. Demons that could change their shape at will and appear anywhere in the world. These could induce the most terrifying delusions in the minds of human beings and control them. A person might think that he was walking along a street when he was walking off a cliff, a woman might think she was feeding her child when she was choking it to death, a child might think he or she was playing with a small brother or sister when he or she was actually drowning it.

Afterwards, if they survived, these abject human beings in which the evil spirits had temporarily made their abode would have little or no recollection of the things they had done. They would be like zombies or half-beings, their souls badly crippled, as in a spiritual car accident, the outer shell maimed and broken until true repentance or death came upon them.

These things Father David had witnessed for himself. He had also seen that the rites of exorcism invariably drove these fell creatures out of the human vessels they sought to inhabit, into colder regions where there was an absence of any human or spiritual warmth.

But of the deep mysteries of the spirit world the priest knew little, nor did he grasp it in any depth. Father David had never seen an Angel of Darkness nor, if he did behold one, would he live. By divine power these presences generally had no means of access into the world and they could not pass the threshold into human reality. In that lay humanity's salvation.

'I'll turn on all the lights,' said Marie, full of angst.

'Fine,' replied Father David. He put down his small bag in the hallway. There was nothing there. He was quite sure of it. No presence. Generally, he would feel a malevolence pervading the place when an evil spirit was present, or even a stench, like that of rotting human flesh. But not here. Nothing. It was very cold, though. A lack of central heating, that was a common-sense explanation.

'Have you a dog in the house?' Father David had known of many cases where cats or dogs had refused to enter rooms or had reacted alarmingly when placed near haunted sites. Another useful pointer.

'No,' said Marie. 'Our Labrador is missing.' For some reason she couldn't quite work out, she'd forgotten to tell him about the animals.

She went into the kitchen. Everything was as it was normally. The dishes were in the dishwasher, a rag doll was propped up against the kitchen sink, the curtains were drawn.

'I'll go upstairs,' said Father David. 'Where did you see this coin?'

'In our bedroom, on the left,' said Marie.

Father David began to ascend the staircase, his bag still in the hall. On the fifth step, the lights went out.

'It's all right, Marie, don't panic. It will simply be a fuse.'

He descended the staircase and went into the living room. Marie stood there, her hand holding on to the phone receiver like a vice. The monk extracted it from her grip.

'Marie,' he said in a very calm voice. 'It's just a fuse. Really, it is. Please don't be frightened. Where's the fusebox?'

'In the cellar. You go through the kitchen.'

'I'll be back in a minute. Just sit down, all right?'

The priest went into the large kitchen and opened the door to the cellar. Then he took a torch and started down the wooden steps. Marie sat on the sofa, but she was no longer listening to his footfalls, for something very strange was happening.

It was getting darker.

However, this was no twilight steadily fading into night. Instead, it was a profound blackness that came into the room like a swirl of fog. Marie blinked. She could no longer see. Not even the living-room door. Not even her hand. She tried to cry out, but she couldn't.

'Father . . . Father,' she gasped. How could she warn him?

The priest inspected the large cellar that ran the length of the house. It was empty save for a few cardboard boxes. By the light of his torch he located the fusebox and opened it.

'There we go.'

The lights flickered on again. As they did so, Father David could see what was appearing on the wall. He staggered back in horror.

'Marie, get out of here, get out,' he shouted, but she couldn't hear him.

The lights went out again. Then a force like the mighty whirl of a tornado swept the priest up into the air and across the room, smashing him against the cellar wall. There was a sickening snap of bone as his right leg broke.

Father David stared in front of him, his mind paralysed with fear. Light was irrelevant now, for the darkness was suffused with a grim, spectral light. On the wall a huge pentacle started to form. The priest tried to say the opening words of an exorcism, but none came. He faced an evil far greater than he'd ever experienced, and in its presence he was incapable of resistance.

The pentacle began to complete itself, its encircling

rings emerging to view, as if etched with sulphurous fire. Father David's eyes were transfixed. Whatever was going to appear came from the outer regions of the spirit world and, when he looked on it, it would annihilate him.

'Marie,' he croaked. He must save her.

Trembling, the priest held up a small vial of holy water. It shattered in his hand, hissing and spitting as the water scalded him. Withdrawing a cross from his pocket, he dragged himself across the floor. The runes on the pentacle filled in as if traced by an invisible hand. Father David clutched at the banister of the stairs. In a whisper he recited from the twenty-third Psalm: 'Yea, though I walk through the valley of the shadow of death, I fear no evil.'

He got no further, for the hallucinations began. The exorcist could no longer see. He was in a vessel in a typhoon, a great avalanche of water hurtling towards him. He waited for it to crush him under its weight, but it did not come. Then he was on the highest of buildings. One more step and he would topple over the side. Father David fell to the ground. Desperately, he began to pull himself up the steps. The hallucinations continued, grotesque and macabre.

He was in a dark wood, on his knees, and he could run no further. There were primeval cries around him. The hunters were fast approaching. He could see them, huge timber wolves loping out from behind the fir trees. Then he was elsewhere. He was in a foul and putrid lake, weighed down with heavy stones, drowning, gasping for breath, dying.

The illusions were so real that Father David experienced them in their plenitude. He cried out in agony as he collapsed, unconscious, unable to go any further. Whatever was there was far more powerful than he and it was playing with him. The cross fell from his hand. From the darkness the spirit of Helen approached, accompanied by other denizens of hell.

It was Marie who found the priest near the cellar door. She discovered more holy water in his bag and poured it over his head. Then she tried to drag the exorcist towards the front door of the house, lost in the fog of night about them. She was frozen with terror, but she knew she had to help him.

Suddenly, she experienced an intense warmth about her heart like a burning flame. Words came into her mind. Where from she did not know, but she shouted them out against the unseen adversary. Words of exorcism: 'I adjure thee, thou old serpent, by the Judge of the quick and the dead, by thy Maker and the Maker of the world, by him who hath power to put thee into hell, that thou depart in haste from this servant of God.'

The words were not Marie's but those of another.

Thousands of miles away in a forgotten convent in Italy a nun at prayer in the deepest of trances perceived Marie and her terrible plight. The presence of the nun entered into her mind and pronounced the words of the exorcism. The battle was on.

Catherine of Benedetto turned to face her foe out on the seventh astral. Two mighty spirits, one armed with death and despair, the other with light. For Helen, to challenge a simple priest of no great spirituality and belief was one thing, to face a living saint quite another. She knew that, without invoking the Coin of Judas, she could not defeat the nun and she might suffer a great loss of her power if this creature were more formidable than she supposed. Yet to reveal the true wielder of the coin now, and kill this woman without having Paul completely in their hands, would be too dangerous.

Marie dragged Father David across the kitchen to the hall, words of exorcism flowing from her. In front of her was pitch-blackness. She could see nothing in the house, no door, no furniture, no walls. Her mind was filled with terrifying images: snakes writhing out of the mist, their eyes imbued with a human-like malice. Behind them, a figure. She was in an ancient temple; a sorcerer's lair from some ancient time, runes and markings on the wall, fires flaring up in the Stygian darkness, the agonised cries and broken forms of other human beings as they lay racked and tortured. The demon began to approach. She dared not look up to contemplate its visage.

'Save me, O Lord,' Marie prayed.

At the same time, the evil broke as the power of Catherine of Benedetto shattered its spell. Marie experienced a searing brightness, then a surge of transcendent joy filled her heart. The love of the nun entered her soul, casting out the terror and deathly fear. Marie cried out and fell to the ground in a faint.

When she recovered consciousness, she was lying on the floor. The lights in the house were on. There was no evidence of what had happened apart from the dying priest who lay in her arms, his face a mask of suffering. Marie cradled him. In her mind an instruction rang out. '*Leave now. Flee.*'

Thousands of miles away Catherine of Benedetto arose quickly from the altar. She had looked on the true face of Helen, a monstrous image. She had also seen the Coin of Judas which she held. But Catherine knew that the one who truly wielded the coin was not Helen. It was another, a dark force much more powerful still. One who came from beyond the astral planes. Catherine could not see its face. But it was approaching ever closer, to enter the world.

One final thing Catherine of Benedetto knew, great soul that she was. She could not defeat it.

For it was an Elemental Spirit.

Sister Martha softly closed the door. From behind her she could hear the last rites being said for Father David, and the sound of weeping. She looked at Marie, her own visage frozen with alarm.

'You and your daughter must not leave this convent under any circumstances.'

'What if we go to another city or another town?'

The mother superior shook her head. 'You don't understand, Marie. Evil spirits are not subject to human boundaries. They are invisible and unlimited by time and distance. You cannot flee from them like escaping from another human being.'

Marie whispered. 'What about my child?'

'Rachel should stay here. You should tell her nothing of what has happened.'

'And my husband?' asked Marie. 'He must not return to the house?'

The nun looked at her curiously. 'You should ask your husband to come here tomorrow, but in daylight.'

Marie said, 'Will he come?'

Slowly, the nun shook her head. Marie gasped, for they'd both read each other's thoughts. Paul would not be able to enter the convent. What she most feared was true.

'Father David?'

'He is very gravely ill.'

'What did he see?'

'I don't know,' said the nun.

There was a noise at the door. Hastily, Sister Martha stepped back inside the small room. The exorcist's face was ashen. Extreme unction had just been administered. His eyes stared blankly as he started on the road to death. Feebly, he motioned the others to leave the room. Sister Martha sat beside him. He tried to speak.

'A coin,' she said, 'did you say a coin?'

The priest assented with his eyes. 'Benelli —'

'I understand,' said the nun, clasping his ice-cold hand in hers. 'I am to tell the Cardinal about the coin.' She paused. 'Was it as the child drew it?'

Again the eyes moved almost imperceptibly. Sister Martha watched the purple colour slowly rise up his face. She spoke again, for the sight and then the hearing were the last senses to go.

'But, Father, what does it mean?'

The priest stared back at her, but in death he could no longer communicate. The nun wept as she witnessed his final moments on earth. If this evil could defeat Father David then, as surely, it could destroy her and her companions.

The trial was upon them.

CHAPTER TWENTY-SIX

*Not even the saints and the faithful wor-
shippers of the one true and supreme God
enjoy exemption from the deceptions of demons
and from their multifarious temptations.*

St Augustine, *The City of God*

CARDINAL BENELLI SAT ALONE IN his study. Outside, in the corridor, he could hear muted noises as
various assistants hurried past on their usual business. It
was a normal day in the heart of the Vatican. However,
for him, it was anything but normal. An hour before,
Benelli had received the phone call about Father David.

The Cardinal was grief-stricken. He blamed himself.
Had he understood his revelation, the Vatican would
have learnt earlier where the coin was. Had he not been
ill, Father David would have been able to contact him.
Because of him, this holy man had died.

Benelli was sure now that the forces of evil were playing
with him, mocking him. Great Cardinal, you think you
are, they whispered, proud man of the cloth, but to us
you are a fool. We trick and deceive you and it is only
later you understand. By your stupidity you will lead
others into the pit.

What should Benelli do? Should he tell the Holy

Father now that he couldn't go on? Surely, John XXV had already noticed this? What other failures would result from him? It was too awful to contemplate and there was no one to help him.

Evil. As to its physical manifestations, Benelli had never had the slightest doubt since he'd become a priest all those years ago. Those who took part in satanic rites, those who used black magic to exalt themselves and to damn their enemies, those who trafficked with fallen angels – they paid an eternal price.

Voodooism in Haiti and Africa, the highly organised satanic lodges that had existed since the eleventh century in Antwerp, Avignon and Rome, the defiling of church altars, the kidnapping and sacrifice of children, the theft of church sacraments: all this still occurred in modern times to a far greater extent than people realised, and it was impossible to stamp out.

This obeisance to Satan was not only communal – it also existed at an individual level. The abominable and horrific crimes committed by many murderers, pathetic specimens of humanity, who then confessed to being goaded on by voices within, were part of the greater whole, an overall demonic intent.

But while Benelli accepted the physical manifestations of evil he now understood that its spiritual reality was even more horrifying in its pervasiveness, its subtlety and its power. It was a living force of immense hate. A previous pope, Paul VI, had emphatically stated in 1972:

Evil is not merely a lack of something, but an effective agent, a living spiritual being, perverted and perverting. A terrible reality . . . mysterious and frightening, this dark and disturbing spirit really exists and he still acts with treacherous cunning. It is contrary to the teaching of the

Bible and the Church to refuse to recognise the existence of such a reality, or to regard it as a principle unto itself which does not draw its origins from God like any other creature; or to explain it as a pseudo-reality, a conceptual and fanciful personification of the unknown causes of our misfortune.

Benelli had seen this evil spirit at work many times throughout his life: in the faces of those who had murdered and tortured, in the almost unbelievable acts of neglect and intentional mistreatment committed by one human being on another, in the bestial cruelties and savagery that emerged during war. He had seen this human element of evil often and he could easily recognise its mark.

However, this time, as an old man, he would witness the actual appearance of these great spirits who trafficked in human misery and directed it for their overlord, for they would enter the world again. No human power or spirituality would be able to withstand them.

Worst of all, the prophecy of Pope Sylvester II had indicated that the Church itself would fall when the one closest to the Pope possessed such a coin. So Benelli himself would now undergo his own trial. He would take up his cross, and he would be found wanting, he was sure.

Comfortable in his Cardinalate, secure in his respected position in the Vatican, smug in his religiosity, Benelli had thought, in his hubris, that the powers of temptation were mostly beyond him. After all, he had no craving for the sins of the flesh, he had no desire for wealth and although he enjoyed his food and perhaps a glass of wine now and again, as his stomach attested, he was, in truth, no glutton.

But this was irrelevant; these were minor virtues. They could not defend him from the claws of the dark powers – that had been his foolish and arrogant supposition. Now they were seeking him out and all that he loved and had dedicated his life to – the Church – might be betrayed and destroyed by his own hand. Somehow a coin would come to him. In his heart Benelli knew this to be true and the certainty of it utterly overwhelmed him.

Let this cup pass from me.

Benelli was also sure that, this time, his prayer would be in vain. This time he would sample the depths of evil and all the temptation it entailed. Moreover, as an individual human being, he would sample it alone. The Head of the Holy Office would himself be judged. This anxiety gnawed at his soul.

There was a knock at the door. Benelli looked up from his desk, at the breathless face of a young priest. 'Cardinal, the Holy Father wants to see you. He has just finished confession.'

Benelli started to walk down the corridor. Had not St Paul once been Saul of Tarsus, intent on destroying the Faith? Had not St Peter, the rock on which the Church was built, denied his own Saviour three times? And what of Benelli himself? Would his fame rest on destroying the foundations of an institution that had taken two thousand years to build?

The Cardinal opened the door to the small private chapel and genuflected. At the altar knelt the Vicar of Christ, head of the Church on earth. As Benelli passed down the aisle the elderly man rose and turned to him. His deeply lined face gave no hint of what the pontiff felt about the greatest difficulty the Church had faced for a millennium.

Dressed in a simple vestment of white, the Pope sat down on a chair that had been placed just below the altar. John XXV was silent; his eyes watched Benelli steadily.

'Have you read the Confession of Pope Sylvester II?'

'Yes, Holy Father,' said Benelli. He also recounted the grisly news of Father David. At the end he asked: 'Do you believe that Sylvester told the truth when he said that no living human can withstand these last three Coins of Judas?'

'I fear so.'

'Then who can oppose this evil?' said Benelli.

'I do not know,' replied the pontiff.

'Could we not employ the Coin of Judas that belonged to Sylvester?' suggested Benelli. 'It's the one coin not buried in the tomb of St Peter. It may still have power; perhaps we could find it. We know from our records that the Pope was buried outside the Lateran Church here in Rome.'

'But suppose the last confession was not true? Suppose Sylvester died entrapped by evil? Will not this coin be one more deadly temptation? And who will wield it?'

Benelli's face reddened, as if with guilt. 'I was not suggesting that I use it, Holy Father.'

John gave him a shrewd glance. 'I was not suggesting it either. Only that we do not know anything of this coin and I suspect that its secret died with Sylvester.'

'Then what can we do? What will happen?'

The Pope paused to consider. 'The Church has had many enemies throughout its long history. But of temporal and spiritual enemies, it is the spiritual enemies that are, by far, the more dangerous. The power of this coin is also growing much more rapidly than I anticipated. It must be stopped before it is too late.'

While they were talking the door at the back of the chapel opened. Benelli waited as the newcomers came to stand beside him. They were the Father Confessor and Catherine of Benedetto.

So here we are, thought Benelli. Facing a power of evil by which the Saviour was delivered unto death. And these are the only people the Church has to defend it – one saint, the Pope's own confessor, and himself – a rather plump cardinal whose only hope had been to stand at the back when the gates of Paradise were opened and the glory of God was revealed to all mankind. What could these frail human instruments do against an Angel of Darkness, an emissary of one who had walked with God before the creation of this world?

'I want you to tell them of the prophecy of Pope Sylvester II,' said the pontiff in a quiet voice.

Benelli nodded and made to speak. Suddenly, a glimmer of understanding entered his mind. He realised now why the three of them had been selected by the pontiff. The choice had been a deliberate one. For had not Sylvester said that the Church would be brought down by one who was 'closest to the Pope'?

The prelate had supposed that this was a reference to himself – the one who, in administrative terms, was the most powerful man in the Vatican after the Holy Father. But these words could mean something else. The 'closest' could also be the one who knew the innermost secrets of the Pope, the Father Confessor. Or it could be the one who was closest to him in spirituality, Catherine of Benedetto. One of these three might betray the pontiff and destroy the Church. One of these might follow in the footsteps of Judas.

'Holy Father,' said Benelli, stammering, 'I'm not sure that we should divulge the prophecy.'

'Tell them.'

'But —'

'Tell them,' insisted the pontiff.

An overwhelming sadness overcame Benelli. He realised that John XXV himself did not know which of these three might betray him.

So, as commanded, Benelli told the other two of the prophecy. He also told them the news he had received from a convent in San Francisco. Of Marie and the child and of Marie's husband, Paul, and the fear that he was the human being through whom an inhabitant of hell would come into the world.

At the end, John XXV asked the nun, 'Can any human being resist this evil?'

She had bowed her head while Benelli had been talking. Catherine of Benedetto now raised it. 'I do not think so, Holy Father.'

'What will happen to Paul Stauffer?' queried Benelli impulsively.

'The Coin of Judas does not belong to this man,' said Catherine. 'He is only the instrument for it to come into this world. Its power is far, far greater. The one who really controls it has yet to appear and its spirit will use Paul to fulfil its will.'

'But why this man?'

'Who knows?' replied Catherine. 'But the mark of these coins is betrayal. Those who betray others and then seek to acquire the things of the spirit for their own aggrandisement.'

'What will happen?'

'The evil will destroy him and all that he loves. Then the spiritual influence behind the coin will seek out the Church. It will come here, a ravening wolf, and its power will be unconfined.'

'What is the spirit that controls this coin?' asked Father Thomas.

'I cannot see it yet.'

They were silent again. Finally, the pontiff spoke. 'Thank you, Catherine.'

The nun knelt before him to kiss the ring. Then she left the chapel.

'We must do everything we can to protect the woman and the child,' said John XXV. 'We must also confirm this really is a Coin of Judas.' He looked at the Father Confessor. 'Will you take up this burden? The decision is yours.'

After an almost imperceptible pause, the monk assented. He also departed once the Pope had blessed him.

Only Benelli and the pontiff remained. The former rose to his feet. His voice was bitter. 'Holy Father, did not Sylvester say that, of the last three coins, if one is held by the person closest to the Pope the Church itself will fall?' He hesitated, unwilling to go on. 'It could be one of us. However, if anyone is sent to determine the nature of this coin it should be I, for I will not betray this Church. I swear that I am no Judas.'

'What I have done, I have done,' replied the Pope simply. 'But I have a burden for you also, if you will take it. You must find the tomb of Sylvester. It may be our only hope.'

He gazed towards the altar. 'And soon, before the Angel of Darkness comes.'

CHAPTER TWENTY-SEVEN

*But in witchcraft, when adults are bewitched,
it generally happens to them that the devil
grievously possesses them from within for the
destruction of their souls.*

Malleus Maleficarum,
'Hammer of the Witches'

PAUL KNEW NOTHING OF THE visit of Father David
to his house, nor of the poor man's death. Even less of
the meeting of the Pope with his closest advisers. These
were things Helen had not the slightest intention of
divulging to him, since her desire was to bind him
in darkness. However, Paul's own mind, while overshadowed, had not yet been wholly obscured. He still
had free choice and he had to be persuaded to give this
up. Not even Helen could change what had been laid
down in the Dawn before the creation of all things.

Where does this force come from? he asked himself.

Paul had no doubt now that the coin had an extraordinary power emanating from a non-human source. He
was captivated by it, greedy for more experiences and
sensations, yet he was no fool.

What does this woman want from me? was the next
question.

Despite Helen's promises of yet more insight and wisdom, Paul needed to assure himself he could get off this cosmic merry-go-round, if so required. Just in case. Not that he believed in good and evil, of course.

So, when Helen disappeared to challenge the priest, Paul had continued his *liaison dangereuse* with Suzanne only for a short while longer. In the early evening he left her. However, instead of making his way home, he headed for the university. There were a number of things he had to find out. Things, he realised, Helen would be unlikely to discuss with him.

'We don't have many books on the occult, sir. But I'll have a look.' The young female librarian studied Paul, curious as to why he'd want to investigate such matters. The library at the University of San Francisco was well stocked. However, black magic and demonic possession were not – presently – topics on the university curriculum, so she had to search for the books. Paul sat in the library, a couple of students and a professor being the only other occupants. He closed his eyes and began to think.

First sensations, then auras, then the ability to travel on the astral planes. What was the effect of this on him? A wonderful sense of elation, of being free to explore the mysteries of the universe without the tiresome restrictions of his physical form. A joy that flowed from the increase of his knowledge to a superhuman level, and a craving for more. All positive features, he considered.

Any negatives?

Paul had noticed that his feelings of charity and mercy became almost non-existent the more he travelled on the astrals. He no longer cared about Marie, his daughter or, indeed, any other person. Instead, he became a dispassionate viewer, interested but unmoved. When he'd seen the child being torn to pieces in the Circus of Nero he'd viewed it with a detached curiosity. If it had been his own child, he'd have done the same. Superhumanity was placing him above the bonds, or beyond the bounds, of pity. Human emotions were leeching out of him, as vices made their secret entrance.

One further thing. Paul knew that Helen was helping him for some, as yet, hidden purpose. There were no free lunches in the universe, he imagined. However, the further out he went on the astrals the more he could divine something of her thoughts, or so it seemed. She'd also admitted to him she was only the guardian of the coin. If he was its master, he could control even her.

Could Paul do it? Dare he risk it? Of course he could. He could outwit even her. Besides, being on the astrals was like a drug – but hundreds of times more powerful than any human concoction. It capivated his mind completely, it shattered all his previous conceptions of human reality. It was truly miraculous. A forbidden wisdom. Yet, although Paul knew it not, his inner thoughts were already being manipulated by the real master of the coin from an unimaginable spiritual distance, beyond time and space. In his covetousness, the sorcerer's apprentice did not realise something rather important. The sorcerer was returning to his lair.

'These are the books you wanted, sir.'

Magic. That was a key. Aided by the power of the coin, Paul quickly absorbed the human record on the subject. He read of Hermes Trismegistus and the occult in Ancient Egypt, of Zoroastrianism and the Magi, of the Kabbala and the Jewish mysteries of God. He read too of the Philosopher's Stone, the Secret Doctrine and the workings of alchemy, of the Illuminati and the Words of Power; of mediums and mystics, of the tarot and divinatory arts, of dreams and clairvoyance. However, in all his reading, Paul discovered no mention of a coin.

Paul also found much of what he read profoundly unsatisfactory. All too often the spiritual power claimed was, in actuality, no more than a human power and one replete with folly and self-deception. Mediums who claimed to see far into the future yet had difficulty avoiding creditors, mystics whose visions would have been cured by a pair of contact lenses, numerologists who couldn't add up, astrologers who couldn't distinguish an eclipse from an ellipse, witches and warlocks whose IQ had given up the ghost before they ever saw one.

And yet, *and yet*, behind all the quackery and self-delusion there was something in it all – the hint of a more mysterious world. But wherein lay the secret to the coin itself?

'The library closes at ten,' reminded the librarian, packing up her things. He was the only one there now.

'I have a pass to stay on.'

The librarian glanced at it. 'That's fine. Oh, Professor Stauffer.' She recognised the name; this was the famous psychiatrist. 'Dreadful what happened, no?'

'What happened?'

'Didn't you see the evening news? It was all over the TV. Toni Brennan was murdered. Stabbed to death. They say his house was a bloodbath. Such a wonderful actor; so sad.'

Paul started to walk away from the table. The librarian was puzzled. 'Don't you want to know who did it?'

'I already know.' So, Julian had slaughtered his nemesis.

Paul returned to his seat in the library. He continued reading. He didn't care a fig for Julian Brennan, but he didn't have much time. Events around him were already quickening.

Sitting alone in the gloom with only a library desk lamp on, Paul read into the early hours, his mind preoccupied with evil and black magic. Perhaps something he'd previously thought didn't exist, did.

Paul devoured Scot's *Discoverie of Witchcraft*, the *Daemonologie* of James VI of Scotland, Sinistrari's *De Demonialitate*, Daugis's *Traité sur la Magie*, Mamor's *Flagellum Maleficorum*, Richalamus's *Liber de Insidiis Daemonium*, Bodin's *De la demonomanie des Sorciers*, Tarrega's *De Invocatione Daemonum*; all works dealing with 'your covenant with death, your agreement with hell', as the Book of Isaiah put it.

He also read of the re-emergence of black magic cults and witchcraft in Europe, particularly from the year AD 1000 onwards, together with the reappearance of Manichaeism – the belief that God was a mixture of both good and evil. He noted the frantic attempts of the Church to suppress this pernicious doctrine – noble efforts that, themselves, soon became twisted and perverted, so that the cure became as bad as, if not worse than, the disease. For the suppression of a false teaching led to widespread persecution of all those who sought to challenge the authority of the Church. *Heresy* became the dreaded watchword and it often had only one consequence – death.

Paul considered the witchhunts – a heady brew of high politics, religious fervour and superstition that raged across medieval Europe like the plague. Thousands of people, mainly old women and children, were hounded to their deaths by mobs or burnt at the stake by an ecclesiastical and political elect seized in the grip of a collective hysteria that the powers of evil had entered the world to drag humanity down to its perdition.

What was the end result? Witchcraft trials in Germany in which more than twenty thousand people perished, torture and burnings at the stake in Spain, the massacre of whole villages in France, the judicial doing to death of witches in Britain, the notorious Salem witch trials in the United States. In all, the slaughter of the innocent by a Church fighting against an imaginary evil.

Or was it imaginary? Why had such people as Francis Bacon, St Thomas Aquinas, Erasmus, Albertus Magnus and Popes Gregory XV and Benedict XII, to say nothing of the mystics and the early fathers of the Church, passionately believed in the physical reality of evil and the ability of the dark powers to enter into this world? And why had they believed it to such an extent that they had been prepared to extirpate it by the most savage and inhuman manner possible? The answer was encapsulated in the words of William Blackstone, possibly England's greatest lawyer, who declared in 1765:

> *To deny the possibility, nay, the actual existence of witch-craft, is at once flatly to contradict the revealed word of God in the various passages both of the Old and the New Testament.*

Paul sat back in his chair. He deliberated. These highly intelligent men were quite certain in their own minds that the devil and his works existed, and the Bible clearly declared it to be so. However, they had no scientific means of proving it. Come to think of it, nor did Paul, even after all his experiences on the astral planes. The spirit world was inexplicable within the parameters of man's thought processes; it seemed that the brain had been programmed to consciously reject it. Why?

Soon, Paul came to the Church's own text against witchcraft, the work *Malleus Maleficarum*, or the 'Hammer of the Witches', written by two priests, Krämer and Sprenger, in 1484, which was expressly approved by Pope Innocent VIII. It stated definitively:

> *The belief that there are such beings as witches is so essential a part of the Catholic faith that obstinately to maintain the opposite opinion manifestly savours of heresy.*

Citing the Book of Job, the text declared that the power of the devil was stronger than any human power, and that evil spirits had influence over the minds and bodies of men, as was clear from many passages in Holy Scripture, for:

> *Satan transforms himself into the shape and likeness of different persons and, in dreams, deluding the mind which he holds captive, leads it through devious ways.*

Paul looked up. Outside it was pitch-black and within the university building there was a deathly hush. Unconsciously, he drew the desk lamp closer to him, as if by way of comfort. He carried on.

The 'Hammer of the Witches' also made it clear that the act of departing from one's physical body could be illusory since the devil had extraordinary power over the minds of those who'd given themselves up to him. More ominously:

> *The devil knows the thoughts of our hearts; he can substantially and disastrously metamorphose bodies with the help of an agent; he can move bodies locally, and alter the outward and inner feelings to every conceivable extent;*

*and he can change the intellect and will of man, however
indirectly.*

Could Paul, using the power of the coin, in some mysterious way, be traversing a threshold that linked the temporal and divine worlds? What was the alternative? To scoff at the mystics, to cast aside the declarations of saints and popes? To declare the Bible plain wrong? To do what he'd been doing for all of his life?

Paul sat back and rubbed his eyes. It was three in the morning. What he'd read profoundly disturbed him. It was time to go home, to return to normality. He'd tell Helen that was enough. She'd been tricking him somehow. Soon he'd wake up from this illusion, this dream, this nightmare, whatever.

'I see you've been busy studying,' said Helen casually. 'My, we are conscientious these days.'

Paul blinked. She stood in the corner of the library, as he'd seen her before on the seventh astral, with a beauty so transcendent and shimmering it could not be adequately captured in human language.

'Books never teach you anything. So don't get muddled by what fools have written. See and judge for yourself. Now, are you coming?'

'Coming where?'

'To the eighth astral,' she said. 'You are still a child. You have so much to learn.'

'But . . .'

'But?' she spluttered, pointing at the texts in front of him in exasperation. 'That is nothing. What do these fools know of these things? Clogging their minds with rubbish. Have you any idea of the power of this coin? Just watch.'

Suddenly, before Paul's eyes, every book in the library

shot out of its shelf to whirl around in the air – an extraordinary paper maelstrom. He looked on, shattered at the sight of hundreds of thousands of books flying silently, not one hitting another, all perfectly co-ordinated by some mysterious hand. Then they returned to their shelves as neatly as before.

'Illusion? Do you still think this is an illusion?' Helen grasped the nearest tome and hurled it at him. 'Select any page and put your hand in it.'

'But . . .'

'Put your hand in it!' she screamed. Paul shrugged. She was mad. He inserted his hand in the open book. It vanished through the pages.

'Now withdraw it.'

He withdrew it. Crawling up his hand was a live scorpion.

'You have no faith, that is your problem,' Helen smirked. 'You don't even know what you want, Paul, but I do. This is nothing. Here's some more to help your faith. You want to be Head of Department and replace Ben. Done. You want Suzanne as your mistress. Done. *Anything* you want the coin will give you.'

Helen eyed a large shrub situated in one of the library alcoves. It burst into fire, the flames roaring dramatically. Then the inferno died away as quickly, leaving the plant wholly unaffected.

'Helen, I . . .'

All the lights in the library lit up, but not in pathetic neon this time. Instead, there was an efflorescence of colour that exceeded a rainbow in its depth and intensity. For added effect, birds appeared from its iridescent beams. Kingfishers, hummingbirds, parrots, golden eagles, flamingos – they circled, wove and dived within the light. Paul felt as though he was no longer in his body. He was there, with them, in their own miraculous world, a world that kept expanding all the time, stepping into yet another reality. Then it all departed as quickly as it had come.

'You're beginning to learn, Paul,' remarked Helen.

She drew close to him, and he felt his whole body consumed by an intense sexual allure. He wanted to possess her too, body and soul. Paul felt the coin in his hand. All human compassion, all concern for his own being and his soul vanished. He grinned. He could still outwit Helen, if needs be.

'Let's go,' he said.

So they left the library. Would that Paul had also read the words of St Augustine:

No Angel is more powerful than our mind when we hold fast to God.

It took some time for the sound of the phone to register in Florence's brain, since she'd fallen into a deep sleep. It had been a tiring day driving to Aspen, Colorado, and they'd turned in early. Locked in her dreams of holiday activities, Florence ignored both it and the agitated movement of Ben beside her. Finally, she awoke. Her husband had gone into the next room.

'Yes?' she heard him say gruffly. He returned to the bedroom. 'Florence!' He shook her. 'Wake up. You must talk to Marie. She's in an awful state.'

Florence got up and went to the phone. The call was a long one and tears poured down Florence's cheeks. Finally, she said, 'Can I speak to the mother superior?'

After many more minutes of conversation, Ben heard his wife say, 'We will come home.'

Florence put down the receiver and turned to her

husband. She recounted to him all that Marie had told her, as well as her conversation with the mother superior. Her husband was silent throughout.

'Can this be true? Is it possible?'

Ben got up and extracted a hotel message. 'There is something else you should know. I was going to tell you tomorrow.' She read about the murder of Toni Brennan.

'Why is this happening?'

Her husband drew back the curtains of the hotel room and looked up at the stars. For some inexplicable reason he knew in his heart what the truth was. Somehow, he'd known it for some time.

'Paul didn't speak out against Kramer even when he knew he was guilty,' he said in a forlorn voice. 'During the trial I think he realised he'd made a terrible mistake, but his pride and his desire for fame stopped him from saying anything.'

'He betrayed Melanie Dukes and her sister?'

Ben nodded. He stared into the night, incapable of saying more. Now Paul would face his own judgement.

CHAPTER TWENTY-EIGHT

It is said that his tomb foretells the death of a
Pope. Shortly before his demise it distils so much
water as to turn into mud the soil near it.
                                    William Goddell,
                              Chronicles Pontiniacensis

ANOTHER DAY IN ROME.

Signora Rossi, the plump Italian tour guide, paused.
She waited until the small group of American tourists
squinted up at the cathedral before them, its grand
façade surmounted with statues of Christ and his
Apostles. Then she raised her voice and began.

'The two most important churches in Rome are
St Peter's Basilica and the Lateran Church. While the
first is familiar to pilgrims, this one is much less well
known, even though it's only a couple of kilometres from
St Peter's, across the River Tiber.'

Signora Rossi glanced at her watch. They were ahead
of time. She could say a bit more before they went off
to the tile shop.

'St Peter's Basilica and this church have much in
common. Both were built by the Emperor Constantine
and in both many popes have been buried. However,
this church, the Church of St John Lateran, to give it its

full title, has had a very unlucky history. Throughout the centuries it has been the scene of much violence and murder. The edifice itself has been destroyed by fire at least twice and rebuilt a number of times.'

As she said this Signora Rossi caught sight of a man who hurried past her. She thought she recognised him. Surely that was the portly figure of Cardinal Benelli? But, of course, it couldn't be. He was in the simple black robe of a priest.

'Now, this cathedral boasts some important features. These include a side door which is opened once every twenty-five years for the Holy Year, a chapel with mosaics and a domed baptistry that has a magnificent octagonal roof dating back to the fourth century.'

Cardinal Benelli heard no more of the tour guide's patter as he moved away from Signora Rossi. He was aware of all the history she was expounding. However, the Lateran Church had one other important feature which she'd not mentioned. Important not to the tourists and the sightseers who poured through its doors on a daily basis, but vital to Benelli.

It was where Pope Sylvester II was buried.

Outside the main entrance to the church, workmen had roped off part of the pavement very close to the façade. Around it they'd erected a screen of black plastic sheeting. There was a small side entrance cut into one of the sheets and by it stood a black-cassocked priest. He smiled nervously as the Cardinal approached. He was not used to encountering such high dignitaries of the Church. He was even more surprised to see that Cardinal Benelli was not in his normal attire. Also, he looked unwell.

They both passed into the enclosure.

Inside, a number of flagstones had been lifted. A few

Vatican workmen gazed at the bare and sandy earth beneath, as they leant on their shovels and conversed. As soon as they saw the Cardinal they straightened up. Benelli said, almost in a murmur, 'Dig.'

Records in the Secret Archives indicated that Pope Sylvester II died on 12 May 1003 and had been buried under the portico, just outside the Lateran Church. It was also recorded he'd been buried hurriedly, late in the afternoon of a day that had been unseasonably gloomy and wet. No inscription had been placed over his grave. Not until three pontiffs later did Pope Sergius IV have an epitaph for Sylvester II engraved on a slab of white marble. This memorial was placed not on the tomb itself, which was hidden from sight underground, but inside the Lateran Church, attached to a pillar on the first aisle to the right (where it was still attached). Among other things the Latin inscription declared:

This spot, wherein are buried the remains of Sylvester, will give them up to the Lord when the Last Trumpet's sound shall announce his coming . . . Whoever you may be who turn your eyes to this monument say O! God Almighty have pity on him!

Why did Pope Sergius pen this strange epitaph and why was it placed in such a manner that it *failed* to disclose the actual location of the tomb? The explanation was well known in medieval times. When Sylvester II died, such was his notoriety, so powerful the rumours of his mastery of the black arts, that none, not even the pontiff who succeeded him, dared place an inscription over his grave. Even in death the rumours did not stop; and they soon spread to cover the tomb as well. A learned cleric, John the Deacon, declared in the twelfth century:

*Even in the driest weather, and though it is not in a
damp place, drops of water flow from it to the astonishment
of everyone.*

And Bartholomew Platina, the librarian who'd looked
into the folio containing the last confession of Sylvester II,
had asserted even more forthrightly in his *Lives of the Popes*:

*From the clattering of this Pope's bones, as from the sweat
or rather moisture of his tomb, people are wont to gather
portents, and those most manifest of the approaching
death of any Pope, and this is hinted in the epitaph on
his tomb.*

Perhaps strangest of all, the Latin epitaph which had
been written by Pope Sergius for his notorious predecessor was deliberately ambiguous. For the words '*ad soni-
tum*' in Latin could refer either to the Last Trumpet or
to a sound within the tomb, and the words '*venturo
Domino*' could refer to the Great Judge in Heaven or to
the next Pope.

Thus the inscription itself lent credence to the rumour
that the tomb of Sylvester would foretell the imminent
death of the Pope by a noise arising from within. Even
in death, the persona of Sylvester II was as mysterious as
he'd been in life. Benelli recalled what he'd read in the
Tower of the Winds about Sylvester's funeral and how
loud groans were heard from the coffin.

Had Sylvester died in sanctity or as the creature of the
devil? wondered the Cardinal. If the former, why hadn't
they buried him inside the Lateran Church, but outside?
And why was there such a delay in preparing an inscription for his tomb? He feared the worst.

Benelli stood by the presumptive burial place and

watched the workmen. Despite digging down more than a metre of thick clay, they found nothing. They continued to excavate. Finally, the Cardinal could wait no longer; he'd another appointment. He told the priest to report to him if they discovered anything.

Late in the afternoon there was an urgent knock on the door. The priest had returned. However, Benelli couldn't be disturbed. He had a meeting with a high dignitary of the Russian Orthodox Church and it was another hour before the Cardinal was able to dispense with his guest. After he did so, he came out quickly into the corridor. The young priest got up from a wooden bench. Benelli looked at his anxious face.

'Well?'

'We've found a marble sarcophagus, a few metres to the left of where we first dug. The lid contains the pontifical arms and a reference to the Pope.'

'Yes, yes. And?' Benelli said impatiently.

'We didn't dare open the coffin without your instructions.'

'I'll come straight away.'

They both hurried over to the Lateran Church. It was late in the afternoon and the November weather had taken a turn for the worse. A storm was approaching and the plastic sheets of the screen were being relentlessly tugged about by the wind. The marble coffin, much discoloured over the centuries, lay within a deep hole that had been dug around it. On its lid it bore the pontifical arms and then, '*Sylvestri pp Secundo*'.

'Why is there water in the pit?'

A workman standing in the hole shrugged his shoulders. 'Don't ask me. It was as dry as anything when we started. When we got to the ground level of the tomb, water began to appear.'

'Could it be a drainage pipe?'

'We haven't found anything,' said the workman, 'and it hasn't rained.'

Benelli realised that they did not know of the ominous legend concerning water in the tomb of Pope Sylvester. Just as well.

'Open the coffin.'

The workmen started to insert wooden blocks under the marble lid so as to be able to cantilever it to one side. Benelli looked up. The sky was darkening as twilight approached. Rain began to fall, slowly at first, then it pelted down. Soon, the Cardinal was soaked, but he wouldn't go inside despite the young priest's protestations.

'This may take a while,' the foreman shouted up from the pit. 'These tops are very heavy and they were usually sealed down in case of plague.'

'Hurry,' said Benelli. 'The tomb must be covered over by nightfall.'

The workmen continued their exertions. Finally, the lid of the sarcophagus began to inch its way across the coffin. By now the storm was breaking. Thunder cracked overhead.

'What's that?' said one of the workmen, startled. They looked towards the far end of the barrier. A plastic sheet was flapping about furiously in the wind. However, it wasn't that to which their attention was drawn. An animal stood there. A large black dog watched them intently, its lips drawn back in a ferocious snarl.

'How did it get there?'

'Ignore it. Carry on, carry on,' cried Benelli urgently.

At last, the massive lid of the coffin was edged to one side. Twilight came upon them. One of the workmen helped Benelli descend the slippery sides into the pit.

Taking a torch, the Cardinal ordered the worker to climb out, so that only he might see the secret of the tomb. Around the men the storm raged.

His heart in his mouth, Benelli bent close to the lid. An icy blast of air struck him as he peered into the sepulchral darkness.

The tomb was empty.

CHAPTER TWENTY-NINE

*For it is the practice of Scripture and of speech
to name every unclean spirit Diabolus, from
Dia, that is two and Bolus, that is morsel;
for it kills two things, the body and the soul.*
                                        Malleus Maleficarum,
                              'Hammer of the Witches'

THE FORCES OF DARKNESS WERE gathering strength.
They had to act quickly since they knew the Church
would try to defeat them before the coin had achieved
its full potency. Yet everything depended on one human
being and his preparedness to become a player in
a cosmic play that far transcended even his wildest
dreams.

After Paul's late-night reading in the university library
and the reappearance of Helen, they headed back
towards his house. Paul drove slowly. He had much on
his mind.

'I know what you're thinking,' said Helen quietly.

'What?'

'You're wondering where your wife is.'

'Is she in the house?'

'No,' said Helen. 'She's at a convent with your daughter. She went there because she's very confused about

things. Of course, Marie's no longer concerned about me or the coin,' she lied. 'She's assumed it was just a hysterical reaction on her part. After all, spirits don't exist, do they? No, she believes you're going to leave her for another woman. Well, are you? What do you make of Suzanne, Paul? Everything in a woman that you've desired, isn't she? I haven't been watching you, I promise.' She giggled.

'How do you know what I was thinking?' said Paul. 'And how come Marie knows about Suzanne?'

Helen chided him. 'I may only be a spirit,' she said, 'but I can read a little of your thoughts. Oh, and Marie knows about Suzanne because your friend Ben told her. One of the student officers saw you going into Suzanne's room and informed him. Gossip is a cosmic quality, I'm afraid.'

'Bastard.' Paul would have something to say to him. He wondered how Ben would react when Helen fulfilled her promise and Paul became Head of Department. He relished the thought.

As they drove, Paul switched his attention to his companion in the car. He'd begun to understand something of the spirit world. Helen could occupy the bodies of others once they allowed her an entrance. Also, in his case, Helen could read some of his thoughts, but not all of them. Why? What was preventing her? It had to be the Coin of Judas; it was more powerful than she was. Helen had confirmed this when she'd told him she couldn't progress beyond the ninth astral since no human being could. However, she'd also indicated that it was possible for Paul. Inevitably, there must come a point in this drama where Helen could no longer control him or the visions he was experiencing. What would Paul do to her when he was her master?

'Why don't you tell me more about yourself? You've been very quiet on that score.'

'Sure,' Helen replied, seemingly without concern. 'We can chat about that later. In any case, using the coin, you'll soon find out.'

Paul deliberated on this. Unexpectedly, he stopped the car. He wanted to test her reaction to his latest idea. 'I want to go to the convent.'

'Oh, I wouldn't do that,' said Helen nonchalantly.

'Why not?'

'You won't be able to get in.' She stared out of the window, her mind elsewhere.

'Why not? There might be someone about, even at this hour.'

'I don't mean that,' said Helen. 'You won't be able to get in because all forces in the universe act and counteract. It's the same with spirits. They react to the presence of others.'

'Good and evil spirits?'

Helen threw back her head. She crowed long and loudly. 'I was waiting for that witticism but it was a long time coming. Tut, tut.' She wagged a finger. 'Remember, I was at your lecture. Since you don't believe in evil, how can evil spirits exist?'

Paul had to smile. 'But they do, don't they? Evil spirits do exist?'

'No, of course not,' said Helen. 'It's more complex than that. You can't just divide the universe into good and evil: those who created it were more imaginative. You'll soon see.' She paused. 'Hey, you're not looking too well. I'll drive you back home. Cars, don't you just love them?' she exclaimed delightedly. 'One modern thing I really like. Great for killing people with.'

Helen drove. Soon, they reached the poorer parts of

San Francisco. Paul felt a profound depression come upon him as he gazed from the car window. He reflected on life. To tell the truth, this world was a shabby place for all its apparent glitter. Nearly two thousand years since the Roman Empire and not much to show for it. Roads little better than in imperial times, houses more cramped and ugly, citizens less literate, and a modern way of life that made people insatiably greedy for more and yet never satisfied. Two thousand years and mankind hadn't wasted a minute in screwing up the planet. Would that he were a god and he could wipe the slate clean. He glanced at Helen.

'I agree,' she said sadly, 'it's nothing to write home about. The system's running downhill at an ever faster rate. Believe you me, I've seen it all.'

They drove through the red-light district. A drunk was fighting over a bottle of liquor with a hoodlum, drug dealers were earnestly gabbling into their mobile phones, and a child prostitute was trying to persuade the most wretched of men to go with her so she could get a bed for the night. Paul sighed. What a world – what an unwonderful world – so shabby, cheap, false, replete with human mismanagement and corruption.

'I'll get you next time,' called out Helen, as she narrowly missed a pimp in flared jeans and purple shirt. Then, 'You're lucky, Paul. You have the choice. With the coin you can change it all. It's a gift given to you.'

'By God or by the devil?'

'Oh, don't be so silly. Neither exists, not in the way humans think of them. Anyway, what does it matter? The coin is a gift. You have come a long way for a person who never believed in any of this. The choice is yours: freedom to live as you want or slavery. No spirit can take that away from you. I made my decision,' she mused in a dreamy voice, 'a long time ago.'

'And you never regretted it?'

'Do I look regretful? All humans, one day, have to elect their own destiny in the universe. I regret nothing.' She leant over and kissed him on the cheek. 'We only come to a few people,' she whispered. 'Don't let the opportunity slip.'

They drew up outside Paul's house. Momentarily, he felt a deep longing to see his wife and daughter again. Yet, in an instant, the emotion passed. He forgot them; he didn't need them now, they didn't need him. He couldn't resist the fatal attraction of the coin with its sweet entreaties of creating a better world.

After all, what was he leaving behind? A reality, yes, the world was a reality, but a poor-quality one – like being brought up in a rundown bar hidden away in a back street. Paint peeling from the walls, tacky pictures, stale beer. It was time to get up from behind the counter and step outside. To get back to the bright regions of the astrals – to dip in and out of life, of time, of other worlds. That was true reality, not here. And whoever was helping him didn't matter; Paul still believed in neither God nor the devil, despite all that he'd experienced. He'd just had a lucky break – that was all. Someone was offering him a prize. Paul wondered how many other people around the world were being offered such a prize like him. Who knew?

Opening the front door to his house, they stepped inside.

'Come with me. We need help to get to the eighth astral.'

'Why can't I just use the coin and close my eyes?' said Paul.

They passed through the kitchen and descended down some steps. Helen shook her head. 'You could do but it would reveal the source of your power. You see, the eighth astral is beyond the reach of the vast majority of human beings, so others would quickly detect you. We need to hide things. Trust me.'

Paul surveyed the almost empty cellar, unaware that the place had witnessed the recent martyrdom of Father David.

'Turn off the lights.'

They stood in darkness. Soon, Paul felt the weight of the coin in his hand. It had come to him again. Gradually, the night around Helen dissolved, to be replaced by a deep, yellowish glow. Entranced, Paul watched as her form and features started to alter. Her clothes too. No twentieth-century human any longer. Instead, a woman clothed in a simple tunic with gold bracelets about her arms and a crown of olive leaves in her hair. She had the majesty of a priestess from a pagan temple of ages past.

Paul's attention shifted as lines began to form on the cellar floor. In front of his eyes, a golden shaft of fire traced out a luminous Pentacle of Solomon. Little by little, a five-pointed star formed, drawn by an invisible hand. When it was complete, a circle emerged to connect its points. Then another, slightly wider. Within these two bands, mystical runes started to appear, divine names not recognisable in any mortal script. As they emerged they flared up in the darkness.

Finally, the pentacle was finished, its clear brilliance bedazzling the eyes like a diamond, two circles of fire encompassing a star of pure white light. Paul was swept up in the glory of it. Only after a while did he notice Helen. Her face was both regal and ancient, with a demeanour and wisdom far surpassing puny human beings.

'Step inside.'

'Why?' asked Paul, though no words were spoken. As before on the astral, they communicated by thought alone.

'I've already explained,' Helen replied impatiently, 'the further out on the astrals you go, the greater the power and the deeper the trance. This power attracts others. They're drawn to it and crave it. The pentacle is to protect you.'

As usual, Helen spoke only half the truth. Those on the outermost astrals, whether good or evil, would be able to sense the enormous energy radiating from the Coin of Judas and so determine the physical location of Paul in the world. For this reason Helen had drawn a pentacle. However, unlike the Pentacle of Solomon used by sorcerers of old to protect them from evil spirits, Helen had inverted the mystic signs so that they formed a wall of deception against the powers of good.

Paul looked about him. On the far side of the pentacle emerged figures, dressed in the same garb as Helen. He couldn't determine whether they were human or spirit forms. Paul watched as Helen crossed the two rings of fire. They parted as she walked through them. She stood in the centre.

'Enter.'

Paul still held back, fearful that he'd be vaporised by the intense heat. Also, something inside him warned him that his human persona was fast ebbing away. He was becoming more spirit than man.

'Come.' Helen held her hand in supplication to him. 'I'll look after you; have no fear.'

Drawn by the intense attraction of the coin to its guardian, Paul edged closer and closer to the rings. He closed his eyes.

Then he stepped inside.

For an age, Paul felt nothing, apart from an immense, raging heat as if he'd been thrown into the centre of a furnace. His mind conjured up the image of a vast circle of fire suspended in space. It began to rise up so high that Paul couldn't see where this molten cylinder ended. It irradiated the very core of his being without consuming him. He felt as if he were no more than a clay figure being burnished in a potter's kiln.

Paul could discern Helen beside him. Her physique had changed once again. It looked neither male nor female. Rather, it had a crystalline nature, as if the flames had stripped away layer after layer of her endless incarnations until only an essence remained. Her expression registered no emotion, no flicker of movement. Yet he could read her thoughts as he began to access her mind. It was like plugging in to a vast computer.

The ring of fire began to expand outwards as a new one formed. Then another. At last Paul could see eight huge rings of fire, one below the other, diminishing into a central core, great spinning concentric circles like the movements of the planets. As Paul passed through each ring, he discerned myriad forms of existence, human and non-human, animal and non-animal. Forms that altered with the consistency of a swirl of gases. Unlike the River Lethe that Paul had experienced on the seventh astral, and which reflected the passing of time on earth, these swirling plumes of heat exuded a stellar creation and an endless cycle of birth and transmutation – of beings, of planets, of minds.

Helen turned to him. They stood face to face. Slowly,

she stepped inside him, inside the very being he comprised. They became one, melded together by heat and act of will. Paul possessed her experiences as if they were his own. Fragments of her reign long ago. Of a vast temple and servitor priests paying homage to her, of deep caverns and forgotten places on earth, of men and women who'd been Helen's playthings and slaves, of bloody wars and battles waged on human and spirit planes throughout the centuries, of her deep knowledge and wisdom.

Paul cleaved to this insight like a child instinctively latching onto the pap of its mother, without any conscious thought. He was her and she was him, inseparable in time and space. It seemed as if they'd always been like this, interlocked and entwined while the great rings of fire spun about them. At some juncture the images of the rings vanished. They were back on earth, though without human form.

'Now you will begin to see how it all works.' The voice was Helen's. Or was it his? They were the same.

Moving as Helen directed, they approached the city of San Francisco, weaving like an eagle through the clouds. Paul felt the flow of the wind, the glitter of car lights and the massy outline of skyscrapers below. There was no separation of the senses. He realised that neither he nor Helen was physically on earth, nor did they even possess a spirit body. They existed in thought alone and when Helen spoke to him, it was his own thought.

'Strange, isn't it?' said Helen. 'Our beings are fused together. Takes a bit of getting used to. Now I'll show you what spiritual power is about. As on earth, a spirit has servants to command, an empire to rule, people to enforce obedience from. The only differences to a temporal ruler are the means of control and the absoluteness of the power. Human beings have no idea of the degree to which we control them. I'll show you one or two tricks of the trade.'

Without any sense of motion, time or distance, they were inside a room. It was a disco in downtown San Francisco – the Temptation of Eve. Whirling about in the kaleidoscopic lights were men and women dressed up for a Saturday night's entertainment. They were decked out in the most lurid of costumes – leather ensembles with spikes and chains, black bodystockings and mini-skirts, face masks and pink fur. All around them was the clink of glass, cries of pleasure and the deep, deep, throb of the music.

'All trying to be someone else,' said Helen. 'They don't know they can be anyone in the universe. They are gods, or rather, they were. Come, let's go in. Inside them. *Into them.*'

Paul began to dance. It was not him dancing, of course. It was a professional stripper whirling about the centre of the disco floor. However, Paul was inside her being. He felt the weight of a woman's breasts for the first time, the tightness of the latex that cut into her buttocks as she swayed to the music, the press of a kiss on her mouth. Paul thought her thoughts, savoured her cravings and desires. Like a thief he perused the inmost secrets of her persona, her hopes and fears. He was inside her temple, even though she was oblivious to him and to his reading her mind.

'Watch that human,' said Helen to Paul, though they now shared the same existence. A pretty girl was approaching the bar, weaving her way through the crowd. She was lithe and slim, with a thick mane of blonde hair; twenty-three years old. At the counter was another woman, ordering drinks, who looked just like her. She turned to her approaching companion.

At that instant Paul felt a tremendous jolt, as if someone had momentarily switched on his mortal emotions again. It was not only disconcerting, it was terrifying to feel vulnerable once more.

'Thought you'd be surprised,' said Helen. 'Look who it isn't?'

The girl at the bar ordering drinks was Laura Dukes and the person who'd approached her, her twin, Melanie.

'Let's see what really happened,' said Helen. Then Paul and Helen were inside Melanie, the girl about to be murdered.

'Hi, sis,' said Laura. 'Found any good men yet?'

Melanie touched her sister's arm affectionately. They were both half drunk.

'No,' replied Melanie with a laugh, 'but tonight's my lucky night. How's Danny?'

They contemplated Laura's current boyfriend. He was arguing furiously with someone at the bar, slamming his fist against the wall. Laura groaned. 'Looks as though he's going to get into a fight as always. I'd better go.' She kissed her sister. 'Be careful.'

Melanie crossed the dance floor, navigating her way through the mêlée of people. She placed her drink on a small bar table. As she did so, a man came up to her.

'I couldn't help noticing you.'

Melanie glanced at him. He was a thickset individual with long black hair tied back into a ponytail. She liked what she saw at first appraisal: a big frame, large eyes with a well-shaped nose and chin. Hunky, she thought.

'I have a boyfriend.'

'Sure you do,' said Karl Kramer easily. 'You're a beautiful woman and I'm just a clumsy fellow. But I'd still like to chat with you. No harm in that, is there?'

'I suppose not,' smiled Melanie. She didn't have a boyfriend at the moment. She bent down to pick up her bag. He wasn't too bad-looking, anyway. Nice bum. 'Like a dance then?'

'A pleasure,' said Kramer.

Helen and Paul stayed with Melanie that night. They experienced her thoughts and emotions as she left the disco, Karl Kramer gripping her hand in his. Melanie was happy. She liked this new guy. She wouldn't go to bed with him tonight, but probably the next time. After saying farewell to her sister, Melanie stood on the disco steps before letting the door swing back. She caught a final glimpse of Laura clutching a tray of drinks. Something prompted Melanie to turn back to the warmth inside, but she didn't.

'Let's get some fresh air,' Kramer remarked.

'OK.'

They started to walk towards Kramer's car. The two spirits watched them.

'I don't want to go any further,' said Paul to Helen in his thoughts.

'But we must,' replied Helen. 'Now you know that Kramer killed her after all. Bit of a misjudgement on your part, wasn't it? Still, we all make silly mistakes. Don't worry about it. Let's wait and see what happens next.'

'No.'

'Let's.'

As the couple neared Kramer's mobile van with its darkened windows, Kramer kissed Melanie and she responded. They stopped, locked in a deep embrace.

'How about a ride?'

'No.' Melanie shivered slightly. She rubbed her shoulders, covered only by a thin satin blouse. 'I promised my sister not to leave without her. I want to go back to the disco. It's cold out here.'

'All right,' replied Kramer in an easy-going tone. 'Let me just get something out the van.'

They walked towards it.

Helen and Paul experienced Melanie's every thought. The young girl had no fear, not even when Kramer opened the van door. Then he turned and came stealthily towards her. However, Melanie didn't see him. Her attention was directed to a blister on her foot, the result of too much dancing. As she straightened up from inspecting it, Kramer suddenly reached out and clamped a chloroformed rag to her mouth.

Paul experienced an agonising panic that surged through Melanie's being as she struggled frantically in the hands of her murderous captor. The lamb and the wolf.

'Mother of God,' she prayed. 'Mother of God, please help me.' But her efforts were in vain and her consciousness began to fade.

'Stop,' said Paul.

'Wait,' said Helen. 'It gets much better.'

'No.' In an instant they were outside Melanie's mind. They watched, invisible spectators, as Kramer thrust the inert body into the van. Paul wanted to stop from happening the horrific desecration he knew would occur to the girl.

'Oh, forget it,' said Helen nonchalantly. 'You're looking at the past. Besides, you'll miss the best bit. It gets very exciting. Kramer was quite inventive. Just wait and see.'

'The past? Who can change the past?' cried out Paul desperately.

'God knows.' Helen laughed.

That night Paul and Helen travelled endlessly on the eighth astral. They entered the minds of human beings, plugging in to their existence for a scintilla of time and reading their innermost thoughts – an old man dying from liver cancer in hospital, a security guard chasing a burglar, a weary commuter on his way home, a belligerent taxi driver, a young boy selling his body for a packet of cigarettes, an old lady sitting in her apartment recalling those she'd betrayed in a civil war, a despairing girl hurling herself under a train.

In doing so, influenced by the power of the coin, Paul's humanity departed from him. He became wholly unconcerned by what he saw, as if viewing creatures – mere ants – from another world. After all, who cares what happens to a single ant, or even five billion of them?

For Paul, such an experience was worth every other possession in the world. It was beyond price. He was each of these individuals, living their lives within them, without their knowledge. Despite that, he'd no responsibility for their bodies, their suffering, nor their ends. It was wholly parasitic; the ultimate trip. Wisdom and insight without any unpleasant consequences.

'Helen, who are you?'

'I'm a woman of thirty-one. That's the body I inhabit. She's a prostitute, a bit rundown, so I'll have to switch soon. As a spirit, you need a human body if you want to continue living on earth. If that body dies, you die to the world as well.'

'So you possess human beings and transfer from them before they die?'

'Yes,' said Helen succinctly. 'When you're inside them you slowly absorb their spirit. It's like drinking water from a well. When it's exhausted they die, so you need to move on.'

'How long have you been doing this?'

'Nearly two thousand years. Every twenty years or so I change body. I don't like old people,' said Helen casually. 'I prefer good-looking ones. Then, just before they die, or if I get bored, I change. Other spirits have survived for much longer.'

'So evil spirits roam around, possessing people and taking them over?'

'More or less,' Helen replied, 'though I don't think the word "evil" is quite the right one, do you? It's like on earth, the strongest take what they want, the weak go to the wall. That's the nature of things. But the pleasure is in your control over them. It's almost absolute.'

'And Suzanne?'

'She's my lover at the moment. I also control her mind.'

'Does she know it?'

'No. Spirits don't disclose themselves save in very rare cases. However, some people are dedicated to us as young children so our hold over them is much greater. Suzanne is one of them. She knows I exist as her lover in human form but she doesn't know that I have power over her to fulfil my purposes, to kill her even. Of course, if you told her she'd never believe you. It's completely outside her frame of reference, just as it was outside your own, until recently. Kramer's the same, but he's more perceptive. His drives make him so.'

'And if you died?'

'If I died without my spirit getting into another body my influence over Suzanne or Kramer would be released, until another spirit inhabited them. Often, a number of spirits can occupy the same body. But I've given her to you, Paul, to do what you will with her. The problem is, if you don't keep a good control over them they tend to follow their own inclinations. They need a lot of watching.'

'How?'

'Look,' said Helen. They were in Suzanne's bedroom. She was cuddled up in bed, sleeping peacefully. However, she wasn't alone. Her arms were round the body of Dave Rattinger, her fellow student in the psychiatry class who'd been keen on her since the beginning. That night he'd got lucky.

'Suzanne couldn't find you,' Helen explained. 'She thought you'd gone back to your wife. Rattinger dropped by with a book by way of an excuse and she decided that she needed some sexual company. I'm afraid you're forgotten, Paul. As her master, you can, of course, make her remember. Wake her up and impose your will on her. Make her scream at him and throw him out of bed.'

Paul concentrated on Dave Rattinger. He wanted to instil a mortal fear in him. However, nothing happened to his enemy in love.

'Why can't I control him? Why can't I make him wake up?'

'Because he's not possessed,' said Helen. 'You can perceive his thoughts but you can't alter them internally. Only externally, using other human beings, can you tempt him into doing what you want and then slowly take him over if he gives in. But it's better to go for the weaker ones. Imagine yourself as a wolf chasing sheep. To get an easy meal you pick off the weaker prey. Possession by a spirit is the same.'

'You eat human beings to survive?'

'Their spiritual energy, yes. You're not the top of the food chain, you know. Just as you eat so we need food. But not physical food. Besides, what are you worried about? Most people don't really value their lives, but we can use their life force to ascend to the higher astrals.'

'You killed Johann Hermanns so I could give the Jung lecture in his place?'

'Of course, because I knew you wanted it. I like to help friends of mine to fulfil their desires. Car accidents, plagues, air crashes – it's all the same to us. The net is cast when people least expect. Which,' said Helen, 'brings me to the final stage.'

'What happens after that?'

'The payback.' She cackled. 'But first, let's enjoy ourselves. Let me show you what it's all about. It's dog eat dog on the spirit planes, just like in the human world. The more powerful spirits dominate the lesser ones. But oh, my darling, it's so much more fun. Come with me.'

They passed from Suzanne's room into the outside world. Helen was searching for someone. She soon spotted him. He was a crack addict, a young man, perhaps twenty, not much older. Scruffy, with needle-thin arms, he was staggering towards an apartment block in a poor area of San Francisco, drugged out of his mind. As he slouched down against a wall Helen and Paul entered him. His thoughts were rambling, incoherent, pitiful and self-deluded.

'See?' said Helen. 'A total wreck. He used to sell drugs and killed a young child. He beat up Suzanne once. Well, there's nothing more for him in this world, a clapped-out old car that won't go much further. But watch, you can still get some mileage out of him. It's just like chariot racing.'

A gang of youths walked past the addict as they made

towards the apartment block. They ignored the heap by the side of the road. Yet, prompted by Helen, the addict sat up. Staggering to his feet he began to weave about the sidewalk, screaming racist abuse at them. Astonished at his audacity, they came over, wielding knives and a baseball bat.

'What did you say?'

The addict spat at the youths; then he began to run away, Helen spurring him on. Suddenly, Helen let go of control of his mind so that the addict's instincts became his own again. The bravado she'd superimposed on his psyche turned to utter panic as he ran for his life, astonished by his earlier decision to pick such a suicidal fight.

As their victim ran, Helen and Paul held on like riders perched on the back of a hunted animal, thriving on the fear the hapless creature gave off, drinking deep of the terror flowing from him. It was as if they were draining a vessel. It invigorated them, making them feel omnipotent.

The gang's boots rang out on the sidewalk as they raced, knives in hand. They caught up with their victim at a bridge. Vengeance was swift: cries of pain as heavy boots smashed into the addict's head, the sound of ribs cracking, blood flowing from a knife wound to his arm.

While he started to bleed profusely, Helen and Paul experienced the perverted ecstasy of evil. For them it was better than any drug in the world – like in a bullfight, the elation and joy of seeing a gored bull fall, stagger to its feet and fall again. Absolute control and no responsibility – unto death.

Now the addict was off once again, stumbling and weaving about. He didn't get far.

'Steady, steady,' said Helen. The gang of youths stood over the bloodied figure, content to leave him half alive.

But Helen forced him to sit up. Ruthlessly, she blotted out his instinct for survival. 'Your turn,' she shrieked delightedly to her accomplice.

For a moment Paul wanted to stop. However, he felt just like a Roman Emperor before a crowd in the Colosseum. They were staring at him expectantly, baying for blood, waiting for him to give the order. In front of his dais was a fallen gladiator. What to do? Satiated as he was with self-love and power, it was obvious; there was no choice. The seeds of pride within him had grown into a great tree. Mentally, Paul gave the thumbs down, though it was Helen, using the power of the coin, who did the dirty work.

'Fucking poofs,' the addict croaked at his persecutors.

The knife went into the boy's chest so deep that the haft broke. As a river of blood jetted out of him, so the boy's spirit left his flesh. It glimmered faintly, a pathetic thing, already much drained of its power. Helen and Paul stepped out of his body as he was dying. They saw the spirit rise up before them.

'Taste,' said Helen.

Ravenously they fell on it, quaffing the former human being's energy into themselves, like a huge draught of fresh red wine. Paul was punch-drunk with pleasure – the joy of an animal devouring its prey, just as the hungry lion had gnawed at the body of the child in the Circus. It was repast with all the elation of a sexual release that went on and on. His concern for the human was no more than that of a carnivore eating. It was the way of the universe: one life for another. The devils feasted.

'Now for the *pièce de résistance*,' said Helen. This one she'd deal with. Paul would still be too squeamish, but he was coming along nicely.

* * *

312

Ben rubbed his eyes.

They'd been driving since three. It was just past six and getting light. Ben looked across at his wife's face. It was etched with lines of tension and she was silent. That, in itself, was remarkable. Ben knew what Florence was thinking; after twenty-six years of marriage it was difficult not to. She was desperately worried about Paul, Marie and their child and she was still very uncertain about what had happened, just as he was. However, the Stauffers needed help and Ben and Florence would give it unstintingly. It was simple: they loved that family.

Florence cleared her throat. 'When you said "it's possible" what did you mean?'

Ben shrugged. 'It's possible, Florence. One thing many years of psychiatry has taught me is to discount nothing. In truth, we know so little – almost nothing – of the human psyche and how it actually perceives things. Carl Jung always maintained that there are psychic truths which can neither be explained nor proved in any physical way. Besides, evil is a spiritual condition, not just a psychological reality. It has a deeper source.'

'And religiously, you believe it?'

'Yes,' said Ben, 'though, of course, Paul never did.' He shrugged. 'The Protestant and Catholic Churches accept the doctrine of evil, as do the Jews. And the Bible makes it clear that Christ cast out demons, which were clearly spiritual entities of some sort. However, I've never really thought how these things might actually take place. It's something none of us wants to contemplate, since it would completely change the whole nature, and direction, of our lives.'

'Do you think Kramer's evil?'

Ben nodded. He didn't want to discuss him. It was too unsettling, what with everything else.

'What will you do?'

'I'll talk with Paul as soon as we get there.' Ben hesitated. Then he said casually, 'Florence, it's best you know now. He's going to be appointed Head of Department. The university board decided it yesterday.'

She looked at him aghast. Ben continued calmly, 'He's a better psychiatrist than I am. I think they made the right decision. My secretary told me.'

Florence started to weep.

'Now, now,' he said. 'You mustn't worry. It's not important.' He caught sight of a diner. 'Let's stop.'

They pulled into the car park of a small shopping mall. Florence's face was still streaked with tears. 'What do you want?'

'Just coffee.'

Florence got out of the car. Then she stopped and turned back to him. Prompted by the mercy of her guardian angel she told him the truth. 'I love you, Ben, and I'm so proud of you.'

Surprised, his voice caught in his throat. 'Honey, I love you too.' Their hands touched.

'I just wanted you to know that, and that it will never change.'

Ben smiled affectionately. She was overwrought. He watched her cross the internal road to the shopping mall. Despite all her foibles he loved her so much. He closed his eyes in weariness.

Two spirits looked on.

'These people mean to destroy us,' commented Helen. 'Your friend Ben told Marie about Suzanne. Soon, they'll turn your wife and daughter against you. They'll get others to destroy the pentacle and to take away the coin. It's them or us, Paul. In their case, I can't influence their minds internally. I need to influence the mind of an agent. Luckily, there's always a few of them around.'

Florence quit the shopping mall. In her hand she clutched her purchases. She was thinking of Rachel. When she saw her again, Florence would hold her so tightly she'd never let go. She'd do everything for her, defend her even before the gates of hell. Florence stepped out into the road.

Ben awoke. He glanced out of the car window, still half asleep. He watched as a camper van came off the highway. It drove into the shopping mall, reducing speed. The driver started to turn into a parking bay and Florence halted to let it pass. At that precise moment she looked across to her husband in his car. Her gaze was fixed on him; he could feel it. It was a look of farewell.

It happened in an instant. The van lurched backwards, accelerating rapidly. Florence turned to catch sight of it, but it was too late.

'Oh, my God, my God,' whispered Ben, as she went under its wheels.

One hour later, the nurse at the nearby hospital came and sat beside Ben in the corridor. She knew what had occurred. They were also treating the driver of the van for shock. His foot had slipped on the accelerator, he said. A freak accident, completely unanticipated. The police were interviewing him, since it was a stolen vehicle and he had a long prison record. The nurse took Ben's hand. People swirled around them, talking loudly. Yet Ben neither saw nor heard them.

'I am so very sorry,' said the nurse gently. Tears came into her eyes. 'Mr Ingelmann, your wife died on the operating table.'

CHAPTER THIRTY

*Even the least Angel is incomparably superior
to all human power, as can be proved in
many ways. First, a spiritual power is
stronger than a corporeal power, and so is
the power of an Angel, or even of the soul,
greater than that of the body.*

Malleus Maleficarum,
'Hammer of the Witches'

THE CARDINAL ROSE FROM HIS evening prayers. He
was in St Peter's cappella, a small side chapel located
within the confines of the basilica. It was richly orna-
mented, the marble decoration having been added in
the sixteenth century.

Strange things were astir, Benelli knew this. It wasn't
the nausea and profound weariness which assailed him
every day, a cancer gnawing his innards. It wasn't the
internal whisperings that had become loud voices, the
cries of the damned and their masters, making sleep and
his ability to concentrate almost nil. It was something
even more disturbing.

There was a deep level of expectation in the air, dark
and mournful, as if the world, seen and unseen, were
preparing for battle: one in which the outcome was

already known. For the Church was going to fight an enemy, whom it had already predicted it would be unable to withstand. A suicidal task.

The choir started on the Agnus Dei. The boys' voices, pure and ethereal, rose high in the air, filling the confined space with the extraordinary power of human adoration, a recognition that man was not the only inhabitant in this universe but that other presences and mysteries were contained within. Benelli closed his eyes. All of humanity was but one vine in a vineyard, a vine that could yet fail.

'Lord,' he asked, 'why now? Why have you chosen this period to allow this trial to come upon us? Why?'

Somehow, Benelli had expected the return of the great powers of evil in other forms: perhaps the destruction of the planet by tempest or war; perhaps the slow decline of the Christian religion and its final snuffing out like a candle, where love was wholly replaced by the worship of technology. But not this – the return of the Angels, so simply described in the Bible and by the early Christian writers.

Their own preparations against the onslaught seemed pitiful. The Pope had cancelled all external appointments, fuelling the inevitable speculation that he was unwell. He'd also instructed Benelli and Catherine of Benedetto not to leave the confines of the Vatican. Finally, the pontiff had ordered that the tomb of St Peter be closed off to everyone, priests and laymen, apart from one person – the Pope himself.

'Cardinal Benelli,' the priest beside him gently nudged his arm, 'it's time for you to say Mass.'

Benelli opened his eyes. They were waiting for him to conduct the service. He rose from his seat. As he did so, his thoughts continued.

During the day they'd been unable to locate the body of Pope Sylvester II, despite exhaustive digging in the area surrounding the Lateran Church and in its crypts. The corpse had been taken. But where and by whom? There must be some writing, some manuscript, to record this event. Even now the Prefect and his assistants were frantically searching the Secret Archives to determine if any mention had been made of this in centuries past. There were only two possibilities. The body of a pope could have been disinterred on the explicit instructions of a subsequent pontiff. Or by the powers of darkness.

Benelli started to consecrate the Host, yet his mind continued to wander. The Pope had imposed on him the task of finding Sylvester II and he'd failed. Even in this relatively small thing he had failed. How worthless was a cardinal's robe after all, he reflected. He should never have desired it. Despite all its outward pomp and majesty, it covered only his unbelief.

With great sadness, Benelli raised the Host to the altar. It was then a sentence formed in his mind, as if someone had spoken quietly to him.

'There is a tunnel under St Peter's.'

Like the Vatican, the city of San Francisco had much to occupy itself with – events both great and small. The serial killer still hadn't been found. The newspaper columnists were starting to speculate that Karl Kramer had been the culprit after all. This was reinforced by comments from Pat Harbison, an ex-warder from the San Francisco High Security Facility, who'd told reporters in detail how other inmates were terrified of Kramer.

That wasn't the big story, of course. Much more significant events were taking place. Outside the city there were increasingly large earth tremors along the San

Andreas fault. Seismologists were predicting that 'the big one' would occur soon, not least since it was long over-due. Everyone knew about the certainty of this event but they'd never thought it would happen while they were living there.

Now it was different; disaster stared them in the face. Hundreds of thousands fled San Francisco, and the air-ports and freeways became grid-locked. People panicked as they always did when they perceived their snug little world was in the grip of forces beyond their control. Yet many stayed on in the city. Some did it for bravado. They didn't think the quake would be worse than in 1906 when it measured 8.25 on the Richter scale and started a terrible fire, destroying the central business district of San Francisco. Others stayed on to protect their property or simply because they were reluctant to leave home and hearth.

All had a degree of fear. For most it was connected with the human rationalisation of terrestrial events. For others, the fear was different, more enduring.

Marie sat at the refectory table in the convent, unable to eat. She was a nervous wreck and even her appetite had been devoured by fear – fear for herself and for her child. She wondered when Florence and Ben would arrive. Soon. They'd know what to do. She smiled feebly at her daughter and ran her fingers through her fine blonde hair. Rachel looked up. Her angelic face was troubled.

'Daddy was here last night.'

There was silence. 'Your father didn't come,' said Marie, looking furtively at the nun who'd sat with Rachel throughout the dark hours.

'I saw him,' said Rachel in an affirmative tone. 'He was in the room. He said he was coming for me soon.'

'It was only a dream, darling,' said Marie. 'The Sister sat by your bedside all night.'

'No,' said Rachel. 'He was there.' She hesitated. 'He said we should go back home. We should leave the convent when it gets dark.'

Involuntarily, Marie shivered. 'Rachel, you were dreaming.'

'He had the coin with him,' continued her daughter, unable to hide the truth. 'He showed it to me.' Then in a quiet voice: 'He is going to kill Ben and Florence as well.'

Marie screamed. 'No,' she gasped. 'No, it's not true, Rachel. It's a lie.' She got up and fled from the room, aghast. For she'd had exactly the same dream.

The mother superior, Sister Martha, rose from her chair as soon as Marie entered her study. She could see that the woman was at the end of her resources, mental and spiritual. It had been a long day. She made her sit down.

'I have just heard some very bad news,' she said, looking into eyes that only reflected anguish. 'Marie, Florence Ingelmann is dead. She died in a tragic car accident this morning. Her husband phoned me.'

The mother superior looked out of the window as she listened to the deep and bitter sobbing. Why did the Almighty permit these things to happen? At times it was beyond all human understanding, try as she might to comprehend it. What had this blameless woman done? Why was she being punished in such a shocking way? Would everything be taken from her? Her husband, her child, her own life?

'God has forgotten me.'

'No, my child.'

'He has deserted me.'

'No,' said the nun, her voice quavering with emotion. 'You must not say such things. There is someone who has come to help you, from Rome. He is an important person, the Confessor to the Pope.'

Marie looked up. Through her tears, she saw a man cross the threshold. She watched as the mother superior made a slight bow to him and left them alone. The Father Confessor sat in a chair beside her and waited. Marie remained with her head bowed. Eventually, there was silence as her crying ceased. She began to feel warmth. It flowed from him and around her, like warm water encircling a cold and shivering body, slowly nursing it back to life again. As his prayer for her continued, slowly Marie's fear of death, the selfish fear of her own death, started to dissipate and the paralysis of her mind and spirit eased.

'The Holy Father sent me to find you and your child.'

Marie whispered, 'Why is this happening?'

'We think your husband has a coin. It contains a very great power of evil.'

Marie looked up sharply. 'It is linked to a woman? I saw a woman. So did Rachel.'

'Yes,' said the monk. 'This woman is connected to it. But she does not control the coin.'

'What will it do?'

'It will destroy Paul by means of false promises and hallucinations,' explained the Father Confessor, 'to enable a great evil to come into the world.'

'Will we be safe here?'

'For a time only.'

'But why Paul? And why now?'

'I do not know,' said the monk. 'These coins contain mysteries the Church does not fully understand. We think its return is connected with cosmic events that we still cannot interpret. However, at the heart of each coin is betrayal.'

Marie started violently. 'Karl Kramer,' she whispered, 'it's him.'

'Who?'

Marie told the Father Confessor about the murders in San Francisco and the court case. When she'd finished, the monk deliberated on all he had heard. Then he concluded, 'It is possible the coin came to your husband if he betrayed Laura Dukes and her sister. However, this is only the beginning. The coin will come to many people around the world who betray, but they need to find one prepared to sell his soul to the powers of evil. I'm sure Paul has not done this yet, though they will offer him everything he desires to gain what they want.'

'And he will kill Rachel and myself?'

'Unless we can stop him. You see, the evil spirit must empty Paul's being of all love before it can wholly possess him. To do that it will make your husband turn against everyone he cares for. It is the path of evil, the eternal struggle of power against love.'

'And who, or what, is this spirit?'

'We think it is of a man who once lived on earth, but we're not sure.' The monk drew a hand across his brow. He did not want to tell her too much, yet he felt compassion for her. 'These things relate to events of two thousand years ago and I need to see this coin. To do that we must return to your house, to the place where Paul first used it. I'll go this evening. Your husband won't be there then.'

Marie was mystified. How did the priest know all these things? What other things did he know that he wasn't telling her? 'Please help Paul,' she implored. 'Please save him.'

'We will do all that we can, but it may not be possible.'

'Why?' Marie cried out. 'You *are* the Church; you must be able to do something.'

The Father Confessor hesitated. Finally he told her, his own voice breaking with grief and emotion. 'Marie, the Church itself is in the greatest peril.'

Paul awoke. He was lying on the cellar floor of his house. It was bare and there was no sign of the pentacle. That didn't trouble him; he knew it was still there but invisible to human eyes. He could clearly recall the early hours of the morning; the visions were indelibly fixed in his mind. The rings of fire, the abduction of Melanie Dukes by Kramer, the death of a drug addict, then that of Florence.

Time to put Helen to the final proof before he made the ascent to the ninth astral. He got up. He felt wonderfully fresh, his mind crystal-clear. With a confident tread he ascended the stairs to the living room and picked up the phone.

'Yes, it's on the back page.' The sub-editor of the *San Francisco Times* spoke in a staccato voice. 'Unimportant news these days, what with the earth tremors. Do you want me to read it to you?'

Paul cradled the receiver. 'Just the general gist.'

'Well, basically, a drug addict was stabbed to death in the early hours of this morning in downtown San Francisco by a gang of drunken youths. Um, what else? Police arrested the perpetrators . . . er, they confessed and can only vaguely recall what happened . . . a mindless crime as always. Any more?' said the editor.

'No, that's fine.'

'Did you know him?'

'I suppose so,' said Paul, 'in a strange sort of way.'

Paul contacted the university. They passed on the news

of Florence's death, which had been conveyed to them by her husband. So it was true; the spirits did not lie. And Florence? She was an interfering old busybody. Come to think of it, he never liked her.

He flicked on the television. Almost half the population had left San Francisco. A massive transmigration of inhabitants was underway; there was misery and fear. The news commented on other events round the world. Civil war in India, riots in Brazil, mud-slides in Colombia, bomb attacks in China, slaughter of the innocents in Indonesia, starvation in central Africa. On and on, a catalogue of human tragedy and woe.

'Enough.' Paul switched off the set contemptuously. He'd free himself, once and for all, from all human limitations.

Paul returned to the cellar and stood where the pentacle had once been. From his pocket he withdrew the coin. Slowly, darkness came until it was pitch-black. The cellar faded from his sight and the pentacle began to re-form. He ascended the astrals.

The grove on the third astral appeared. He stood gazing in wonder at the ancient trees surrounding him, their mildewed trunks and great spreading branches reflecting their timelessness. He breathed in the scented air of the wood, musty and dew-filled. Would that he could stay here for ever. Helen approached along a path, the Helen of Greek myth. Paul ran to embrace her; her kisses were soft and perfect on his lips.

'Why did you go?' She already knew the answer. She never left his side now.

'I wanted to check it was true.'

'It's all true. I do not lie, Paul. With this coin you will have the power to smite your enemies and to exalt whomever you wish. It creates the world you desire, *your* world. There's only the ninth astral, then you will begin to see it all. It is miraculous.'

'How do we get there?'

'By using the pentacle, but we need a vast concentration of spiritual energy. Also, we need to go to Rome. There's something that could disrupt our plans. I must locate a tomb.'

'A tomb! Rome! Why can't we go now?' he said petulantly. He craved to return to the joys of the spirit world immediately.

'No,' replied Helen. 'I have to see inside a source of spiritual power and I cannot do that without the help of other spirits, ones mightier than I. They are hiding something from me.'

'They?'

'People who want to take the coin from us.'

Helen had been expecting this. The Vatican was now aware that Paul was the holder of the coin; the killing of the priest disclosed it. Also, and this concerned Helen more, great spirit of evil that she was, it was just possible there were other spirits still on earth that could defeat her. So they must take no risk.

Helen kissed Paul. 'Will you come with me? It'll be nice to go back to where I once lived. To bring back happy memories.'

'Of course.' Paul didn't hesitate. When his influence matched hers he'd forge his own destiny. He didn't realise Helen could read his every thought.

'Go and prepare things.'

Helen watched Paul quit his house to undertake the practical arrangements for the trip. Hardly a thought of his former life remained in him. Only an irrepressible desire to ascend to the highest spiritual plane of all, and to look down on man.

Helen turned her speculation away from her victim. There were other things to attend to and one concerned her deeply. The Vatican was not reacting as she'd expected.

Why was it searching for the tomb of an old pope?

Ben Ingelmann sat in the hospital in a town midway between Aspen and San Francisco. He scrutinised the face of his wife. It had a marble hue, a deathly beauty no living face could replicate.

Ben thought of the past, their past together. Memories of how they'd first met. A chance encounter all those years ago, when Florence had bumped into him, a young and gawky psychiatry student, as he was running to class. The hours they'd spent in the university coffee shop, his hand in hers. His proposal to her on a hilltop one windswept autumnal day, just before his finals. The extraordinary sense of joy he'd experienced when she'd put on the cheap engagement ring that he'd given her, all he could afford.

Memories of the dignity with which Florence had faced the doctor's declaration that she would never be able to have children. The thousand small kindnesses she'd undertaken during her life which she'd kept hidden from the world. The fierce love she had for their friends, especially Marie and her child. Her warm-heartedness and empathy with those less fortunate than her.

Final memories. Of her love for Ben, abiding, never waning to the end.

It was impossible to sum up the life of another and Ben didn't seek to do so. Instead, he sat for an hour beside her, reflecting on their time together. It had been worth it all. A life spent quietly. No great fame, no riches – Florence knew these things wouldn't come her way when she married him. Instead, she had dedicated her time to looking after Ben and, together, they had achieved a love and happiness that made it as fulfilled as those who achieved the victor's laurels in this world. Even more so. Insignificant it might be, but he thanked God for their lives. It was enough.

Ben rose from the bedside when the undertakers came. Tomorrow, he'd return with the body to San Francisco; he was too exhausted today. After booking a room in an hotel, he went and sat in the town's small park, his mind in a whirl as he ruminated on the extraordinary events of the last few days.

It was only after some time, as he sat on a park bench, that Ben noted the presence of a large black dog. It stood there, almost hidden by the foliage of some trees, watching him steadily. Among his other concerns, he pondered on this. Then he set off for the local library, the dog following him at a distance. Perhaps the explanation he needed to all these events, in some strange way, had something to do with animals.

In the library, Ben opened the autobiography of Carl Jung, entitled *Memories, Dreams, Reflections*. There was one section in this intensely personal memoir which had always puzzled him. He flicked to the relevant page and started to read:

I once had a case, which I have never forgotten. A lady came to my office. She refused to give her name, said it did not matter, since she only wished one consultation . . . She had been a doctor, she said. What she had to communicate to me was a confession; some twenty years ago she had committed a murder out of jealousy. She had poisoned her best friend because she wanted to marry the friend's husband. She had thought that if the murder was not discovered, it would not disturb her. She wanted to

*marry the husband, and the simplest way was to eliminate
her friend. Moral considerations were of no importance
to her, she thought.*

*The consequences? She had, in fact, married the man
but he died soon afterwards, relatively young. During the
following years a number of strange things happened. The
daughter of the marriage endeavoured to get away from
her as soon as she was grown up. She married young and
vanished from view, drew further and further away, and
ultimately the mother lost all contact with her.*

*This lady was a passionate horsewoman and owned
several riding horses of which she was extremely fond. One
day she discovered that the horses were beginning to grow
nervous of her. Even her favourite shied and threw her.
Finally, she had to give up riding. Thereafter, she clung
to her dogs. She had an unusually beautiful wolfhound
to which she was greatly attached. As chance would have
it, this very dog was stricken. With that, her cup was full.
She felt that she was morally done for. She had to confess,
and for this purpose she came to me. She was a murderess,
but on top of that she had also murdered herself. For one
who commits such a crime destroys his own soul . . . it
comes out in the end. Sometimes, it seems as if even animals and plants know it.*

Odd, wasn't it?

Ben closed the book. Hastily he walked back to his
hotel; he wanted to get there before twilight. As he did
so, Ben reflected on how curious it also was that animals
could also appear as manifestations of evil. For he had
noticed something strange about the mastiff that had
followed him all afternoon.

It had no shadow.

*   *   *

In the convent Marie tucked her daughter up to sleep, hugging her long and hard. She stepped outside the door into the passageway. The Father Confessor approached.

'It's time for me to go.'

Marie shivered. 'I'll drive you to the house.'

'I don't think you should.'

'I insist.' She clenched her fists. 'I want my husband back.'

Eventually, the Father Confessor agreed. 'Very well, but stay close to me at all times. And don't react to whatever you see, or you think you see. These spirits are very dangerous indeed. They can influence and alter the mind.'

'What exactly are you looking for?' said Marie as she drove. This journey was so like a replay of the journey she'd taken only two days before with Father David, it scared her even to think about it. But she loved Paul and she'd do whatever she could for him. But did she love her daughter more?

'I need to see the coin,' replied the monk. 'It exists both on a physical and on a spiritual plane. At first, it's a simple coin, a silver denarius of the time of Christ. Then it becomes an image, as its power grows and it bridges the gap between the terrestrial and cosmic worlds. If the coin we're seeking has attached itself to Paul, its image should be detectable in the house.'

'How do you know Paul won't be in the house?'

'Because he's gone to Rome.'

'You say it as if you could see these things,' commented Marie helplessly.

'The powers of good have a few weapons in their own armoury,' replied the monk. 'Like evil they can comprehend many things not readily understandable to most human beings. The coin gives off a vast energy when used, enabling its source to be detected. It is not I who have seen this. It was a nun.'

'What sort of woman is she?'

The car sped through the outskirts of San Francisco. For once all the traffic was leaving town. The Father Confessor shrugged. 'She's a simple woman, a mystic. A nun who belongs to a closed order. It is not only the powers of evil that have revelations; those who follow the path of good do so also.'

'The same images?'

'No,' he retorted emphatically. 'They can perceive the tricks evil creates, but they know that they are delusions. Their own revelations are centred on the divine.'

'Why is this nun not here?'

'You mean why did they send a poor priest like me and not a great saint?' said the Father Confessor with a faint smile.

'Oh, I'm sorry. I didn't mean to say that,' said Marie, though that had been her thought. 'I mean why doesn't she come and destroy the coin?'

'Because the Holy Father has asked her to remain in Rome for the present. Besides' – the priest lowered his voice – 'I'm not sure we can extinguish this coin, Marie.'

'Why?'

'It descends to the very roots of original sin and is part of the deepest of mysteries; a paradox for us. You see, Marie, in a way, love is powerless, since God is the most humble being in the universe. Love will not destroy; it will not use evil to fight evil. And yet, incomprehensibly, love is also the most powerful thing in the universe because, when souls are united in love, nothing, not even the greatest evil, can affect them. There is no space, no crevice, for it to latch on to.'

'How can the coin be defeated then?'

The monk didn't reply for some time. Then, as if musing to himself, he said, 'I don't know. But I believe that if a human being turns their soul to God with complete faith, the coin loses its power over that person's mind and, having no foothold on which to grip, it dies.'

'But who can do that? Can you?'

Sadly, the monk shook his head, measuring up his own worth. 'I do not think so.'

Eventually, they walked up the drive. Marie inserted the key in the lock and they entered her home. She looked about her. There was no indication she'd ever been there with Father David. In one corner a sweater was draped over a chair. It was Paul's. He must have cast it there just before going out. Surely, in a moment he'd pop his head around the living-room door and say, with a smile, 'So, you're back?' Yet, as Marie gazed at the sweater, her heart felt an unbearable loneliness. Paul wasn't coming back. She knew in her heart that he'd never come back. He was lost. The terrible evil he was helping to unleash would never reunite them in this world.

Together they walked down the wooden stairs. The cellar was empty and pristine, as if it had been swept that morning. Marie turned to the priest.

'There's nothing here. It's gone, whatever it was.'

The Father Confessor shook his head. 'Watch.'

He held out his hand. In an instant, a pentacle flared up as if etched deep into the concrete with molten metal. Marie stepped towards it involuntarily, fascinated by its strange and wonderful design. It beguiled her, like a fly drawn to a web.

'Don't touch it!'

The monk extracted a silver crucifix from his pocket.

331

He cast it so that it crossed the outer circle of the pentacle. When it passed through the rings, it flared brilliantly and melted.

'They have inverted it. I fear the worst.' The Father Confessor turned. 'Come, we must hurry. We should leave now.'

They exited the cellar. In the far corner and almost hidden in the gloom stood a large black dog. Its malignant eyes were fixed on Marie's, its maw drawn back in a mask of hate.

'I'm frightened.' She gripped the monk's arm. Together they ascended the stairs into the hallway. The lights went out. The monk lowered his head in prayer and they came on again, though not back to their full strength. On the first landing, they entered Marie's bedroom.

'Is this where you saw the coin?'

Marie wasn't listening. 'Father!' she gasped.

In a corner of the bedroom the wall started to dissolve and vanish. Shapes emerged. Macabre and twisted, half-human, half-devil, they hurtled towards her as if running along a path, about to penetrate into Marie's world. She screamed out in fear.

The monk made the sign of the cross. Slowly, the phantoms dissolved with a dismal shriek.

'Over there!' The Father Confessor directed Marie. On a dresser there was an intense red beam of light that was so brilliant that it hurt the eyes to look at it. Yet, as they both continued to stare, its glow gradually diminished.

Finally, Marie saw a coin, the perfect replica of the one her daughter had drawn. Its sides were uneven and it bore on its face the visage of an emperor from Roman times. It glistened as if it had been freshly minted. The coin began to flip over, rotated by an invisible hand.

Marie glanced at the priest and knew, in some extraordinary way, that he was doing this. On its reverse she saw it had been badly disfigured. Someone, or something, had scratched deep into its face the letters SMRM. She didn't know what they stood for.

'It is a Coin of Judas,' said the Father Confessor in a tone of dread. 'There is no doubt.'

Suddenly, Marie heard a noise downstairs – the heart-rending anguish of a child in distress. 'Help, Mummy,' it screamed out in agony. 'Help me!'

'Rachel!' Marie's hand flew to her mouth. She rushed from the room.

'Don't go!' shouted the Father Confessor, all his will having been concentrated on the coin before him. 'It's a trick.'

But it was too late.

Paul and Helen had arrived in Rome. They were taking a taxi from the airport into the city centre. Helen had been insisting to Paul that their flight had been so smooth only thanks to her help – why suffer turbulence when you can do something about it?

Suddenly, she leant forward in the taxi and bawled to the driver, 'Stop!' The vehicle screeched to a halt. She pulled Paul out, ordering the driver to go on to her apartment.

'What's happened?' Paul asked, bewildered.

'They've found the coin! A monk is there.'

Helen pushed him towards some trees. Her eyes glazed over completely. She was no longer in Rome but in Paul's house in San Francisco watching the two intruders. Her visage became distended with rage.

'Sit down here,' she spat.

In the Roman darkness in which the first flicker of

morning had yet to appear, they sat on a bench. They needed to be alone, but they soon had company. There was a rustle of branches and a tramp emerged from the undergrowth, clasping an empty wine bottle. He lurched towards them with a liquid grin but it was not the best time to exchange greetings with an evil spirit.

Helen turned to their unwelcome guest, her face divulging her intentions. The drunken tramp stumbled over a tree branch that flicked up in front of him. He slipped and fell directly on top of the bottle he was clutching. There was a hideous gurgle as broken glass severed his windpipe in one fell blow. Helen ignored the death rattle.

'A priest has entered your house. He's searching for the coin.'

'But I have the coin,' said Paul numbly and drew it from his pocket.

'Not the physical coin, idiot,' Helen snapped. 'They can detect the astral projection where it was first used.' She looked at him, her eyes aflame with malice. 'We must combine our forces or they will kill us. Now is the period of real danger. Let us go to the eighth astral.'

Although Helen and Paul remained on the park bench physically, their spirits were soon far away in Paul's house, with the Father Confessor and Marie.

After she heard Rachel's scream, Marie ran out of the bedroom and onto the landing. At the bottom of the stairs she could see her daughter struggling in the half-light in the arms of a man. The monster glanced up. It was Kramer. Marie cried out in horror, then the lights went off. Pounding down the stairs she tripped and fell, hitting her head soundly. She tumbled to the bottom. Lying at the foot of the staircase, she floated in and out of consciousness.

'Marie.'

Before her eyes two luminous forms approached. One was her daughter, the other was Paul, his arms wrapped protectively around the child. He gave a warm and slightly mischievous smile that Marie knew so well.

'Come with us,' he said to his wife. He extended his arms in a loving gesture. 'Come, I'll show you things beyond your wildest dreams. Rachel is with me now.'

Marie started to get up, drawn by a will that was not her own, her physical pain forgotten. A hand gripped her.

'Stand back. It's an illusion created by evil.'

The Father Confessor made the sign of the cross and pronounced some words of exorcism. With a horrible screech the spectres began to waver and die. Then everything changed. Marie was in her house no more, she was *within* the vision. About her were rings of fire, burning and flaring in the deep darkness. Marie stood on the ring of the eighth astral. Beside her was the Father Confessor, but his cassock was a worn brown no longer. Instead, it was a profound blue, light streaming out from it with a great pulsating glow.

Opposite them, within the circumference of the ring, were Helen and Paul. However, they appeared to Marie as images of darkness, shadows that held athames, great swords of flame. They came towards her, uttering words of death.

'Do not be afraid!' The words came from the monk but she received them without any human voice.

His form changed so that it became a pillar of pure white light. Against him, the shadows began to quiver and distend. Paul no longer saw rings of fire as the Father Confessor imposed his will. Paul was in a garden. Its flowers and trees radiated lightness and beauty, just as he'd perceived on the third astral. Yet this garden was truly alive; it radiated an indescribable sense of joy, one that permeated everything like the flow of living water. A woman, a nun, stood close beside him. Her voice was calm.

'Paul, listen to me. They're deceiving you.'

'How can you say this?' he retorted. 'You haven't seen what I have.'

'Listen, since we haven't much time,' said the nun. 'You're being deceived. I will try and explain as simply as I can. There are two worlds – a physical earth and a spiritual one. The first is the physical earth, its temporal master is evil, the "master" of the Field of Blood. The second world is the spiritual earth. It has an eternal master, the master of the Field of Life.'

'What is this to me?'

'Everything. Like all human beings you live and work on the physical earth and, at the end of your life, you will receive payment. But you also exist and work on a hidden spiritual earth, for which you will receive payment as well. Yet the wages are different depending on your choice. Those of the master of the Field of Blood comprise power over all the kingdoms of this world, a power he has only for a limited time. The coins lie at the heart of this.'

'And the other?'

'The wages comprise love. But they can only be earned by love. Yet even this will be given to you, if you ask for it. With these wages you can acquire a great treasure.'

'Treasure? What treasure?'

'A treasure hidden in the Field. Not in the physical earth itself, but in that which was created by God from the dust of the earth, mankind. It lies within you, Paul, and it is the greatest gift of all, the gift of eternal life.

However, the master of the Field of Blood covets this treasure – for Satan himself has fallen, fallen into time. Let him possess your soul and you lose eternity. If you use the coin you are sold into slavery; you will till the Field of Blood until the ends of time.'

Paul looked down and in his hand was the Coin of Judas. Something deep within him told him to give it to the nun. To have done with things too powerful for man. To accept humility and to receive true life.

Helen materialised beside him, incandescent with fury. 'Don't show them the coin, idiot. Do not challenge them.'

'But . . .'

Within the space of a thought, Paul found himself once again in the park in Rome. Helen was beside him, her face twisted in agony, her power drained. Eventually, she spoke.

'You fool. Didn't I make it clear that spirits further out on the astrals can destroy you? They can steal the energy that sustains you. That's what they were trying to do. The brilliant light about them indicates that they were on the very edge of the eighth astral. What did the monk tell you to do?'

'To cast away the coin. Who is the nun?'

'All that they've told you are lies,' ranted Helen. 'We must be careful until you pass the ninth astral; then no one can challenge you.'

'What did they want?'

Helen looked up. He must not know the truth.

'They are searching for the coin,' she said. 'They want it for themselves, to gain wisdom. But if they obtain it, they will annihilate us.'

'Why?'

'Because our destinies are inextricably linked to the

Coin of Judas, Paul.' She cackled. 'You see, we no longer control it. It controls us.'

Marie sat on the staircase in her house. The Father Confessor looked exhausted, as if a huge amount of energy had been withdrawn from him.

'They have gone. But they will return.'

'Does it exist?' she said.

'Exist?'

'The garden. I felt I was in a garden. It was so vivid and so strange. Like magic.'

'It was a vision,' replied the Father Confessor. 'Just as evil can create hallucinations to enslave people, so the good have other revelations. But unlike those of evil, these phenomena are true ones, they exist within the world of the spirit. You see, evil is the perversion, the twisting of good. It mimics, it distorts. It cannot create anything new.'

'Will they come back tonight?' asked Marie.

'I don't think so,' said the Father Confessor, 'but we must leave. I am sorry, but this has become a wicked place.'

'And the woman?'

'The woman you saw is very formidable indeed,' said the Father Confessor. 'However, she was holding back from using all her force.'

'Why?'

'Because she did not want us to know the name of the true holder of the coin.'

'Why do we need to find this out?'

The priest got up wearily. 'It is our only hope. Only then will we know if there is any way to defeat it.'

'But you've discovered something else, haven't you?' Marie studied his face anxiously. 'You are sure of one other thing? About who truly holds this coin?'

In a voice replete with sorrow the Father Confessor declared the truth.

'Yes. *It is a great Angel of Darkness.*'

CHAPTER THIRTY-ONE

*God's great mercy is needed to prevent anyone
from supposing that he is enjoying the friendship of good angels when in fact it is evil
demons that he has as his false friends, and
when he thus suffers from the enmity of those
whose harmfulness is in proportion to their
cunning and deceit.*

St Augustine, *The City of God*

'They've found a tunnel!'

'Where?'

'In St Peter's!'

Cardinal Benelli stared at the messenger. It had been
an extraordinary day: one filled with remarkable news,
all of it bleak. That morning, when the doors to the
Pope's private chapel had been unlocked by staff, they'd
discovered two of the stained-glass windows close to the
altar had been smashed. How? It was impossible for out-
siders to get into the chapel. Yet it had happened. News
of this dreadful omen had spread quickly throughout
the Vatican. A great disaster was predicted. But where?
No one seemed to know.

Benelli did. They had received confirmation from
the Father Confessor in San Francisco. A Coin of Judas

was in the world. It existed. Now they were certain.

The Cardinal had cancelled all his morning appointments after Mass and hurried over to St Peter's Basilica. His mind was aflame. Could the body of Sylvester II, the last person to have held a Coin of Judas, yield any clue as to how the present coin might be defeated? Or were they pursuing another false trail?

As Benelli went down the worn stairs to under the high altar, the Prefect of the Secret Archives followed him. He said: 'I don't know, Cardinal, how you made such an inspired guess. We've only just discovered a seventeenth-century map in the Secret Archives. It suggests there was once a subterranean passage from the grotto of St Peter's Basilica to the obelisk located in the piazza outside.' He continued, his voice as dry as ever: 'They must have dug the tunnel when they relocated the obelisk to the front of the square in 1586. But why the tunnel was later bricked up I can't imagine.'

They descended into a mayhem of noise and dust. Workmen with hammers were breaking down a lime and brick wall at the far end of the grotto. It had been thought this wall was part of the original Roman graveyard under the basilica. Yet when the plaster was removed, it was clear it had been disguised to appear so. Why? Directly in front of this false wall, at a distance of less than ten metres, lay the tomb of St Peter. Was there some reason for the location, or was it just fortuitous?

Questions, but no answers.

Benelli sat down on some steps and watched the workmen. At least, he now knew *when* the body of Pope Sylvester had been removed from his tomb. The Prefect had discovered an account in the Secret Archives by the historian Rasponi who indicated that, in 1648, the grave of the Pope had been reopened. The account had declared:

The corpse of Sylvester II was found in a marble sarcophagus, twelve feet below the surface. The body was entire and clad in pontifical robes, the arms were crossed, and the head was covered with the sacred tiara.

So, Sylvester's body had not been cut up as the legends had suggested. Yet surprisingly, Rasponi didn't say where they had reburied Sylvester's body. Why? Benelli watched impatiently as the workmen started to clear away the rubble, for the sight being disclosed in the haze of dust was indeed a tunnel. They continued to excavate until the Cardinal announced, 'Everyone, please leave now.'

The workmen and the Prefect turned round to him with astonished expressions. However, he was under strict orders from the Pope. Reluctantly, they quit the scene. Benelli knelt in prayer. Then he walked towards the narrow aperture and squeezed through the gap.

In the light of a workman's lamp he could see that the tunnel was of brick and large enough to hold a man. The walls were coated with a skim of whitewash and they, as well as the floor, were caked with grime. No one had been in it since it had been sealed up hundreds of years ago.

Benelli began to walk along the passageway, his feet kicking up clouds of dust. According to his calculations they were passing straight under the foundation walls of St Peter's Basilica, proceeding in an easterly direction. More than two hundred metres into this murky darkness the tunnel ended and Benelli saw the base of the obelisk before him. So, they had built the tunnel to be able to inspect the foundations of the obelisk. Quite extraordinary. Then, he caught sight of a date stamped on the brick wall before him. It was 1648.

However, the obelisk had been moved in 1586. Why

would they have built the tunnel sixty years *after* moving the obelisk from the side of St Peter's Basilica to the middle of the piazza? What happened in 1648?

There was another mark to the right of the obelisk. Benelli reached out and, with his hand, swept away the dirt of ages. He started back in shock. Painted on the wall in red was the sign of a huge cross and underneath an inscription: *pp Sylvestris II*.

It became clear to him. They'd built the tunnel for the *sole* purpose of relocating the tomb of Sylvester here, underneath the obelisk outside St Peter's, where no person would possibly think of finding it. What was so special about this particular location? Benelli's speculation soon ended. Written below the cross, also in blood-red letters, were the same words as on the Coins of Judas: '*Salva me, Redemptor Mundi*': 'Save me, O Redeemer of the World.'

Benelli drew in his breath sharply. Then he started back, to report his find to his master.

When he had got half-way along he heard a noise in the direction from whence he'd come. His heart thumping, the Cardinal shone the workman's lamp back down the passageway towards the tomb. With a shiver, he returned to the safety of the basilica. At the same time as he'd made his discovery so had someone else. Or, rather, something else.

A large black dog.

Pope John XXV listened carefully to all his Cardinal had to say. Even as Benelli asked for permission to break into the tomb he realised that the discovery of the body raised more questions than it answered. Why had they moved the corpse from the Lateran Church to this even more secret location? More worrying, if this Pope had, in fact, been a good man and not an evil one, why didn't they rebury him *in* St Peter's Basilica – perhaps even close to the tomb of the Apostle? Yet, if he had been evil, why bury him anywhere near a church?

The pontiff reflected on their dilemma for a long time, his eyes closed, deep in thought. Finally, he told Benelli that his request to open up the tomb was refused. Despite all their investigations they still had no idea of whether the secret it contained would assist their cause or that of evil.

Benelli also told him about the black dog he'd seen. 'Surely this man was evil? Why else the presence of the dog?'

The Pope shook his head. 'We do not know the condition of Sylvester's soul when he died. Only God knows that.'

'But,' said Benelli helplessly, 'whatever is in the tomb may help us. Holy Father, time is running out.' Why was the pontiff so cautious on this matter? Why didn't he do something? 'Do you think that the powers of evil know what is in the tomb?'

'I do not think so,' replied John XXV. 'At least, not yet. Like us, I think they have just rediscovered its existence. Perhaps, the body of Sylvester II was moved for this reason. They will now use all their powers to penetrate its secret, especially since the grave is located outside the confines of the basilica and not on hallowed ground. That may be the reason why they've decided to come to Rome.'

'When will they try to break into the tomb?'

The pontiff did not speak for some time. Then he said abruptly, 'Tonight.'

That afternoon an order went out from the Vatican to the guardians of the basilica. The doors of St Peter's were to be sealed with the papal arms. No one was to enter it that evening without the express permission of the Pope himself.

Almost at the same hour as the workmen were breaching the wall of the tunnel, Ben returned to San Francisco with his wife's coffin. Once he'd made arrangements for her burial the following day, he went over to the convent. Before he met Marie and Rachel, he called on the mother superior. It was she who introduced him to the priest from Rome.

Ben and the Father Confessor talked for a long time – about Paul, about the nature of evil, about the death of Florence. By the end of it, Ben had formed his own conclusions. Perhaps he was assisted by the fact that wherever he went, the form of a large black dog now followed him. He didn't mention this to the monk since he thought the latter had enough concerns with Paul and Marie. Yet it was curious that, while he was in the convent, the animal didn't appear.

At the end of their conversation, the monk asked Ben for his help and he agreed. Together they left the convent. Soon, they were travelling down a long and dusty road. It had only one destination.

Hanlon Dawes, the aggressive Warden of the San Francisco High Security Facility, was taken aback at the unexpected arrival of two visitors. He was also uncertain what he should do in light of their strange request. This annoyed him, since he knew the answers to most things and, when it came to something concerning his prisoners, the answer was invariably negative.

The Warden turned away from the window of his office. Outside, he could see only the bleak inner walls of the prison and the anonymous buildings marked

A to D. Even within his own sanctum, he'd made few concessions to creature comforts: a wooden desk, many books (for he loved reading) and a couple of chairs. If truth be told, Dawes was a man who made few concessions, even to himself. He was a born ascetic anyway and his sense of justice was biblical – swift and full of wrath.

The Warden sat down at his desk. He considered Ben Ingelmann and the slight figure beside him. Finally, he commented, 'It's a very unusual request, Professor Ingelmann. I'm happy to let *you* visit Kramer. However, not this gentleman.' He nodded curtly at the Father Confessor. 'I don't think Kramer has time for priests. I imagine he doesn't even know what they do. It'll only antagonise him and he's a dangerous enough man as it is.'

When they'd first arrived and made their request, the Warden had known what his answer would be. It was obvious. Kramer had made no formal application to see anyone and he was still in disgrace after the attack on the student – though a stint in the underground dungeons of E Block was beginning to teach even Kramer that you couldn't mess about with Hanlon Dawes.

However, he wasn't so sure now. There was something about this priest that made him want to agree with him. He continued to focus his eyes on the Father Confessor. The monk had a strange and persuasive quality about him. He must be a remarkable man.

'Well . . .' Dawes drew a hand over his chin again. Irritated, he pressed a buzzer and snapped at his secretary to find the Head of E Block and pass on some instructions. He said to his small audience, 'OK, you can both have twenty minutes with him, but only *if* Kramer consents.'

He watched Ben's disappointed face, knowing that Kramer wouldn't possibly agree.

'I'm sorry.' Hanlon leant forward in his chair. 'We go back quite a while, Professor Ingelmann, but as Warden of this prison I can't bend the rules for anyone. Not even an emissary of the Pope. That's what rules are for. By the way, how's Paul?'

Ben glanced at the Father Confessor. 'Paul's ill,' he said.

'Nothing serious?'

'He's really quite ill.'

Dawes mused on this. Perhaps he should tell them his suspicions about Kramer being the serial killer. Further conversation was precluded by a knock on the door.

'Come in,' Dawes bawled.

The Head of E Block entered. He was built like a gorilla and had the brain to match. 'I've talked with Kramer, sir. He will see them.'

'Oh,' said Dawes. He flushed angrily, his face registering his complete astonishment. 'You've twenty minutes, so you'd better get on with it.'

He watched the odd couple depart. Strange really. He'd hardly talked to the monk, yet when he'd mentioned earlier to him that in running a prison obedience was the key, the Father Confessor had immediately replied, 'No. Truth is the key.'

Strange, since Hanlon's father often used to say that. But the priest wouldn't have known.

They stood outside the underground entrance to E Block.

'I must speak with Kramer alone.'

'I understand,' said Ben. 'I hope you find what you're looking for. I have to go to the university now. Please

347

tell Marie I'll come and see her later this afternoon, to talk about Florence's funeral and many other things.'

The Father Confessor shook his hand. 'Ben, I want you to be very careful. You are in great danger. These evil spirits will destroy anyone who was close to Paul or who loved him. Don't go to Paul's house under any circumstances. I also think you should stay at the convent tonight. You'll be safer there.'

'I'll be fine.' Ben looked at the pained face of his companion. 'See you later.'

Ben watched the priest walk down the grey-painted corridor, as if proceeding to his doom. Then he turned away.

'Well, well,' said Karl Kramer. 'The servant of Christ has come at last.' He sniggered. They were alone. The prisoner's arms and legs had been locked to an iron table in the centre of the room so that he couldn't move. If he could, he'd have killed the priest as easily as swatting an insect. He said, 'I know who you are.'

The Father Confessor made no reply. Despite the lack of any visible sign of his office, the murderer would know all about him; the devils would have told him that. Then Kramer began to blaspheme. In a low voice, urgently, the words slipping from his tongue in an unknown language. The glossolalia of the devil. The monk ignored it; the prisoner couldn't control this manifestation. The devils controlled him now like a child in its mother's womb.

'I also know why you've come,' said Kramer. He spoke in Latin, the eyes sparkling with demonic intent. 'It's about the coin. You're all afraid. She offered it to me first, but she tricked me and gave it to him.'

'Be quiet.'

The Father Confessor let the power flow from him.

He didn't watch Kramer's face but he knew what would happen.

Within a few moments the murderer's eyes glazed and his head rolled back. His mouth opened in a horrifying rictus, the head twisting to one side, saliva flecking the lips and tongue. Kramer sat there, like some grotesque puppet, his body rigid and cutting savagely against the iron ties that restrained him. However, the monk had no fear of Kramer, for he was gazing into the shattered remnants of a human spirit. In his vision, the Father Confessor began his descent – into the hell of another human being.

Even though only a minute or two passed within the cramped prison walls, the journey was a long and frightening one. Although the Father Confessor went far out onto the astral planes of evil, he could not determine the identity of the one that controlled both Kramer and Helen, for it hid itself from him, as if behind a veil. My name is unknown, challenge me not, it willed into his mind.

At last, the priest could proceed no further, for the spirit dwelt far beyond the outermost ring of darkness so that even he could not perceive it. Finally, the Father Confessor opened his eyes again.

He'd failed.

The confessor's power over him released, Kramer straightened in his chair. As he did so, the monk perceived Kramer as he truly was. The carcass of a human figure, a wrecked ship endlessly tossed by the tide, his soul close to dissolution. Soon, the evil spirits would return to their abode to continue his final torment and destruction. There was no hope for him in this world.

'Karl, listen to me,' said the monk in an urgent tone.

'You must fight against them, you must not let them destroy your soul. Do you understand? You must do some acts of good, make some penance.'

Kramer surveyed him mutely. He made no movement. There was the sound of doors being unlocked; the warders had returned. The monk stood up. Within this wretched specimen of humanity lay a great secret. He was sure. Yet this man would not disclose it. It would die with him.

Slowly, he made the sign of the cross over the murderer and departed.

Ben walked round his office, packing various books and papers into a cardboard box. It was time to leave. With the death of Florence any desire to carry on at the university had gone and he'd inform the Faculty tomorrow. To remain with memories of Florence in every aspect of his life would be unbearable. He didn't know what he was going to do in the future; that didn't matter. What did were Marie and Rachel. He'd do whatever he could to help them, even though he was now dealing with things far beyond his ken. Florence would have done the same. Loyalty unto death. He would not betray those he loved.

Ben picked up the box of papers. Sadly, he walked down the stairs of the university building for the last time. It was an empty place anyway – like the rest of San Francisco. There'd been another earth tremor this morning measuring over six on the Richter scale, and the US press and TV were concentrating on little else. It was rumoured the President was going to order the forcible evacuation of the city. They were waiting for the hammer blow. The big one.

'Professor Ingelmann?'

A pretty girl sauntered up to him.

'Hi, I'm Suzanne Delaney.' She added immediately, 'A close friend of Paul's, a very close friend.'

Ben stopped. So this was the student whom Paul was rumoured to be having an affair with. He must warn her in some way; she could be in danger. 'Yes?'

'I wanted to speak with you. I've been having a difficult time lately. It's about me and Professor Stauffer.'

Ben hesitated. He must talk with her. However, he had to talk urgently with Marie as well; he was so worried about her and the child. 'Very well. Tonight.'

'Couldn't you make it earlier?' Suzanne adopted a meek tone of voice. 'I may have to leave town soon. You know, with the earthquake.'

Ben had reached his car. Opening the boot he thrust the cardboard box into it. He scratched his head. For some absurd reason he couldn't come to a decision.

'Please, Professor Ingelmann. Please.'

As she said this, in a daze, Ben got into his car and switched on the ignition. It wouldn't start. Damn, that was all he needed. Was there anything else that could go wrong in life? The battery was flat. How could that possibly be? It had been running perfectly the last few days.

'You seem to be having a problem.' Suzanne gave a kindhearted smile as she drew near to the window. 'My car's just over there. We could go for a coffee and chat.'

She pointed to a red sports car gleaming in the autumn sunlight. It was only a few metres away.

'That's an idea.' Ben loosened his seat belt and made to get out. Suddenly, he exclaimed, 'Look, I'll see you at my clinic, this evening.' His voice was harsh and dismissive. He closed the door to his vehicle hurriedly.

A furious expression flickered across Suzanne's face. 'Sure,' she said in a soft voice. 'Goodbye, my friend. Oh, and regards to your wife.' She strolled away.

Ben watched her depart. Although it was a November day he was sweating profusely. There was a reason. In the back of Suzanne's vehicle he'd espied something.

It was a large black dog.

Only after the car disappeared down the drive did Ben get out of his vehicle. Then he began to run – back to his office. He must contact the Father Confessor and Marie; he had some vital information. He'd worked something out.

Kramer, Helen and Suzanne were all connected.

'Hey there, look where you're going.'

Ben raced up the stairs to the third floor, oblivious to the person descending. He reached it panting heavily, his pulse erratic. Then he made towards his office. Perhaps he was too late. Perhaps Marie and Rachel had already left the convent. As he passed Paul's room a voice cried out, 'Ben!'

Stunned, he halted in his tracks. Paul was back. It was his voice, unmistakably. Should he go in or not? Or should he make those phone calls? Anxiously, he ran his hand through his sweat-filled hair, debating the matter. Then he approached the door. Cautiously, he opened it, his heart thumping at a furious tempo.

'Hi, stranger.'

Ben gawped at the figure, then at the large black dog at her heels. The room started to spin before his eyes and an agonising pain shot across his ribcage like a lightning strike. He clutched at his chest. His heart started to die.

'Florence,' he murmured; then, 'Marie.' His last thoughts were for her – for a meeting which would never take place in this world. He had failed her. An overwhelming sadness covered him.

Idly, the spirit of Helen watched the dying figure on the floor. She'd seen so much death in two thousand years of murder it no longer interested her. That was the problem with evil – it always deceived. False revelations, false voices, false prophecies. And these humans always fell for it – ah, such children. Why had the greatest treasure in the universe been given to them to guard in their hearts? What a foolish thing to do – God himself had erred.

While Ben completed his death throes, Suzanne entered the building and slowly made her way up the stairs. When she opened the door to Paul's office, Helen's spirit form faded and disappeared from sight. Her slave took over. Suzanne tidied her hair as she inspected the still warm corpse. Then she stepped out into the corridor and screamed out in a hysterical voice, 'My God, help me, help me! Professor Ingelmann's having a heart attack.'

Acting. Now that was Suzanne's forte.

CHAPTER THIRTY-TWO

On the Tibertine Island, which lies in the river like the hull of a grey stone ship, there stood . . . the luxurious palace of a Jew who had tried to buy with gold and precious stones the powers of the Apostles. With him was the beautiful Helena, whom he elevated from the status of a courtesan to the dignity of the primordial idea of God.

Ambrosini,
The Secret Archives of the Vatican

'ROME, THE ETERNAL CITY. DON'T you just love it?' Helen turned back from the window of the sumptuous apartment. 'But it's nothing now. You do not know how it was, Paul, to be alive in its heyday. Under the Emperor Nero, Rome was simply the best place to be. The best city in all the world and of all time. You can't imagine what we got away with. Pure murder.'

Helen came and sat down on the bed. She was naked, her sleek body and delicate thighs glistening in the moonlight. She ran her hand through Paul's dark hair, while he lay sleeping. Then she pinched him hard on his shoulder so that he stirred and woke up. Outside, lights gleamed all over the city.

'Time to get dressed,' she said. 'It's not far.'

'Where are we going?'

'We're going to visit where I once lived. In olden times when the coin first came into my possession to guard.' She kissed him. 'Missing Suzanne? I'm not as good, eh? Less satisfying? Old flesh?'

'You were wonderful.'

She smirked. 'Remember, the body's not mine. But I've had two thousand years of experience, believe you me. Anyway, don't worry, you'll soon be back in San Francisco.' She pouted. 'Though you'll find it's changed a bit.'

'Changed?' He leant on his arm. 'What do you mean?'

Helen laughed merrily. 'On earth everything passes, everything is vanity. And, of course, we spirits always talk in riddles and parables, which doesn't help. The difficulty is that you humans can't see what we do. If you did, all would be clear.'

'What about this coin? When did it first appear?' Paul said, drawing her to him. He no longer had a wife; his mind had no recall.

'It belonged to a friend of mine who's dead now.'

'But why did it come to him?'

'Because it was foretold in the stars.'

'Stars?' he said incredulously. 'That's impossible.'

'Paul, have I ever lied to you?' said Helen, lying. 'Look, when a small child sees a map of the world it only see shapes and colours. However, you know, with your human intelligence, that the map represents countries that actually exist. Well, it's the same with the stars. When you view them, your vision is a child's vision. They are just bright dots, with no apparent sense of order or relationship. But when I look at the stars I see something completely different.'

'What?'

'Ah,' she said in a dreamy tone. 'You wouldn't believe what I see, Paul. You see stars, I see Angels and Archangels, I see Thrones and Powers. I also see a mighty Temple perfect in its symmetry. And much more – the twelve tribes of Israel, the kingdoms and the Ark. Oh, I see so many things.'

'The coin lets you see these?'

She nodded. 'With this coin one can behold when the past, present and future were one. Your problem on earth is that you comprehend everything in terms of time: you think one event follows another, but it doesn't. Everything is interwoven like a seamless garment. The past is always driven on by the future, the future always follows on the heels of the past and both the past and the future have their beginning and their end in the eternal present. And' – she produced the Coin of Judas from her hand, like a magician – 'thirty coins like these purchase the greatest treasure of all: eternal life.'

'So what the nun said was true?'

'No.' Her lips curled with distaste. 'These people are meddlers, they don't understand.' She paused. She had to tell him more, since he must be allowed to make a free choice. 'How can I explain this to you when you know nothing of the spirit world?

'Well, here goes. Here's a riddle for you, a sort of child's tale. Someone I know was once promised a field in which a wondrous treasure was hidden, in return for some silver. But the field was not like an ordinary field, OK? It was one field, but it was both a physical and a mystical field; that is, it existed both in heaven and on earth, since what is above is reflected below. And the promise was sealed in a temple. One temple, but it was both a physical temple here on earth and a spiritual one up there in the heavens. The coins reveal all this; they act like mirrors.'

'But what happened?'

Helen's face became fraught with bitterness. 'The promise was a fraud. The thirty coins bought only the field below, which is the earth and all that is contained therein, including man, who was created from the dust of the earth. It also bought a slave who knew where the real spiritual treasure was hidden. However, this slave had wickedly dissipated the treasure among all those he loved. Of course, the buyer, the one I know, demanded that the true bargain be upheld. He'd been misled and a promise once made in the temple cannot be revoked. It is eternal. And it wasn't as though the treasure had been lost, just scattered in time.'

'And?'

'There was a great battle in heaven and on earth, which is continuing. The slave was crucified for his treachery; the temple below was broken. But nothing is ever lost in eternity. Just as the coins can be painstakingly gathered up, so can the treasure be recovered.'

'And when it happens?'

'The bargain holds. When the coins are returned, the treasure must be handed over by those to whom it was wrongly distributed – it will belong to the one who owns the field. He will receive his due.'

Paul pondered on this. 'The field and the temple above are reflected below – I can understand that. I can also understand that the buyer thought he was buying a heavenly field as well as an earthly one. But did he discern the true nature of the bargain? Did he buy what he saw or what actually *was*? If he bought what he saw, it was his own fault. Anyway, who really owns the field in which this treasure is still supposed to be hidden?'

Helen kissed him. 'Clever clogs. That, my darling, you are going to find out. When each coin releases its awesome power, Paul, the world feels it. Tonight, you will see the kingdoms of this world, I promise. It's already beginning.'

'I don't see anything.'

'That's because you're in the wrong position, lover,' she said, 'as usual.'

The earthquake struck the city of San Francisco in the early evening, when the traffic was at its greatest. It recorded 8.5 on the Richter scale. Within one minute, forty-five seconds, three hundred and eighty thousand people were dead.

Not long after, in Rome, at six o'clock in the morning, Cardinal Benelli stood before the Pope. A short while later he arrived at the Vatican observatory.

'Cardinal!'

The observatory technician was the same man with the bald pate and beady eyes Benelli had met on the last occasion. This time he was less assured. He'd been summoned out of bed on the orders of the Pope only a few minutes before and he was very nervous as a result.

'Cardinal, how can I help you?'

Benelli looked at him, equally bewildered. How could he explain without sounding mad?

'Signor . . . ?'

'Pundi,' said the technician. He could see the prelate was flustered and unsure of himself. What was going on?

'Signor Pundi,' said Benelli. 'A few months ago I came here with a monk. Do you remember?'

'Of course.' The technician had been very impressed to have received the second most important person in the Vatican.

'You showed me some planets.'

'I showed you a conjunction of the planets. In fact, there was an interesting retrograde loop between —'

'Stop!' shouted Benelli. 'Stop! What did I see?'

'See? What did you see? Well, as I said, planets.'

'No!' cried Benelli. 'In my vision, I saw stellar constellations, I saw planets, I saw animals.'

'Animals?' The technician fiddled with his clipboard. 'Er, yes, I will try and help you,' he said, overwhelmed. Obviously, the good Cardinal was having a breakdown.

Benelli nursed his head in his hands. 'I saw stars. I saw planets. I saw animals.' He started. 'You told me that the planets were the same as before.'

'Yes,' said the technician, frightened now. 'The same as before. You saw the same conjunction of planets as in AD 66. The seventh of March. A close alignment between Mars, Neptune and Uranus. I told you, but of course you know, that a conjunction is a close apparent approach between celestial objects . . .'

'That's it,' said Benelli, almost weeping. 'But I also saw stars.'

'But there are billions of stars, at least a hundred billion.'

'Yes, but on that day, the stars and the planets were aligned in a special relationship,' said Benelli. 'You have to help me find them.'

The technician looked on helplessly. 'I could phone the observatories around the world,' he said, 'but what shall I say? How can I describe the stars you saw? It is like looking for a needle in a haystack. They are just points of light.'

Benelli stared wildly about him. Out of one hundred billion or more stars he had seen some of them, as well as these planets. He had seen a snapshot of a moment in time on earth and now he was trying to repeat it.

'Kneel,' he said desperately.

'Kneel?'

So they knelt and Benelli prayed. Soon he had his original vision again. But now, he also understood how to interpret it. He should not look at all this from the perspective of the Church, but from the perspective of the powers of evil. The Cardinal seized the poor lab technician, still on his knees. 'Pretend that you are a sorcerer in ancient times, one of the Magi, people who could read the stars. Pretend that you are looking at the sky on the seventh of March in AD 66. What do you see?'

'Er, I see the planets, er, Mars, Neptune and Uranus, in conjunction.'

'But where?'

'Er, in Pisces. These planets are in the star sign Pisces.'

'Yes! And what is Pisces, but the fish? And the fish represents the fisherman, St Peter. What does Mars represent?'

'Er, war.'

'And Neptune and Uranus?'

'Um . . .' The technician frantically tried to recall. 'Neptune represents the mystic and Uranus the magician.'

'Don't you see?' whispered Benelli. 'A magician and St Peter, the mystic, fought a battle in AD 66.'

'Who won?' said the technician, perspiring heavily. The Cardinal was quite clearly off his ecclesiastical trolley.

'St Peter,' cried Benelli, 'because it was fought in the constellation of Pisces, the fish. The fisherman won; the magician's power was overshadowed. But that's not the point, don't you realise? That was then. The vision is trying to tell me who the magician was, what creature of evil is coming!'

'Creature of evil . . .' The lab technician rose from his knees. 'Cardinal, forgive me, but I really think that . . .'

Benelli did not hear him. He remained on his knees. He was weeping bitterly. Now he knew who the Angel of Darkness was.

The Acts of the Apostles had made it very clear.

'Did you see what has happened?' Paul said in an incredulous voice, staring at the television set.

'Yes,' said Helen as she came out of the bathroom. 'There's been an earthquake in San Francisco, and thousands of ants have perished.' She lied, 'I could have told you that a while ago.'

'How do you know this?'

'The coin, of course.' She slipped into her muslin dress. 'I told you, it increasingly manifests its strength. But that's nothing. Come on, we mustn't be late.'

They left the expensive block of apartments. 'Turn down here,' she said. They passed along a grimy back street, crowded with tavernas and cafés in front of which sat sullen-faced men, nursing their brandies. The haunt of the local mafia. The murderers glared back at them, their faces closed, cruel and merciless.

'They won't harm us.' Helen passed a gang drinking from wine bottles as they sat on a sidewalk. Ostentatiously, she flaunted her sapphire and diamond ring at them. One or two stepped forward. However, as quickly, they slunk back into the shadows.

'They're afraid,' Helen said, 'and so they should be.' With her influence she could easily disable or destroy them. By distracting their minds so that they'd step off the pavement into the passing traffic. Or making herself invisible to their eyes, even when in human form. The evil spirits in the mafiosi recognised her anyway, and they were obedient to her will. They always obeyed their masters. They had no choice; their thoughts were no longer their own.

Paul and Helen came to the River Tiber and began to walk along its banks.

'That's where we're heading.' Helen pointed to a bridge further down river. It was the Ponte Fabricio, the oldest bridge still in use over the Tiber, built in 62 BC. As they approached it, Helen began to reminisce.

'I remember crossing this bridge on my first visit to Rome. It was early in the morning and packed with people coming into the city for market day. The stench from the river got me and I felt quite sick. It was so different from the port of Tyre where I used to live. There we had decent sanitation at least.'

A moment later, from out of the shadows a figure emerged and stood in their way. He pulled heavily on a cigarette and studied them both. Rino Marcelli was a stocky man of fifty-three with a saturnine complexion and the face of a thug, characteristics that complemented his nature. He was a mafia godfather and into every vice. Helen had helped him build his little empire. They belonged to the same secret society in Rome and he treated her with the greatest respect.

Rino didn't speak to Helen but walked in front of them both. They crossed the bridge onto the Tibertine Island.

'This island's been populated since early Roman times,' continued Helen conversationally. 'There was a temple to Aesculapius, the god of medicine, over there.' She pointed. 'It was put up long before I was born. And there was a slave market over here. You could get some good bargains if you came early and pre-empted the buyers for the gladiatorial displays.'

Paul and Helen began to walk down the left-hand side of the Tibertine Island. She slipped her hand into his. They strolled like a wealthy couple out for an evening walk, without a care in the world. They walked on, to the northern tip of the island, past the houses of fishermen and boatmen.

'The palace was situated here,' said Helen. 'They levelled it not long after he died.'

Paul looked. All he saw was a small park with trees and stone benches for people to sit on. Helen directed him to one corner of the park and they approached a concrete bunker with a massive steel door. It had been drawn back to reveal a flight of very old and worn steps. Evidently they led to somewhere underneath the park. Helen continued to chat as they descended.

'Directly across the river is the Trastevere area, where his greatest enemy used to live. Of course, it's changed over the centuries. In my time it used to be the Jewish section, a ghetto. They had tanners, moneylenders, coppersmiths. We never knew when he first arrived. We didn't expect a challenge from an illiterate fisherman.'

They passed along a narrow corridor with many openings, a number of which appeared to be false trails. Finally, the corridor opened out into a huge cave. Paul gazed with awe, for it was not just a cave, it was an underground temple, hollowed out from the bedrock of the island, a small replica of a mighty temple that had once existed in the palace above. No true light penetrated this infernal gloom. Instead, the place was bathed in a curious yellow glow that arose from no discernible source.

Paul peered about him. In the centre of the cave, seats carved from a dark, lustrous granite surrounded a huge pentacle etched into the floor with gold lettering. On the walls frescos depicted scenes from an ancient time.

They revealed a pagan place of worship in which acolytes were performing human sacrifices while a woman and high priest looked on. The scenes were filled with blood; unmistakable signs of terror were etched on the faces of their victims.

Paul gasped in amazement as he fixed his attention on one scene that was particularly vivid. For the face of the woman in the painting was Helen's, while the features of the high priest were not dissimilar to those of Paul.

Yet, even as Paul watched, the picture rippled slightly like an image in a pool, as if the painting were a living one. The visage of the high priest assumed a crueller aspect and his stature became taller. The clothes altered as well. The sorcerer's robe of pure gold metamorphosed into one of pitch-black. A new image emerged before Paul's eyes – a haughty and mighty figure of pagan times, a king of old.

'Who is it?'

'You'll soon find out,' said Helen in a sharp tone. 'Come.'

Helen stood in the centre of the temple, inside the pentacle, Paul beside her. What he'd supposed were dark shadows along the walls of the cave now stepped forward. They were men and women dressed in the ancient vestments Paul had seen once before when he'd been about to ascend to the eighth astral.

Two servitors approached Helen and Paul and stripped them of their clothing. Two more placed vestments on them, similar to those of their companions, as well as gold and silver ornaments. Paul made no resistance. His mind and his movements were lethargic and unquestioning, obedient to the will of the coin.

The atmosphere in the underground temple became

warm and close. The yellow light that permeated the darkness slowly began to diminish until there was only the faint flicker of black candles at the back of the temple. Paul stared ahead of him. There was nothing there, no ornamentation save the glistening rock of which the Tibertine Island was formed. Helen turned to Paul.

'Before you ascend to the last astral, we need to use the power of the coin to see inside a tomb. It lies not far from here. Whatever you see do *not* let your mind be deflected. Do you understand? One mistake and it could destroy both our physical and spirit bodies.'

Paul nodded. Only one thought dominated his mind: ascending the last astral. Why Helen should wish to search within a tomb he didn't know, or care. About them the other members of the temple gathered in a circle and started to chant in an unknown tongue.

For some time, Paul perceived nothing. Helen then passed him a cup and told him to drink deeply from it. Paul drank. The taste was sweet and a great tiredness flowed through him. He was no longer conscious of his limbs; his mind concentrated on the wall before him. He peered into the blackness like an astronomer trying to detect a star in the deepest wells of space.

Then slowly, from the nothingness, there emerged a temple of old, similar to the one in which they now stood, but far larger in size, with a ceiling that towered above it. It was full of people. All around Paul were many slaves and minions, bowing in worship. The air was heavy with incense and the smell of human sacrifice; the floor was bespattered with blood. Then this image faded and the rock before him became like a curtain of velvet, high-lighted only by a slight diminution in the blackness surrounding it. Paul made towards it.

'Paul, you must tell me what you see. I cannot go;

I am only the guardian of the coin. You must wield it.'

Although Helen's spiritual power was very great, she was reluctant to enter the tomb herself, so close to the heart of the Vatican. She was uncertain what they might find. Better for him to go first.

Suddenly, Paul was elsewhere. He stood in a corridor, narrow and dusty. It seemed to be a tunnel that had just been opened up, for at one end, bricks lay scattered on the floor. Paul looked towards the opening. From it radiated a source of light, brilliant and pure. It strained Paul's eyes even to look at it. It seared into his soul.

'Turn away, turn away,' cried Helen. If he walked into St Peter's Basilica itself, to the tomb of the Apostle, he would be lost to them.

After some hesitation, Paul averted his eyes. He started to proceed along the tunnel much as Cardinal Benelli had done the day before. Reaching the base of the obelisk, he saw a huge cross painted in red on the wall and the inscription '*pp Sylvestris II*'. Paul made ready to pass through the tunnel wall into the tomb of the medieval Pope. It was then he became aware of a presence. A physical presence and a holy one. For the Pope had placed someone there after all.

Catherine of Benedetto.

She stood alone, but uncowed, in that narrow tunnel in the depths of night. Desperately, she tried to look beyond Paul to determine who was the true wielder of the coin. She also sought to prevent Paul's entrance into the last resting place of Sylvester II to divine its mighty secret.

'You shall not pass,' said the nun.

'Paul, get back, get back!' screamed the voice of Helen. 'Do not challenge her.'

But it was too late. Paul continued forward. Abruptly,

he felt the presence of Helen beside him. Taken by surprise at the unexpected appearance of a mortal enemy, the sorceress had thrown herself across the dark curtain. Now the antagonists faced each other on the outermost rim of the ninth astral. A figure of light and a figure of darkness.

'You shall not pass! *You shall not pass!*'

Paul saw the conflict only dimly, warriors struggling in a spiritual field; the figure defended by her faith and a monster that relentlessly sought to destroy her, rapidly transmogrifying from a snake to a scorpion to a wolf.

Paul's spirit was so rocked that he did not know whether he was in the body or out of it. In his ears rang cries of pain and suffering. At one stage he saw the faces of Rachel and Marie, as the saint sought to help recover his freedom of will. Yet Paul still held onto the coin and fixed his will on passing into the tomb. Slave to his own ambition and pride, he could not escape. He had enslaved himself.

There was a tremendous scream, one of agony.

Paul woke to find himself in the underground temple again. Helen was beside him, acolytes crowding around her. She was deadly pale. Having suffered a mortal wound, her power and her lifespan on earth had dramatically diminished. But she was alive; just.

'The fools, the fools,' she croaked. 'They've revealed the only power they have. The woman can defeat me but she cannot defeat our master. Born into the world, she cannot protect them against the Angel.'

Helen's eyes smouldered with evil.

'They have lost. Nothing can stop us now.'

It was Cardinal Benelli who found her in the morning, before the tomb of Pope Sylvester. He was sure she was dead. However, eventually, Catherine of Benedetto stirred.

'Tell the Holy Father,' she murmured. 'Tell him that I have seen the Angel of Darkness.'

She spoke again and Benelli's blood ran cold. For she confirmed what he already knew.

'It is Simon Magus.'

THE FISHERMAN

CHAPTER THIRTY-THREE

There was a man named Simon who had previously practised magic in the city and amazed the nation of Samaria, saying that he himself was somebody great. They all gave heed to him, from the least to the greatest, saying, 'This man is that power of God which is called Great.' And they gave heed to him, because for a long time he had amazed them with his magic.

The Acts of the Apostles 8:9–11

HIGH PRINCE OF SORCERERS, THE greatest black-magician who ever lived.

Of Simon Magus, the first heretic, the Church knew much; not least since the Bible and the Apocryphal New Testament recounted the dreadful tale. A master of illusion, a diabolist of the first order, the Magus lived at the same time as St Peter. Claiming to be the Son of the Most High, he was found guilty by the Church of the greatest heresy of all, that of falsely asserting that he was divine. In this he had committed a spiritual sin against the Holy Ghost for which there could be no forgiveness.

The Secret Archives in the Vatican contained much testimony against him and the unrivalled powers of evil he exercised in his attempts falsely to usurp the role of Christ. In the first list of prohibited books, the *Decretum Gelasianum*, drawn up by the Church in the fifth century, the writings of the Magus were banned and declared 'damned for eternity' along with their author.

Simon Magus, the son of Antonius and Rachel, was born in Samaria, modern-day Israel. He became versed in the mysteries of the occult from an early age and he joined a sect led by one Dositheus, which comprised twenty-nine males and a woman called Helena or Helen. Soon the Magus (meaning 'magician', as he became known to one and all) had supplanted his teacher and taken Helen, said to be a prostitute from Tyre, as his lover. He came to Rome, where he built a palace on the island located in the middle of the Tiber. It was from here that the Magus expounded his doctrine of gnosticism, the mystical knowledge of spiritual enlightenment.

Simon Magus preached that the world had been created by a power that believed itself to be god, but which was, in fact, nothing but a pale reflection of the true God. He also alleged that human souls had fallen from grace onto earth and that only the redeemer of mankind could bring them back to their former perfection. The redeemer in question was, of course, Simon Magus, who claimed to be the son of the true God. As for Christ, he alleged that Jesus was not crucified, but that it was only an illusion and that he was not born of the Virgin Mary.

The Magus asserted that his lover, Helen, was the fount of all wisdom. She had fallen from her celestial seat into the world, betrayed by the Angels she had created, who forced her to live in human form, to prevent her returning to the true God. She would become Helen of Troy and the Magus prophesied that she was doomed to be a prostitute for centuries afterwards, the common property of mankind. Finally, through the power of the Magus, she would return to her rightful seat.

All this dogma, the cruellest mockery of the incarnation of Christ, the Magus preached far and wide. It was eagerly embraced by people in a time when each and every cult was given credence by a highly superstitious population. Soon, Simon became famous throughout Samaria and his legendary powers were spoken of with awe. For it seemed that, like the Messiah, he could raise the dead, perform miracles, make the lame whole and the blind see, and command spirits to appear.

Where this diabolical power came from no one knew apart from his lover, Helen. The Magus had only revealed to her that he had found a Coin of Judas, which he was at great pains to keep secret from the rest of mankind. It was in Samaria that Simon Magus first met the true Apostles and he was both astonished and fascinated by the incredible power of the Holy Spirit that worked through them. Wanting this magical power for his own, he offered the Apostles money for it. However, he was told:

Your silver perish with you, because you thought you could obtain the gift of God with money . . . repent therefore of this wickedness of yours.

Yet the Magus did not repent of his simony. Instead, his heart was suffused with the deepest malice and hate. He vowed that what he could not have, he would destroy.

He would bring down the Christian religion – by turning the might of the Roman Empire against it. And no one on earth could stop him. For the Magus was certain of the invincibility of his Coin of Judas – no human being could oppose it. Yet, he was wrong in this. One could.

A humble fisherman. An old Jew.

Simon Magus remained in Samaria, where he was worshipped as a god, until there arose, in those dark times of the Roman Empire, another great force of evil that drew him to the capital of the world like iron to a magnet – the Emperor Nero.

Often called the Antichrist, a man whom the historian Pliny the Elder described as the 'poison of the world', this paunchy and thin-legged Emperor with the neck of a bull, the crimped blond hair of a charioteer and the blotched skin of a dissolute, was to make himself famous in history, less for his mediocre acting talents than for reducing the citizenry of Rome to the very depths of cruelty and degradation.

It was Nero who encouraged all manner of evil. Dressed as a gladiator he frequently led the slaughter in the Circus Maximus; dancing in the blood of his victims with rapture; using Christians as human torches to light his gardens; raffling off others to be raped. Nero was a monster when it came to the extremes of cruelty and profligacy.

Able to corrupt the human world, Nero did not have the one thing that might enable him to extend his corruption and persecution eternally. Yet he thought he knew someone who did, for Nero was searching for a coin.

The Emperor begged the wizard to appear before him. The journey from Samaria to Rome was a long one. Finally, however, the Magus crossed the Ponte Fabricio and entered Rome – the sink of iniquity, the new Babylon, as the Christians called it.

The meeting of these mighty spirits of darkness was a

momentous one and, together, they planned to ensure that their evil became a permanent feature of the empire, making Nero's current wickedness appear child's play in comparison. However, in perhaps one of the strangest events of human history, even as these two devils met, there came an Apostle who passed over that same bridge; and he came secretly.

Across from the island where Simon Magus was soon to build his palace and temple, in the Jewish section of Rome, the Trastevere, among the publicans, the coppersmiths, the moneylenders and the boatmen, an illiterate and white-haired fisherman, together with his secretary, Mark, made his home behind the shop of Aquila and Priscilla.

For St Peter was searching for the coin.

Within a short time the Magus became famous in Rome, fêted by the rich and powerful. He rapidly became Nero's favourite. Always accompanied by his faithful Helen and a large black dog, at dinner parties he entranced and frightened the citizenry. It seemed he could communicate with the spirits, conjure phantoms from the air, raise the dead, turn stones to bread. More than that, he could read the stars as easily as a human map.

Simon Magus could be challenged by no one, for he brought fear and death in his footsteps. He even boasted that he could create human beings with souls. 'I am the Word of God,' he told them. 'I am the glorious one, I am the Paraclete, the Almighty, I am the whole of God.' It was impressive stuff and Nero loved it. He knew, of course, that only he, Nero, was truly divine. However, it was fun to have some competition. For a while, that is.

Yet all good things come to an end.

One afternoon, Nero summoned the Magus to attend

on him the following day at the Campus Martius, a military parade ground in Rome. Why? To face a contest with another magician. It was, of course, a huge joke, the monarch told his courtiers. He let them in on the secret. The most powerful sorcerer in all the Roman Empire was going to compete against a wretched Jew who – laugh, O you Romans – had told Nero that he could vanquish the Magus.

The night before Simon left his palace, Helen came to him. She told him that she'd had a terrible dream. She had seen in the heavens that he would be defeated by a man bearing the sign of the fish. She begged Simon Magus not to go, but he ignored her. It was impossible. She'd read the stars incorrectly. He didn't bother to check.

'I will return, I promise,' he said. He set off over the Ponte Fabricio for the last time.

The scene that greeted the sorcerer in the field of battle was a happy one. Nero was resplendent in his latest cloak of the finest gold thread (a present to himself as usual). About him were soldiers from the Praetorian Guard as well as senators, knights, ambassadors; all fawning and servile, anxious to curry favour. Finally, there were the multitudes, avid to see this, the latest comedy act, before they hurried off to the races in the circus. Once the Magus had finished his witty introduction, the Emperor produced his joke, his mighty magician, from the back of the crowd. Truly, it was a wonderful jest and the audience adored it.

There stood an old Jew, still smelling of the Trastevere one imagines, and beside him Paul of Tarsus. How the crowd roared with delight. Once the merriment had subsided, the Magus turned to go. He'd various other entertainments planned that day. Yet the Emperor called him back with a slight crook of his finger. He pointed to a high wooden tower that had been constructed by his soldiers before them.

'If you are who you are, then you can fly,' Nero said to his favourite magician.

Encouraged by the delighted calls of the crowd, Simon Magus, the erstwhile Son of God, went to climb the tower. When he neared the bottom, a figure broke from the crowd. Helen was distraught. Tormented by her dream, she'd followed him from his palace.

'Do not challenge this man, Simon,' she beseeched him. 'He is far greater than you.'

The Magus laughed with the crowd. 'Who can oppose me? Am I not the Christ?'

But he was wrong. One man could oppose him. He had no coin, no power, no things of the world. But his magic was greater than the universe itself.

Faith.

The Acts of the Holy Apostles Peter and Paul state it thus:

Then [the Magus] went up upon the tower in the face of all and, crowned with laurels, he stretched forth his hands, and began to fly. And when Nero saw him flying, he said to Peter: 'This Simon is true; but thou and Paul are deceivers.' To whom Peter said: 'Immediately shalt thou know that we are true disciples of Christ; but that he is not Christ, but a magician and a malefactor.' Nero said, 'Do you still persist? Behold, you see him going up into heaven . . .'

Peter, looking steadfastly against Simon, said, 'I adjure you, angels of Satan, who are carrying him into the air, to deceive the hearts of the unbelievers, by the God that created all things, and by Jesus Christ, whom on the third day He raised from the dead, no longer from this hour to keep him up, but to let him go.' And immediately, being let go [Simon Magus] fell into a place called the Sacra Via, that is, the Holy Way, and perished by an evil fate.

Infuriated by the death of his favoured magician, Nero vowed revenge. He got it. Within a few months, St Peter was crucified, upside down, in the gardens of Nero. He did not resist, he did not use his spiritual power, which puzzled Nero even more. However, try as he might, Nero could never find the Apostle's body. There was one other thing that Nero could not find, despite his insatiable searching, until his own suicide a year later, in AD 68.

The Coin of Judas held by the Magus.

Benelli stood before the Pope. The task was hopeless. They were doomed.

'Holy Father, we are facing the destruction of the Church. Only St Peter had the ability to defeat Simon Magus. I beg you command the tomb of Sylvester II to be opened. It may contain something which can help us. Or, at least, summon the Father Confessor back to Rome.'

The pontiff was silent.

'Holy Father, is it also true that Catherine of Benedetto has left the Vatican?' Benelli asked.

'She has done what she can for us in Rome. You and I must oppose the Magus in this place.'

Benelli could see the doubt in his eyes. The pontiff did not know what course of action to take. An ability to see into the future had not been given him and he gave the impression of a man rent with indecision in this crisis.

'What can we do?' said Benelli. He was agonised. It

was as if the pontiff were accepting their doom, as if he had already given up.

John XXV thought for a long time. 'Let us see whether this man, Paul, takes the final step and the coin becomes complete. Only if he willingly agrees to sell his soul can this happen. Perhaps he will not permit this evil to come into the world even at this late stage.'

'But, Holy Father, what if he does?' said Benelli desperately. 'Who can oppose the Magus?'

'No one can,' said the pontiff. 'No human being can. I believe this to be true.'

Benelli hesitated. Yet, he had to declare what was on his mind. 'You believe that one of us – the Father Confessor, Catherine of Benedetto or I – may betray you? You believe Pope Sylvester's prophecy, that if one of the remaining coins comes into the hands of the one closest to the Pope, the Church itself will fall?'

'Yes.' The dreadful truth was told.

'So, what do we do if the Magus comes?'

'We wait.'

'For whom? For whom?' cried Benelli.

'For the fisherman,' replied the Pope softly.

CHAPTER THIRTY-FOUR

> *[God] does not propose to restrain the human*
> *sins which are possible to man through his*
> *own free will, such as the abnegation of the*
> *faith and the devotion of himself to the devil,*
> *which things are in the power of the human*
> *will.*
>
> *Malleus Maleficarum,*
> 'Hammer of the Witches'

'WE MUST GO TO THE ninth astral.'

Helen and Paul sat in the underground temple. He could see she was mortally ill. In her battle with Catherine of Benedetto before the tomb of Sylvester II she had lost a huge amount of her spiritual energy. It was as if, in some invisible fashion, the power of the saint had cracked the vessel that contained her soul and its essence was slowly leaking away. Yet although Helen's face had aged and her physical body seemed to have shrunk, her malevolence remained. So did her imperative need to return the Coin of Judas to its master. For her own sake.

'I thought we were returning home.'

'There is no time,' said Helen. 'These spirits may attack again and summon others to help them.'

She rose from one of the black granite chairs and stepped into the pentacle.

'Paul, listen to me,' she said, coughing badly. 'You are on the final part of your journey. Beyond the ninth astral no human being can pass, only you. The coin will take you. After that nothing, no one on earth, no creature on earth can stop you.'

'And if I do?'

'You will acquire the power and the insight of an Angel and you will be able to look deep into the cosmic reality of things. The decision is yours. It is your choice.'

For Paul there was no longer any decision to be made. He could not elect otherwise, the evil of the coin had warped and corrupted his core. Humanity, the world, his loved ones – none of these had the least hold on him. To have the power and insight of an Angel, yet still to be in the world: it was a gift impossible for him to refuse – whatever the consequences. He would be the greatest, and wisest, of men. He would raise up and cast down those whom he desired. Helen watched him keenly. He didn't yet appreciate the consequences of this gift.

'Where is the coin?' Paul asked anxiously.

'It exists wholly in the world now. You have only to think of it and it is with you.'

Paul closed his eyes. Before them appeared the Coin of Judas. It had the deepest red glow to it, the colour of blood. 'Let us go,' he said simply.

Together they stepped into the pentacle again to visit the last astral of all – the ninth astral.

Paul stood with Helen beside him. They were passing through a curious snowstorm. There was nothing else, no sense of time, no points of reference save for the snow that fell all around them. Paul realised it was a cosmic vision and that the 'snow' he was witnessing constituted constellations and planets without number.

After the snowstorm there was the darkness. Finally, a comprehension of his own being, and that of Helen, returned back to Paul – as if he were making an impression on the face of the deep itself, making a mark on a blank slate. Helen had only the faintest yellow outline to distinguish her from the nothingness that surrounded them. His own form was sheathed in a pale red light.

'Look.'

From the darkness came light. Then Paul perceived the Way. It appeared like a huge path, vast beyond all human or angelic measurement. Spreading out across the eternal darkness, it shimmered faintly. Wherever Paul stood on the Way it would be the same – without beginning, without end – the eternal road of all spirits. Even as Paul contemplated it, the mystical vision altered. Now the Way seemed like an endless ladder. Then it comprised circles of light that expanded upwards and outwards forever, a whirlpool of infinite height and depth.

'Where are we?'

'You are perceiving the Way,' said Helen. 'The path along which all spirits journey. All the things you have seen on the astral planes and all the levels of the universe are comprehended within it. It is one and many, depending on the perception.'

'But it seems to be a circle at times, and not a path.'

Helen replied, 'This is because it can only be truly seen by those beyond all human and angelic limitations, so my master taught me. It changes even for the Angels and the Archangels. All things comprehend the Way differently. Your revelations are not the same as mine and, even within your own insight, the perception of the Way is infinite.'

'And beyond the perception of Angels and Archangels?'

'There lie the Principalities, the Powers, the Virtues
and the Dominions.'

'And beyond them?'

'The Thrones. Then the Cherubim and the Seraphim.
There are nine orders in the angelic hierarchy. And
beyond these nine orders are more mysteries that progress into the mind of God.'

'So there is a God?'

'Oh, yes,' said Helen. 'Both good and evil accept there
is a God, an essence without being and limit, from which
all things are derived. It's just that their perception of it
is so different.'

'How?'

Helen continued to lie: 'The basis of all things which
we call God is unconfined, it is an infinite nothingness,
yet it contains everything. It has no boundaries, whether
of good or evil. It flows without restriction and the Way
that you see is part of it. It cannot be contained and it
has no disposition. It neither loves, nor hates. It neither
craves, nor desires. It simply is. It has no conflict or
opposition. It embraces everything – every thought, every
being, every world, every power, every concept. It is the
Word that defines everything. This is what I was taught
by one much greater than I, one who is my master.

'But from this Word came the angelic orders and in
all of them there was contradiction for, not being the
whole, they comprised parts. Being parts they yearned
for the whole and in that way contradiction was born.
And each fought to rejoin the source, and from this came
into being the paths of good and evil.'

'And what of humanity?' asked Paul.

Helen said, 'I was taught that from the tiniest of tiny

particles of the Way the world was created and it contained contradiction for, like all the parts, it craved to return to the whole. Then the powers beyond even the angelic, the two Sons, both sought it and its creatures, but for different reasons. The Son of God sought it so that all men would glorify him. He also sought to impose conditions. He falsely told mankind that the path to God could be achieved only through him, by following in his footsteps.

'But the Other Son imposed no such conditions. He allowed mankind free choice to do as they wished; for the Other Son knew that God was beyond limitation, beyond strife, beyond contradiction, beyond argument, beyond beginnings and ends. It simply was. And the Other Son also taught that mankind should freely choose, and by doing whatever they chose, in that way to find God.'

'So there is no good and evil?'

'You have said it,' said Helen. 'Ultimately, there is no contradiction. God is not divided and freedom of choice is not limited. All men can follow the path to God in their own way. You see, Paul, they have falsely taught you that evil has a negative meaning, a pejorative tone, an antagonism. But it does not. It does not seek to divide man; it imposes no moral limitations, no restrictions, no punishments, no disobedience. It asserts only that human beings are free to do all that they wish and they will not be punished for it. With this coin you can find out this for yourself. You do not have to believe what I say.'

'But what are these coins?'

'They are coins but they represent far more. They are the price Judas Iscariot was paid to bring Christ to judgement.'

'But Christ was betrayed.'

'No, of course he wasn't,' said Helen. 'He arranged it all himself. As a Son, one above all human and angelic orders, Christ could raise himself up from the dead without the need for the power of God. You see, Christ demanded that all worship him as the *only* path to God. Yet he failed, for mankind judged and condemned him for this false doctrine. You see, the one thing he cannot take away is your free choice, to behold God independently of him. You can have all this.'

'If only I deny?'

'Yes, if you only deny here, on the Way, that he has power over you. With that, the coin will give all that you want. Just as it condemned him, it will set you free.'

'And the words?'

'The coin itself will give them to you. Paul, I can go no further for it is not given that I should influence you in your decision.'

With that, the faint yellow glow about her faded and to Paul it was as if her spirit were no longer there. Yet Helen remained beside him. Although not the possessor of the coin, she was still its guardian for a while longer.

In spirit, Paul stood on the outermost rim of the ninth astral. On earth, Catherine of Benedetto prayed before an altar in her convent. As Paul held up the Coin of Judas, he perceived her, a frail old woman. 'The spirit lies, Paul,' she told him. 'If you use the coin you will become the slave of the master of the Field of Blood. He seeks a great treasure which was freely given to you, eternal life.'

'I see no such treasure. How can I find it?'

'Only through love and faith, and these will also be given to you if you ask. There is no other way, no other path. It cannot be bought, it cannot be seized, it cannot be stolen. There is no power on earth or heaven that can wrest it from its hiding place. You are not the master of this coin, Paul. Its true master will control you, just as it controls others. For the one who wields this coin seeks to destroy your soul and all that you love, to command you as a vassal of his own. I beg of you, do not do this act.'

Paul felt the words of the holy one penetrate deep into his soul. Yet even as she sought to persuade him, on the other side the endless power of the coin, its self-love, poured into him like water filling a jug. Paul made his decision. All for him.

Holding up the coin and in a tongue never heard on earth, he cried out: 'I deny the power of God. I deny the salvation of my soul for all eternity.'

With that Paul was no longer standing on a path that went forever onwards; he was standing at a fork in the road that bifurcated to the right and left. Again, a prayer of Catherine of Benedetto came urgently to Paul's mind. 'Do not do this, I beg you. If you do, you can no longer save yourself.'

Continuing to hold the coin in front of him, Paul asserted, 'I accept the power of this coin. It is my choice freely made.'

The crossroads faded. The Way was a single path again. Paul started down what was the left fork, for the right was lost to him. As he advanced, it changed in appearance. The fork became a vast tunnel. Through it radiated the narrowest of bridges, a thread through the eye of a needle. For the road into the Abyss was a deception unto the last – a mockery of the path of Light, since, in truth, it was sufficiently wide and broad to encompass all humanity within its scope. Helen watched Paul go.

'Farewell,' she said.

When he returned to the world of men, Paul would no longer be as before. He would be the servant of the Magus and, at the next nightfall, the sorcerer would possess him wholly.

One other human soul bore witness to this terrible event. Before the altar of God, Catherine of Benedetto looked down that narrow path, far into the depths of the chasm, before it closed. She saw the presence of the spirit that would afflict the world, the true master of the coin. Her heart was bereft.

For Simon Magus, the Angel of Darkness, had started on his journey.

CHAPTER THIRTY-FIVE

Therefore, the devil can, by moving the inner perceptions and humours, effect changes in the actions and faculties, physical, mental and emotional, working by means of any physical organ whatsoever, and this accords with Saint Thomas. And this sort we believe to have been the acts of Simon Magus in the incantations which are narrated of him.

Malleus Maleficarum,
'Hammer of the Witches'

RACHEL FLED INTO HER MOTHER'S room in the convent. Marie awoke with a start.

'They're here.'

'Who?'

'Evil spirits. Outside.'

Bewildered, Marie sat up. She arose from her bed and looked out of the window. In the darkness, she could see the astral projections clearly now, as the forces of evil impinged directly upon her mind. They were dragging her into the world of the spirit. The images she witnessed were as vivid as on earth but with an additional intensity. Wolves prowled about in the garden, vultures perched on the roof, snakes slithered along the guttering, scorpions began to crawl out of the woodwork. They waited for the command of their master.

There was a noise at the door and they started back, grasping onto each other.

It was the mother superior. 'It's not safe to remain here.' Quickly, she led them down the stairs and into the living quarters of the nuns. 'Rachel, you should sleep here.' Then, more quietly, 'It is next to the chapel.'

'Where's the Father Confessor?' asked Marie. She could not remove the images she'd seen in her mind. They were going to drive her insane; that was their intention, she was sure. She could no longer see things in the human world properly; they were becoming blurred as if her sight were going.

'Come with me,' replied the nun. As they walked the mother superior looked at Marie, her voice crackling with strain. 'Their power is becoming very great.'

'What can we do?'

'Prayer is the only thing. Spiritual forces cannot be opposed in the same way as human ones.' She looked at Marie. 'But, my child, you are not forgotten. Remember, the Holy Father has sent someone to look after you.'

They climbed the stairs and entered her study. Within a few minutes the Father Confessor arrived. His face told Marie all.

'Marie.' He gently held her hands. 'The spirit will come here – soon.'

Marie wept. 'Tell me,' she said, 'why must I and my child suffer in this way?' She shook her head. 'It is unjust, he is an unjust God; he has betrayed me; he has led me into the hands of my enemies.'

The monk said nothing.

She continued wildly, 'Paul did wrong; he betrayed the murdered girl and her sister. They have a right to ask for vengeance. But I have had no part in this. I have a right to beg for mercy. Is that not so?'

'Marie,' the monk replied, 'I do not know the workings of God, nor do you. This coin is not just for Paul, it is for us all. God teaches humility to the Church as well as to individuals. No one escapes death or temptation in this world, not even the Vicar of Christ. Yet we must judge things at the *end* of the matter, not as they unfold. What I also believe is that you and Rachel are innocent of any wrongdoing.'

Marie rose to go. 'I no longer care about myself, but promise me one thing. That you will stay with my child until the very end.'

The Father Confessor looked into her worn and haunted eyes. The face of Job stared back at him. 'I promise.'

Benelli awoke. He retched into a basin. It was getting worse. Would that he die soon. His sleep was now constantly disturbed by dreams. Macabre dreams, dreams so frighteningly real that they made him return to wakefulness soaked with sweat and the deepest sense of dread.

In one dream he was in a crowd. They were jostling and laughing. He was laughing too, happy to be with them on that sunlit day, though he didn't know why.

Suddenly, someone cried out, 'Verbera! Strike!'

The Cardinal heard the cry and, like all those around him, he took it up, repeating it. Then he was screaming it out at the top of his voice, his face lit up with a frenzied delight.

Then he discerned the object of his pleasure. To his grief, he saw before him a small child, in total fear, fleeing for its life before the merciless race of a lioness. His mind and soul were filled with an unutterable shame. I was there, he thought. I am condemned as well.

Benelli groaned and got out of bed. He looked about his simple bedroom in the Vatican. He felt too ill to lie down, too drained of hope, too full of despair. You were there, the voice told him, you were there. It talked to him now from within.

The Cardinal left his room and crossed the piazza to St Peter's Basilica. It towered up before him in its majesty. As he entered the church, he started to reproach himself.

'You are a sixty-five-year-old man, and you've achieved nothing. You have a cardinal's robe, but you do not merit it. You are the Head of the Inquisition, but you have failed. You're the one who was meant to confront and destroy this evil. Yet, you have achieved nothing. You ignored the revelation given to you. The Holy Father knows this, and of your inadequacy.'

Benelli went to the high altar, then down to the grotto beneath it. He continued to disparage himself. 'Who are you, Benelli, to compare yourself with Catherine of Benedetto or the Father Confessor? You have high office but no sanctity. They have no office yet they fulfil their promise to God and more.'

He crossed over the fallen bricks and into the tunnel. 'You were given a talent and, in truth, you buried yours. God has no need of administrators, of pen-pushers, in his kingdom. When did you last help the poor? Tend the sick? Love the unloved?'

Benelli started down the corridor. He seized a hammer that one of the workmen had left in the entrance.

'Achieve something; do not fail them. Open the tomb of Pope Sylvester. Take the coin and destroy it by placing it with the others in the tomb of St Peter. Then, at least, the Magus cannot use this one.'

Benelli stood before the foundations of the obelisk and the great red cross. Picking up the hammer, he smote the wall again and again.

Suddenly, he stopped. His eyes had fallen upon the words 'Salva me, Redemptor Mundi'.

The Cardinal moaned and sat down. It took him many minutes to come to himself again. They are tempting me, he realised. They are tempting me to take the coin for my own; and they are winning. It is I who will betray.

He threw aside the hammer.

Sadly, he retraced his steps back along the corridor.

Helen stood in the underground temple, waiting. The candles in the pentacle began to flicker and go out. Finally, the pentacle itself vaporised as if hidden in a thick mist. From within it, a plume of thin black smoke issued, then rose and thickened. To Helen's sight it formed into a mighty spectral figure in black, about whose head was a golden crown. The Magus was already beginning his long journey from the underworld.

Finally, the mist cleared and Paul stood in the pentacle once more.

'Don't leave it yet.' Helen was scared. What would happen when he stepped out of it, before the Magus came, she didn't know. A human being with the insight of an Angel was beyond even her comprehension. 'Now you know the truth.'

Paul's voice was full of remorse. 'The coin was not meant for me, was it? It was to bring Simon Magus into the world, through my body and spirit.'

'He is my master. Look.' She drew back part of her dress and showed him a mark on her left shoulder, a mark he'd been unable to see before. It was burnt deep into her flesh, a great scar. 'He's your master as well now.'

Paul was silent. Eventually, he continued, 'Tell me of the coin.'

Helen hesitated. She could no longer see into Paul's mind, since he had become more powerful than she. Why did he want to know this? Surely he could read her thoughts? Or had the coin, by seizing him, freed her from the overlordship of the Magus? An unanticipated hope flickered in the depths of her being.

'I was there, Paul,' she whispered, 'when my beloved master fell and his soul departed from the world.' She groaned at the memory. 'When I saw what had happened I fled Rome, since I knew his victor would destroy the coin as well. I hid it in the earth in a land far away and I waited. When Nero imprisoned the Apostle I came back to savour my revenge.' She coughed, her body racked with pain after the depredations of the saint on her energy.

'I was also there, Paul, when he was crucified one evening before the obelisk, with others. In death his mind sought me out. He told me the coin would stay with me until I wearied of it to the depths of my soul. He also told me that I would be its guardian only, unable to wield it until its true master returned. So it has been. I've wandered the earth, occupying the bodies of others until the Magus returns to claim his own.'

'Why me? I was not the only one you approached, was I?'

'No. You are one of many. The Magus can return only when the cycles of heaven dictate. Within that short period I needed to find a human whose body the Magus could occupy. It had to be a betrayer and one who, through pride and self-love, was prepared to sell his soul. You were the only one who has travelled so far. No one can save you now. You have denied yourself. It is irreversible.'

'And if I step from the pentacle?'

'You will have the vision of an Angel, but not the power, for that belongs to the Magus. When he comes you will be extinguished. By the end of the night you will be no more.'

Paul listened to this. Then he smiled. It was a wonderful smile, of benevolence and understanding.

'This is all true,' he said. 'But I am already the Magus. I was simply testing you. Enter the pentacle and you will be united with your lover once more. But, my darling, this time, I will be your equal, not your master. You have done well. You have waited for me.'

Helen saw the mighty figure of the Magus before her. She cried out in ecstasy, despite all her pain. They'd be united again; her servitude gone. She'd progressed one step further down the path of evil and even more souls would become hers to command. They'd rule together. Angels of Darkness.

'Step within.'

Helen crossed into the pentacle and the Magus embraced her in the mist. He kissed her for the last time in the world.

'What is it like to be an Angel in human form?' Helen said as his arms folded about her.

The Magus laughed softly. 'I will tell you, Helena.' He caressed her. 'As an Angel, I've travelled the paths of darkness further than you and learnt much. In this world there is love even as there is evil. But in the Abyss there is none; love is utterly extinguished there. Only self remains. You see, my darling, we destroy what we most love to make us what we are – the deceivers of mankind. In that alone, there is no deception.'

Helena began to struggle frantically but it was futile. The Magus placed his fingers about her neck and strangled her. Now they were united, body and spirit. Lover no longer, slave for ever.

At that moment, in his prison cell, Helen's servant, Karl Kramer, felt her death in the marrow of his being. He experienced both joy and fear. Joy in that the one who'd imprisoned him had died. Fear in that Helen's master, the shadow of death, was fast approaching.

Soon, the Magus would claim him too, as his own.

CHAPTER THIRTY-SIX

*Far more grievous and violent is the torment
of those who show no sign of being bodily
possessed by devils, but are most terribly possessed in their souls, being fast bound by their
sins and vices. For according to the Apostle,
man becomes the slave of him by whom he is
conquered.*

*And in this respect their case is the most
desperate, since they are the servants of devils,
and can neither resist nor tolerate that domi-
nation. It is clear then that, not they who are
possessed by the devil from without, but they
who are bewitched in their bodies and possessed from within to the perdition of their
souls, are, by reason of many impediments,
the more difficult to heal.*

Malleus Maleficarum,
'Hammer of the Witches'

THE INSIGHT OF AN ANGEL.

Paul found himself lying on a floor. The pentacle and
the body of Helen were nowhere to be seen. Even the
temple about him was hidden. His mind was clear, beautifully clear, like spring water bubbling in a fountain.

However, his body lay rigid as if paralysed. All his senses were also lost to him. For what need of these had an Angel, who could see the world without the need for a human medium? Paul had never considered this aspect of his damnation. They didn't require his flesh at all; they were after his soul.

In his state of paralysis, Paul contemplated the Way, that great path of the spirit. All humankind walked it. Some walked in light, others in darkness – yet all walked that path until they came to the crossroads where they must make their choice. Angels walked it too; Paul could see them, great presences of light and dark, without human aspect but capable of assuming any terrestrial form. As he discerned these things, Paul perceived his own world, a single vine in a vineyard, some of its leaves fresh, others tattered.

Paul also experienced more of the true nature of the Coins of Judas. For they had a mystical as well as a physical reality. They represented the attempt by human beings to buy with money the goods of the spiritual world – faith, hope, charity and love. They also represented all the evil in the world, the price for the making of that dreadful bargain, to enslave the Light and bring him to judgement at the command of another who had no authority over him.

Paul began to experience the fruit of these coins and it was acrid, a distillation of darkness. Only as an Angel could he sample the plenitude of the sufferings of humanity, since he could not die. Immortal, he must sustain the weight of just one thirtieth part of a coin, through his own choice. Wars without count, cruelty, torture, starvation, neglect – unimpeded by time, this limitless misery, the raw sewage of mankind poured into Paul's soul – for the deepest spiritual knowledge came at a price, and it was a truly awesome one.

As Helen had promised, Paul felt the suffering of Melanie Dukes the night Kramer had taken her life. The unbelievable torment she'd experienced as Kramer tortured and killed her. Paul also saw her sister Laura, when she had stood in the church and called on God to exercise his vengeance – both on those who had committed the crime and on those who had protected Kramer from its consequences. As Paul recognised this he comprehended another truth in all its starkness, a truth his mind had resolutely refused to concede while in human form, but which his opened soul could not reject.

Paul had known that Kramer had been guilty.

Before the trial began, Paul had known in his heart that his advice was flawed. Yet he'd said nothing. To admit an error at so late a stage would have been to lose his reputation, to incur humility, to recognise he was not so gifted as he'd supposed. So he had denied this, even to himself. When Suzanne had been attacked by Kramer, the powers of darkness had shown him the truth even as they sought to bind him. Even at that late stage Paul should have admitted the error and done something to ensure that Kramer was never freed, but he had not. In his pride, he had failed them, both the dead girl and her sister. Did they not have a right to call for vengeance? Was God not just?

Paul surveyed a great Field – that of the earth, and as human beings progressed along the furrow of life in which they laboured, Paul saw the changes wrought. Disfigurations to the spirit, worse than any external disease, as the snakes of self-love lashed out, the scorpions of avarice stung and the wolves of hate tore away at the inner being. He saw the sickness that resulted, for, in Truth, the rich were poor, the powerful weak, the greedy unsatisfied, the wise foolish, and all blind. But there was a justice. The devils were forced to feed eternally on the sins they inspired, yet this food never satisfied. Like eating dung.

The pentacle began to emerge and form about him on the temple floor once again, its golden light flaring up as the first of the molten circles completed its orbit. Should Paul lie within its infernal embrace once more, so would he lie in a lake of darkness until the end of time.

In San Francisco, by Presidential decree, the city was ordered to be evacuated. The military were removing by force those who sought to stay. Earth tremors were increasing and the whole country was gripped with a sense of expectation that a second, massive, earthquake was imminent. Bad weather was also expected. Despite this, some people did stay on, their presence undetected. They had no choice, for other reasons.

Marie and Rachel looked out of a convent window as the afternoon slowly moved towards twilight. They could see a storm was approaching. The weather itself seemed to herald the arrival of the Angel and they watched the clouds in silence.

Marie held her daughter in her arms, unable to give her any further comfort or consolation beyond her love. She knew there was no hope of avoiding the fate which approached them, as implacable as death. Marie reflected on the Bible as she stroked her daughter's hair. Poor Job. An innocent man who had had the temerity to challenge God in his suffering. It was Job who had dared to suggest to the Almighty that the fountain of all mercy was itself unjust and unmerciful; that God was a cosmic tyrant – as bad as tyrants of the human world whom he permitted to wreak havoc and inconceivable pain on the lives of others.

Tormented in his misery, Job finally demanded of his creator, 'Are you not ashamed to wrong me?' And God answered him. From out of the whirlwind he asked a question in return: Who is this that darkens counsel by words without insight? Did Job know of the deepest mysteries of things, the innermost workings of evil and their relationship to God? Had he been there at the foundation of the heavens and the earth?

Have the gates of death been revealed to you, or have you seen the gates of deep darkness?

When you know the mind of God you can be the judge, he was told. Job conceded the wisdom of the reply and admitted, 'I have uttered what I did not understand.' Poor Job, poor Judas, poor Paul, thought Marie, all parties in a mystical play of a cosmic and eternal nature which they could not possibly understand.

What would she say to the Angel of Darkness when it came for her and her child? Even more, when it came in the guise of the one she had most loved on this earth? Would Marie curse God and die, as Job's wife told him to do, or would she also say: 'I have uttered what I did not understand?' And if she did, would God compensate her as he had done Job? How would he give back to her even more than she had lost? How would, how could he repay?

And what of all those who suffered around the world without apparent rhyme or reason? What of those who watched their loved ones being slaughtered or destroyed before their eyes? What of those who bore the most dreadful of diseases? What of those destined to starve or to die alone and unloved?

What did they say to their creator in their final

moments on earth? Did they, in faith, bless him for their salvation – even though they knew not how it would occur – or did they curse God and die?

The Father Confessor was also in the convent as that fateful day drew to a close. He knew of the agonies of Marie and Rachel and his prayers were with them. He also knew that the Church itself was in the very greatest danger and, in their hour of need, they appeared to be lost. The physical manifestations that would occur with the arrival of the Magus would be nothing in comparison with their spiritual effects.

It was late when he took a phone call from Hanlon Dawes. The Warden was even more brusque than usual.

'Kramer's dying. They were evacuating the prison. Against my orders, he was placed with other prisoners and an inmate with a grudge against him stabbed him in the chest with a skewer. Anyway, he's a goner. We've taken him to the city hospital and he wants to see you. He'll die tonight.'

The monk exhaled audibly. He might have known the powers of evil would produce their final trick to lure him away from Marie in her most tragic hour.

'I cannot come.'

'You must,' said Dawes angrily. 'He wants to talk to you.' He paused, 'Look, I know it's only to mock you, but the prison rules say that a dying prisoner may request a priest and he's requested you. That's the rules, so you must come. Rules are rules.' Dawes continued sardonically, 'Personally, I'm glad it's happened. The bastard's got what he deserves and it's been a long time coming.'

If Dawes had his way, murderers would be shot immediately after sentence. No point in inconveniencing the world any further.

'I cannot,' said the Father Confessor. Abruptly, he put down the phone. How could he go to Kramer, a man of such monstrous evil, and break his promise to Marie? He started to ring for other priests. Yet, as he heard the soft burr of the unanswered phones sounding in his ears, he knew he must make a choice. Be deceived again by the powers of darkness or perhaps deny a man absolution when he most needed it? Lord, he thought to himself, why do you never speak to me in a way I can understand?

The Father Confessor made for the door. He could still be back before twilight. In any case, the Magus would come for him wherever he was. He had no doubt of the consequences.

Slowly, the pentacle completed itself.

Lying paralysed on the cellar floor, suffering pouring through him now like a mighty ocean that carried him helplessly along in its wake, Paul's soul was close to its dissolution. It was impossible for him to save himself.

Yet, another tried to save him before the night came. A vision came to Paul as an act of grace by one who loved him, though he knew it not.

In his last revelation on earth, Paul stood in the Basilica of St Peter's. For now this, the greatest church in Christendom, was unable to resist a being who held one of the last three Coins of Judas. Paul recognised its mighty columns, the Pietà of Michelangelo, the Chapel of St Peter, the eighty-nine candles flickering quietly at the high altar. Under this hallowed ground lay two thousand years of human history, two thousand years in which the smallest of churches had become the greatest. While Paul looked towards the high altar the modern basilica faded before his eyes, an insubstantial vision. He travelled back into the past.

Paul saw the basilica of the sixteenth century, the older church torn down on the imperious orders of Pope Julius in 1506. The great dome of Michelangelo had gone and the architecture of the old basilica was simpler, with its long vaulted roof and thick columns. Then, the high altar itself vanished, to be replaced by the marble altar of Pope Callistus II erected in 1124. The pews were absent and small groups of pilgrims knelt on the stone floor.

Time flickered back and Paul perceived the high altar of Gregory the Great erected in AD 594, over which the Pope had placed a silver canopy, its columns twisted with vine leaves. Further back. The basilica just after it was constructed in the fourth century by the Emperor Constantine, its silver altar inlaid with four hundred precious stones. There were mosaics on its walls, depicting cedars and palm trees in an earthly paradise.

Back. The basilica itself faded. Paul gazed on as thousands of labourers started to lay down its foundations on the Vatican Hill. It was a cold December day in AD 320 and Paul could see them in rags as they struggled with horse-drawn carts, carrying the bricks and tufa stone. Human history rewound once more. A large and straggly Roman graveyard. Finally, Paul saw the beginnings of it all. He stood among the Roman tombs, a shallow trench close by.

That night, after St Peter's crucifixion in the Circus of Nero before the Emperor, it was the faithful Marcellus, a Roman convert, who smuggled the broken body of St Peter past the guards. Paul watched two men carrying a corpse wrapped in a simple woollen winding shift. They lowered it into a makeshift grave, which was no more than a trench dug from the bare earth, and a cheap marble slab was placed on top. A hurried prayer was said and a sign scratched on the wall nearby: the chi-rho – the mark of Christ, to identify the site of the first Apostle's resting place.

However, for Paul, there was no need for such identification. The light from the tomb told him who lay there. Brighter than that of an Archangel it seared, and burnt like a furnace. It was then that Paul perceived the man who had given him this final revelation and who, even now, was trying to save him. Before the tomb of St Peter in the modern-day basilica knelt the figure of Pope John XXV. He prayed.

'I beg you, Paul, cast the coin into the tomb. St Peter has the power to bind and to loose. He alone in our world can destroy these coins and free you from your suffering.'

Paul had only to walk forward and hurl the coin into the divine light. But he did not, for the vessel which comprised his spirit was full.

'Throw away the coin.' The words of John XXV came even more urgently to his mind. 'Child, save yourself.'

There was a huge thundering in Paul's being. The Angel of Darkness approached.

'*I repent.*' Paul did not, could not, say it. Even as the thought fashioned in his mind, so did the enormous power of the Magus fill him like a reservoir released from behind a broken dam. Hurled back from the tomb, Paul's perception of his own salvation evaporated. In the darkness he heard the unearthly cry of the Magus.

He was lost.

Along the narrowest of bridges, from the depths of hell, came the spirit that was Simon Magus. Mighty in the demonic arts, a crown of gold about its helm, the Angel of Darkness came, a warrior that could be withstood by none in the human world. The vast, dark wings of the Elemental Spirit brooded over the Abyss and in its hand it held the flaming sword of death. The air was rent with tormented cries from the pit.

At the crossroads to the Way the Magus stopped. In front of him appeared the image of a human being that had once been Paul. The Angel of Darkness spread out its wings. Then it covered the tiny form, absorbing the essence of man into its own being. There was a triumphant cry. Simon Magus had returned.

With that the Angel of Darkness passed over into the human world.

CHAPTER THIRTY-SEVEN

He destroys both the blameless and the wicked.

Job 9:22

FRANTICALLY, BENELLI RAN ALONG THE passage leading to the tomb of St Peter.

John XXV started up when the Cardinal reached him. The Pope's face was lined with the deepest grief and pain. They both knew what had happened. Benelli was distraught. 'What shall we do, Holy Father?'

The pontiff paused. He must make his decision now. 'Bring me the coin from the tomb of Pope Sylvester.'

'No,' replied Benelli, shaking his head repeatedly. 'Not I, Holy Father, not I,' he stammered. 'Do not ask this of me.' He bent his head in shame. 'I am sure it is I who will betray you and the Church. The Magus will come to me. Do not lay this temptation before me. Let me not be a Judas.'

His eyes bright with tears, John XXV replied, 'Temptation is given to each of us. It is your destiny. Go.'

After Benelli departed, the Pope left the tomb and went upstairs to the chapel of St Peter. He knelt down again before the small altar. Swiftly, his mind sought out the great spirit of evil. As the enemies faced each other across the Abyss, the Pope began to pray. By prayer alone could he, and one other in this world, maintain the cloud of unknowing about the convent and delay the Magus from perceiving the whereabouts of Marie and her child before the Father Confessor could come to their aid. It was a hopeless task, yet the time for battle had come.

As the Pope prayed for the soul of Paul, throughout the world so did millions of others pray for help in the light of their temptations, and their prayers were taken up by the Angels, those messengers of good and of evil.

'Are you ill?'

Hanlon Dawes stood beside the Father Confessor. They were about to enter the hospital room where Kramer lay dying, surrounded by armed guards. The journey across the city had taken the monk much longer than expected with every delay as he struggled to get past military checkpoints. San Francisco was almost deserted now.

Suddenly, the Father Confessor collapsed and fainted.

'Do you want some water?'

'No,' gasped the monk, as he struggled to get to his feet. 'I must see Kramer.' Outside, the dark was thick. The Magus was crossing the Abyss.

In the small bedroom, Karl Kramer lay. It was strange to see that bulky frame and arms engorged with muscles, which had wrought so much misery in the world, bound now by the soft sheets of a bed from which he would never escape. His visage had changed. The large face with its well-shaped nose, almost feminine chin and dark eyes, no longer glistened with vitality. Instead, it had assumed a deep purple hue as the life drained from him and the necrosis began. His eyes were closed and his breath laboured with the beginnings of the death rattle.

Kramer was dying. His heart was dying. So was his spirit. With the extinction of Helen, the energy of hate that she'd helped pour into him had been savagely extinguished and it had broken him, as it had her. Death was cruel to the evil as well as to the good. It came when least expected, to snatch life away just when one assumed it would continue.

At a nod from the Warden, the guards beside the murderer's bed filed outside. Kramer wouldn't cause problems any more; they were glad to get away from his foetid presence. The Father Confessor and Hanlon Dawes were left alone with the wolf.

The monk looked at the human being before him. It was very difficult not to hate him. During his time on earth this man had caused such incredible suffering, such inhuman misery, and he had done so until the very end. Even now, as the Father Confessor stood by this monster, he perceived that he had failed both Marie and her daughter because of Kramer. He had broken a promise he had made to the innocent in their time of greatest need to give succour to a guilty man who cared nothing for it.

'Please wait outside,' the monk said to Hanlon Dawes.

'No. He's not asked for confession and it's prison rules that I be present at his death.' The Warden gripped the monk's arm. 'It's too late. Can't you see he's on the point of death? Whatever he was going to say to you is lost.'

'No.' The Father Confessor thrust aside the restraining hand angrily. 'I will give him confession.'

He bent down to the face of the dying monster. 'Kramer, Karl Kramer. Can you hear me? Do you confess your sins? Do you seek pardon for all the evil that you have done? Do you repent and ask God for forgiveness?'

There was no sound but the laboured breathing. Hanlon Dawes shook his head. Prisoners. He knew his prisoners.

'Kramer, do you ask for forgiveness for your sins?'
Once again the monk asked him, his voice full of misery.

Silence. Only silence.

'Kramer, do you repent?'

Silence. The Father Confessor turned away.

'Yes.' The mumbled sound, uttered so quietly, was electrifying. Hanlon Dawes looked at the monster lying before him in utter amazement. Then he watched as tears started down the face of the monk who, with a choking cry, continued:

'Karl, just before you are about to meet your maker, is there anything you want to confess?'

The dying man was incapable of words. They could hear the breath becoming more and more shallow.

'Karl, if you want to confess that you killed Melanie Dukes, if you wish to confess this crime and others, then just say "Yes".'

The soul of Karl Kramer stood at the crossroads of the Way. Freed now from the chains of evil that had bound him for so long in his life of spiritual and physical incarceration, he looked deep into the realms of the spirit as he made his choice and his repentance. Then, very slowly, he whispered, 'Yes.'

The monk knelt by his bedside and wept. But even as he wept, Kramer was to offer him one more insight into a mystical world that defied all human rationalisation. An insight that not even the Father Confessor could fully comprehend, so that, from the greatest of evil, might flow the greatest of good.

Karl Kramer spoke his final word on earth, delivered to him by the Angel of Light that now guarded his soul. He whispered it to the Father Confessor, and to him alone.

'Sylvester.'

Then Kramer died.

Hanlon Dawes stared out of the window into the darkness, as he listened to the weeping of the monk. He later confessed that he had tears trickling down his own cheeks. He had learnt one thing this night, after all.

Prisoners, yes, Hanlon Dawes knew his prisoners. But souls, God knew his souls.

In the convent, Marie gripped the nun's hand. 'Where is the Father Confessor? Why is he not here? Why has he deserted us?'

'He hasn't deserted you,' said the mother superior. 'But you must leave. The Magus will come here first.'

Seizing Marie and Rachel by the hand, the nun fled down the stone corridor of the convent. Outside, a mighty storm was brewing and they heard the wind raging. In the chapel, Marie saw that the nuns had gathered about the altar in prayer. Against the deepest powers of evil there was no army, no weapon, but faith alone, and these women had chosen to stay, for the love of Marie and her child.

'Come.'

From the chapel, the group descended the winding stairs into the crypt. Light emanated from one corner. Catherine of Benedetto knelt at the altar. Rachel rushed up to her and embraced her, bathing in the warmth of the love that streamed freely from her, as the worlds of man and of the spirit began to coincide. The nun turned to Marie and took her hands in hers.

'God has failed me,' whispered Marie.

'Do not say such things. Your time of trial is at hand. It comes to all human beings, though in many different forms. God will find a way.'

'I have no faith.'

'Then look to your child. In your, and her love, Paul still lives, for without it we are nothing. You must go to the cathedral. The Father Confessor will be there. Go.'

'Come with us,' Marie pleaded.

'No.' Then, more quietly, 'Goodbye, Marie.'

As Marie stared into the eyes of this, the servant of God, so was her own future shown to her. She knew her fate and she accepted it. God had indeed repaid her. The nun said, 'Pray for the soul of your husband. He stands before judgement now.'

Holding Rachel's hand, Marie departed.

At 7.41 p.m., the city of San Francisco was hit by a second mighty earthquake measuring 8.7 on the Richter scale. At the same time, there was a great storm. Yet this was but a minor incident in a cosmic play. On the occasion of the earthquake, as the physical and spiritual worlds united for a moment in human time, the shadow of the Magus materialised before the convent.

Sheets of lightning leached from the sky like the thrashings of a whip, and the whirlwind began. The roof of the convent chapel burst into flames. Within seconds the structure collapsed, burying the nuns inside. Amid the fire and the falling stonework, the majestic form of the Magus passed into the sanctity of the convent itself.

In the crypt, with a fire raging about her, and the stone pillars beginning to crack from the heat of the flames and the weight of the collapsing chapel above, Catherine of Benedetto turned to face her unequal foe.

The Magus appeared before her as he'd once stood before Nero so long ago, a sorcerer in his long robe, a being who even then had been mighty in the black arts, his power hugely augmented by the Abyss. Once he had been vanquished by a man greater than he. But that simple fisherman was no longer on this earth. Now he, Simon, would be the vanquisher.

The Elemental Spirit beheld the presence of the saint: a crucible of light so pure that she had been able to cast about her a cloud of unknowing which not even the Magus had been able to penetrate from afar – a cloud he must disperse before he could divine the place to which Marie and the child had fled.

The saint and the Angel of Darkness looked on each other. Bound as if on a wheel of fire, Catherine of Benedetto began her final trial of faith, her mind locked into the image of the fisherman.

'Catherine.' The words of the Magus were honeyed and wise. 'I seek not to destroy you. Show me where the wife and child are and I will protect you, I promise.'

The nun said nothing. Then the Magus revealed to her the Coin of Judas. He was now a great Angel of Light, a messenger, a counsellor.

'I have been sent. It is God's will that you take this coin, Catherine. In your hands it will be converted to good. Take it, child. Become one of us, know now the mind of God, for we are both his servants.'

The nun said nothing. Above them the chapel finally collapsed, its masonry breaking through into the crypt. Fire began to lick the fabric of the altar and crept about Catherine of Benedetto, its heat burning her body. The Magus tempted her once again.

'You are only human, I am a spirit. You have done enough, you cannot do more. Remember, it was I who encompassed the death of even the first Apostle. Try not my patience.'

The saint was silent.

'So be it,' said the Magus, unable to find a foothold in her soul. 'So be it, great saint. Die and fail.'

With that the Magus held up the coin in one hand. Then, as the roof of the crypt fell in, with his wings of darkness he covered her. Around them, the chairs, the stations of the cross on the wall, the altar itself, were irrevocably smashed to pieces.

In the Chapel of St Peter, as he prayed, John XXV groaned and clutched at his heart. For the one who he hoped might be able to withstand the coin, if any on earth, had passed beyond.

Cardinal Benelli entered the corridor with a workman. He stood before the plaster wall with its great red cross, already damaged by the blows he'd previously delivered against it.

'Breach the wall.'

The workman looked at him apprehensively.

'It is by order of the Pope.'

Within a minute there was enough of a breach for a man to enter. Benelli and the workman passed into the dusty chamber. The Cardinal could see in the murky light there lay an alabaster coffin on a plinth. It was wholly unadorned.

'Open the coffin.'

The workman inserted a crowbar and wrenched the lid away from its seal. Then he pushed aside the lid.

'Now go.'

Benelli hurriedly drew back the shroud. He gasped. For despite a millennium the body had scarcely corrupted and the narrow and bony face of Pope Sylvester II stared back at him from down the centuries, dressed in his papal robes, the great mitre of office folded across his breast.

'Oh, Holy Father, we have found you.'

Then he saw what he was looking for. In the withered hands of the Pope there was a golden chalice. Benelli looked at it, too frightened to touch it. Finally, he drew it from the lifeless fingers which, even now, seemed to grasp it tenaciously. Holding his breath, Benelli opened the vessel.

Before him, still in holy water, lay a coin of silver, extraordinarily bright and pure, set into a small cross. A Coin of Judas with the extraordinary marks scratched on it by the betrayer of the Light of the World. Benelli stared at it, bedazzled.

Suddenly, the Magus, so far in distance, so near in spirit, locked into his mind as this coin, freed from the presence of Sylvester, was revealed to the Angel. A coin whose power had not been destroyed by being placed in the tomb of St Peter, a coin whose continued existence the Magus, mysteriously, had known nothing of. An insatiable urge came upon Benelli to pick it up.

'Take the coin.' The words of the Magus rang out loud and clear in his mind. 'Take the coin and you will have the force of an Angel.'

Benelli reached out. Perhaps this truly was the will of God. He could use this coin to oppose the Magus; to acquire a mighty wisdom and power to challenge the Angel of Darkness. Was this not a divine instruction to him?

Suddenly, Benelli drew back his hand and closed the chalice. He began to tremble violently. Then he stepped out of the tomb and into the corridor. Opening the chalice once more, he dipped his finger in the holy water and wrote on the wall of the tomb in the dust the letters on the coin: SMRM, 'Save me, O Redeemer of the World.'

This marking though was not for Sylvester, it was for

him. Now Benelli knew the pain of Judas. Now his own trial was upon him.

The Cardinal made his way up the stairs, his back hunched as if carrying a mighty burden, his mind torn between the desire to open the chalice and take the coin as his own, and the desire to cast out this devil. And with every step the Magus whispered to him in his heart.

'*You will betray. It cannot be changed. It is your destiny.*'

Marie ran with her child. They fled down the pathway to the cathedral, gasping for breath.

Around them was a scene of utter desolation. Crumpled buildings, roads and pavements slit open, gaping holes, houses on fire as the aftershocks of the earthquake continued. In the distance there were the shouts of military personnel as they sought to determine whether there were any other people in the city who needed help. The air was filled with panic and an inability to come to terms with what was happening to one of the most materialistic places on earth. Marie heard the mighty cracks of thunder in the sky and saw the jagged strikes of lightning, but she did not look back. Suddenly, Rachel tripped and fell. 'Mummy!'

Marie knelt down beside her fallen daughter. In so doing, she glanced down the path along which they had just come. She saw what she most feared in the world as death approached. Marie clutched her daughter to her and looked into her eyes for the last time.

'Run to the cathedral. Do not look back.'

Rachel clung to her, weeping. However, Marie broke her hold. Then she seized her once more in her arms, stroking her hand through the child's hair. With that, she pushed her on. '*Do not look back.*'

Finally, she stood to face her foe.

In the road before her, there was darkness. From it came a sound like the flapping of wings as the Magus loomed up before her, a mighty Angel, dark even against the night. The sorcerer locked into Marie's consciousness. In her mind it conjured up a vast spiritual host. Great wolves standing to the right and left of the spectral figure, ready to tear her to shreds. Behind them the twisted and changing forms of men and beasts swirling in a deep mist, their cries and movements betraying their merciless intent. The Magus approached. With each soft step, so did her extinction draw near.

'Give me the child.'

Marie called out Paul's name. It was answered by hideous laughter, the cackling of the guardians of the damned.

'Paul no longer exists,' the Angel told her. 'He is dead and with him will die those he once loved. For this world belongs to the master of the Field of Blood.'

Marie gazed towards the cathedral. Her daughter had almost reached its steps. Then Rachel turned.

She looked back.

The Magus cried in triumph; held by the force of his will, the child was also caught up in his spell. Seeing her daughter's plight, Marie walked towards the Magus, abjuring the figure of evil before her. But it was too late; her efforts were in vain. In the hand of the Magus appeared a flaming sword.

Simultaneously, before Marie's eyes, the vision of the future the saint had shown her in the crypt began. Yet, to the child, the perception was so different. As she witnessed her mother's dying form, a spirit arose from it, similar in outline to her physical form. It raised its arms as though trying, even in its death throes, to protect the child.

But it was not to be. The wolves beside the Magus hurled themselves at the spirit, tearing it to the ground in a frenzy. Suddenly it vanished.

The Magus and his host swarmed on.

Cardinal Benelli staggered along the tunnel to the basilica. It seemed an eternal journey and, with every step, the Coin of Judas weighed more heavily on him.

For the powerful Cardinal, tucked away in the Vatican, it had been easy to avoid many of the sins that afflicted his fellow human beings. However, from the sin of pride, by which Angels themselves fell, there was no escape. Relentlessly, the voice of the Magus urged him to open the chalice and to use the coin to fulfil his destiny. Caught in a vice of wanting to help others by way of self-aggrandisement, the Cardinal felt the full weight of his own ambition.

The voice of the Magus whispered to him, and was it not his own? 'You are destined to become Pope. Is this not your secret desire? That's why John XXV told you to fetch this coin. He will die soon.'

The Cardinal halted in the underground tunnel. His whole body began to shiver and tremble. The walls changed before his eyes: no longer dusty plaster, but vivid scenes as, in a moment of time, the kingdoms of the world flickered before him. The pomp, the power and the glory.

'Pick up the coin, pick up the coin!' the voice of the Magus thundered in his heart.

'I cannot go on,' wept Benelli. Yet stumble on he did.

As Benelli trod his *via dolorosa*, bowed down by his own pride, he did not realise that he bore but the tiniest part of the true weight of the coin. For, although Benelli knew it not, another walked beside him.

Nearly two thousand years before, a simple fisherman had taken that same path as they led him to his place of execution, to be crucified for the pleasure of the mob. His crime was unknown, but Nero had long remembered how the first Apostle had brought down his favoured sorcerer, and he'd sought his monstrous revenge.

A simple fisherman, although he lived in a different time from the mighty Cardinal, bore across his scarred shoulders the weight of Benelli's temptation and, as the first Apostle sought to save him, so his own sins were carried by One whose love would never fail, though the cosmos itself might pass away.

In front of the cathedral, the Magus approached the child, his mind unmoved by the agonies of Benelli. Rachel stared at the Angel. Then, directed by a force that was not her own, she turned back to the steps of the cathedral.

On them stood the Father Confessor.

CHAPTER THIRTY-EIGHT

And I saw also another place over against
that one, very squalid and it was a place of
punishment, and they were punished and the
angels that punished them had their raiment
dark according to the air of the place . . . and
there was a great lake full of flaming mire,
wherein were certain men that turned away
from righteousness; and angels, tormentors,
were set over them.

The Apocalypse of Peter,
Akhim Fragment, v. 21

RUNNING TO THE TOP OF the cathedral steps, Rachel
buried her face in the monk's robe.

About the Magus writhed up creatures from the outer
darkness, their features distended and warped by malice
and hate. Also human beings or, rather, the semblance
of human beings, their spiritual form deformed by their
own misdeeds, a plethora of snakes, coiling and un-
coiling about their limbs. Behind lay an army of lost souls
that the Magus had gathered unto his own until the Day
of Judgement.

Rachel watched the spectacle, the uncertainty and

horror reflected on her features, her moon-shaped eyes staring brightly into the darkness. This time she was experiencing no story but a reality, a super-human one.

She was no longer on the steps of a cathedral. Instead, she stood on the steps of a temple of sacrifice in Rome, its floor and walls drenched with blood, as her cruel executioner made his way towards her, promising her the most grisly of deaths.

'Do not look at them!'

The monk stretched out his hand and, with a roar, the steps of the cathedral were encircled with fire. The flames rose high into the night, causing the creatures of evil to draw back. The Magus snarled in anger. From out of the darkness on either side of him came two other forms, summoned by the power of the coin, their heads bearing crowns of gold. Together, the three entered the flames and began to ascend the steps. The fire dampened and failed.

Slowly, the monk and the child gave ground before the awesome power facing them, retreating back into the cathedral itself. The priest began the words of exorcism: 'I exorcise thee, O impure Spirit, who art the phantom of the enemy. I exorcise thee, O creature of Fire, by him who hath made all things. May all malice pass out herefrom, may it be blessed and sanctified in thy most powerful name.'

At the command of the Father Confessor the cathedral's oak doors swung to and closed. However, within an instant, the doors were riven down their centres and hurled to one side. The Magus passed into the cathedral. Then he spoke. No words came, but his thoughts radiated clearly in the mind of the Father Confessor: 'You cannot prevail against the coin. Give me the child. It is her I seek.'

Inside the church all went dark. The paintings on the

walls, the statues, the font, everything faded and disappeared as the Magus penetrated the Confessor's and the child's minds, superimposing his thoughts on theirs. They stood now in a temple, near its bloodied altar. About them, on the walls, the scenes of sacrifice came alive. Amid the carnage another form emerged, dark and mournful. The phantom of Marie gazed at her child and beckoned to her.

'Rachel,' shouted out the monk, 'it is a false image, an illusion.'

However, her will almost subject to the power of the Magus, the child started to loosen her grip on the hand of the monk. The Father Confessor sighed. He felt his spirit weakening. He closed his eyes in prayer.

Suddenly his garments became suffused with light as that great saint revealed herself. Like a mighty sea, the love of Catherine of Benedetto filled up his spirit – a great tidal wave driving onto the shore. Unstoppable and sublime, her love pierced the monk's being and his robes changed to radiate the purest light.

The Magus perceived them on the mystic planes, two forms slowly merging into one through the force of love, a force that even an Angel of Darkness and its companions could not challenge. Stretching out his hand, the Father Confessor called on the spirit of Marie, the power flowing out far into the realms of light.

'Child, thy mother.'

A pillar of fire appeared beside the monk. Perceiving the radiant vision of her mother who had died in grace, feeling the love flow from her beyond the confines of death, in her mind Rachel shattered the apparition beside the Magus. Yet even as this occurred the Father Confessor and Rachel were steadily driven back to the high altar of the cathedral. They had expended all their strength; the Magus had not yet revealed his.

Now he held up the Coin of Judas and invoked its power.

The cathedral became lost to them. Its floor liquefied, its walls glowed, the air began to darken and become all the more noisome. The two spirits – the monk and the child – walked across a molten lake as they descended into the deepest pits of hell. The thin and luminous path that had been before them began to fade and disappear as it sank into the quagmire.

The spirit forms of the priest and the Magus changed as they fought the last battle. The spirit of the dead Catherine of Benedetto within the priest challenged the Angel of Darkness itself on mystical planes that lay far beyond the ninth astral, even as the priest's own faith began to diminish and to fail.

Rachel descended into the deepest layers of revelation known to man and to Angel. The Magus now appeared before her in the most basic forms by which evil was recognised in the physical world. He transformed himself into a mighty serpent, coiled and ready to strike, yet the monk beside her became as an eagle. Then the Magus was a wolf, slavering and ravenous. The monk became as a lion. The Magus transformed into the hideous image of a goat. The monk became a unicorn.

Finally, all about the Father Confessor and the child became the blackest night. Still they descended down the left path of the Way, each moment the power of monk, and the saint, weakening. The vision of evil that the Magus had imposed on them increased ever more as the coin belched forth its poison.

Pope Sylvester II had spoken the truth after all.

No living soul, not even the soul of the Father Confessor, imbued with powers brought from beyond the world, could withstand the power of this coin, a coin by which the Redeemer himself was betrayed.

At the back of the chapel a door opened. The Pope turned to face Benelli.

What changes the last minutes had wrought on the mighty Cardinal. His face bore dreadful suffering – that of the spirit. His eyes could reflect only some of the pain. With trembling hands he carried the chalice containing the coin held by Pope Sylvester. 'See, I have not betrayed you,' he whispered.

John XXV looked at him and his eyes filled with tears. 'Bless you,' he said.

Taking up the chalice, the pontiff turned to the altar and he closed his eyes. Then he cried out, 'Father, thy Holy Church itself is in peril.'

For John XXV knew that the mighty edifice that was St Peter's Basilica, and all the Church, rested on one human foundation, and one alone. Faith.

Against that rock evil could not prevail. Further, of one thing the Church's text on witchcraft, the *Malleus Maleficarum*, had said little and deliberately so:

> *It is not seemly to discuss the Power of the Keys granted to the Head of the Church as Christ's Vicar; since it is known that, for the use of the Church, Christ granted to the Church and his Vicar as much power as it is possible for God to grant to mere man.*

John held up the chalice containing the Coin of Judas and sought faith. 'If thy servant Sylvester converted this coin to good so that it might cancel out the coin which seeks to destroy thy Church, in thy name I seek to redeem the soul of Paul, lost unto God.'

When the Pope mentioned Sylvester II before the altar, Benelli comprehended the true nature of that man. A great soul; one who had borne throughout his papacy the taunts and catcalls of others as they sought to denigrate him and his love of God. To these shocking accusations Sylvester had made no reply. Until his last confession, he had remained silent.

Instead, he had quietly carried a Coin of Judas, embedded in a silver cross, against his breast throughout his life, in order that its wickedness might drain out and be replaced by love; this to occur covertly so that even the Angels of Darkness would be unable to detect the change, so it could be used in its predestined time. This coin too Sylvester II had blessed before the tomb of St Peter before he died. Only at the end had this remarkable Pope told the truth about himself, to the world and to God: 'My mind never consented to that oath, nay, that abomination.'

For Sylvester II had sold his soul to no one. He had given it freely to his Saviour.

Cardinal Benelli, who had experienced the temptation of the coin for only a short time, marvelled at how one could have carried such a cross for so long. It humbled him.

John XXV lowered the chalice. He closed his eyes.

In another place, standing at the high altar of the cathedral with Rachel beside him, the Father Confessor raised his hands, the path now wholly lost and gone. In his death agony, he summoned up an image of a cross, yet it shattered and broke.

'You have failed,' said the Magus. 'The power of this coin cannot be defeated.' He pointed to Rachel. 'With it, this child's father denied God and his salvation. By that choice he forfeited his soul, and all that he loved, including his daughter, will be extinguished.'

The Father Confessor looked towards Rachel. In his blindness nothing else could he see. All about him was darkness and flames. Love, friendship, hope, charity, the perception of his own being had been stripped away. Cut off from God, he stood alone. Yet from his mouth, his spirit spoke for the last time. He turned to the girl.

'Child,' he said. 'Your father will be saved.' Then, in a loud voice: '*Salva me, Redemptor Mundi.*'

The Magus brought down his sword. Rachel watched as the priest was struck down at the altar by the Magus. The Coin of Judas fulfilled its grim prophecy. No human power could withstand it. Finally, the Magus turned to Rachel, the last crucible of Paul's love. He knelt down before her. 'Little child,' he said. 'Though they know it not, at the moment of death I come to all mankind. I offer you, as I offer to every one of your race, the kingdoms of the world. In return, I ask only that you serve my master.'

There was silence.

Rachel did as her mother told her. She turned to the altar and she directed her soul, like a mirror, to God. In her innocence she sought one thing.

'Save my father.'

Even as the prophecy of Pope Sylvester II was satisfied, so did John XXV, successor to the one on whom Christ had built his Church, finally reveal his own power. It also comprised magic, but it was true magic. The deepest magic unknown to the Magus. It existed even before his physical being, before time, before creation, before thought. It lay within the Godhead itself.

Unconditional love.

As the forfeited soul of Paul lay in its lake of perdition, John XXV, in an act of unconditional love, joined his spirit to Paul's. This selfless act formed a tiny thread between the saint and the sinner. A bond of love.

Slowly, the souls of Catherine of Benedetto, the Father Confessor and Marie locked onto those of Paul and John XXV. The bond became a ring – a ring of unconditional love – and the ring expanded as the souls of Ben and Florence joined them. So did others, for before the very throne of God, Melanie and Laura Dukes, victims who had sought judgement, forgave what only they could forgive. The ring became a knot.

About that knot there formed another and another and another as millions of human beings on earth prayed for the Holy Father, his predecessors and his cardinals. Yet more, as the souls of past pontiffs, including the saintly Sylvester II, unhindered by time and the devil, testified to their love and to their faith. And yet more!

These human knots, small and insignificant in themselves, formed a net, a net of love, but a net so tight and strong that not even the smallest and weakest of minnows could escape, and certainly not one the Almighty had deigned to save long before he was born. For vengeance was his alone.

As the Coins of Judas cancelled each other out, the Magus, who could induce such terrible images of evil in others, now had his own vision. Mighty Angel of Darkness that he was, the Way also began to open before him.

Simon Magus saw that, while the spiritual distance between a man and an Angel was vast, that between an Angel and an Archangel was greater still. Even more again between the other angelic orders and the Cherubim and Seraphim. And yet more into the very Temple. Despite this path being eternal it was also cognisable in an instant, since all human and spiritual beings passed along the Way into light – though some dwelt in darkness for a very long time.

Beside the lake of despair, a humble fisherman walked, impervious to evil. The Magus felt fear when he saw his former adversary, and he cried out. However, his master heard him not; for his hour was not at hand. Then St Peter, that great fisher of men, cast his net into the lake.

From the darkness came light. It was the last thing Paul ever saw. Ineffable, transcendent, merciful beyond all human conception of mercy, this light would never leave him. Unlike the perception of human beings or of Angels, this *was* reality. The only one.

The light of the true Master of the Field.

EPILOGUE

The end of the matter; all has been heard.
Fear God, and keep his commandments; for
this is the whole duty of man. For God will
bring every deed into judgement, with every
secret thing, whether good or evil.

Ecclesiastes 12:13

CARDINALS BENELLI AND HEWSON SAT in the
Vatican gardens.

His tale of the Coin of Judas finished, Benelli looked
about him – at the vivid colours of the tulips and daffodils
as they swayed gently in the breeze, at the clouds as they
scudded across a pale blue sky, at the magnificent dome
of St Peter's Basilica rising before them. Then he looked
at his companion and sighed. 'For it is through the love
of others that our own souls are saved.'

They meditated on this for a while. Finally, Benelli
rose. 'It is time for me to go,' he said. 'Old men must
retire. Even I.'

They walked back through the garden. Benelli mentally bade farewell to it. Hewson strolled beside him.

'So the girl that I saw this morning at the tomb is
Rachel?' he said.

'Yes,' replied Benelli, 'and the tomb before which she

was praying is that of her parents. She has gone there every day for the last six years. Paul and Marie are buried together in a place where evil can no longer touch them. Close by is the tomb of the Father Confessor. It was the will of the Holy Father.'

'And Catherine?'

'In the priory of Benedetto.' Benelli looked up at the figures on the colonnade of St Peter's. 'Many saints in his world are known only to God.'

'What of the remaining two coins?'

They crossed over the threshold of the veranda windows, into Benelli's study once more. From the light into shade. The Cardinal shrugged his shoulders.

'Who knows? It is unlikely we shall see them for many years. Yet all men are subject to temptation. That is the one great certainty, besides death. Evil can also reach into the heart of the Church. We should remember this and always be on our guard.'

From around his neck Benelli took a silver cross and placed it on his desk. It was curious in that it had a gap in its centre, in which a coin had once been located.

'It's time to leave you, Cardinal. I hope your inauguration goes well tomorrow. I trust you will wear this cross as a small reminder of my affection and of the great secret that I have told you. It was worn by Pope Sylvester II. May he bless you.'

Hewson looked at Benelli. A mighty Prince of the Church no longer, a simple priest once more. O vanity of vanities. How quickly passed all temporal pomp and power. Hewson said, 'Bless you, for all that you have done for us. I hope you have a wonderful retirement.'

Benelli gave a regretful smile. 'I've done so little for the Church in reality,' he said. 'Indeed, I was thinking I have learnt only two things after all these years.'

'What are they?' said Hewson. The old man was becoming maudlin.

'There is but one God, and he loves every one of his children unconditionally.'

'I understand,' said Hewson.

'I wonder,' replied Benelli. He looked at him shrewdly for a moment. 'I wonder, for if we really understood, how different our world would be. Well, goodbye then, Cardinal.'

Hewson watched the old man depart down the corridor. He went and sat in his predecessor's chair. He did not pick up the silver crucifix, since his mind was on other things. Soon, there was a knock on the door. Two young priests entered, their arms full of books from Hewson's library.

'Where would you like us to put them? We've been asked to help you unpack.'

The Cardinal eyed the top shelf of one of the empty bookcases. 'How about there? Pass them to me.'

Hewson climbed a small set of wooden library steps. Taking some books in his arms, he placed them on the top shelf. One of the priests went outside to get some more while the other passed up another armful to the Cardinal. Hewson stretched out to grasp them in his hands. Suddenly there was a metallic sound as something struck against the floor.

The young priest bent down and picked it up. 'It fell from your pocket, Cardinal,' he said as he inspected it. 'It's a coin. Very old, most unusual.'

Hewson looked at him with a glint in his eye.

'Yes,' he said. 'It *is* a most unusual coin.'

AUTHOR'S NOTE

THIS BOOK IS A WORK of fiction and does not purport to represent the doctrine of any church. However, a number of features in this novel are based on fact or ecclesiastical legend. These include:

- St Peter's crucifixion and tomb
- Obelisk in front of St Peter's
- Secret Archives (including the Tower of the Winds and Room of the Meridian)
- Legends of Pope Sylvester II and Simon Magus
- Purges against the Church initiated by Diocletian and Julian the Apostate
- Disreputable life of Pope John XII and the Sack of St Peter's by the Saracens
- Emperor Nero and the Circus of Nero
- Coins of Judas
- The ecclesiastical text, the 'Hammer of the Witches' (*Malleus Maleficarum*).

Further details are provided below:

1. St Peter's Crucifixion and Tomb
St Peter is thought to have been buried in a trench located in a pagan graveyard close to the Circus of Nero,

in an area outside Rome known by the Etruscan name of Vatican Hill.

His grave is believed by the Catholic Church to lie some ten metres under the present high altar of St Peter's Basilica, below various altars dedicated by Popes Clement VII (AD 1594), Callixtus II (AD 1124) and Gregory the Great (AD 594); a monument erected by the Emperor Constantine in c. AD 315; and a shrine (called the Tropaion or Victory monument) erected by Pope Anicetus in c. AD 160. This shrine was built into a Roman brick wall erected over the grave only a few years after St Peter was buried there. Excavations in 1940 revealed the bones of a man in his late sixties (with feet missing) who appears to have been wrapped in a robe lined with gold thread. For further details see:

- Guarducci, *The Tomb of St Peter* (Harrap, 1960)
- Toynbee & Perkins, *The Shrine of St Peter and the Vatican Excavations* (Longman, 1956)
- Walsh, *The Bones of St Peter* (Victor Gollancz, 1983)

Church sources have it that St Peter was crucified upside down c. AD 67 in the Circus of Nero, the remains of which currently lie under (or very close to) St Peter's Basilica. His body is thought to have been buried by Marcellus, a Roman convert. See generally:

- Rhodes James, *The Apocryphal New Testament, Acts of Peter* (OUP, 1924)
- *Encyclopedia Britannica*

For the quotation from St Peter (p. 55 of the novel) see Rhodes James op. cit. On St Peter's ability to withstand the gates of hell (pp. 128 of the novel) and his power to bind and loose (p. 404 of the novel) see the Gospel according to St Matthew, Ch. 16, vv 18–19.

On the refusal of Pope Julius II to move the tomb of St Peter (p. 130 of the novel) see the Roman historian Egidio de Viterbo. On the old St Peter's Basilica and the former adornment of St Peter's tomb (pp. 403–404 of the novel) see generally Toynbee & Perkins, op. cit., Seldes, *The Vatican* (Kegan Paul, 1934) and *Encyclopedia Britannica*.

2. Obelisk in front of St Peter's
This 15–18th century BC Egyptian obelisk used to stand in the Circus of Nero (pp. 250 & 341 of the novel). Currently, it stands in the piazza of St Peter, being moved to its present location in 1586.

3. Vatican Library and Secret Archives
On the Vatican Library and the Secret Archives (including the Tower of the Winds and the Room of the Meridian) see Ambrosini, *The Secret Archives of the Vatican* (Eyre & Spottiswoode, 1970). The Tower of the Winds currently comprises papal apartments.

4. Legend of Pope Sylvester II (AD 999–1003)
Even during his lifetime this Pope was rumoured throughout Europe to have satanic powers, including a black dog which always followed him. For the nature of these legends (and the quotation on pp. 209–210 of the novel about his pact with the devil) see:

- Butler, *The Myth of the Magus* (Cambridge, 1948)
- Platina, *Lives of the Popes* (*Liber Pontificalis*, 1479, in Latin)

In his work, Platina, the papal librarian, included his allegation that Sylvester was aided by the devil (p. 208 of the novel) and the reputed content of Sylvester's final confession (p. 211 of the novel). As to Sylvester's ambiguous epitaph in the Church of St John Lateran, the words of John the Deacon and the legend about his tomb foretelling the death of Popes (p. 289–290 of the novel) see:

- Mann, *The Lives of the Popes in the Early Middle Ages* (Kegan Paul, 1932)
- Döllinger, *Fables Respecting the Popes of the Middle Ages* (Rivington, 1871)

For a more balanced view of Sylvester II see Lattin, *The Letters of Gerbert and His Papal Privileges* published in 1961 and Mann, op. cit. On the rediscovery of Sylvester's tomb in 1648 and its description by the historian Rasponi (p. 342) see Mann, op. cit.

5. *Legend of Simon Magus*
For this arch-heretic and his fall see:

- The Acts of the Apostles 8:9–24
- Rhodes James, *The Apocryphal New Testament* (OUP, 1924)
- Butler, *The Myth of the Magus* (Cambridge, 1948)
- Palmer, *The Sources of the Faust Tradition* (Octagon Books, 1936)
- Mead, *Simon Magus* (London 1892, reprint Kessinger Pub.).

For the philosophy of the Magus, his magic powers, his use of the money disdained by St Peter (p. 373 of the novel and quotation from The Acts of the Apostles, 8:20) to purchase a prostitute, Helena, who became his lover, as well as legends about the black dog that always accompanied him, his palace on the Tiberine Island and his fall before St Peter, see generally Mead, op. cit. Also, Palmer and the *Catholic Encyclopedia* (1913). The Church of Santa Maria Nove in Rome currently stands where the Magus is alleged to have fallen to his death in the Campus Martius. As to the quotation on p. 377 of the novel from the Acts of the Holy Apostles Peter and Paul, see Rhodes James op. cit.

6. Diocletian and Julian Apostate
Both Diocletian and Julian the Apostate have come down in history as great persecutors of the Christian faith. On them generally see:

- Williams, *Diocletian and the Roman Recovery* (Batsford, 1985)
- Eusebius, *History of the Church from Christ to Constantine* (trans., Baltimore, 1965)
- Bowersock, *Julian the Apostate* (Duckworth, 1978)
- Browning, *The Emperor Julian* (Weidenfeld and Nicolson, 1975)

On St Jerome's allegation that Julian was the betrayer of his own soul (p. 173 of the novel) see Browning op. cit. On the final words of Julian (p. 173 of the novel) see *Encyclopedia Britannica*.

7. John XII and the Sack of Rome
On the shocking life of Pope John XII see Mann, op. cit., the *Catholic Encyclopedia* (1913) and Rosa, *Vicars of Christ* (Bantam Press, 1988). On the sack of Rome by a Saracen

army and the desecration of St Peter's Basilica see both Platina and Toynbee, op. cit.

8. Emperor Nero and the Circus of Nero
On Nero generally see:

- Tacitus, *Annals* (Penguin, 1956) including the quotation on p. 159 of the novel
- Suetonius, *Lives of the Caesars* (Penguin, 1937)
- Griffin, *Nero: The End of a Dynasty* (Batsford, 1984)

9. Coins of Judas
On the betrayal of Christ for thirty pieces of silver, Judas's repentance and the purchase of the Field of Blood (pp. 156–158 of the novel) see the Gospel according to St Matthew, 26 and 27. As to the nature of these coins (and their destiny) I know of no Church legend.

10. Malleus Maleficarum etc.
The original text of *Malleus Maleficarum*, approved by Pope Innocent VIII, was published in Latin in 1484 (for English translation see Rodker, 1924). This work became notorious as the standard ecclesiastical text for the detection and punishment of witchcraft. It has never been formally repudiated.

On the nine orders of the angelic hierarchy (p. 383 of the novel) see *Pseudo-Dionysius: The Complete Works* (trans. Colm Luibheid, Paulist Press, 1987). On the quotation from Pope Paul VI on evil (pp. 269–270 of the novel) see Stanford, *The Devil: A Biography* (Heinemann, 1996). On Jung's perception of evil and the paranormal see generally:

Jung, *The Undiscovered Self* (Routledge, 1983)

Jung, *Memories, Dreams, Reflections* (Fontana Press, 1974, inc. quotation on pp. 327–328 of the novel)

Jung, *Answer to Job* (Routledge, 1979).